A CLAN CHIEF'S DAUGHTER

SHE WHO RIDES HORSES
BOOK TWO

SARAH V. BARNES

HEART SOUL HORSE
PUBLICATIONS

ISBN 979-8-9927690-0-5 (soft cover)
ISBN 979-8-9927690-1-2 (eBook)
Library of Congress Control Number: 2025909849

Cover and interior design: Jane Dixon-Smith / www.jdmith-design.com
Editor: Page Lambert / www.pagelambert.com
Cover artwork: Diana Lancaster / www.dianalancaster.com
Author photography: David Barnes

Author website: www.sarahvbarnes.com
Substack: www.substack.com/@heartsoulhorse

DEDICATION

For Prada

Watching you go
Off to live your best life,
You took my heart with you,
leaving me the moon.

Warning:

This novel includes a depiction of sexual assault.

Discretion is advised.

Contents

Characters

Naya: A girl of fifteen summers
Amu: Naya's dog and devoted companion

Naya's family:

Awija: Naya's paternal grandmother, medicine woman and
                 wife of the old clan chief
Awos: Naya's paternal grandfather, the old clan chief, head of
                 the Plānos tribe
Sata: Naya's mother, originally from the southern
                 mountains
Potis: Naya's father, son of Awos, has succeeded his father
                 as clan chief
Tausos: Naya's uncle, Potis's younger brother
Glōs: Naya's aunt, Tausos's wife
Sunus: Naya's cousin, Tausos and Glōs's oldest son
Swesor: Naya's aunt, Potis and Tausos's sister
Elēn: Naya's cousin, Swesor's daughter

Other members of the clan:

Bhermi: Potis's cousin and best friend, killed in a bear attack
                 before the story begins
Vedukha: Sata's cousin, widow of Bhermi
Melit: Vedukha and Bhermi's daughter, Naya's second cousin
                 and best friend
Maqā: Melit's younger sister, a girl of ten summers
Kawona: Melit's oldest brother, a skilled archer and tracker
Bhlaghmn: Awos's brother, the clan's senior priest
Uksor: Bhlaghmn's wife

Skelos:	Potis's enemy and rival for leadership within the clan, brother of Bhermi
Krnos:	Skelos's son, Naya's childhood tormentor
Saurosa:	Skelos's much-younger sister
Oyuun:	A trader from the far north who helped to save Naya's life
Aytal:	Oyuun's oldest son, a young man of seventeen summers
Dayan:	Oyuun's stepson, adopted by Tausos's family

Other members of the Plānos Tribe:

Regos:	Another powerful clan chief, Potis's rival to succeed Awos as head of the Plānos
Wailos:	Son of Regos
Unksra:	Wailos's cousin, son of Regos's sister

Members of the Dānus Tribe, whose territory lies to the south:

Ceru:	Head of the Dānus, Potis's friend
Elōr:	Ceru's wife
Reiwos:	Ceru and Elōr's oldest daughter, a young woman of seventeen summers, known as Rei
Perqos:	Ceru and Elōr's oldest son, a young man of nineteen summers
Swelā & Aknā:	Ceru and Elōr's younger daughters
Weri:	Ceru and Elōr's younger son
Árdejā:	Ceru's great-aunt
Awontlos:	Ceru's younger brother, father of Ceru's nephews Merkō and Mikāmi

Horses:

Réhda:	The red filly
MeHnd:	The mare, Réhda's mother
Šuurgan:	The gray stallion
Rebhjo:	The yellow mare, protector of the captured herd
BeHregs:	The herd stallion, killed in the round-up

Pontic-Caspian Steppe

c. 4,000 BCE

Prelude

The clan's settlement, late winter…

"I'm here, my chief."

Awija left off adding wood to the fire and returned to her husband's side. Awos lay on his pallet, buried under two heavy fur blankets. Despite the coverings and the blaze Awija kept stoking in the hearth, he shivered, his emaciated form unable to retain warmth. Weakened even before the trek to the clan's winter settlement, once they arrived, the old clan chief had not been expected to live much longer. Yet somehow his spirit had endured, remaining with them throughout the long, cold season. He'd been especially restless tonight, moaning and calling out. Reaching for his withered hand, Awija gave it a tender squeeze, reassuring him of her presence. She hoped her affectionate use of his title would bring a smile to his face. Despite his former status as leader of the clan, they both knew who had truly been in charge between the two of them throughout their long marriage. She realized he was trying to speak and leaned close to make out the words.

"The boys," he rasped.

"They're at the council," Awija answered, guessing he wanted to speak to their sons.

"A vision… must tell only you and them… no one else. You must all do as I say."

"They're at the council," Awija repeated. Although the periods when Awos was coherent had grown fewer over the last several days, she was reluctant to intrude upon the meeting taking place in the men's tent. Whatever their father wanted to say to Potis, the current clan chief, and his brother Tausos would have to be important to warrant the interruption.

"Must tell them… now," Awos whispered. He opened his eyes and, for a moment, Awija glimpsed the spark of the man he'd once been, accustomed to command.

"Alright," she agreed. "I'll fetch them."

Shivering in the cold air, Awija pulled her bison robe more closely around her shoulders and hurried to traverse the distance between her family's dwelling and the men's tent where the council was taking place. She regretted having to leave Awos alone but there was no one else to go. The other women and children were retired for the night. Only the men and older boys who were not out with the herds were still awake, attending the council. Even had there been someone else to send, Awija recognized that she alone possessed the temerity to intrude upon the meeting.

She had no difficulty finding her way, at least, even in the dark. The waning sliver of moon that hung over the settlement may have been too feeble to illuminate the hard-packed earth, but she did not have far to go. The *Starving Moon*, Awija thought ruefully, pausing to look up. This year the name seemed particularly apt, for after a winter more severe than anyone could remember, the people were indeed starving. The worst of the storms had abated, and temperatures had become more moderate, but spring was still another moon away. Food stores were perilously low. The land was barren of game and the icy river, just beginning to thaw, had become too treacherous to yield many fish. Despite the best efforts of the disheartened herders, nearly half the clan's cattle, sheep and goats had perished, buried in drifts or so weakened by lack of fodder that they collapsed and froze where they lay.

At least their deaths were not a complete waste, Awija reflected as she resumed her errand. They'd fed the people for a time. But the clan had lost many of their most valuable breeding stock. To rebuild the herds with the few animals who remained would take more than a single season. To lose even one more would be unthinkable.

As she approached the large circular tent, Awija heard the sound of raised male voices. *How like them to argue*, she thought, *as if fighting ever solved anything*. According to what her sons had told her, the debate among the men about how to prevent further disaster had been going on for several nights, with opposing positions beginning to harden. Predictably, the older men were taking sides, with Potis's cousin Skelos and his followers advocating for one solution, while Potis, his brother and brother-in-law and their remaining cousins held out for another. The young men – Awija supposed she must no longer think of them as boys, now that they'd been through their initiation ceremony – tended to side with their fathers. Meanwhile the two priests, ostensibly playing a mediating role, lent their support to Skelos's faction, as usual.

Awija paused at the entrance. How could she alert her sons to their father's request without making the other men, especially the priests, suspicious? Like vultures, they were waiting for word that Awos's death was at last imminent. Bhlaghmn, the clan's senior priest, had gone so far as to insist that he must be present for his elder brother's transition, as though he alone could oversee the old chief's safe passage to the other world. *That time has not yet come*, Awija thought. She would know when Awos was ready to draw his final breath. Only then would she decide whether or not to call her brother-in-law. In the meantime, she must fetch Potis and Tausos at once, before their father lost what little ability he had left to communicate. But what excuse could she give?

Just then, someone inside must have gestured for silence, for the shouting subsided. Had they heard her approach? Awija was about to announce herself when a voice she recognized as belonging to her brother-in-law began to speak. Crouching, she cautiously pulled aside just enough of the tent flap to peer in without being seen.

The men of the clan were gathered in two semi-circles around the central hearth, Potis and his supporters together on one side, Skelos and his supporters on the other, with Bhlaghmn and the younger priest in between. Missing was Skelos's son, Krnos, even though as one of the clan's newly initiated young men, he should have been present. *Up to mischief, no doubt*, thought Awija. Bhlaghmn had risen to his feet. Shrunken with age, he held himself very erect, as though what he had to say was of utmost importance. With his dark robes hanging from his gaunt frame, he did indeed resemble a vulture.

"The land withholds her bounty at the behest of *Dyēus-Ptēr* – Sky-Father – and the other Shining Ones, the *Deiwos*," he declared. "They challenge us to demonstrate our resourcefulness in a time of scarcity. They are testing us. We must be sure not to neglect our sacred duties, no matter the cost. Otherwise, how are we to retain the gods' favor?"

Murmurs of agreement from both sides of the circle accompanied the old priest's words. No one doubted the severe winter had been intended as a test. The only question was how they were to respond.

"Above all," Bhlaghmn went on, "we must secure the animals required for the clan's contribution to the solstice rites. Only thus, by fulfilling our responsibilities, shall we prove our worthiness, not only to Sky-Father, but to the other clans of the tribe as well. I need remind no one that as the hosts of this year's Gathering, our obligations must take precedence over all else."

At the old priest's words, Awija saw her oldest son stiffen. She knew Potis did not agree with his uncle. In his view, the clan's best hope for the future was to care for *all* of their remaining animals. This included those designated for *Sāwel-Dom* – the summer solstice rites – but not at the expense of the breeding stock. In particular, the cows, ewes and she-goats recently delivered of this year's offspring must be cared for and guarded, along with the young bull, the two rams and the most potent of the buck goats. The future depended on their survival. Surely the gods would understand.

Perhaps, indeed, this was the test. Yes, the gods had sent a terrible winter, worse than anyone could remember. But if they could all manage to survive through another moon, the snows would recede, and the wild herds would return. Grass would grow once more. Soon the Rā would be free of ice and fish would again be available in abundance. They had only to trust in the bounty of the earth and the renewal of the seasons. If worse came to worst, the animals meant for *Sāwel-Dom* would have to be sacrificed earlier than intended, in order to feed the people. This too, the gods would surely understand. But no matter what, the breeding males and the newborns and their mothers must be protected.

More than once in the last several days Awija had overheard Potis make this argument to those who approached him, asking what he thought they should do. As chief, his words carried weight, and she felt proud of him. Heir to his father, Potis followed the example Awos had always set, humbling himself before the awesomeness of Sky-Father's capricious power, but he was also his mother's son, reminding the people to accord equal faith and honor to the unconditional generosity of *Cita-Amsus*, the Great Goddess, whom Awija had taught him to revere as the life-force imbuing all of creation.

Despite the cold and the urgency of her errand, Awija hesitated to announce herself, both curious and apprehensive about what the senior priest would say next. She doubted Bhlaghmn shared her son's balanced approach to handling the current crisis. Never had she heard a word of reverence for the Goddess, in any of her forms, pass willingly from her brother-in-law's lips. Such neglect, she feared, would have consequences for the clan's well-being, not because the Goddess was a vengeful being like Sky-Father, but rather because *Cita-Amsus* represented the sacred spirit infusing all of creation. To dismiss the Goddess was thus to dismiss the essence of life itself.

What the old priest said next increased Awija's misgivings.

"The gods expect the men of the clan to prove their worthiness not merely as herders but as warriors," Bhlaghmn admonished, looking pointedly at Potis and his supporters, as though to quell any dissent. "That means not only protecting our own herds from theft but doing whatever it takes to acquire the livestock we need to meet our obligations."

Potis met his uncle's gaze in silence, expression inscrutable. In the short time since taking over as chief, Awija observed, her son had become more adept at hiding his thoughts, at least so long as he retained control over his temper. The restraint was hard won, she knew.

"I would remind us of what the stories teach," Bhlaghmn continued, turning to the other half of the circle. Skelos, surrounded by the members of his own faction, returned the priest's regard. Awija thought something seemed to pass between the two men, but it was hard to discern. Whatever its meaning, the expression that flitted across Skelos's face served to accentuate the scar he'd received two summers ago in the vicious bear attack that had killed his older brother, Bhermi. Skelos blamed Potis, Bhermi's best friend, for his brother's death, one of the many reasons the two men did not get along. Awija turned her attention back to the priest.

"Harken," he commanded, his tone leaving no doubt about the importance of what he was about to say. "Harken again to the truth of how the world began."

Awija remembered the first time, as a young bride, she'd listened to her brother-in-law, newly ordained in his role as priest, recite the clan's version of the world's origins. Out of chaos, the story began, there arose first air, then water, then land, but as yet no life existed. Next, according to Bhlaghmn's account, Sky Father's twin sons, *Manu* and *Yemos*, had come into being.

"*Yemos* was intended to be the ruler over all the earth," Bhlaghmn was saying now. "But he saw that in order for there to be life, there must also be death, otherwise there would be no balance. In order for there to be a beginning, there must first be an end. It was thus at *Yemos's* behest that his brother *Manu* made the first sacrifice, killing his twin as well as a sacred cow which had been a gift to *Yemos* from Sky Father."

No mention was made of the Goddess, an omission which at first had shocked Awija but all these years later no longer surprised her, given who was doing the storytelling. Outside the tent, she held her breath, hoping that Bhlaghmn would not launch into the tale of *Trito* and the first cattle raid, which often followed the story of the world's origins, but the priest seemed satisfied for the moment. Relieved, she was about to get to her feet and announce herself when she realized that Skelos had risen to take over from the senior priest, as though by mutual agreement. Despite her mounting impatience, Awija remained where she was, under the pale light from the waning moon, and listened as her son's principal rival began to speak.

"Sacrifice," he intoned, picking up smoothly from where Bhlaghmn had left off. His voice was deep and sonorous, well able to command men's attention, persuade their thinking and inspire action. Awija wished Potis had spoken up instead. Sometimes her son was too respectful towards his uncle. Skelos, in contrast, was obviously in league with the old vulture.

"We've heard the wise words from our senior priest," he was saying, "reminding us that sacrifice is necessary to maintain balance in the world. We must be willing to consider all our options in order to replenish our livestock. Given the number of animals we've lost this winter, we're going to have difficulty meeting our obligations, especially since we're the hosts for the Gathering. We will lose standing and respect. But if we were to undertake a raid against a foreign tribe..."

Awija had heard enough. If Potis wouldn't interrupt, she would. Rising stiffly to her feet, she made a great show of coughing and stamping her feet before pulling wide the tent flap.

"Pardon me," she said when all the men turned to look at her. Voice firm, her tone was polite but not especially deferential. She focused her gaze and her words on her two sons. "Potis, Tausos – your father would like to speak with you." Simplicity seemed the best tactic. The fact that she had come looking for them would have to be sufficient to excuse the clan chief and his brother from the meeting. Let the others speculate as to why. As she hoped, the two rose, wrapped their cloaks around their shoulders and followed her out into the night.

No one spoke as they crossed the short distance to the dwelling where the old chief awaited. At the sound of them entering the tent, Awos stirred and tried to speak.

"Boys?" The lone syllable came out in a whisper.

"Yes father," Potis and Tausos replied in unison. "We're here."

Awos's eyes opened briefly, long enough for Awija to glimpse the spark she'd seen earlier. Whatever he had to tell them seemed to be burning from within, as if it were all that was keeping him alive. She was glad she hadn't delayed any longer than she had before interrupting the council.

"He's had a vision," she told their sons, hoping to relieve Awos of the necessity of trying to explain. "He insists that we must all do as he says."

"Nothing changes," quipped Potis, apparently hoping to bring a smile to his father's face.

As he and Tausos knelt next to one another at their father's side, Swesor, their sister, emerged from the shadows at the back of the tent, holding a small pot of herb-infused beeswax. Awija realized with dismay that Swesor must have been up late and had come to see if she could help. Finding Awos by himself, she must have decided to stay until Awija returned. Did Awos realize Swesor was there? He'd wanted to speak to Potis and Tausos alone, but Awija couldn't very well ask their sister to leave.

"Swesor, Tausos and Potis are here now," she said instead. "All three of your children have come." Kneeling opposite her brothers, Swesor was about to apply the soothing balm to her father's parched lips. Awija shook her head to dissuade her. *Not now*, she mouthed silently.

Awos's eyes were closed. "And Naya?" he asked.

"Your granddaughter has not yet returned," Awija answered gently. From her place beside Swesor, she reached for her husband's hand. His skin felt slack against hers, but he responded to her touch with a strength that surprised her.

"She will," the old chief said, opening his eyes. The certainty of his words matched the force of his grip. The others looked at one another. How could their father know his missing granddaughter's fate?

"This is what I've seen," he said, as though in reply.

A pause followed. Everyone waited for Awos to speak. Although the old chief's eyes remained open, his gaze had become lost somewhere in the middle distance. Awija wondered if he might have forgotten their presence. At last, seeming to have gathered what remained of his strength, he went on.

"My granddaughter will return," he proclaimed, "and with her will come the horses. The horses are a gift to the people. With their help, we will become more powerful than can be imagined, able to transform the world. We must never forget the horses' gift. To them we shall owe our lives and our future." Having delivered this pronouncement, the old chief fell silent.

From opposite sides of Awos's pallet, Awija exchanged a look with her oldest son. Of those gathered to witness what were likely the clan patriarch's final words, she and Potis alone knew about Naya and the red filly. Almost imperceptively, Awija shook her head. Now was not the time to speak of the girl and her other-worldly experiences, even to others in the family. Swesor, especially, had a loose tongue and could not be trusted. Following Awija's unspoken warning, Potis ignored his siblings' obvious curiosity about Awos's strange words, instead turning his gaze back to his father's still form. Although open, the old chief's eyes were once more unfocused.

"Father?" he asked quietly. "The livestock are dying. The wild herds, even the horses, have disappeared. Soon the people will go hungry. Skelos and his followers are arguing that the only solution is to take what we need from some other tribe, otherwise we cannot survive."

And Naya and her mother may never return, Awija imagined Potis wanting to add. She saw him swallow hard. "What should we do?" he asked his father.

"The horses," Awos answered in an almost inaudible whisper. "The horses." Too weak to do otherwise, he closed his eyes.

The old chief did not open them again, nor speak. Awija and the others stayed with him throughout what was left of the night, taking turns keeping watch and tending the fire in the hearth. At last, toward dawn, when the lag between each of Awos's inhalations began to lengthen, Awija sent Swesor to fetch the rest of the immediate family. "Summon Bhlaghmn, as well," she had added reluctantly. "And bring Vedukha too, and her children. They'll want to be here when he crosses over."

Soon everyone was assembled around Awos's pallet, silent and solemn, the younger children still rubbing sleep from their eyes. Only Potis's wife, Sata, and their daughter Naya were missing. Awija sent up a prayer for her oldest granddaughter's safety, telling herself she must hold fast to Awos's faith regarding the girl's homecoming, as well as remember the words of his final prophecy.

As she did, she noticed Vedukha, standing behind Potis's kneeling form, place a hand on his shoulder. Potis, without turning around, reached up and covered Vedukha's hand with his own, giving it a squeeze. Nothing more than an innocent gesture of comfort, offered and acknowledged, Awija conceded. After all, Vedukha was the widow of Potis's best friend, and she was Sata's cousin; she and her children were considered part of the family circle. Still, Awija prayed as well for Sata, wondering if her son's wife had any idea what awaited her return – assuming she and Naya has survived the long winter alone on the steppe, with nothing more than the company of two strangers to assist and protect them.

A short while later, just as Awija thought Awos might be nearing his last breath, the tent flap opened, revealing the gaunt figure of the senior priest, fully garbed in his ceremonial attire. Obviously, he'd delayed in order to dress for the occasion. *How typical*, Awija thought. When Awos passed, Bhlaghmn would become the clan's eldest male member, the last of his generation of five brothers who represented the core of the clan. As such, Awija could not deny her brother-in-law's right to bear witness, however she felt about him personally.

"It won't be long now," she said in place of a greeting. Bhlaghmn nodded in reply and moved to claim a place at the head of Awos's pallet, requiring Potis and Tausos to shift aside to make room for him. A skin rattle, lavishly adorned with raven feathers, appeared from beneath his robes and the priest drew himself up, as though about to speak, or perhaps chant. Before he could open his mouth, however, Awija sent him a quelling look. She would tolerate the old vulture's presence, but not his ceremonies.

"It won't be long now," she repeated firmly, before he could object. "The door is already open. He does not need your help to pass through." *The Goddess is waiting to welcome him*, she wanted to add, *unbidden by the likes of you.*

Moments passed. How many, Awija couldn't be sure, but at some point she became aware of a subtle shift, deep within her heart. She'd been so focused on caring for her husband throughout his decline that she hadn't allowed herself to think about him actually being gone. Now she recognized the first stirrings of grief. The pain was not unwelcome. It spoke of the depth of their feelings for one another. She and Awos had loved long and well. She would mourn his passing from the earth, yet his spirit would always be with her. Who knew how many more moons she herself had left?

Not long now, she said again to herself, reaching to cradle her beloved's nearly lifeless hand in hers. *Not long*. And in that instant, just as the flaming orange disk of the sun appeared above the eastern horizon, the old clan chief released one final breath before departing from the land of the living.

Afterwards, Awija would remember that her husband's death had coincided with the spring *Aiqos*, one of the year's two points of equilibrium, when darkness and daylight were evenly matched. Much later, looking back, she realized the portent had been clear. With the old chief's departure from the earth, the forces responsible for keeping the world in balance must have lost their hold. How else to account for everything that followed?

PART ONE

Chapter One

The first of the calamities presaged by the old chief's passing occurred four days following his death, on the night of the dark moon. The young herders charged with guarding the clan's cattle, sheep and goats, pastured some distance from the clan's winter settlement, had just settled into camp for the evening when vicious marauders disguised as wolves attacked them. The unsuspecting boys were quickly subdued. Beaten, bound and gagged, they looked on horrified as the thieves slaughtered the newborn lambs and kids, then made off with the choicest of the remaining livestock. Two days passed before the herders managed to free themselves. By the time they stumbled into the clan's settlement, battered and bruised and driving before them the few animals the thieves had left behind, seven days had gone by, giving the raiders a substantial head start.

The herders' tale of the attack was met with shock and disbelief. How could such a thing have happened? What had become of the dogs, who should have sounded the alarm? Most disturbing of all was the raiders' senseless slaughter of the newborn lambs and kids. Even the most stoic among the boys broke down when relating this aspect of the thieves' treachery. Who in the sight of the gods would do such a thing? Offering an adult animal, chosen and sanctified, as a sacrifice to demonstrate the people's gratitude to Sky Father and ensure the gods' future favor was one thing. What the raiders had done to the newborns was outright butchery – malicious, evil, unforgivable.

Potis, the clan chief, stood alone in his tent, contemplating the herders' grim news. He'd sent for his brother, Tausos, wanting to confer in private before discussing with the other clan members what to do in response to the raid. With his back to the door flap, he heard his brother enter and turned.

"We'll need to send out a tracking party." Potis spoke without preliminary.

"Agreed," Tausos replied, "and I should be the one to go."

Potis considered his brother's words. Tausos's middle son was one of the young herders who'd been attacked. Neither the boy nor his companions had suffered any permanent physical harm, but all felt ashamed. Potis had been forced to intervene to stop Skelos, his cousin and archrival, from needlessly berating them. The raid had not been the young herders' fault. Still, the clan chief was not surprised that his brother would want to lead the hunt for the perpetrators. Unfortunately, he would have to disappoint him.

"No," Potis answered. "I understand why you want to go, but I need you here."

"Skelos is saying he should be the one to lead the tracking party," Tausos countered. "Is that what you want?"

"Of course not." Potis turned away and started pacing. He did not need reminding of why allowing his cousin to chase after the thieves would be a bad idea. Skelos might easily take matters into his own hands, either by retaliating without consideration for the consequences, or by deciding to conduct his own raid against another tribe, as he'd been advocating for some time. Both options were likely to prove disastrous.

"Given the brazenness of the attack," Potis said, continuing to pace, "the marauders almost certainly had the backing of powerful allies. We're going to need help – warriors from our entire tribe. We'll have to wait for the Gathering, when all the Plānos clans will be assembled. In the meantime, someone with discretion needs to track the thieves and identify them without tipping them off or doing anything reckless." Potis stopped and looked across the hearth at his brother. He didn't want to be without him by his side, but whom else could he trust to send?

"Exactly." Tausos raised a brow in acknowledgment of what the clan chief had left unsaid. "With Father so recently passed, you want your supporters around you," he sympathized, "but that's exactly why Skelos thinks he can take advantage. Better he stays where you can keep an eye on him and send me instead. I'll take Sunus, and Vedukha's boys. We can rely on them not to say anything. We'll discover who's responsible. When we return, you can decide how to respond. I'll back you up with the others."

Potis held his brother's gaze, weighing his advice. Sunus, Tausos's oldest son of nineteen summers, was nearly as skilled a hunter and tracker as his father. Vedukha's boys, while younger than Sunus, already showed considerable promise. More importantly, they could be counted on to be loyal to Potis, whom they looked up to as a father, ever since their own father had been killed.

"Alright," Potis said after a moment. "Thank you."

Skirting the hearth, Tausos came around to lay a hand on each of his brother's shoulders. "It will be alright," he said, looking him in the eye. The clan chief wished he could agree.

A short while later, Potis stood outside his tent, watching along with the rest of the settlement as the tracking party prepared to depart. They would travel light, taking only weapons and basic necessities. Potis glanced at the sky and pulled his cloak closer around his shoulders against the fresh breeze. If the unseasonably dry streak of early-spring weather held, the trackers' journey might be easier, as would their task. To a skilled tracker, hard ground could reveal a wealth of information, even when the trail was old. More likely they'd have rain or even snow, he speculated gloomily, erasing all sign of the thieves, given their long head start, and making travel miserable.

Potis's thoughts strayed to his wife Sata and daughter Naya. He wondered how they had fared over the winter – if they were still safe and if they might have taken advantage of the break in the weather to start for home. Were it not for this more urgent errand, he would have sent Tausos to fetch them. He sighed. His family would have to wait, and he would have to continue to rely on the good will of the strangers to whom he'd entrusted them.

Having said their goodbyes, the trackers awaited only the clan chief's blessing. Potis stepped forward. "Take care, brother," he said, wrapping Tausos in a one-armed hug.

"Take care, yourself," Tausos replied, his gaze cutting to where Skelos and his son Krnos stood a little apart. Having lost the argument about leading the tracking party himself, Skelos had insisted that Krnos, as one of the clan's best trackers, should at least be sent along. When Potis pointed out that the young man's scouting and sentry skills would be needed closer to home, Skelos had given in, although with great reluctance. Subsequently, Potis had observed father and son in whispered consultation and knew Tausos had noticed as well.

"Watch your back while I'm gone," he added now.

Following the direction of his brother's glance, the clan chief frowned. "Don't be away too long," he replied.

Nearly a month later…

When the trackers returned, they brought disturbing news: the stolen animals were in the possession of *ghosti* – foreigners – who appeared to be members of the powerful Dānus tribe, whose territory lay some distance to the south.

"We can't say for certain who stole our livestock – the thieves had too long a head start for us to be able to confirm their identity or follow them all the way back to the Dānus camp without risking detection," Tausos reported, speaking to the assembled clan shortly after the tracking party arrived back at the settlement. "But we definitely know where the animals ended up."

"Good job," Potis said, clapping his brother on the back and congratulating the other trackers as excited conversations broke out among the crowd. "We'll meet after supper to decide how to respond," he announced, raising his voice to be heard. Then leaning close to his brother's ear, the clan chief murmured, "follow me," and indicated his tent. He wanted to talk privately, without risk of being overheard.

"So, what did you *really* learn?" Potis demanded as soon as the door flap dropped behind them. "Because you know as well as I do that Ceru would never do such a thing."

The Dānus tribal leader was an old friend, he and Potis having first met as youngsters when their fathers had visited one another's territory. Over the years, the two had stayed in contact, meeting occasionally, sharing intelligence, and generally looking out for one another's interests. The connection was not common knowledge, however, particularly beyond their immediate families.

"Boyhood loyalties aside," Potis continued from the far side of the hearth, "why would Ceru send raiders all the way up here? The Dānus have more than enough cattle of their own."

"That's just it," Tausos explained. "The Dānus didn't steal our livestock. Once I realized where the animals ended up, I managed to get a message to Ceru. We met in secret, well away from the Dānus camp. According to him, a group of young warriors, purportedly from our tribe, showed up with an impressive number of cattle, sheep and goats. They said they were emissaries from a powerful chief seeking to establish an alliance through marriage – Ceru's daughter to be wed to the leader of the band of young warriors, who claimed to be a Plānos clan chief's son. The livestock were meant to be the bride price."

"Which Plānos clan chief? Whose son?" Potis sounded incredulous.

"Yours."

Potis stopped pacing and stared at his brother in disbelief. "But…" he began. Tausos said nothing, just raised an eyebrow.

Turning away, Potis began running through the implications in his mind. Ceru knew he had no sons, only his daughter Naya. Someone unaware of their friendship had stolen his clan's most valuable livestock and tried to pass-off the animals as their own while assuming the identity of Potis's non-existent son. Who would do such a thing and believe they could get away with it? And why? What was the point?

"Did Ceru have any idea of the thief's true identity?" he asked. "How did he respond?"

"Ceru knew the animals belonged to us – he recognized the young bull from the description you gave him last summer, when you and I took that hunting trip south and we crossed paths," Tausos answered. "He also obviously knew the young warrior claiming to be your son wasn't telling the truth."

Tausos paused, looking around for a place to sit. "Do you mind? I'm exhausted. We really pushed to make it back as soon as we could."

"Of course," Potis replied, contrite. He pulled two piles of furs closer to the hearth. "Are you hungry? Thirsty?"

Tausos shook his head as they both sat. "No – just happy to get off my feet."

Groaning, he stretched out a leg and began unlacing one of his hide boots. "To answer your question, Ceru did not recognize the young warrior. But Ceru's as wily as a pike, as you know," he went on. "He played along with the raiders and agreed to the whole arrangement. The young warrior promised to return with his father, the chief – meaning you – in time for the wedding to take place as part of the Dānus tribe's annual festival. It's their equivalent of our Gathering and takes at the autumn *Aiqos*."

"And meanwhile our animals were to be left behind, as security?"

"Exactly."

"At least they're safe with Ceru," Potis observed, "but the whole thing still doesn't make any sense. I can see someone stealing our livestock to use as a bride price – an alliance with the Dānus would be valuable to just about anyone – but why pretend to be my son?"

"Unless an alliance was never the intent." Tausos pulled off his second boot and looked up. "The theory isn't mine," he confessed. "Ceru came up with it. He said to ask you if there's anyone who would want to harm our clan, and you in particular, by stealing our livestock and not getting caught with them. Anyone who might benefit?"

Potis looked at his brother. Neither spoke. They both knew the answer to Ceru's question.

"Without proof, we can't be sure," Potis said after a moment. "Although that would explain why Skelos was so keen to lead the tracking party or at least send Krnos along."

"My thoughts exactly," Tausos concurred.

"Even so, we have to know for certain who else is involved before we confront anyone," Potis cautioned. "To start making accusations otherwise would be ill-advised, to say the least."

"Ceru knew we'd need evidence," Tausos replied. "He's planning to come to the Gathering and bring the livestock with him. Assuming the young warrior who led the raid is who we think he is, Ceru will be able to identify him – and everyone will recognize the young bull as the one you traded for at last year's Gathering."

"But Ceru is a *ghostis* – the head of an unallied foreign tribe," Potis objected. "He can't attend the Gathering without joint agreement among all the Plānos clan chiefs. Otherwise, his presence could be construed as a hostile act. He'll need a plausible excuse for showing up."

"Ceru thought of that as well," Tausos assured him. "His story will be that he's heard that you replaced Father last summer as chief of our clan and are to succeed him as head of the entire Plānos tribe at this year's Gathering. He'll say he has come to be first in line to seek an alliance with you through the marriage of his oldest son, Perqos, to your daughter Naya. As proof of his sincerity, he will have brought a choice offering of cattle, sheep and goats to serve as the bride price."

Potis looked up, a reluctant smile creasing his features. "That's brilliant," he conceded. "Leave it to Ceru. He and I have discussed the possibility of such a match, but never publicly. Still, the story is entirely plausible."

Sobering, Potis waited a beat before continuing. "Of course, in order for Ceru's plan to work, Naya and Sata will have had to have returned by the time of the Gathering. Unfortunately, that's far from guaranteed." He sounded grim.

"They'll be back," Tausos reassured him. "Give me a day or two to recover and I'll go after them."

"Would you?" Potis gave his brother a grateful look. There was no way the clan chief could go himself.

"Of course," Tausos reiterated. "Meanwhile," he went on, returning to the problem at hand, "we at least know our animals are safe with Ceru."

"Which gives us even more incentive to convince everyone else to wait before trying to reclaim them." Potis tented his fingers, thinking. "When we meet tonight," he said after a moment, "if you could repeat what you reported when you first arrived, I'll take it from there."

Tausos nodded. "How do you think Skelos will react?"

"He's never been known to go along me willingly," Potis acknowledged. "But who knows how he might want this to play out? Whatever he says, our objective is to convince our fellow clansmen to wait until after the Gathering to respond to the raid, without letting on about our suspicions. Agreed?"

"Agreed."

Later that evening…

Following the evening meal, which had been eaten in family groups, Potis, Tausos, and the other men of the clan returned to gather around the central fire. Some of the women joined the council circle as well, including Awija, Vedukha, and Skelos's younger sister Saurosa, but by custom the men were expected to do most of the talking.

Once everyone was assembled, Potis asked Tausos, seated at his left, to recount again what the trackers had learned. While embellished with a few more details, the essence remained the same: regardless of who may have stolen the clan's animals, they were now in the hands of the Dānus. When his brother finished, Potis raised aloft the *tloqai-koljō*, a straight thick alder branch wrapped in leather strips and adorned with feathers, signaling that he would be the next to speak.

"As I feared all along," he began, "our best livestock have ended up in the possession of a tribe too powerful for us to confront on our own. Only with the backing of the other clans of our own tribe can we muster the force needed to secure the animals' return. With a show of strength, we will be able to successfully negotiate, rather than risk actual violence. In the meantime, a counterraid would only make a permanent enemy of the Dānus, which serves no one's interest. Once our fellow Plānos warriors have learned of our need, they will surely come to our aid, but we cannot reasonably seek their assistance until we are all present for the Gathering."

Potis paused, letting his words sink in.

"The situation is clear, my friends," he concluded, voice firm. "Only with the support of our allies can we hope to reclaim our herds without the risk of starting a war. We must be patient and solicit their help at the Gathering."

Lowering the *tloqai-koljō*, the clan chief surveyed the faces around the circle. Expressions were difficult to read in the semi-darkness, but at least some clan members were nodding their heads in agreement with what he'd said. Others had turned toward Skelos, seated on the opposite side of the central blaze, wanting to hear from him before making up their minds.

Potis eyed his cousin. Skelos returned his gaze with a sardonic half-smile that accentuated the jagged scar across his left cheek. Holding out a hand, he gestured for the *tloqai-koljō*. Surrendering the ceremonial branch, Potis watched as it passed from hand to hand around the circle, knowing that his rival was likely to oppose everything he had just said. If only his fellow clan members would recognize the folly of his cousin's insistence on seeking immediate revenge.

To Potis's surprise, instead of debating, Skelos began by agreeing with him. "Our *Dukos* is correct," he declared, using Potis's official title without apparent irony. "Under the circumstances, we have no choice but to enlist the help of the other clans within our tribe."

Murmurs broke out around the circle. The clan chief wasn't the only one surprised by his rival's words. Awija, seated nearby with the other women, caught Potis's eye and raised a single skeptical brow. *What is he up to now?* Potis wondered the same.

"We still have a problem, however," Skelos continued. "Even if we wait until after the Gathering to go after the raiders, we'll have nothing to offer the other Plānos clans in return for helping us. We won't be able to repay them unless we're prepared to trade away a good portion of whatever livestock we recover."

"This is what I've been saying all along," Bhlaghmn interjected. Seated halfway between Potis and Skelos, the old priest didn't bother waiting to be handed the *tloqai-koljō*. His hooded eyes, sunk deep in his lined face, gleamed in the reflected light of the fire. "If we're to contribute our share as hosts of the Gathering," he warned, "we'll have no choice but to sacrifice our remaining animals, leaving us unable to compensate the rest of the tribe for their assistance in recovering the stolen livestock, unless we hand them over too."

"My point exactly, Uncle," Skelos agreed, smoothly resuming control of the discussion. "Is this what you would have us do?" he inquired of Potis. "Wait, like powerless weaklings, until our debt is so heavy that it cannot be repaid?" Skelos no longer bothered to mask his derision. His question hung in the night air, along with a silent accusation aimed at the clan chief: *this is all your fault.*

Part of Potis wanted to agree. In the time since he had taken over from his father as chief, less than a year ago, the clan had gone from being prosperous and respected to losing nearly everything. As their leader, he bore responsibility. Yet accepting his rival's judgment would mean not only forsaking his father's legacy, but going against everything the old chief had taught him – an even bigger failure.

Rising, Potis gestured for the *tloqai-koljō*, his eyes never leaving his cousin's face. If Skelos and Bhlaghmn and their followers thought he would cede his position as head of the clan, they were mistaken. Too much depended on winning this fight.

"Friends," he began, holding the stick aloft. "Despite our present misfortunes, I stand before you as Awos's chosen successor. I am determined to protect all that he stood for from being destroyed, which it will be if we abandon his example.

"Most of us grew to manhood watching the old chief nurture ties of reciprocity and mutual assistance," he reminded his audience. "Never did we hear him speak of debts owed in return for favors granted. He built a reputation for being trustworthy, generous and fair. Over and over, these qualities ensured not merely power for one family, clan or tribe over another, but lasting prosperity and peace for everyone. Such is the true measure our wealth and inheritance, not the present paltry size of our herds."

Potis lowered the *tloqai-koljō*. He'd spoken honestly, from the heart, as his father would have counseled. He prayed to the old chief's spirit that what he'd said would be enough.

He was about to resume his seat when Skelos's son, Krnos, who was on sentry duty, came running to announce the arrival of visitors. Two young men followed in his wake. The appearance of travelers this late in the evening was unusual. Even so, Potis noted, neither Skelos nor Bhlaghmn seemed surprised.

He remained standing to confront the newcomers. "They've surrendered their weapons?" Potis spoke curtly, looking to Krnos for confirmation. Krnos nodded.

"Please." Potis gestured, giving the visitors leave to enter the circle and identify themselves. Those seated around the fire shifted, making room.

Only when the pair stepped into the light did Potis recognize them: Wailos, son of Regos, and his cousin, Unksra. Head of an allied clan whose territory lay on the eastern side of the river, Regos was Potis's main opposition to be chosen as tribal leader of the Plānos, now that Awos had passed.

Potis noted that Wailos appeared to have inherited his father's considerable presence. Entering the circle with the predatory confidence of a young wolf, he effortlessly drew everyone's attention. No one even glanced at his cousin, who all but disappeared in his shadow. Nor had Wailos any need of an introduction – everyone knew him, if not personally, at least by reputation.

The young warrior was strikingly handsome, Potis had to grant, with bronzed skin, high angled cheekbones, and straight brows over piercing eyes as black as jet. Yet, for all Wailos's good looks and evident charisma, something about the thin set of his lips hinted at the potential for cruelty, not to mention treachery. The young wolf was not to be trusted, Potis was certain, any more than his father, Regos.

Sweeping Potis a courteous salute, Wailos proceeded to acknowledge the others gathered around the fire, grasping wrists with those who were friends of his father's, including Skelos and Bhlaghmn. He saved a wicked, white-toothed grin for the cluster of women, singling out Saurosa, Skelos's much-younger unmarried sister. Potis wasn't surprised when he saw Saurosa return their visitor's bold regard. He'd seen the two together at last year's Gathering.

Potis traded looks with his brother, seated beside him. Given the suspicions raised by Tausos's conversation with Ceru, Wailos's arrival constituted a surprising development.

Greetings having been exchanged, the clan chief addressed the newcomers. "Wailos, son of Regos; Unksra, nephew of Regos," he began with appropriate formality, nodding to each in turn, "we are pleased to honor you as our guests. To what do we owe the favor of your visit?"

Wailos acknowledged his host's welcome with equal courtesy. "We accept with gratitude your hospitality," he replied, bowing, "and would beg your assistance as well. We've come at my father's behest to seek out new summer pastures for a portion of our herds, as our usual grasslands have become too dry to support them. Knowing our explorations would bring us close to your winter settlement, we have come seeking permission to journey through your territory, as well as gain advice on where we might go in search of better grazing for our livestock."

As Wailos spoke, striking just the right note of polite deference, Potis observed how much the young man's polished delivery recalled his father's oratorical gifts. On more than one occasion, Potis had witnessed Regos wield charm and apparent sincerity with the skill of a warrior handling lethal weapons. The reminder only served to put the clan chief further on his guard.

"But first, may I inquire what is amiss?" Wailos went on. "Your sentry hinted that some adversity has befallen your clan?"

Suppressing a scowl, Potis searched for Krnos among those gathered at the fringes of the circle, but the erstwhile sentry had returned to his post. He sighed. At this point there was nothing to be gained from concealing the raid. Besides, the clan chief was interested in Wailos's reaction once he'd been officially informed of the situation. First, however, the requirements of hospitality needed to be observed. Saurosa and Vedukha had already risen to fetch mugs of spring water and trenchers of leftover stew.

"Please," Potis said again, gesturing. Resuming his own seat, he indicated the place of honor to his right. "Allow us to offer you food and drink while we share with you the story of our misfortune." As Wailos and Unksra seated themselves, Potis noted the travel-stained state of their clothing, which would seem to indicate the two had been living rough for some time.

"Before you arrived," he began, once they were settled, "we were deciding what to do about the brazen theft of the best portion of our livestock, those animals who remained after the earlier losses suffered as a result of the hard winter…" Potis paused long enough for Saurosa to hand Wailos his food, not failing to note the exchange of flirtatious glances.

"Not only did the scurrilous scoundrels abscond with all of our breeding stock," he went on, making sure to sound suitably outraged, "but they left behind the carcasses of this year's newborns." He would have preferred not to dwell on the latter atrocity, which could only serve to stir up Skelos's faction, but leaving out any reference to the slaughter would have been too obvious an omission.

"Of course we sent out a tracking party immediately," he continued, "and thanks to their good work, we've discovered the whereabout of our animals. All that remains is to reach agreement on how to respond."

As Potis spoke, he watched for changes in Wailos's demeanor. Upon being told of the raid, their guest adopted an expression of concerned sympathy. Hearing mention of the massacre, he looked appropriately shocked. Learning that they'd identified the thieves – or at least those currently in possession of the livestock – he seemed gratified but no more. *Nothing conclusive, one way or the other,* Potis thought. *Time to raise the crucial question.*

"You see," he went on, "the tribe in possession of our stolen livestock is among the most fearsome and powerful to roam the steppe – the Dānus. Therein lies our dilemma, as we were just discussing. The timing of your arrival is indeed fortuitous. Perhaps you could speculate as to whether, following the Gathering, your father would be willing to send warriors to join us in seeking restitution from the raiders?"

"He might," Wailos answered diplomatically. "In any case, I'm sure that he, along with our entire clan, will be most aggrieved to learn what has befallen you."

No doubt, Potis thought cynically.

"But there is a more pressing concern," interjected Bhlaghmn. "Something that cannot wait until after the Gathering. We must have animals for *Sāwel-Dom*, and for my brother's funeral."

"Forgive me," remarked Wailos, looking from the priest to the clan chief in evident surprise. "Must I assume from your words that Awos, our most revered leader, chief of chiefs of the Plānos, has made his final passage from this world?"

Potis fumed at his uncle's lack of discretion. He'd hope to avoid mention of the old chief's death but now that Bhlaghmn had spoken, ignoring the news would be disrespectful. "Yes," he replied tersely. "My father's spirit departed at dawn on the morning of the spring *Aiqos*. His body lies in a temporary grave, awaiting the ceremonial burial that is his due, once the whole tribe is present for the Gathering."

"My sincere condolences." Wailos's sympathy appeared genuine. Around the circle, heads bowed in a customary sign of respect for the departed chief. Watching as their guest dropped his gaze along with the rest, Potis wondered again what he was up to. Awos's death, along with the clan's other devastating losses, assured Regos's path to power, but why take the risk of showing up to verify the situation in person?

Potis needed to think. Noting the trencher of stew sitting untouched in Wailos's lap, he decided to call for a break. "Let us allow our guests to eat and rest after their long trek," he suggested once the moment of silence for the old clan chief had ended. The invitation was met with general agreement. A few people rose to take care of personal needs, while others lapsed into conversation with those seated nearby.

As Potis watched, Wailos held out his mug for Saurosa to fill, which she did with an obliging smile. Unksra ate in silence next to him. The clan chief pondered their presence. With the help of the information Tausos had gleaned from Ceru, the broad outlines of the conspiracy were becoming clear – the pieces all falling into place. Yet even so, the last thing Potis would have expected was for Wailos and his cousin to show up, unannounced. Moreover, much as he may have wanted to confront their visitor, to do so without more proof would be foolhardy.

Surveying the rest of the circle, Potis could easily speculate as to the price the clan would be forced to pay if they had to depend on Wailos's father to provide their contribution to this year's rites – their full support in backing Regos's ambitions. The conclusion left a hollow pit in his stomach. He looked across the fire at Skelos, laughing quietly at something Bhlaghmn said. His cousin, his uncle, their followers – Regos himself, for that matter — they all viewed the world in terms of competition for scarce resources, whether livestock, grazing rights, hunting territory, even the exchange of women in marriage. If Regos became head of the tribe, Potis was certain the Plānos would be led down a path of intrigue and conflict, ending ultimately in outright war.

He looked over to the women and caught his mother looking back at him. Awija wore that knowing expression of hers, as though she could guess his thoughts. Perhaps he should talk the situation over with her. If his wife Sata were available, she would have counseled him. His gaze shifted to Vedukha, seated next to Awija. Meeting his eyes, she sent him an encouraging smile. He smiled back.

"*Dukos?*" The polite inquiry interrupted Potis's thoughts. Wailos had finished eating and laid his trencher aside. "May I share an idea which might perhaps be an answer to your predicament?"

"Certainly," Potis replied, wondering if Wailos had somehow guessed at the questions running through his mind. "We welcome any suggestion you have to offer."

Conversation around the circle ceased. Everyone was curious to hear what the visitor might have to say.

"If I understand correctly," Wailos began, "the most pressing problem is that your clan no longer possess the sheep, goats, and above all the cattle required for *Sāwel-Dom*, as well as for the old chief's funeral celebration."

A murmur of accord arose from the audience.

"While a counterattack could be mounted with assistance from my own clan and others in the tribe," Wailos continued, "it would have to wait until after the Gathering, which will be too late to solve the immediate need."

More nods from around the circle.

"Well then," Wailos paused with a rhetorical flourish, "if cattle and other livestock suitable for the rites are lacking, why not acquire an even better alternative?"

"What did you have in mind?" countered Potis, unsure of where this was going.

Wailos replied with a query of his own. "Of all the creatures of the earth," he asked, "which pleases the gods the most, even more than cattle? Which is the most noble, the most beautiful, the most esteemed?"

He paused again, holding everyone's attention.

"The answer is, of course, *the horse*."

A jolt of surprise traveled through the assembly, followed by a wave of agreement as everyone recognized the undeniable truth of Wailos's pronouncement. While the tribes of the steppe cherished their sheep, goats, and especially their cattle as befitted valuable gifts from the gods, and were grateful for the presence of deer, bison and other game, the majestic herds of wild horses with whom they shared the vast grasslands held a special fascination and significance. No doubt the gods agreed.

Where is he going with this? Potis wondered again, the hollow returning to the pit of his stomach. He thought of Naya's strange visions of the red filly, and of his daughter's quest, kept secret from the rest of the clan, to tame the filly and her herd.

"As we all know," Wailos went on, "the challenge *Sawel-Dom* is to bring a living creature before the people to be consecrated and sacrificed."

This was also true. To count as a true sacrifice, the animal's spirit, while still living, must be entreated to carry the people's prayers of gratitude and supplication to *Dyēus-Ptēr* and the *Deiwos*. Only then could the animal's body be ritually slaughtered under the direction of the high priest. Normally, individuals were selected from among the choicest livestock and carefully raised from an early age with such a fate in mind. For obvious reasons, wild animals, including horses, were much more difficult to sacrifice properly. But perhaps this made them all the more pleasing to the gods? Potis watched as everyone's gaze turned toward Bhlaghmn, wondering what the old priest would say. Ignoring the looks cast in his direction, Bhlaghmn's attention remained fixed on their guest, a speculative gleam in his eye.

Wailos continued. "While regrettable that treacherous foreigners have stolen the animals intended for this year's rites, there is a solution: capture a herd of wild horses. Trap them and keep them alive until the Gathering. There is still plenty of time, and the other clans will be coming here, so no need to travel a long distance with the horses in tow."

Unprecedented as their visitor's idea might have seemed, the possibilities were immediately obvious. Everyone began talking at once.

"Quiet!" Potis demanded, hiding his mounting dismay behind a show of irritation at the loss of decorum. "How, exactly, are we to accomplish this feat?"

"A large corral," Wailos replied, "constructed at the back of one of the ravines that cuts into the bluffs along the river and disguised so that the horses can be driven inside and trapped."

Potis was not alone in raising concerns about the difficulties involved in executing such an ambitious undertaking, but Wailos seemed able to meet every objection with a persuasive solution, almost as though he'd had plenty of time to consider the matter. His case was strengthened when Krnos chimed in that he knew of a band of horses who seemed to have become accustomed to humans and might therefore be easier to catch. When Bhlaghmn, after appearing to listen carefully to all the arguments for and against the scheme, at last gave his blessing, the clan chief had little choice but to agree as well.

Later that night, lying alone in his family's tent, staring up into the darkness waiting for sleep to come, Potis reflected on the day's unexpected turn of events: first Tausos's disturbing news, followed by Wailos himself showing up with his seemingly original solution to the clan's problems. The clan chief felt certain their guest's proposal was not what his father, the old chief, had meant when he'd spoken of horses on his deathbed. He was also quite sure that his daughter would be appalled – assuming she still lived. But he could find no grounds on which to reject the idea of capturing and sacrificing a wild herd without risk of betraying Naya's strange encounters with the red filly, along with her grandfather's portentous visions of the future.

Whatever their visitor was up to, at least he would remain where Potis could keep an eye on him. Wailos and his cousin had offered to stay on, avowing their errand of searching out summer pastures could easily be accomplished in the course of assisting in pursuit of the wild horses. Potis's misgivings notwithstanding, for the moment he had little choice but to go along, regardless of Wailos's true motivations and whether or not the plan worked.

Chapter Two

Six days later, on a bluff top near the clan's settlement…

Stretched out on her stomach, sharp rocks biting into her hips and forearms, the smell of damp soil and crushed weeds mingling in her nostrils, Naya lifted her head just high enough to see down into the ravine from her hidden perch. Even from this distance, she felt a constant buzz of anxiety coming from the herd of horses trapped below.

With no breeze stirring, the heat of the mid-morning sun was becoming uncomfortable, but she remained as she was. If she sat up to ease her position or remove a layer of clothing, she might be spotted from below. She wished she could get closer but as it was, she was testing the limits of the strict orders her father had given her yesterday to stay away from the corrals.

Restless, the horses circled, and circled again, their hooves churning the rain-soaked earth into a quagmire as they searched for a way to escape. Occasionally, one or two at a time would stop to grab mouthfuls of grass hay from one of several scattered piles, before resuming their incessant pacing. A large clay basin near the corral gate held clean water, untouched. Every now and then, one of the mares, always the same one, lifted her head and gave a loud whinny, full of nervous tension, calling to the stallion to whom she and the others had looked for protection. The mare's desperate cries were futile; the stallion could no longer answer. The sound rent Naya's heart. These horses were her friends.

She could envision all too clearly what must have happened the previous day, not long before her return to the clan's settlement after being away all winter. Too late, BeHregs, the stallion, had understood the danger toward which he and his family were being stampeded. Before he could turn them back, he'd been cut down by the men's spears. Panicked, the rest of the herd had galloped on, chased by more men and their dogs, leaving BeHregs's body trampled in their wake. Now the mares and the youngsters were trapped inside the corral into which they'd been driven. At first, Naya imagined, they must have raced frantically around the perimeter of the enclosure until eventually, exhausted, they'd had to stop. Even after a night in the pen, she could see they remained unsettled. Anyone approaching the fence set them off running again.

Rebhjo, largest of the mares, was the most upset, calling repeatedly and threatening to kick her herd mates if they strayed too close. The others who Naya recognized – Mus and Ghrasom, along with their yearling offspring MiMus and Bhrounos – did their best to give the big mare space but in their own agitation could not always stay out of her way. Rebhjo's filly, Melos, seemed to have attached herself to a new member of the herd, a small, pale-coated mare with an even paler star-shaped mark on her forehead, who was heavy with foal. BeHregs must have added her to his band since Naya had last seen them. Another addition, a golden dun mare with a dark dorsal stripe, had a tiny foal at her side who couldn't have been more than a few days old.

Seeing the little one, Naya pushed the image of another small, vulnerable creature out of her mind. Only two days had passed since the awful morning of the lion attack, when she'd held the blood-soaked body of MeHnd's month-old colt as he died in her arms. The other horses who'd been with them – the colt's mother MeHnd, the outcast gray stallion Šuurgan and MeHnd's three-year old red filly Réhda, with whom Naya had a special bond – had disappeared immediately afterwards. *Only two days!* Naya thought. Yet so much had changed. For the first time since Réhda and the others had vanished in the wake of the attack, she was glad there'd been no sign of them. At least they weren't trapped with the herd below.

Naya pressed her forehead into her folded arms and squeezed her eyes shut, willing the dizziness she felt looking down at the horses to stop. Wishing she could block out the memory of the dead colt as well, she recalled instead everything that had happened since yesterday, when she and her mother and the others had arrived at the clan's settlement.

Rather than the warm welcome they'd expected after their long absence, they'd found the encampment temporarily deserted, with no one on hand to greet them. Climbing up to the bluff top above the settlement, they discovered the whole clan gathered on the opposite side, looking over the cliff's edge into a steep ravine, pointing and exclaiming about whatever was below. At first, no one had noticed their arrival. As soon as Naya spotted her father, she'd raced across the distance separating them and thrown herself into his embrace. As much as she'd anticipated the triumph of riding into the clan's settlement astride the red filly, she longed even more to feel her father's strong arms wrapped around her. Safe in the protective circle of his love, she could forget the anger, grief, betrayal and guilt of the last few days and cling to him instead.

"What is everyone so excited about?" she'd asked him once he set her down.

"We've captured a herd of wild horses."

"Let me see!" she begged, trying to get a glimpse down into the ravine.

"Not now," he'd insisted, pulling her away from the cliff's edge. "First, we need to celebrate. Thank the gods, you're home!"

Joy lighting his face, he'd picked her up again and spun her around, just as he'd done when she was a little girl. Afterwards, they were both swept along by the crowd, so that she had no chance to go back and see the captured horses for herself, and once they'd returned to the settlement, her father kept her with him, even dissuading her when she would have gone in search of her grandmother.

"Awija will greet you soon enough," he told her. "Right now, you and I must oversee the festivities."

He'd made clear that she was to remain by his side, and she felt flattered to be given a seat next to him in front of the central fire. The place of honor to his right, however, was reserved for the clan's distinguished guest, the young warrior who, she learned, had been visiting for several days and was responsible for the plan of capturing the wild horses. Even before being officially introduced to him, she recognized the young warrior as Wailos, son of one of the tribe's other clan chiefs. Her cousin Melit had pointed him out at last year's Gathering, remarking on how handsome he was, but at the time Naya hadn't paid much heed. Now, however, his feat had become the focus of everyone's attention, including her father's, thereby overshadowing her own homecoming. Worse, along with her father's admiration and respect, the clan's visitor had evidently stolen Naya's idea, or at least a version of it.

If only I could talk to Papa alone, she thought. She wanted it to be just the two of them so she could tell him about everything that had happened with the red filly over the winter while she'd been away. She would explain to him that her vision for the horses had nothing to do with taking away their freedom. But the filly was only part of the reason she wanted to speak to her father in private. He deserved to know the truth about what she'd witnessed going on between her mother and Oyuun, the stranger who had stayed with them throughout winter, keeping them safe.

Instead, Naya had been required to remain demurely by her father's side, surrounded by other people, behaving politely while trying to hide her mounting impatience. She'd grown especially frustrated listening to the other men extoll Wailos's knowledge of the nature and habits of wild horses and asking for his views about how to tame them – for what purpose Naya still wasn't exactly clear. *She* was supposed to be the one with the special relationship with the horses. *She* was the one who knew how to tame them, how to *ride!* As badly as Naya had wanted to interrupt, however, she'd held her tongue, afraid no one would give any credence to what she had to say. After all, she was only a girl.

Almost as irritating, she'd had to endure watching Krnos, her childhood tormenter, be recognized for his contribution to the wild herd's successful capture. Apparently, he'd been the scout credited with sighting the horses and alerting the others. Watching as he ducked his head in feigned modesty while Wailos sang his praises, Naya could see Krnos had become a great favorite of the clan's esteemed guest, whom he clearly hero-worshipped in return.

As if Krnos felt her eyes on him from across the fire, he'd pinned her with a derisive smile. "Naya," he'd called, loud enough to be heard above the babble of voices, his tone just shy of mocking. "Tell us, how did you manage to make it through the winter?"

Caught off guard, Naya stared back. With everyone's attention focused on her, she'd stubbornly refused to look away, which made her failure to respond seem rude. In reality, she hadn't trusted herself to speak. Before the moment could grow even more awkward and her father find it necessary to rebuke her for her lack of manners, her mother stepped forward and offered to tell the story of their survival.

Naya should have been relieved – grateful even – but she wasn't. Listening to her mother's account of what had befallen them, she'd grown even more upset. On top of giving all the credit for their survival to Oyuun and Aytal – the stranger and his son who'd rescued them – her mother managed to avoid mentioning the red filly and the other horses entirely, not even the poor colt. Outraged, Naya wanted to object to her mother's version of the story but was afraid that she might burst into tears. And so she sat there, letting her mother speak in her stead.

The only person to whom she might have turned for sympathy was off limits. Even had both her parents not warned her against speaking to Aytal, neither need have worried. Now that they had returned to the settlement, Naya wanted only to avoid him. Not because of Aytal's errant arrow that had almost ended her life. She'd forgiven him for that, unlike her father who had made clear that justice still needed to be served. But after everything else they'd been through, including the lion attack, Naya's feelings for Aytal were complicated. She needed time to sort them out before confronting him.

He and his father had found a place at one of the smaller fires surrounding the central blaze where they stayed throughout the evening. At one point Naya saw Aytal's younger brother Dayan join them, but after a while the boy left to rejoin her uncle's family, with whom he'd been living. As the festivities wore on, Naya found her gaze turning in Aytal's direction but whenever he looked up, she quickly glanced away. She wished he would stop wearing that remorseful expression, which just made her feel more irritated. If only she could bring herself to be truly angry with him, things would be so much easier.

Eventually, tired of brooding and as annoyed with herself as with everyone else, Naya decided to go back to her family's dwelling where she could at least pretend to sleep. By now, she was sure, she had little hope of attracting her father's attention, let alone talking to him. *Why couldn't he understand?* She wanted him to tell him how she'd succeeded in taming not only the red filly, but the mare and the gray stallion as well. She was even willing to give Aytal his share of the glory. She wanted to describe what it had been like to ride, galloping across the vast grasslands, as free as an eagle soaring on the wind. She wanted to confess what had happened to the colt, how guilty and devastated she felt about his death, and she'd wanted to warn her father of her mother's betrayal.

Absorbed in talking to the other men around the central fire, her father didn't seem to notice her unhappiness. Not until she rose abruptly did he put out a hand to stop her, asking where she was going.

"I'm tired Papa," she'd said, evading his grasp. Swallowing hard, she managed the smile she knew he would want to see. "It's been a long day," she apologized. "I need to go to bed."

Hurriedly, before the light from the fire could betray the tear-tracks staining her cheeks, she'd excused herself, disappearing into her family's shelter.

Back at the bluff top, overlooking the ravine...

From below Naya's hidden perch, a loud and disgruntled *moooo* echoed off the limestone walls. Lifting her head, she scrubbed away grit and tears with her knuckles. *Enough*, she admonished herself, determined not to give in to her feelings. She looked down once more into the steep-sided gorge. Next to the large corral that held the horses stood a smaller pen, also constructed of brush and saplings bound with stout rope, containing what remained of the clan's livestock. A pair of her male cousins had taken down the enclosure's makeshift gate and, with the help of a couple of dogs, were driving the animals through the opening. As they passed, Naya counted: ten *lāpos* – young female cattle – one bullock, eight ewes, and seventeen she-goats, including the two she and her mother had brought back with them. The *lāpos* were too immature to have been bred this season, which accounted for the lack of calves. But no new lambs or kids cavorted at their mothers' sides either. Missing as well were the clan's two rams, six buck goats and the magnificent young bull who had cost her father so dearly when he'd traded for him at last year's Gathering, not to mention the majority of the clan's other cattle as well as the most productive of the dairy goats and the best wool producers among the sheep.

The loss, Naya realized, was staggering, especially the absence of youngsters and breeding males. Without them, there would be no means of rebuilding the herds, and little likelihood of the remaining sheep and goats continuing to produce milk. As for the upcoming rites of *Sāwel-Dom* – the sacred marking of the sun's still point in the summer sky – her people would be unable to make their expected contribution unless they gave up nearly all the animals that remained. Even if the other clans attending the Gathering could be persuaded to help, Naya knew her family's future looked extremely uncertain. The alternative was for them to go back to depending solely on hunting, fishing and gathering what they could from the land, with all the loss of status such an existence entailed.

From what Naya had gleaned last evening listening to the talk around the fire, her clan's only hope of avoiding such an outcome had something to do with the captured horses. Did her father know that the animals trapped in the corral belonged to the red filly's band? That they were *her* horses? If she'd been allowed to see them for herself yesterday, she could have explained to him how special they were.

She watched now as the mother of the new foal finally stood still long enough for the youngster to nurse. Dark patches of sweat stained the mare's flanks. The sun had gained in height and the cliff wall no longer cast much of a shadow. Naya worried about the lack of cover for the horses. She looked over to where a group of men stood several paces away from the corral gate, enjoying the shade of a large oak tree. They'd been there all morning, talking. Clearly, they were discussing the horses, but Naya was too far away to hear their words. At the moment, her father, her uncle Tausos, and two of her father's cousins were listening intently to Wailos. As had been the case last evening, the other men apparently regarded their guest as the expert.

All of this is my fault, Naya thought, looking down at the captured herd. First the colt, then poor BeHregs, and now the rest of the mares and youngsters – trapped, desperate to escape, bound for some fate she did not yet understand. The horses' disquiet continued to waft up like a hot breeze from the ravine floor. Naya was still dizzy, her head had begun to throb and her throat felt parched. Perhaps it was time she returned to the settlement. The sun's arc told her she'd been gone too long. People would wonder where she was and she needed a drink of water.

"What are you doing?" called a voice. Startled, Naya rolled off her stomach and sat up. Coming along the path from the settlement was her cousin Melit, her long black braid swinging behind her as she walked.

"Watching the horses," Naya replied, furtively wiping her cheeks. She crawled away from the cliff edge so she wouldn't be seen from below and stood up, brushing dirt and dried grass from the front of her tunic. Melit hurried forward. Throwing open her arms, she swept Naya into an enthusiastic hug. Although they'd exchanged waves from a distance the night before, they hadn't been able to talk to one another. Unable to resist her friend's genuine affection, Naya returned her embrace.

"I missed you so much!" Melit said, stepping back. The expression in her deep brown eyes matched the wide smile dimpling her pretty face. "A lot has happened since you've been gone."

"To both of us," concurred Naya, wondering where she would start if she were to try to explain to Melit about what she'd been through. Putting on a smile she hoped would hide her inner turmoil, Naya linked arms with her cousin as they turned to walk back in the direction of the settlement. "You talk first," she said with false brightness. "Tell me about all of it."

Words tumbling over one another, Melit began to recount the details of everything that had occurred during Naya's absence. In addition to descriptions of the winter's hardships and gossip involving their other female cousins, she gravely relayed to Naya the circumstances of her grandfather's passing. With a shock, Naya realized his death had occurred the same night that the colt was born, just as she and the others were preparing to set-off from the clearing. Four nights later had come the disastrous raid on the clan's livestock.

"They decided to lay your grandfather's body in a temporary grave," Melit explained, "until the rest of the tribe can be present for an official funeral befitting his status as chief of chiefs. He's to be formally interred on the second day of the Gathering." Melit turned to look at Naya. "No one as important as your grandfather has died since before you and I were born," she pointed out, sounding both solemn and excited. "His funeral is bound to be quite an occasion."

Listening to her cousin, Naya's mood sank even further. So many terrible things had happened while she'd been away. No wonder her father seemed even more burdened and preoccupied than usual.

"But Wailos and his cousin arrived just in time," Melit was saying, interrupting Naya's gloomy thoughts. "Capturing the wild horses was all his idea – although someone was saying your grandfather had some kind of dream about horses before he passed. Either way, Wailos was the one who came up with the plan. Isn't he handsome? And he's always so friendly. He certainly seemed interested in you last night."

Stopping for breath, Melit gave Naya a sidelong glance. They had reached the opposite edge of the bluff and were about to start down the narrow path, full of switchbacks, leading to the settlement. From here they would have to travel single file until they reached the bottom. "Has your father said anything to you?" Melit asked over her shoulder as she began to descend the rough trail.

"Said anything about what?" Naya replied, still distracted. She was used to listening with only half an ear to Melit gushing about attractive young men. At the moment, thoughts of the horses and her grandfather's dream preoccupied her. Had he spoken of her and the red filly before he died? Surely, he had not given anything away.

"Silly," Melit, teased her, looking back over her shoulder. "I meant has your father said anything about you and Wailos. Everyone is talking about how advantageous a match it would be. I'm sure it would solve a lot of difficulties for your father. I've heard him discussing it with my mother when he visits our tent in the evenings. They whisper and assume I'm asleep, but I still hear a lot of what they say. Mostly what they talk about is boring, but I pay attention whenever the topic is marriage.

"That's when your name comes up," she continued. "Of course, I haven't heard them mention Wailos *specifically*, but now that you're back – alive – and with the whole clan talking about how much your father respects Wailos and what a good alliance it would make – well, all I can say is that I'm sure your father would be really happy if you two were to wed."

Naya halted midstride, speechless. Did her father really want her to get married already? And to Wailos? The son of one of the tribe's wealthiest and most powerful chiefs? But maybe that was the point, the reason her father needed to create such an alliance. For the first time since being introduced to Wailos, instead of resenting him, Naya began to see the young warrior in a different light. Cocking her head to one side, she caught her lower lip between her teeth, considering. Even without understanding all the dynamics at play, Naya had more of a grasp of tribal affairs than her cousin, enough to realize that her grandfather's death would be the cause of upheaval and uncertainty, with the question of her father's future position at the center.

More than anything else, Naya wanted to help her father. If she could show him that she could be an asset to him, instead of always being an embarrassment, maybe she'd be able to make up for having been born a girl, her father's only child, the one to have survived instead of her twin brother. She'd tried for most of her childhood to be as good as any boy, but that had gotten her worse than nowhere. If what Melit said was true, maybe as Wailos's wife she could finally be useful to her father, serving as a liaison between their two clans. And she'd have status. Krnos and the others would no longer be able to taunt her. She might even be able to influence what happened to the captured horses, or at least prevent others, including the red filly, from suffering the same fate.

She hurried to catch up, slipping a little on the steep slope.

"Of course, if I were you," Melit was saying, "I wouldn't take it for granted that you'd be the only option for Wailos to marry, especially if you keep acting like you used to before you left."

Her tone was light, but her message was clear. Before last winter, in addition to trying to compete with the boys, Naya had been prone to spending a great deal of time alone on the steppe. That was how she'd discovered the red filly and her herd in the first place. Melit often teased her good naturedly about her solitary behavior, but others had not always been so kind.

"Seriously though," Melit went on, "my aunt Saurosa seems to have caught his eye. She's not too old to snatch him up."

As they reached the bottom of the trail and neared the edge of the settlement, Melit turned to Naya, her expression earnest. "If you want to please your father," she cautioned, "my advice is to be nice to our guest. Who knows, you may turn out to like him."

Before Naya could respond, her cousin was off on another subject. The path leading the remainder of the way to the settlement widened. Walking abreast once more, Melit linked arms and leaned in, her voice dropping to a conspiratorial whisper.

"Tell me about the young stranger," she urged, then proceeded with her own observations on the new topic of interest. "I can't imagine having to spend all winter with someone who'd almost killed me. It must have been awkward. He doesn't seem to have much to say for himself, from what I can tell. He is good looking, though, in a rough kind of way. At least he has a nice smile."

Stopping once more, Melit turned to Naya. "They say your father will announce his sentence today, just before the contest," she observed. "Do you think he'll be allowed to participate? Dayan, his brother, has been bragging all winter about what an accomplished bowman he is

– although shooting a defenseless girl in the back doesn't seem like very good aim to me."

"What contest?" asked Naya, finally getting a word in.

"The archery contest, of course, like we have every year before the *Wesr-Admn* feast," answered Melit, resuming their pace. "While you were up on the bluff all morning, the rest of us have been busy preparing. After such a long, hungry winter, it will be wonderful to have plenty to eat and to really celebrate. My mother had me and the other girls cleaning fish all morning, while most of the boys have been collecting wood for the bonfires. The others set up targets for the competition on the floodplain down by the river. Wailos and his cousin have said they'll take part. I bet Wailos is a good shot, although I doubt anyone will be able to best my brother, Kawona. You remember, he won last time."

"I wonder if my father would let me take part." Naya hadn't meant to speculate out loud.

"You?" replied Melit, sounding scandalized. "First of all, as you seem to keep forgetting, you're not a boy and only the boys and young men compete in the *Wesr-Admn* contest. Even Saurosa has never entered, despite being pretty good with a bow and arrow. And second, while you may be able to handle a hunting spear, you'd make a complete fool of yourself in front of everyone in an archery competition. You don't know how to shoot!"

"But I do," contradicted Naya. "Aytal – the young stranger – taught me. I even have my own bow and arrows…" *We made them together*, she almost added, thinking of the days she and Aytal had spent crafting her weapons and then attempting to perfect her skills. Naya pushed the memories away. She was too upset with him to want to want to remember the good times. "I bet I can hit at least the closer targets," she said instead.

"Well, if I were you," Melit dismissed the idea, "even if you've got better aim than all the men and boys combined, I'd keep it to myself. Neither Wailos nor your father is likely to be impressed."

"Perhaps you're right." *Oh course she is,* Naya told herself. Look what happened the last time she'd missed where she was aiming. If only she'd been able to hit the lion, the colt might… But she wouldn't let herself go there. As for Aytal, she thought bitterly, he'd been worse than useless. She almost hoped he *was* allowed to participate in the contest, just so that someone – Wailos, or Melit's brother – would put him in his place.

But more likely he would refuse to take part, using the vow he'd supposedly made against drawing his bow as a convenient excuse.

Naya swallowed hard, once again forcing back tears. They were approaching the edge of the settlement. She couldn't risk giving way to all the emotions threatening to overwhelm her. Instead, she must be brave and strong, so that her father could be proud of her. Melit was right. She needed to grow up and start acting like the daughter of a clan chief.

Chapter Three

The previous evening…

Even if no one had tried to stop Naya from retiring before the celebration had ended, others took notice of her departure. From the doorway of the women's tent where she'd been sitting unobtrusively for most of the evening, Awija had watched her granddaughter leave. The old woman's vantage point, hidden deep in the shadows beyond the circle of light cast by the central fire, afforded her an unobstructed view of the festivities. Although her hearing might not be as acute as it once was, her eyesight was still sharp, with the result that she missed little of what transpired as the night progressed.

She noted, for instance, the esteem with which her son, the clan chief, treated the clan's guest, inviting Wailos to the seat of honor at his right hand, where the young warrior remained throughout the meal and lingered afterwards. She observed the pride with which Potis introduced his daughter, before drawing Naya down to a seat at his left. Although Awija could not make out Wailos's words, she could tell that he must have been doing his best to charm her granddaughter, no doubt complementing her on her fortitude in being able to survive the winter with only the assistance of the two strangers. She thought Naya looked uncomfortable being the focus of his attention.

Awija also noted that another young man – the stranger's oldest son, relegated with his father to a place at one of the smaller fires outside the central circle – could not take his eyes off her granddaughter. From early on, when the stranger had first sought help for Naya last fall, Awija had harbored a good feeling about the man. She recognized a kindred spirit. She had entrusted him with the sack of precious grain for Naya and the horses, all those moons ago. Now she was curious about his son. Yes, the young man must be held responsible for almost killing her beloved granddaughter, but she would reserve judgment regarding his character until she knew more about him. He was striking to look at – thick hair, black as a raven's wing, falling haphazardly over dark brows and broad shoulders. And those eyes – the same blue as Naya's. Beneath the ragged, travel-stained clothing and deferential demeanor, she sensed strength, loyalty, honor, perhaps even a touch of pride. Yet a cloud shadowed the young man's features. He carried himself as though weighed by a heavy burden. No doubt he was dreading whatever justice would be served against him.

Studying the young stranger, Awija detected something else in his expression. Following the direction of his gaze, she saw that he watched Naya stand to leave, say something to her father, and then turn and walk away without once glancing back in the young man's direction. Not yet schooled in guarding his features, the expression he wore – disappointment mixed with utter devotion – was not difficult to interpret. *By the Goddess*, Awija thought, *he's in love with her*.

Much later, after the feasting had ended and most of the women and children had retired to bed, leaving the men to continue their talk around the fire, Awija saw Sata heading in the direction of the family dwelling. Her daughter-in-law had seemed withdrawn throughout the evening, keeping mostly to herself or speaking quietly with one of her sisters-in-law away from the main circle around the fire, except when she'd stepped forward to rescue Naya from having to share the story of their survival over the winter. Awija imagined that for Sata, rejoining the clan and claiming her place might feel awkward after such a long time away. She doubted that there had been an opportunity for a private reunion with her husband. A frown creased Awija's forehead. When the two finally talked, she hoped Potis would be honest with both his wife and himself. Sata deserved no less.

Catching her daughter-in-law's attention, Awija motioned her closer. "Come," she said, inclining her head in the direction of the entrance to the women's tent behind her. "I want to hear more about everything that happened while you were away."

Sata acceded to the request, but not before Awija noted the look she cast in the direction of the smaller fire where the stranger and his son still sat by themselves. Awija wondered briefly if anyone had thought to provide them with a place to sleep. *Ah well*, she thought, *they'll be comfortable enough where they are, at least for a night or two.*

Barely had the tent flap dropped behind them when Awija turned. "I want to hear about my granddaughter and the horses and about the young man who almost killed her," she said. "But let's start with you and the stranger. What's going on?"

Sata gave her a startled glance, then looked away, as though considering how to respond. Awija supposed her daughter-in-law might be offended by the question, or at the very least wonder how Awija could have guessed her secret. Over the years Sata had made a habit of disguising her true thoughts and feelings and she'd done nothing overt since her return to signal anything amiss. Awija often noticed what others overlooked, however, and rarely avoided asking a direct question.

But perhaps in this instance, her daughter-in-law's hesitation in answering was merely about getting her bearings. *She's been away a long time*, Awija thought. *Coming back must seem strange.* She watched as Sata took in her surroundings. At least the interior of the women's tent looked much as it always had. Worn hides carpeted the floor and stuffed cushions lay scattered. A small fire burned low on the hearth, providing just enough light to throw shadows against the tent's dark recesses, which held clay vessels and woven baskets of various shapes and sizes as well as leather sacks of wool, waiting to be carded. Bunches of drying herbs hung from the tent poles, their pungent aroma filling the air. Awija hoped Sata derived some comfort from the familiar space.

"His name is Oyuun," she finally answered, her back to Awija as she bent to pick-up a bison fur robe. Turning, she offered it to her as protection against the nighttime chill. "He is a good and honorable man," she stated simply. "Both he and his son, Aytal, have more than kept their promise to see to our welfare and safe return."

Taking the proffered hide, Awija regarded her daughter-in-law thoughtfully. "He does seem like an honorable man," she agreed after a moment. "But honor can be a difficult thing. It sometimes gets in the way."

"Oh?" replied Sata. "How do you mean?" She returned Awija's gaze openly, almost defiantly.

Awija studied her daughter-in-law for another long moment. Did

Sata suspect how well she understood the sorrows the younger woman harbored? How much she appreciated the sacrifices Sata had made? The sympathy she felt for her circumstances? Knowing Sata as she did and trusting her own instincts in regard to the stranger, Awija doubted there was anything truly egregious with which to reproach either of them. But the Goddess was not always kind.

Not commenting further, Awija merely nodded before changing the subject. Gesturing toward two cushions pulled close to the hearth, she indicated that Sata should take a seat beside her. "Now," she said once they were both comfortably settled, "tell me about my granddaughter."

Awija listened without interruption, giving Sata time to describe all that had transpired while they had been away. She spoke of her fears for Naya's survival and the *etmn-itājō* – an other-worldly journey – undertaken by Oyuun's son, Aytal, to find her daughter's spirit. She spoke of a storm and appearance of the horses on the night of the winter solstice, followed by Naya's gradual recovery and the slow, careful process whereby she and the red filly established a relationship of such mutual trust.

"You should have seen them galloping freely across the open steppe.," Sata concluded. "They were magnificent, as though they shared one heart."

"And then what happened?" prompted Awija. "Why didn't the horses come back with you?"

She listened as her daughter-in-law described their last days on the trail home, how the horses – including the red filly and the gray stallion, plus the mare and her foal born just before they'd started out – had stayed with them almost the whole way.

"But just as they'd nearly made it back to the clan's winter settlement, the horses were attacked by lions. The colt was killed," Sata explained, shuddering at the memory. "The horrible thing is that it wasn't the lion who caused his death. An arrow pierced his throat, and the poor thing bled out, with Naya holding his head in her lap."

"Was it the young stranger?" asked Awija. On more than one occasion, he seemed to have had extremely unfortunate aim.

"No, that's just it," replied Sata. "It was Naya's arrow. Oyuun told me afterward. But Aytal tried to cover it up and take responsibility, rather than let Naya know the truth and blame herself."

"Foolish boy," commented Awija. "Obviously in love. Does Naya feel the same about him? My guess would be yes, even if she won't admit it."

"I would share your guess," concurred Sata. "But she is so upset – over the death of the colt but also over something she must have witnessed between me and Oyuun and misunderstood. She's barely spoken to me since the day before the lion attack, so I've had no chance to explain."

"Do you have an explanation to give her?" Awija raised an eyebrow. "You don't need to answer," she went on. "I'm not the one who needs to know. Just be sure when you *do* talk to Naya, you tell her the truth. Your truth. As a mother, that's the best you can offer her."

Awija wanted to suggest to Sata that she be just as honest with Potis, and with Oyuun for that matter, but held her tongue. There was only so much advice her daughter-in-law could be expected to accept at the moment. She'd keep the rest of her thoughts to herself and wait until another opportunity arose.

"It's late," she said instead. "You are welcome to stay with me tonight if you wish. Since Awos passed, I find I sleep better here in the women's tent." The invitation was sincere, and for a moment Sata seemed to consider accepting, but Awija guessed that her daughter-in-law knew as well as she did what kind of statement would be made if the clan chief's wife spent her first night home anywhere other than with her husband.

"Thank you," Sata responded, "but I should go to my own shelter." Rising, she took Awija's hands in hers and squeezed them gently. "Thank you," she said again, then turned and ducked through the door, stepping from the dim interior of the women's tent into the darkness of the night. Awija watched her go.

The following day…

Just after noon, having spent all morning helping her sisters-in-law with preparations for the impending *Wesr-Admn* feast, Sata slipped inside the tent she shared with Potis, intent on finding a clean change of clothing before heading down to the river for the festivities. Everything she'd brought back with her was either filthy or worn-out. Perhaps she could locate something serviceable to wear from among the things she'd left behind, at least until she'd had time to fashion fresh garments for herself.

How strange, she thought, looking around the immaculately ordered shelter. It had been too dark to see much when she'd entered the tent late yesterday evening and she'd headed out early this morning, before sunrise. Now, in daylight, she almost didn't recognize her surroundings. Other than her traveling pack, which lay beside the bedroll she'd slept on, she could find no trace of herself. Where were the bundles she'd packed before they'd set-off last fall to make the return trip to the clan's winter settlement? Had Potis even unpacked them? Apparently not, which must mean her belongings were tucked back in a corner somewhere, perhaps behind the extra hides.

As she considered where to start her search, Sata's thoughts strayed to the conversation she'd had with her mother-in-law the previous evening. While Awija had been up to her usual inquisitive talk and opinionated observations, delivered with all of her customary candor, Sata's own reaction, especially to the old woman's interest in Oyuun, had surprised her. Rather than becoming annoyed and defensive, she'd realized with a wave of affection just how much she'd missed her mother-in-law. And even if she hadn't said much in response to Awija's elliptical remark about honor, she hadn't tried to hide anything either, as she would have in the past. After all, of what did she have to be ashamed? A longing for home? An ache of loneliness so deep it went to the marrow of her bones? A wish, however futile, that her husband might show a stranger's interest in what was in her heart? She'd felt too weary – and too much had happened – for her to want to maintain a wall between her mother-in-law and herself.

In contrast, Sata reflected, the distance separating her and Potis only seemed to have grown during her absence. Since returning yesterday, she had not had a moment alone with him to talk – too many people constantly surrounded him, soliciting his attention, keeping him up past when she'd fallen asleep last night and requiring his presence before she'd been awake this morning. True, when she and the others first arrived and Potis eventually made his way across the bluff top to where she waited, he'd folded her into his arms in a fierce hug. Yet there had been a distractedness about him, as if he didn't really see her, and Sata couldn't help wondering whether his embrace spoke of passion or mere possessiveness. Was he truly glad to have her home again? As pleased as he'd been to greet Vedukha, before realizing his wife and daughter had returned and were waiting to be reunited with him? And poor Naya. The girl had been desperate for her father's attention, wanting to tell him about everything that had happened.

Sata could see that Potis was clearly filled with joy at his only child's safe return, yet she knew he had not found time, with all his responsibilities as clan chief, to listen to Naya's account of what she'd accomplished with the red filly. Nor had he allowed her to leave his side long enough for the girl to greet her grandmother and share the tale with her. At least Awija had made an effort to find out what she and Naya had been through, Sata thought. While her mother-in-law's questioning about Oyuun had caught her off-guard and she'd needed a moment to consider how to respond, Sata had no doubt that Awija cared.

She sighed and looked once more around the tent. This space was supposed to be hers, as much as Potis's, yet it held no sign of her. The irony did not escape her. For what seemed like forever, she'd kept up appearances but her time away from the clan – truth be told, her time in Oyuun's company – had made her realize just how exhausted she'd become by pretense. Now that she'd returned, she couldn't bear to face going back to how things had been. Erasing her true self. She no longer had the energy to be anyone other than who she was. Dropping to her knees, she began pulling aside hides, searching for her belongings and going over again what she wanted to say to her husband, if and when he made time to see her. An honest conversation between them was long overdue.

Later the same day…

It was early afternoon when Potis returned from the corrals to find Sata in their tent. He'd gotten so used to her absence over the winter that her presence surprised him. "Sorry, I didn't know anyone was in here," he said, starting to withdraw through the door flap without entering. "I can come back later."

"No," she replied, rising from she'd been doing. "Come in. Stay. Don't feel you need to leave on my account." She sounded flustered, Potis thought, which made him feel even more awkward. He shouldn't let it irritate him, but it did. Everything seemed to irritate him these days.

Taking a breath, she tried again. "Please come in," she repeated, more calmly this time. "I would like for you to stay for a moment." Putting down the hides she'd been folding, she gestured toward two seats near the cold hearth. "May we talk?"

They hadn't had a moment alone since she returned. His fault, Potis admitted, but he'd been busy with managing his duties as clan chief. Still, he was reluctant to be diverted from his current errand.

"I really only came to fetch the torque and mace for the ceremonies," he explained, referring to the precious copper necklace and heavy stone hammer, symbols of his authority. "I don't have much time," he continued. "The day's events will be starting soon, and I still need to have a final conference with Bhlaghmn about sentencing the young stranger."

Sata looked dismayed, whether about the young man's fate or about his own excuses, Potis couldn't be sure. Either way, he felt guilty for not being able to stay, which only served to further aggravate him. He knew they should talk; she had something she needed to tell him. Perhaps now was as good an opportunity as any to have this conversation. He'd already made up his mind to be magnanimous. Besides, there was something he wanted to discuss with her as well.

He looked at her, granting her the privilege of being the first to speak. An uncomfortable silence ensued.

"We never used to have nothing to say to one another," Sata observed at last, gazing back at him, her expression indecipherable. "Aren't you glad to see me?"

"Of course," he answered, annoyed for sounding defensive. She looked exhausted, he thought, noticing more gray threads amidst the auburn in her hair. He'd have to make sure she rested now that she was home. Taking a breath, he tried to sound considerate. "I thought you might be tired from the journey and want some time to settle in. You and Naya were both already asleep when I came in last night and I had to be out early this morning." All of which was true, so why did he feel like he needed to apologize? "My mother mentioned you might want to stay in the women's tent for a while," he added.

"Is that where you'd like for me to stay?"

"Wherever you'd be most comfortable," Potis replied stiffly. What was the point of this conversation, if *she* was going to pick a fight with *him*? Maybe this was bad timing after all. He needed to get on with the day. He should look for the items he'd come for.

"Wouldn't people talk?" Sata asked, not letting the subject drop. Potis, who had gone to rummage amongst his things, was now squatting with his back to her.

"Not if there's nothing for them to talk about," he said without turning around.

"You're not worried there might be gossip?"

"Sata, what are you getting at?" He'd found the heavy polished stone mace but was still searching for the twisted copper torque.

"So, Naya hasn't spoken to you yet?"

"No, not yet. Like I said, you were both still asleep when I left this morning and I've been down with the horses until just now. I know she wants to talk, and we will as soon as I have a spare moment."

"Mostly she wants to tell you about the red filly," Sata said. "What she managed to do – she and Aytal – it's truly amazing. But it's her story to tell."

"Then what is it that you want to talk to me about?" He glanced back at her over his shoulder. "The priests are waiting for me," he went on. "I need to be officially attired. We'll be announcing the terms of the young stranger's punishment just before the archery contest."

Sata held her husband's gaze, willing him not to turn away. The conversation wasn't going anything like she'd intended – she hadn't meant to start out by baiting him – but she wasn't going to give up.

"You'll be lenient?" she asked. "Aytal and his father did everything in their power to care for us. They've more than earned your mercy."

"Have they?" Potis raised an eyebrow, and something in his tone made Sata wonder if he knew more than he was letting on.

"Naya and Aytal became quite good friends," she said, pushing ahead anyway. "She's upset with him at the moment – I'm sure your brother told you already about the lion attack and the death of the colt – but I don't think she will want for you to punish him for injuring her. It was an accident, and she has forgiven him."

"Be that as it may," Potis replied, going back to his search, "there is still a price to pay. And it's not up to her – or you – to dictate the terms."

There it was again, the hint of a challenge in her husband's voice, backed by a note of hostility, aimed not only at Aytal and Oyuun, she felt, but also at her. Sata forced herself to remain calm. They needed to get everything out in the open. Before she could decide what to say next, however, Potis spoke again.

"If you're worried about what Naya might tell me about you and the stranger, you don't need to be. Tausos already filled me in on that as well."

"What do you mean?" *So, he does know.* An instant of panic in Sata's mind gave way to indignation, followed by dismay. What could her brother-in-law possibly understand about the situation between her and Oyuun? What could he have said? Sata's whole strategy depended on being the first to explain to Potis what Naya had seen and that it hadn't meant what the girl assumed. She'd practiced the words in her own head enough times to know exactly what she wanted to say. Now, she realized, she'd lost control of the story.

"Only that it was obvious to him that the stranger has feelings for you," Potis answered matter-of-factly. "But that's understandable, given all the time you spent together. And I imagine you developed feelings for him, at least on some level. But I also know that you would never betray me or our marriage. It's not in your nature. Now that you're back where you belong, he'll be on his way."

Speechless, Sata stared at the back of his head as she tried to absorb the words. Apparently assuming the absence of a response from her meant that she agreed with him, Potis went on looking for the copper torque. *As though he's done us both a favor by clearing the air,* she thought. *As though I should be relieved by his generosity and grateful for his trust. As though nothing further needs to be said on the matter.*

Instead, he changed the subject.

"What would you think of letting Naya stay with Melit for a while?" Potis asked. "If you want some time in the woman's tent anyway, it would provide an opportunity for Vedukha's boys to stay here with me. Peikā will be preparing for his initiation next year and Kawona could still benefit from some teaching and supervision. I owe that to Bhermi. Better me than their uncle Skelos."

Again, Sata didn't know what to say. It was a common practice to send older boys as well as recently initiated young men to live with male relatives, providing a transition away from the influence of their immediate families, particular their mothers, and helping to create closer ties with the other men of the clan. She knew Potis felt a particular responsibility toward Kawona and Peikā, the two fatherless sons of his best friend.

"Vedukha and I have been discussing the idea," Potis went on. "She agrees that it would be good for her boys to stay with me, and she and I both thought that once Naya returned, spending more time with Melit would be good for Naya as well. From what Tausos told me, you and Naya don't seem to be getting along all that well at the moment anyway, so maybe some time apart from each other isn't a bad idea. And I know my mother would probably welcome your company."

Sata felt knocked off balance and almost put out a hand to steady herself against one of the tent poles. The implications were inescapable. Her husband and her cousin Vedukha had everything all worked out, the best arrangement for all concerned. She opened her mouth to defend her right to remain with her family, to go back to how they had been before Naya's accident, but when she tried to speak, no sound came out. The ground felt as though it was shifting beneath her feet. The sensation reminded Sata of when she was a little girl and the earth would tremble, moving in rolling waves until she felt dizzy and had to get down on her hands and knees to keep from falling over. Just as suddenly, the shaking would stop, and her surroundings would be left in ruins.

"Ah – here it is," said Potis, holding up the copper torque.

Sata still said nothing. To question Potis now about his relationship with Vedukha would seem petty. On the surface, the plan they'd come up with was reasonable for everyone concerned – except that it made her feel superfluous.

"What does Naya think of this idea?" she finally asked.

"I'm sure she'll be fine with it," Potis replied. "She and Melit have always gotten on well and the training for their presentation is likely to begin almost immediately, so they'll be together anyway."

Sata waited for him to add that Vedukha would be a better influence on their daughter than she would, as Naya prepared for the next stage of her life as a young woman. He didn't say it, but Sata was sure it was what he thought. He was just too diplomatic to point it out to her. "Well," she said finally, "it sounds like it's all decided."

Turning away, she bent as though to examine the largest of the bundles she'd found heaped in a corner. "How convenient," she went on without turning around. "I haven't had a chance to unpack yet. It will be easy to move my things into the women's tent right away."

"Would you like help?" asked Potis solicitously.

"No thank you. You said you were in a hurry. I can handle it." Some detached portion of Sata's mind was impressed with how practical she sounded – entirely reasonable, completely unemotional. "You go on," she added, straightening but with her back still turned. "I'll be down for the celebration shortly."

She waited, back rigid, until she was certain Potis had left the tent before sinking once more to her knees. Silent, head bowed, hands covering her face, she remained motionless for several long moments until finally a deep shuddering breath wracked her body. After that, the next breath came more easily.

Chapter Four

The flood plain of the great river Rā was a swarm of activity as Sata made her way down from the clan's settlement a short while later. Sheltered by birch- and oak-clad bluffs to the west, the plain was an open expanse, its boundary nearest the river marked by an almost vertical cliff, the height of two men, where the land dropped abruptly to the riverbed below. In late summer, when the Rā's waters flowed calm and placid, a narrow strip of sandy beach bordered the water's edge. This time of year, swollen with melting snow and rushing furiously southward, the river climbed the steep side of its western bank and there was no beach to be seen. Occasionally the river in full spate overtopped the edge, inundating the flat expanse beyond and leaving behind a stinking layer of mud and debris after the water receded. More common was for the Rā to spread through the innumerable shallow channels cut into the eastern shore, where fewer impediments existed to redirect the river's energy down-stream. Here the ground often remained marshy well into summer, full of tall cattails and other reeds and alive with animals, insects and birds who loved the semi-aquatic habitat the river provided.

Pausing in her decent from the higher ground where the settlement was located, Sata scanned the wide, flat valley below. This year, despite the heavy snows, the Rā did not seem inclined to spill over its western bank, leaving the clanspeople free to use the plain for their own purpos-es. In less than two moons, the area would be the site of the Gathering, bringing the entire Plānos tribe together to observe the most sacred event of the ritual calendar – *Sāwel-Dom*.

Today marked *Wesr-Admn*, a smaller and less elaborate celebration of the arrival of spring after the deprivations of winter. In addition to invoking the promise of the earth's bounty, *Wesr-Admn* was the occasion when the priests sought blessings for the clan's livestock, entreating Sky Father and the Shining Ones to grant the animals protection and oversee their health and safety throughout the ensuing year.

Sata could see that most of the other members of the clan had already made their way down to the festival grounds and were busy with final preparations. In the middle of the plain, several enormous granite boulders formed the outline of a large circle. The original megaliths had been placed generations ago by the Plānos ancestors and even the flood waters of the Rā could not shift the heaviest. Smaller stones, still weighty enough to require two men to lift, were added periodically to fill the gaps. Within the sacred circle, wood for two large bonfires had been laid, waiting to be lit.

Unfortunately, Sata reflected as she surveyed the scene, this year's blessing ceremony would be rather unimpressive. Normally, the clan's substantial flocks and herds were collected at the north end of the plain. Once it became full dark, the animals would be driven in a long, snaking line between the twin bonfires burning in the center of the stone circle, with the priests overseeing the livestock's safe passage between the flames. Today, she could see that the clan's few remaining cattle, sheep and goats had been brought the long way around from the corrals and were picketed off to one side, well away from where the archery field had been set up, so that if an arrow or two went astray during the contest, no harm would come to the animals. *There aren't enough of them left to make much of a procession*, Sata thought with a sigh. She resumed her descent.

The horses, too wild to be led in the procession, had been left behind in their pen, no doubt with a contingent of young herders to take turns keeping an eye on them. Sata wondered how much Naya knew at this point about what was in store for the herd. Sata had recognized most of the individuals as soon as she'd seen them from the bluff top yesterday but had only learned the full truth of Wailos's plan last evening from Glōs, Tausos's wife. Although she'd hidden her distress from her sister-in-law, she shuddered now to think how Naya would react when she found out.

Whether through luck or foresight, during their initial reunion, Potis had somehow managed to prevent Naya from looking over the cliff edge and seeing the horses for herself, but Sata doubted he could shield her for long, despite keeping her by his side all last evening and ordering her not to visit the corrals. When Naya discovered that the trapped horses belonged to BeHregs's band and the stallion had been killed during the stampede, she would be devastated. When she learned the intended fate of the others, Sata could only imagine her daughter's fury. Worse, Naya would feel responsible, and with good reason. Because of her, the herd had become habituated to humans, making them that much easier for Wailos and the other hunters to trap.

Stopping again to gaze out over the flood plain, Sata tried to spot Naya among those who had left their preparations and begun to make their way in twos and threes toward the stone circle. She hadn't laid eyes on her daughter since just after sunrise. Knowing Naya, she'd gone to the blufftop, despite her father's orders, which meant she'd figured out by now that the horses in the corral belonged to BeHregs's band. At least the red filly, the gray stallion and filly's mother were not among the captured herd. Potis might stand a chance of reconciling Naya to the necessity of what was to happen to the remainder – provided he could convince her to listen to him long enough to explain.

Still searching for Naya in the crowd, Sata's eyes were drawn toward a rise of higher ground to the south that commanded a view of the entire flood plain. Atop the rise stood a large earthen mound containing the graves of Potis's forebears. Of all the clans of the Plānos, her husband's held stewardship over not only the most desirable pastures on this side of the great river but also the best ceremonial site, watched over by the tribe's ancestors. If this plan with the captured horses were to fail, not only would Regos, Potis's main rival, have a greater claim to be named as the tribe's chief of chiefs, but Potis's clan would likely have to forfeit oversight of territory that had been in their custody for as long as anyone could remember. Such an outcome was not the legacy Potis wished for himself. Nor, Sata knew, could he afford to consider the sympathies of his only child. Regardless of her personal frustrations with her husband, she did not envy his position.

One question nagged at Sata. *Why would Wailos promote a plan that worked against the interests of his father, Regos?* Looking down on the stone circle, she spotted the clan's distinguished guest standing near the entrance, surrounded by an admiring group of other young men. Potis must be wondering about Wailos's motives as well. She saw her husband mount the temporary dais that had been constructed in the northwest quadrant of the circle, providing a vantage point upwind of smoke from the fires. From here, the clan chief, along with the senior priest, would preside over the *Wesr-Admn* festivities. How impressive Potis looked, standing erect, garbed in his finest clothing, including the voluminous bison hide cloak that had been his father's. His presence commanded attention. This was the first time, she realized, that she would witness her husband rather than his father officiating during one of the clan's sacred rituals.

Although too far away to see the detail, she knew the cloak was fastened across Potis's broad chest with an elaborately braided thong she had made for him years before. The thong, in turn, was secured by a delicately carved antler tip that had belonged to the massive buck Potis had taken as a young man on his first solo hunt. The precious copper torque encircled his throat and in his left hand he held the ceremonial mace, its heavy variegated stone head carved in the shape of a horse's skull, to which generations of handling had imparted a dull sheen. If she'd been closer, she could have made out the curving interlaced lines tattooed across his cheeks, further signifying his status as chief.

Beside Potis stood his uncle. Much more simply attired, at least for now, and holding only his gnarled wooden staff, the senior priest looked shrunken, almost inconsequential, by comparison. Sata knew appearances were deceptive, however. While the winter had clearly aged him, she had no doubt Bhlaghmn retained every attribute of the power he had long wielded, even if for today's events he had yet to don his raven-feather cape and peaked ceremonial headdress. During her father-in-law's lifetime, Sata reflected, the old chief had been able to counter his younger brother's influence, but that dynamic had now shifted. If Potis and his uncle disagreed, as was inevitable, with whom would the rest of the clanspeople side? Despite her husband's imposing presence and official regalia, the answer to that question was far from certain.

Just then the younger priest, who stood below the dais and off to one side, used a mallet made from a bullock's thigh bone to strike several blows against a massive auroch-hide drum. A deep *boom, boom, boom* reverberated off the limestone bluffs flanking the flood plain, calling the clanspeople to order so that the festival could begin. Hurrying, Sata covered the remaining distance in time to take a place just inside the margins of the stone circle.

She scanned the crowd, still searching for Naya, and finally spotted her standing to the left of the dais with Melit and Vedukha. A pang gripped Sata's chest. Fearing that if she allowed her attention to linger, her daughter might feel her eyes on her and send her one of those cutting looks, she quickly glanced away. Instead, she tried to locate Oyuun and Aytal. She found them across the circle from her, with Tausos and Skelos standing guard on either side. The drumming ceased and everyone's attention shifted to the dais, where Potis had raised his right hand for silence.

"*Gentis!*" he called in a loud voice. "People of the clan. We are gathered for ceremony and celebration. But before the day's events begin, we have an additional matter of importance to address. Bring forward the young stranger."

As people stepped aside to allow them to pass, Aytal, flanked by his two escorts, approached the open space in front of the dais. Sata wondered if Potis would require Aytal to kneel before him. Closing her eyes, she sent up a prayer for mercy.

When she opened them, she noticed that Oyuun had disappeared from the opposite side of the circle. Before she could wonder where he'd gone, she realized he stood beside her. Although she wanted nothing more than to turn to him, Sata kept her eyes straight ahead, trying not to betray that she'd noticed his presence. A hand reached unobtrusively for hers and she felt a gentle squeeze. She could not help but return the gesture.

Eyes forward, gaze fixed on the dais, Oyuun spoke quietly in his own tongue. "I need to see you before I leave. I've been told I should plan to be gone by tomorrow or the following day at the latest."

Sata's breath caught in her throat, but she willed her features to reveal nothing of the turmoil she felt. She assumed Oyuun wanted to say a final farewell somewhere private. For a long moment she kept him waiting for her reply, long enough that she was sure he must be worried she would not agree to meet him. In truth, she needed time to think of a safe place where they could talk without being disturbed.

"Alright," she finally whispered back. "Come to the women's tent tomorrow night, after everyone has gone to bed." Silently acknowledging her instructions, Oyuun gave Sata's hand another reassuring squeeze and then was gone. Letting out a breath she hadn't been aware she'd been holding, Sata turned her attention back to Potis, who had resumed addressing the crowd.

Near the dais, Naya fidgeted. People were staring at her, and she didn't know how to stand or where to look. She still felt the effects of her morning on the bluff top and wished she could sit down somewhere. Forearms folded tightly across her stomach, she tried to quell the persistent dizziness by focusing on the patch of bare ground at her feet. She overheard whispered exchanges – speculation running rampant about what Aytal's sentence would be.

Her father had begun speaking. A hush fell over the assembly and his voice carried easily to the far edges of the stone circle. "By the grace of the gods," he was saying, "my daughter has survived. Were this not the case, the punishment, fully justified by the customs of our tribe, would have been death. Yet her survival is not enough to allow the one who so gravely wounded her simply to go free. Rather, he must pay a price that fulfills his debt – not just to her but to her people."

Despite having almost convinced herself that she did not care what her father's pronouncement would be, Naya held her breath in anticipation, along with everyone else.

The clan chief paused, allowing the suspense to build. Naya risked lifting her gaze enough to catch a glimpse of Aytal's face. He stood no more than a few paces away. She was relieved to find that he was looking not at her but up at her father. Shoulders straight, spine erect, chin ever so slightly elevated, he met the clan chief's stern regard with no sign of flinching. Naya could not help but admire his poise. More complicated feelings threatened to stir but she refused to acknowledge them.

Aytal must have sensed something, however, because he turned to her and for an instant their eyes locked. Naya felt something surge between them and had to take half a step backward to avoid losing her balance. Flustered, she lowered her eyes, vowing not to raise them again. Another wave of dizziness washed over her. She mustn't pass out, she admonished herself. She'd only draw everyone's attention and embarrass her father. She shifted her gaze back to him.

"Aytal, son of Oyuun." The clan chief's tone was solemn as he lifted the mace overhead.

Sata wondered if her husband had observed what had just transpired between their daughter and the young stranger. Even from where she stood, she'd seen Naya's face when she and Aytal had looked at one another, as if the girl had been struck by a bolt of lightning. But if Potis had noticed, he gave no sign. Voice measured, he spoke the terms of the sentence.

"As restitution for your carelessness and the harm you have caused, you shall, without hesitation or complaint, labor as required for the length of a full year in the service of this clan."

Potis paused, letting the words sink in. A year was a long time in a young man's life, thought Sata.

"Being merciful," the clan chief went on, "we shall consider the term of this service to have begun last winter, when you and your father together were tasked with caring for the welfare of both my daughter and my wife. The sentence will be considered complete upon the occasion of next winter's solstice. Until then, you shall do whatever is required of you by any member of this clan. Do you understand?"

Sata watched as Aytal, bowing his head slightly and lowering his gaze, nodded to indicate his understanding and acceptance of the clan chief's words.

"Should you fail to obey a request or act otherwise than directed," Potis continued, "you shall be brought before myself and the senior priest for judgement. Do you understand?"

Keeping his eyes respectfully downcast, Aytal again nodded his assent.

"Should you try to leave the clan or otherwise evade your punishment before the end of your term, you shall be pursued without mercy and marked forever as an enemy of this clan. Shame and dishonor will stain not only you, but the members of your family, including your father, who, so far as we know, has committed no crime against us, and your brother, who has found a place for himself with my brother's family, with whom he is welcome to remain for as long as he chooses. Do you understand?"

Another wordless nod. Sata could see Dayan, standing in the crowd beside Tausos's youngest son. The boys, she gathered, had become very close. She thought Dayan looked uncomfortable at being singled out for mention by the clan chief and wondered if he would choose to leave with his father or want to stay behind – and what Oyuun would have to say about the matter. She also wondered if anyone else had taken note of Potis's elliptical reference to unknown crimes of which Oyuun himself might be guilty. Perhaps no one else had noticed – the turn of phrase was innocuous enough to be tossed off as meaningless – but still she could not help feeling as though, in warning Aytal of the consequences of shame and dishonor, her husband intended to send Oyuun and herself a subtle message as well.

"Finally," Potis concluded, "you have been assigned your first task. For what remains of the next two moons, until the time of the Gathering marking *Sāwel-Dom*, you shall be charged with the care of the herd of horses now contained in the corrals. Daily you will gather enough forage for the animals to eat, ensure at all times they have fresh water, and clean the muck from their enclosure. By night, you shall keep watch in the ravine, seeing that no harm comes to them from either man or beast. During the duration specified for this task, no one shall be permitted to make any request of you that would prevent you from carrying out these duties. Do you understand?"

This time Aytal looked up, once again meeting the clan chief's stern gaze. "*Jai, Dukos,*" he answered. "Yes Sir."

While the crowd remained riveted on the exchange between the clan chief and the young stranger, Sata's focus had shifted back to her daughter. How would Naya react to Aytal's sentence? But Naya seemed not to have taken note of her father's words. Instead, she was looking into the far distance, toward the blufftops that towered over the floodplain. Following the direction of her gaze, Sata struggled to see what had caught her attention. On the ridge above the ravine where the corrals were located, she noticed three shapes, hard to distinguish in the glare of the afternoon sun. Putting up a hand to shield her eyes, Sata thought she caught a flash of copper. In the next instant, a sound tore at her heart.

"Noooo!"

Hearing her daughter's anguished moan, Sata turned in time to see Naya collapse in a heap beside the dais. Pushing through the crowd to reach her, she could see Aytal kneeling next to her inert body and then Potis, who had jumped down from the dais, roughly shoving him away. Just as Sata gained the girl's side, she opened her eyes and sat up, looking dazed but otherwise unhurt. Nonetheless, a commotion ensued, with Potis ordering everyone to give his daughter space and Naya insisting she was fine and just needed water. By the time Sata thought to look back toward the blufftop, the shapes had disappeared.

Chapter Five

Later that evening…

"Everyone assumed Naya was upset by the judgment against Aytal," Sata remarked. "I don't think anyone besides me noticed what she was looking at, up on the bluff. She tried to brush the whole thing off by saying she'd gotten overheated from being out in the sun all morning and called out because she was about to faint."

Sata and Awija were alone, seated beside one another in front of the hearth in the women's tent, the soft glow of a low-burning fire illuminating their features. As she spoke, Sata reached for a pot of water just beginning to boil, removing it from the coals and tossing in a handful of dried herbs. Hopefully the brew would help her to sleep.

Although darkness had fallen some time ago, the rest of the settlement was nearly deserted, with most of the clanspeople still down at the stone circle enjoying the *Wesr-Admn* festivities. As was customary, there would be feasting, drinking, music, dancing and storytelling long into the night, until at some point the revelers fell asleep beneath the stars, waking to return to the settlement well after the start of the next day.

Weary, Sata had slipped away to the sanctuary of the women's tent as soon as she thought she would not be missed. In contrast to earlier in the day, when she'd deposited her belongings and given Awija a cursory explanation of why she was moving in, she now found herself grateful for the new arrangements. She needed time to herself to sort out how she felt and decide what to do, but she'd also realized she might actually welcome her mother-in-law's company and advice.

First, however, Sata needed to satisfy the old woman's curiosity.

Although Awija had exercised her prerogative as a widow-in-mourning to remain in seclusion rather than attend the festivities, she still wanted to know about the day's events and plied Sata with questions, all of which had to be answered and discussed before Sata could bring up what was troubling her.

"Hmph," Awija replied in response to Sata's account of Naya's fainting spell. "We'll come back to my granddaughter and what you think you both saw. What about the young man – how does he feel about his sentence?"

"Aytal's relief was obvious," Sata admitted. "At least to me, but then I've come to know him fairly well. I'm not sure anyone other than his father and Naya would have understood what a reprieve it is for him to be assigned to care for the horses. Everyone else would see it as the most demeaning of tasks. But I could also tell he was trying to hide his relief at the sentence, not to mention his concern over Naya when she collapsed. He understands enough to realize the wisdom of concealing how he feels."

"Do you think that when Potis proposed the sentence, he guessed Aytal might prefer the horses to any other task that could have been devised?" Awija inquired.

"If so, then he's been merciful," Sata conceded. "But he would have had to keep that part of it to himself. If the others suspected Potis was attempting to spare Aytal – or Naya – I'm sure they would have argued for a different punishment."

Sata did not have to specify the 'others' to whom she referred. She and Awija both knew.

"And it's not as if Aytal's gotten off easily," she went on. "Looking after those horses from now until the Gathering will be backbreaking. Along with guarding them overnight, he won't have time for much else." Sata moved the pot of water back to a place among the coals where it would stay warm.

"Perhaps that was part of Potis's calculation as well," observed Awija. "Assuming his aim is to keep them apart and keep Naya away from the horses. He's forbidden her to go to the corrals, is that right?"

"Yes," replied Sata. "At least for the time being. Hard to know whether she will obey him or not. I'm almost certain she was on the blufftop this morning, which means she at least knows the horses are from the red filly's band." Using a wooden spoon, Sata stirred the brew, raising a cloud of aromatic steam. She would need to wait for the leaves to settle once more before pouring the tea.

"But Naya doesn't know yet about the rest of the plan?' Awija asked.

Sata shook her head. "As far as I know, not yet," she replied, "but she's bound to find out."

"And you think she saw the red filly and the other two horses on the blufftop this afternoon?" Awija's sharp eyes held Sata's, green flecks glinting in the firelight.

"Possibly," Sata answered, returning her mother-in-law's look. "It would explain why she cried out."

"If it is them, what do you think Naya will do?" Awija asked.

"Truthfully, I'm not sure." Turning away, Sata poured a small amount of tea into one of two clay mugs. Deciding the herbs needed longer to steep, she poured it back. She was at a loss for what to tell her mother-in-law.

"Naya's completely shut me out," she lamented. "I don't know what to expect from her. I tried to keep an eye on her today – she spent most of the festival with Melit and some of the other girls. I didn't see her try to confront her father about the horses, or talk to Aytal, which surprised me." Sata thought of the look that she'd seen pass between Naya and Aytal just prior to Potis's pronouncement of the young man's sentence, followed by Naya's fainting spell. Afterwards, Sata recalled, there'd been a further incident, which she also wasn't sure how to interpret.

"Something else happened," she said to Awija, thinking her mother-in-law might be able to provide some insight. "After the sentence had been handed down, once Naya was back on her feet and order had been restored, someone in the crowd – I think it might have been Krnos – called out, wondering if Aytal would be allowed to participate in the shooting match."

"And what did Potis decree?" Awija inquired.

"That's just it," Sata answered. "He left it up to Naya to decide."

Realizing that in order for her mother-in-law to grasp the signif-icance of what ensued, Awija would need an explanation of the sur-rounding circumstances, Sata briefly shared what Oyuun had revealed about Aytal's troubled past amongst his own people, the secret vow he made on the night of the winter solstice while journeying to find Naya's spirit, and his subsequent reticence to use his bow.

"So you see," Sata concluded, "asking Naya to determine whether or not Aytal should compete was rather fraught. I wanted to suggest to Potis that he ban Aytal from participating in the tournament in order to avoid all this, but I didn't have the opportunity."

"So what did my granddaughter decide?" Awija inquired. "And stop fussing with the tea," she added, holding out one of two waiting mugs. "I'm sure it's fine."

Acknowledging her own restiveness with a rueful smile, Sata poured the tea while replying to her mother-in-law's question. "Not what I would have hoped or expected," she admitted. "To be honest, Naya's answer surprised and disappointed me. For all her faults, she's generally not given to being deliberately unkind. Maybe she didn't think through the implications – but still. Rather than taking responsibility and perhaps sparing Aytal from embarrassment or worse, she told her father that as far as she was concerned, Aytal could decide for himself whether or not to compete."

Awija sat silent for a moment, letting the mug warm her stiff hands as she took in what Sata had said. Watching her mother-in-law's features, Sata could easily guess the older woman's thoughts – the same ones she'd had herself.

"Naya is well-aware of Aytal's reluctance to use his bow," Sata remarked. "Even if she doesn't fully understand his reasons, she should have realized that she had an opportunity to save him from an impossible choice. All she had to do was decree that he not be allowed take part in the contest. Instead, by leaving it up to him, Naya forced Aytal either to appear as a coward for refusing to compete, or to go against the vow that led him renounce his bow in the first place.

"I'd hate to think Naya could have acted so heartlessly," Sata continued, not hiding her dismay, "But perhaps if she believed it had been Aytal's arrow and not hers that felled the colt, she assumed he had already reclaimed the use of his bow. In that case, leaving the decision up to Aytal about whether or not to compete might have been Naya's way of punishing him over the colt's death. Honestly, I don't know what to think."

"Or maybe she knows it was her arrow that killed the colt and she's angry with him for *not* shooting and leaving her to try to fend off the lion by herself," Awija suggested. "At least she didn't order him to participate. That would have been truly cruel, mocking even, given all you've told me. What did the young man decide?"

"This part is also difficult to fathom," replied Sata, swallowing a sip of tea. "Before Aytal could be compelled to make the choice for himself, Wailos spoke up."

"Our distinguished visitor, hmm?" Awija lifted a brow. "And what did he have to say on the matter?"

"He finally did what both Potis and Naya failed to do," Sata answered. "He argued that Aytal should not be allowed to take part. Who knows what his motives were – perhaps he worried Aytal would beat him. I doubt it had anything to do with compassion, since Wailos would have no way of knowing that Aytal would rather not have to enter the contest. In any case, Wailos voiced the argument that Potis should have made in the first place: that a stranger, especially one under the shadow of a crime such as Aytal had committed, should not be given the honor of sharing the field with the warriors of the clan. And that was that."

"No one objected?" Awija sounded mildly surprised. "Given all the talk over the winter, I would have thought the others would have wanted to prove themselves against the young stranger's purported prowess."

"I heard no objections from where I stood," Sata replied. "It's quite striking how much influence our visitor seems to have," she added, giving Awija a sidelong glance. She wondered if her mother-in-law was as impressed with Wailos as everyone else seemed to be.

Awija answered Sata's look with a roll of her eyes. "I assume Wailos took part in the contest himself," she said. "Did he win?"

"It came down to him and Kawona, the only two left at the maximum distance. Kawona drew the short stick, so he had to go first, which is normally a disadvantage. Even so, he managed to put his last arrow in the exact center of the target. Then Wailos did something else unexpected – he conceded."

"Really?" Awija's reaction sounded less incredulous than speculative. "Why, do you think?"

"If I had to guess, I'd say he decided he didn't have that much to gain by winning," Sata answered. "He'd already demonstrated his skill by defeating everyone in his earlier matches. No one doubted his ability. And Kawona's last shot was outstanding. By acknowledging as much, Wailos acted as the gracious guest. He also gave the impression that he's confident enough not to need to prove anything."

"Well, well, well," mused Awija. "We must keep an eye on that one. According to the tales Swesor brings me, I gather Wailos may be expected to start taking a more-than-casual interest in Naya." She took a last swallow of tea.

"I've heard those rumors as well," Sata admitted. "But I'm not sure there's much I can do about it. Naya barely acknowledges me these days and Potis seems more interested in Vedukha's advice than mine on how to deal with her." She allowed a hint of annoyance to creep into her voice.

"There is less going on there than you might imagine, and also more," Awija remarked, holding out her empty mug for a refill. "The important question is, how much do you care?"

Avoiding her mother-in-law's astute gaze, Sata poured more tea for both of them, giving herself time to consider how to reply. As usual, Awija had gone straight to the heart of the matter. How much *did* Sata care? The issue was not so much what, if anything, may have happened between her husband and her cousin – the widow of his best friend – as how Sata chose to view the situation.

Even before Bhermi's death, the two couples had been close and afterwards, both she and Potis had always gone out of their way to include Vedukha and her children in their wider family circle. Was it so surprising that during the extended period of separation over this past winter, Potis might have turned to Vedukha for support, just as Vedukha so often relied on him? Could Sata blame either of them?

Moreover, leaving aside the exuberant kiss she'd witnessed on the blufftop yesterday, she had no evidence that anything truly untoward had happened while she'd been away. Such a thing could not be hidden from the rest of the clan, and she'd been back long enough that someone would have told her, if only out of spite. Yet the potential was there, whether or not her husband and her cousin admitted as much, even to themselves. Apparently Awija thought so as well. Moreover, Sata couldn't in good conscience ignore her feelings toward Oyuun, even if she'd done nothing of which to be truly ashamed, regardless of what Naya had witnessed and whatever Tausos thought he'd surmised.

Sata took a sip of tea and stared into the embers glowing in the hearth. What answer could she give her mother-in-law? How *did* she feel about whatever was developing between her husband and Vedukha?

After her conversation with Potis earlier in the day, she'd been upset. But if she were honest, once she'd let go of her pride and taken that second breath, hadn't she experienced something more akin to relief, as though tension pulling tight against a frayed rope had at last caused the rope itself to unravel? And to the extent she was still bothered, wasn't it less about admitting the possibility that she and Potis were growing apart, than that their daughter seemed to want nothing to do with her? Was she in fact more perturbed by Vedukha taking her place as a mother than as a wife? Equally irritating was Potis's assumption that she would simply renounce whatever misplaced feelings she might have developed for Oyuun and resume her role as Potis's faithful spouse. Did feeling taken for granted justify abandoning her responsibilities, her identity, her position?

"*Dhugter.*" Awija's voice broke in on Sata's confused thoughts. She felt the touch of a kind hand on her arm. *Daughter*, Awija had called her, not daughter-in-law.

"In all the time I've known you, you've always put the needs of others first, ahead of your own." The old woman's grip tightened with gentle insistence. "Tell me now," she demanded, "what is it that *you* want?"

Sata lifted her gaze from the hearth. Compassion warmed her mother-in-law's hazel eyes. She had asked the question that no one ever asked, the question Sata had long ago stopped asking herself. Awija was right. Sata couldn't remember a time when she'd thought about her own wishes apart from the requirements of those around her. Even the decision to marry Potis in the first place had not really been hers. Yes, she'd agreed. Who would not have wanted to become the bride of the handsome herder, son of a renowned chief? Yet some part of her had also known that the choice was never entirely hers to make. She'd done what was expected of her.

And it wasn't that she'd been unhappy in her marriage. Not exactly. She and Potis had been through a lot together. He was a good man. They loved each other. She had been content. Or at least made herself believe so. But lately she'd been forced to admit that beneath the contentment lay feelings whose existence and power she had long suppressed. Sorrow and longing to be sure, but also joy and hope, buried deep, then safely overgrown with day-to-day cares and concerns, until there was hardly any sign of where to look for the pathway to her heart.

Sata looked past Awija, unseeing. Searching. The answer, when it came to her, was as distinct as the memory of a kiss.

"Home," she said simply, looking once more into her mother-in-law's wise face. "I want to go home." Back to the mountains, far to the south, where she'd been born.

With a small nod, Awija withdrew the hand she'd placed on Sata's arm but did not otherwise reply, giving Sata time to acknowledge the truth of her own words.

"When?" the older woman finally asked. "How will you get there?"

"I suppose more or less right away," Sata answered. "If ever I *am* to go." Realizing she hadn't mentioned Oyuun's connection to her home-land, she explained. "I knew Aytal's mother, Zerashsha, as a girl. Her name means 'great beauty' in my tongue. She died giving birth to Aytal. Oyuun goes now to bring word of her fate and of their son to Zera's family. He has asked me to accompany him."

"And will you go?" Awija's tone was neutral, free of either assumption or judgment.

Gazing down at the half-empty mug held in her lap, Sata again did not answer immediately. Before today, she had thought she was certain of her response. As certain as she'd been when Oyuun had first proposed the idea, on the night of the colt's birth. As certain as she'd been when he'd asked again, just before their return to the settlement. Could only three days have passed since she'd insisted on bidding him goodbye?

Now she was no longer so sure. The ties she had always believed bound her seemed to be coming loose. Perhaps she *could* actually go, at least for a visit. She would not have to decide anything else right away. She would not have to commit to leaving behind her current life forever. But what would Potis say? What would the rest of the clan think of her? And Naya. Would her daughter judge her even more harshly than she had already? More importantly, who would watch over her precious child? How could she possibly leave?

"I don't know," she confessed. "What do you think I should do?"

Awija raised her mug to finish the last of her tea before responding. "Explain to Potis that you're homesick for your family and fate has provided you with a way to visit them," she advised, lowering the mug and giving Sata a frank look. "Promise him that you will return before making any other decisions about your future together."

"And Naya?"

"As her mother, you can do little at this stage of her life either to influence or protect her. She must find her own way. If you reach out to her, she will only push you further away."

"But if I leave with Oyuun, won't I just be confirming all the terrible assumptions Naya's made about me?" Unable to sit still any longer, Sata got to her feet. Looking for something to do, she began folding a pile of hides that had been left in a heap near the entrance of the tent.

"Before you go, you must tell your daughter that you are setting forth on a journey to discover your heart's longing. That's the truth and all she needs to know. As her mother, it's the best explanation you can give her, the best example you could set." Sata could feel Awija's eyes on her, watching from beside the hearth as she placed the hides in a neat stack.

"What about the rest of the clan?" she asked over her shoulder. "The gossip and speculation? Potis's reputation, and mine for that matter?"

"Do you want to be ruled forever by the judgment of others? Besides, what is so awful about taking advantage of an opportunity to be safely escorted to your homeland after an absence of twenty years? I know you know how to hold your head up and carry on regardless of what other people may think. I've seen you do it."

Reaching over to gather up the discarded mugs, Sata gave her mother-in-law another rueful smile.

"If anyone can pull off a dignified departure, you can," Awija insisted, returning Sata's smile with a wink as she passed the mugs to her. Sata placed them next to the entrance, where she would remember to take them outside to be rinsed in the morning. She was about to begin laying out the sleeping mats when Awija patted the cushion beside her.

"Come," she said, "that chore can wait."

Giving in, Sata sank back onto her seat.

"Seriously," Awija continued, "as long as Potis publicly gives his blessing, which he will if you're both honest with one another in private, then the others will have nothing to say about it." She chuckled. "I must admit," she confessed, "I will look forward to seeing the expression on Uksor's face when you go. *Setting a bad example*, she'll say."

Uksor was Awija's sister-in-law. As the wife of Bhlaghmn, the senior priest, she considered herself responsible for enforcing what she deemed a proper standard of decorum among the girls and young woman of the clan. Naya, especially, was a frequent target of her great-aunt's disapprobation. Awija's mention of her highlighted another of Sata's concerns.

"What about Naya?" she worried out loud, turning to face Awija. "Will you be able to protect her from Uksor's ill-will and convince her to stay out of trouble? Even if Naya no longer wants anything to do with me, she'll still listen to you."

"Yes, I will watch out for Naya." Awija took Sata's hands in hers and gave them a reassuring squeeze. "And Potis will look out for her too. Despite what you might fear, you must know he would never allow anything or anyone to harm her. He does want what's best for her."

"But he also has to consider what is best for the clan," Sata countered. "You know he does."

"Either way," Awija pointed out, "there is little you can do, beyond trusting that a father's love will outweigh a clan chief's necessity. Perhaps the two will align – you never know. In any case, you must have faith that the Goddess has a plan for her."

Sata must have looked skeptical, for Awija squeezed her hands again. "Awos received a vision before he passed," she explained. "Tausos and Swesor heard his words, but only Potis and I understood their significance, and we've told no one." Voice dropping to a whisper, Awija repeated the old clan chief's deathbed prophecy, not only that his granddaughter would return, but that the horses would accompany her and change forever the future of the clan, and perhaps of all the tribes of the steppe.

"So you see," she went on, "if there was ever any doubt, we now know for certain that some great destiny lies in store for Naya – for her and for the horses. Her own spirit-journeys and her grandfather's dying words have revealed as much. But if she is to have protection and assistance in accomplishing the task she has been set, she must find them elsewhere than from her mother. You have done your part and can do no more, at least at present."

"*A't Munar Urug.*" Sate pronounced the foreign words with an air of resignation.

"Indeed," agreed Awija once Sata had explained the meaning of the title the young stranger had bestowed upon her granddaughter.

"Although I don't think Aytal's ever called her *She-Who-Rides-Horses* to her face," Sata added.

"Wise choice," the old woman observed with a chuckle. "If he tried to address her with such reverence, she'd probably bite his head off – and if he did it in public, they'd both be nothing but the target of ridicule."

Awija paused. Her tone when she continued was more sober. "While Naya has already accomplished much, she has more challenges yet to overcome. Only then will she be able to accept with grace the truth of her destiny. But it will happen."

"So will Awos's prophecy indeed come to pass?" pondered Sata, still anxious. "Naya and the red filly? The gray stallion and the mare? The rest of the herd, now that they've been captured? What will happen to them all?"

"A great deal will depend on Naya herself," Awija answered. "We shall have to see what unfolds."

"And how, then, can I bear *not* to be here?"

"To that question you alone can seek an answer," Awija replied. "I have no more advice for you tonight. Give it to the Goddess for now. Perhaps by morning you will have been shown more clearly the path that is yours to follow."

"Oyuun's coming here, to the women's tent, tomorrow night. He thinks it's to say goodbye." The look Sata gave her mother-in-law held both anguish and uncertainty.

"Then you have until tomorrow night to decide what's in your heart," Awija observed. "Best to start by attempting to get some rest."

Chapter Six

Despite her fatigue and the calming effect of the tea, Sata feared she would lie awake, mulling over all that she and Awija had discussed. Instead, almost as soon as she retired to her sleeping mat and pulled the hide blanket over herself, she'd fallen into a deep slumber. She awoke near dawn, feeling remarkably refreshed, as if the Goddess had indeed been watching over her.

Although unable to recall the substance of any dream that might have been sent to provide guidance about her choice to stay or go, she'd arisen knowing what she needed to do before making a final decision. She must have another conversation with Potis – give him a chance to offer his understanding and support– and if he would not, then do her best to persuade him to allow her to leave anyway, if that's what she chose. Equally important, before even bringing the subject up with her husband, she must confirm with Oyuun that his offer to take her with him to her homeland – an offer made well before they had returned to the settlement – still stood. Otherwise, there was no point in confronting Potis. At some point, Sata thought, she would also need to speak with Naya. Throwing off the hide blanket, she sat up, took a deep breath and rose to face the day.

Careful not to disturb Awija, who still slept, Sata tiptoed to the entrance of the women's tent. Pulling aside the door flap just enough to see out, she peered into the golden light of early morning. Shadows cast by the other tents spread across bare earth still marked by footprints from the most recent rain. The chilly air smelled green and damp, like spring. Sata pulled her cloak more tightly around her shoulders. Her best chance of catching Oyuun for a moment alone would be when he came for fuel for a morning fire. She shouldn't have long to wait.

Sure enough, just as the orange disk of the sun appeared beyond the river, a figure appeared silhouetted against the eastern horizon. Oyuun was making his way toward the communal woodpile. Slipping out of the women's tent, Sata joined him. Their meeting might have been entirely accidental, except that Sata had been watching for him. Although most of the clan was no doubt still sleeping off the previous day's festivities down at the stone circle, Sata was disinclined to risk more than the briefest of exchanges.

They bent next to one another beside the neatly arranged stack of birch logs. "Did you mean what you said?" she whispered.

Caught by surprise, Oyuun waited half a heartbeat, studying Sata's face to discern her meaning, before giving a silent nod.

"Then come tonight as we planned," she instructed. Quickly gathering an armful of wood, she straightened and turned away.

Moments later, Sata entered her family's dwelling carrying the load of firewood. She intended to replenish the dwindling supply beside the hearth and then retrieve her spindle and distaff, which had been left behind when she'd moved her belongings into the women's tent the day before. Expecting to find the shelter deserted, she didn't bother to be quiet. Potis wasn't likely to appear until mid-morning. As for Naya, Sata assumed she also would have spent the night at the stone circle, or possibly with Melit in her family's tent if the two girls had decided to return early to the settlement. She was thus surprised to find her daughter in her own bed, Amu curled at her feet. The dog was not fully recovered from his battle with the lion and had spent much of the time since their return resting and licking his wounds. Sata reminded herself to check the lacerations.

Naya lifted her head when Sata entered the tent, then rolled over, turning away.

"How was your evening?" Sata asked, trying to make conversation as she stacked the wood. No reply. After a few similarly pleasant inquiries also failed to elicit an answer, Sata confronted her daughter. "Naya," she said, standing over her motionless form. "This can't go on. You and I need to talk."

Naya's only response was to pull the hide blanket over her head.

"Well at least you can listen to me." Sata sighed, wondering where to start. Best to come straight to the point. Naya was not likely to tolerate anything else. "You're wrong about Oyuun and me, no matter what you think you saw the other day. I was upset and he was comforting me. That's all it was."

No response.

"Naya!" Sata exclaimed in exasperation. "Talk to me!"

The girl sat up, throwing the blanket back, and turned to face her mother. "Do you love Papa?" Her tone dared Sata to be anything less than fully honest.

"Of course."

"Then why does *he* make you happy, and Papa doesn't? Don't try to pretend it's not true."

Naya looked mutinous, prepared to reject whatever explanation her mother might offer. What could Sata say that her daughter would understand?

"It's not that your father makes me unhappy," she began at last. She could have added that, at the moment, Naya was the one vexing her. Her daughter had a legitimate question, one which Sata had been asking herself for some time, with no easy answer.

Crouching, Sata scratched Amu behind his torn ear, giving herself another moment to consider what to say. How could she explain to Naya what she'd only just begun to admit to herself? Years of unacknowledged sorrow had a stranglehold over her. It hadn't been so terrible at first, when she'd been a new bride come to live among her husband's people, full of hope for the future. But as she'd grown older, with only her daughter but no other living children to surround her, with less and less to bind her and Potis to one another, the sense of loneliness and loss had settled into her bones. Potis had never overtly blamed her for her failure to give him a larger family – to give him sons – but Sata blamed herself. The absence of Naya's twin haunted her. How had she managed to keep going after the boy's death, not to mention the others who had never even drawn breath? Grief had become a habit so ingrained she'd stopped paying attention to her feelings, let alone expressing them. She'd grown more and more desolate. Oyuun had brought it all to the surface – and now Sata couldn't rebury what had been laid bare.

"Well?" Naya had grown impatient.

"I suppose if anything, it's that I miss my home," Sata finally replied. It was the closest she could come to giving voice to the longing she felt in words her daughter might accept. "I miss the mountains where I grew up," she elaborated, continuing to stroke the dog's rough coat.

"I don't believe you," Naya spat. "I think being homesick for where you came from is just an excuse. You made a promise and now you're going back on it. I'm not going to be selfish like you. I'm not going to disappoint Papa."

"Naya!" Sata exclaimed. "You're not making any sense. Where is this coming from?" Amu whined, looking first at her, then at Naya.

"Just go away! I hate you!" Naya rolled over again, pulling the blanket back up over her head, shutting her mother out. The dog turned back to Sata, whined once more, then laid his muzzle between his paws.

Later that morning…

Naya's words still seemed to reverberate within the walls of the empty tent when Sata returned just before midday. She looked around, noting the girl's rumpled bed roll with mild exasperation, a welcome substitute for the stab of hurt she'd experienced earlier. She'd spent the morning telling herself that she mustn't dwell on her daughter's outburst, or she wouldn't get through the next confrontation awaiting her. At least the painful exchange with Naya would give her a starting point for the conversation she needed to have with Potis. Knowing that her husband's first errand upon returning from the *Wesr-Admn* celebration would be to put away the ceremonial torque and mace, she'd decided to wait for him here, in the one place likely to afford her an opportunity to speak with him alone and uninterrupted. Hoping he wouldn't be much longer, she set about straightening up the tent, all the while mulling over what she intended to say.

Despite her determination, when Potis did eventually appear, looking tired and disheveled, Sata hesitated, wondering if she'd chosen the best moment. Returning his silent nod, she watched as he replaced the sacred items, then rose and turned to depart the way he'd come. Sata summoned her courage and plunged ahead.

"We have to talk," she blurted. "Please don't put me off."

With his back to her and obviously in a hurry to go, everything about Potis's posture conveyed a desire not to be bothered.

Sata insisted. "Please."

He turned around, obviously ready with an excuse, but when he looked at her something must have convinced him that whatever she needed to say required his full attention. He waited.

"I've been thinking about what we discussed yesterday," she began, intending to sound composed but her voice quavered. "I think you're right. There's not much I can do for Naya right now."

"Oh," Potis replied carefully. "What's happened?"

"I tried to talk with her earlier this morning – tried to explain about everything. It didn't go well."

Potis listened in silence as Sata recounted her exchange with Naya.

"…*I hate you.* Those were her exact words."

"You know she didn't mean it." Still standing near the entrance of the tent, Potis spoke soothingly. "You just need to give her some space."

Sata pressed her lips together in a tight line, willing herself to regain her composure.

"Yes, that's just it," she agreed, once she trusted her voice. "She needs space, but Potis…" Another pause to gather courage. "Potis, I need space as well. I want to go away. I want to go home."

"What do you mean go home? You are home. After being away all winter." He sounded confused.

No air moved in the tent and Sata felt stifled. Wishing she could sit, she remained standing. "No. My home. Where I come from. The mountains. I miss the mountains. I miss my family." How could she make him understand, any more than she'd been able to explain to their daughter?

"But your family is here. You've been away all winter." Potis was repeating himself, Sata noted, as though his mind insisted on rejecting what his ears were hearing.

"I think being gone made me realize how much I want to go home," she ventured. This was at least partly true, although perhaps not the entire story.

"Is this about the stranger?" Now Potis was beginning to sound angry – accusatory in fact – as well as bewildered. "Have you decided you'd rather be with him?"

Leave it to her husband to go to the heart of the matter, Sata thought, like his mother. What could she tell him? She looked down at her hands, clasped together to keep them from shaking. *I must be honest,* she reminded herself, *with myself and with him.*

"I don't know," she finally answered. She glanced up at him, wondering how her confession had landed. Potis turned away, as if he didn't want to hear, or accept, what she had to say. For a long moment he stood with his back to her, silent, before turning to face her once more.

"I don't understand." His voice was tight. Beneath the accusations lay confusion – and hurt.

Sata's heart broke. She had not wanted to wound him. But how could she explain the sensation of being slowly strangled by years of swallowing her own pain, without seeming to blame him for her unhappiness? How to make him see that if something about her life didn't change, she thought she might suffocate?

"Do you love him?" Potis asked quietly, but there was an edge to his tone. This time while waiting for her answer he did not look away. His amber eyes held hers, fierce, hawk-like, demanding a response.

"I don't know," Sata said again. And it was the truth, she suddenly realized. Earlier in the day – talking to Naya – she would have denied it. Now, asked point blank by her husband of twenty years, what could she say?

"I might," she admitted, forcing herself to meet Potis's gaze. Despite a reflexive stab of shame, she would neither deny how she felt nor endure self-reproach, not any longer. Doing so would only serve to tighten the noose around her neck.

"So, you would rather be with him – give up your life, everything you have here, abandon me and our daughter?!" Potis's voice rose, anger fueling the hurt. At his sides, his hands clenched into fists.

"No," Sata responded emphatically, her voice wanting to rise to match his. She inhaled deeply, reaching for calm. "That's not what I'm saying. I'm saying that all I know right now is that I want to go home – for a visit – not forever."

"But you would go with him." It was a statement, not a question.

"It's the only chance I'm ever likely to have," she countered. Silence ensued, as they both considered the legitimacy of her observation.

"He has to come back," she pointed out at last. "His sons…"

Potis interrupted, pacing despite the small space. "What about Naya? Can you really just walk away from your own daughter?"

"I can't do anything for her right now. She's made that clear," Sata rejoined, watching him move about like a caged animal. "You seem to think that Vedukha might have more influence over her," she pointed out, recalling his proposition from the day before. "And you'll still be here. And your mother. Awija told me that Bhlaghmn insists that Naya and Melit and the other girls be presented at this year's Gathering, in which case their training has to begin immediately. Your mother will have much more opportunity to keep an eye on Naya between now and the Gathering than I would. I don't want to miss Naya's presentation to the tribe – or your father's funeral – but traveling with Oyuun is the only opportunity I'll have to return to my homeland."

"And what about me?" The words were forced. Potis stopped and pinned her again with his hawk's gaze.

How typical! Her husband made no effort to understand how she might be feeling; instead, it was all about him. But then, behind those fierce amber eyes, she saw something vulnerable stir, causing her to discard the bitterness as unworthy of them both. Rather than engage in unproductive recriminations, she needed to make him see that a change might be for the best for everyone concerned.

"Vedukha..." she began.

"Don't bring her into this." Potis snapped, sounding defensive as well as angry. "She's the widow of my best friend, my cousin."

"Bhermi may have been your cousin, but Vedukha is *my* cousin, *my* friend," Sata reminded him. "Have you forgotten?" She thought of the embrace she'd witness on the bluff top – recalled the initial stab of it – and reminded herself of the realization she'd come to since: although painful, seeing Potis and Vedukha together did not hurt in the way it should have.

"I love you both," she continued, meaning the words sincerely. "If I'm willing to accept that the two of you may need each other more than either of you needs me, perhaps you should admit the possibility as well. She might even give you more children."

Her words hung in the air between them. For a long moment neither looked away, until abruptly Potis turned his back again, as though suddenly aware that his face might betray what he would rather remain hidden.

"I promise I'll come back," Sata said at last. She hadn't moved from where she was standing, hands now at her sides. "I won't make any other decisions until I return, until we talk again," she offered. It was what Awija had advised, and she knew her mother-in-law had been right. "But I have to go. Can you let me go?" She forced herself not to reach out to him, to keep the pleading tone from her voice. She'd found the courage to ask; she wouldn't beg.

More silence. Sata couldn't see Potis's expression, couldn't tell what his answer would be, couldn't decipher from the rigid set of his shoulders what he might be feeling, beyond anger and a need to defend himself. She pressed ahead anyway.

"If you agree," she said, "there are two things I would ask from you while I'm gone."

Potis's response was a sharp nasal exhale, indicating she had some nerve to be demanding favors. Not allowing herself to be deterred, Sata continued.

"First, please be honest with yourself and with Vedukha," she insisted. "I mean it. For too long there's been too much buried under the weight of duty, for all of us."

Sata paused, waiting for a reaction. *It would be nice if you would at least turn around,* she thought. Potis remained with his back to her, posture unchanging and indecipherable. *Look at me!* she wanted to shout. *Say something!* Moments passed. At last, he sighed and she thought perhaps some of the tension might have begun to drain from his body.

"What's the other thing?" he asked, still without turning around.

"Don't make Naya marry until after I return."

Now Potis did turn to face her; in fact, he rounded on her. "What makes you think I'm planning to marry her off?" he demanded. "And how can you suggest that I would *ever* make her marry against her will? What do you think I am?"

"You are a clan chief, with pressures and responsibilities," Sata answered, stating the obvious as reasonably as she could manage in the face of his ire. "I'm not naïve. I know she has to marry for the good of the clan. I'm just asking that you agree to wait until I return."

"I'm afraid you're right," he replied, voice shading into sarcasm. "That's a lot to expect from me, given all the 'pressures and responsibilities' as you call them."

"She's barely fifteen," Sata implored, ignoring his tone. "She will just have been presented. If she has to be betrothed to Wailos or someone else, at least put off the wedding itself until I can be there. Is that really too much to ask?"

"You're the one who's leaving," he'd pointed out bitingly.

"Potis, please."

"All I can offer is this. Only if she herself decides to marry before you get back will a wedding take place. That's as much as I'm prepared to concede."

"Do I have your promise?"

"As long as I have yours that you will return."

"Then we are agreed."

Potis departed immediately for the corrals and Sata spent the remainder of the day going about what, under normal circumstances, would have been her usual activities – helping her sisters-in-law to gather fresh greens for the evening meal as well as various other tasks around the settlement – all the while anticipating her meeting with Oyuun later that evening and calculating what she might want to pack for another long journey, assuming she made the final decision to go. She caught sight of Naya several times throughout the day, always in Melit's company, but had no further chance to speak with her.

The evening meal, a generous fish stew, was a communal affair. Sata, Potis, and Naya were joined by Awija and the rest of the extended family, including aunts, uncles and cousins, plus Vedukha and her children. Wailos and his cousin Unksra were included as well. Dayan, who normally would have eaten with them, had gone instead to sit by his father's fire, since this was to be Oyuun's last evening before setting out again on his journey south. Aytal, who had already assumed his duties with the captured horses, was not free to leave the corrals. Earlier in the day Sata had watched from a distance as he and Oyuun said goodbye. She regretted not being able say farewell to the young man as well. She had come to care for him, almost as a son.

At supper, Sata felt grateful for the laughter and conversation generated by the small crowd. No one appeared to notice her silence throughout the meal, nor remarked when she followed her mother-in-law in retiring early to the women's tent rather than joining the other clan members around the central fire. Once sheltered within the privacy of the tent's thick walls, she confessed her plans to Awija: while regretful about being absent for Naya's presentation, as well as missing the old clan chief's funeral, she intended to depart with Oyuun in the morning. She reminded her mother-in-law to expect a clandestine visit from him later that evening and hoped Awija wouldn't object, assuring her that

Oyuun would have the good sense to wait until he could enter without being seen.

Far from seeming shocked or even mildly disapproving at the prospect of a man – a stranger to the clan – entering the forbidden sanctum of the women's tent, her mother-in-law had merely nodded and offered to help her to pack. Not until after the last of the few belongings Sata planned to take with her had been safely stowed, did Awija so much as mention Oyuun and then only to say that she had one or two important questions to ask him. "Be sure to wake me when he shows up," she insisted. With that, the old woman settled herself by the hearth and, closing her eyes, drifted off to sleep.

Much later, sitting in the firelit darkness of the women's tent, Sata waited for Oyuun to find his way to her. Although the night had grown old and she'd been expecting him for some time, she wasn't really worried that he would not appear. More likely the delay was due to the last group of stragglers lingering around the central fire. Still, Sata found passing the time difficult. While her mother-in-law snored in her accustomed place beside the warmth of the hearth, she'd tried to occupy herself with spinning raw wool into thread but her fingers, uncharacteristically clumsy after months without practice, kept tangling the fibers, forcing her to start over. She'd finally given up.

With the spindle laying idle in her lap, Sata's thoughts continued to whirl. When she imagined leaving, something in her chest fluttered. Whether with excitement or trepidation – perhaps some combination of the two – she couldn't be sure, but she also could not remember the last time she'd felt such a not-altogether-unpleasant sensation. In contrast, when she contemplated staying behind, a sickening knot formed in the pit of her stomach and she experienced a horrible, panicked reaction, like an animal caught in a snare. If she went with Oyuun, she would feel guilty for leaving. If she stayed, sacrificing her deepest longings, something inside her would shrivel and die. Perhaps Awija was right. The best gift a mother could give her beloved daughter, poised on the threshold of womanhood, was to honor her own desires, even if doing so went against everything she had ever believed about obligation and duty.

Finally, just as Sata thought she couldn't bear the wait and her own indecision a moment longer, the door skin lifted, and a dark shape ducked inside. She held her breath, waiting while the shadowy form fumbled to retie the thongs holding the tent flap closed. Straightening at last, the figure turned and stepped toward the circle of light from the dying fire. Oyuun had come as promised, and Sata's heart rejoiced.

Chapter Seven

Early the next morning…

"Naya?"

Standing next to her father, Naya kept her eyes on the ground.

"Naya?" her mother repeated.

Naya didn't want to answer. She didn't even want to acknowledge that she'd heard her mother. Her aunts and uncles and cousins formed a cluster to one side of her family's tent. Awija waited next to Oyuun. His travel pack, and her mother's, were on the ground at his feet. Her mother had stepped forward. Opening her arms, she offered a parting embrace.

"Please?"

Other clan members lurked nearby, watching surreptitiously as the clan chief's wife said farewell to her family in preparation for setting off on an unthinkable journey with only the stranger for company. Naya could imagine their disapproval. She shared it. But she didn't want to embarrass her father, who'd apparently given Mama his blessing.

"Please?" her mother asked again, this time in a whisper.

Relenting, Naya allowed herself to be hugged. Still, she refused to return the embrace, or to look her mother in the eye. No matter what Mama had said earlier that morning, when she'd tried again to explain about being homesick for her own people and for the mountains where she had spent her youth, and about making the choice to honor her heart's deepest longing, as far as Naya was concerned, her departure was a betrayal and she'd vowed never to forgive her.

As soon as her mother released her, she turned away, ducking inside the tent so that she didn't have to watch her leave.

Later in the day, while restocking the woodpile in their family shelter as her father had instructed, Naya realized that she and her father would have the tent to themselves, at least for a night. She'd be moving in with Melit and her mother and sister the next day, but this evening, she and Papa might finally be able to talk, alone and uninterrupted. When their paths crossed at midday, she'd mentioned the possibility to him and he'd agreed, promising not to let anything interfere.

Naya planned to tell her father everything – all the good that had happened while she'd been away, and the bad. She wondered how much he knew about her mother and Oyuun and if what she had seen between them would have changed his mind about allowing Mama to leave. More pressing, she needed to convince her father to allow her to go in search of the red filly, the gray stallion and the mare before hunters found them or they wandered too far from the settlement.

Naya also wanted to ask her father about the captured horses. Before she went looking for Réhda and the other two, she had to know what was going to happen to the rest of the herd in the corral. All she'd overheard were rumors about something to do with the Gathering. So far, whenever she'd tried speaking to her father about the subject, he'd put her off, saying he didn't have time to explain but then he'd made her promise not to talk to anyone else and risk revealing her mysterious connection to the red filly. Naya didn't dare bring up the subject with Melit, who was too good at prying secrets out of her, especially since she had already caught her spying from the bluff top. *Why are you so interested in those horses?* she'd want to know. When Naya had asked Awija, her grandmother had given a disapproving sniff and told her to speak to her father.

Then this evening, while clearing up from the evening meal, she overheard her aunt casually mention the herd's intended fate. Shocked, she managed not to erupt in front of the rest of the family, but her heart leapt to her throat.

After supper, when she and Papa were alone, she confronted him. "Is it true?" she demanded, letting the door flap drop behind her as she followed him into their tent. "What Swesor said, that the horses are going to be slaughtered?"

"Your aunt Swesor doesn't know when to guard her tongue." Obviously irritated, her father turned to face her, then sighed in resignation when he saw the look on her face. "Not slaughtered," he clarified. "Sacrificed. There's a difference. But yes, it's true. And the ones not sacrificed will be traded away."

Naya stared back at him, speechless. After a moment, she lowered herself to her bedroll beside the hearth and gazed with unseeing eyes at the banked embers of an earlier fire, still not uttering a sound.

"I know these horses are special to you," her father went on, attempting to explain. "Your mother told me they're part of the red filly's band. I wish there was a way to set them free but the situation is complicated. There's a lot at stake." He avoided looking at her and began moving around the tent, putting things away. Lifting her eyes from the smoored fire, Naya followed his actions, so overwhelmed by what he'd just confirmed that she had to struggled to pay attention to what he was saying.

She listened and asked questions, all the while experiencing a strange sense of detachment. He didn't tell her everything, but enough for Naya to grasp the serious consequences that would follow if the clan lost standing with the rest of the tribe. What he didn't say, but Naya guessed, was that her father's reputation, not to mention his position as clan chief, were also at risk. In the end, she told him she understood and promised again not to go the corrals.

"Don't get involved," her father warned. Naya agreed.

"I'm tired, Papa," she said. "I want to go to bed." She no longer felt like talking. Lying down, she pulled her sheepskin cover around her shoulders and turned away.

Waiting for sleep that did not come, Naya thought of everything she'd wanted to share with her father. None of it mattered anymore. Her mother had left with Oyuun and might never come back. Trying to convince her father to allow her to look for the red filly, the gray stallion and the mare was worse than pointless. Perhaps she'd only imagined the three figures silhouetted above the ridgeline on the day of Aytal's sentencing – hopefully Réhda, Šuurgan and MeHnd were far away by now, out on the open steppe – but if not, and they were still close by, did she really want to bring attention to them, only to have them captured as well? Hadn't she caused enough trouble?

As for the rest of the herd down in the ravine, her worst nightmares had come true. Following her heart's desire had led to nothing but disaster, all her fault. Instead of proving horses could be tamed and ridden, she'd only guaranteed that the herd she'd befriended would be more easily sacrificed. Better not to go near any of the horses again.

Naya stifled a sob. *Better for everyone*, she told herself, *especially the red filly*. She should leave her dreams and visions in the past and concentrate instead on the future. Her future, as the daughter of a clan chief.

Vedukha's tent, a few days later…

"What do you think?" Arms outstretched, Naya turned in a circle. Vedukha, Melit, and Melit's younger sister Maqa looked on critically. Naya wore one of Melit's dresses. The garment, belted at the waist, reached just below her knees. Although the deer skin was soft and well-cut, the bodice felt tight across Naya's breasts. She used to be flat-chested compared to Melit, but no longer. She smiled tentatively.

"Too small," Vedukha pronounced. "You can try one of mine. Maqā – fetch the one with the colored thread and shells sewn around the neck."

Maqā – a girl of ten summers who shared her older sister's dark hair and dimples – had been observing the proceedings with interest. At her mother's request, she went to rummage through a small stack of clothing piled against the back wall of the tent, returning with another dress, this one longer and more generously shaped. She passed it to her mother, who shook it out and handed it to Naya.

"Try this one," Vedukha urged. "It will be too big, but I can alter it for you. While I'm doing that, Melit can fix your hair."

Obediently, Naya switched garments and stood while Vedukha took the measurements she needed. Afterwards, wrapped in a blanket, she sat on a cushion by the hearth, determined to be patient as Melit, kneeling behind her, began the laborious process of detangling her unruly mane. Maqa sat close by, ready with delicate elmwood hair pins as well as a wide-toothed comb in case the one Melit was using, carved from a deer's shoulder bone, happened to break.

Normally Naya couldn't be bothered to do more than tie her long thick hair with a thong at the nape of her neck, or finger-comb it into a loose plait to keep it out of her way. Although she hated the coppery shade because it set her apart, she'd long ago decided that she couldn't do anything about it, any more than she could change the color of her blue eyes, so why spend time with brushing and braiding? Much the same was true of her clothing. As long as what she wore was functional, allowing her to move comfortably and stay either warm or cool as required, she hadn't given it much thought. As she'd matured, however, her clothing had become as much a topic of derision among her peers as her flaming tresses. Before being away all winter, she'd been teased frequently, both for continuing to garb herself like a boy long after the other girls her age had adopted dresses, and for apparently allowing birds to nest atop her unkempt red head.

Naya winced as Melit pulled at a knot but otherwise submitted meekly to her cousin's ministrations. Since she'd moved in with them, Melit and her mother had set to work convincing her that the time had come to make a change in how she behaved and presented herself. *If not for your sake*, they'd reasoned, *think of your father*. Once Naya would have resisted their arguments, but now that she'd foresworn pursuing her own selfish desires, she'd come to agree.

All her life, she'd sought her father's approval, desperate to make up for not being the son he deserved. More often than not, she'd failed. She'd lost count of the number of times she'd embarrassed him or caused him worry and trouble. After everything she'd put her father through – all the mistakes she'd made – she was determined going forward to render him her unconditional loyalty and obedience. She would not betray him, as her mother had done. Instead, she vowed to do whatever was necessary to be the kind of daughter of whom a clan chief could be proud. If that meant putting away her tunic and leggings, constraining her wayward hair in a neat braid, and otherwise respecting her father's wishes, so be it.

"There!" Melit said, tying off the last braid and tucking in the ends. "What do you think, Mama?" Naya looked around to see Vedukha's reaction as well. She started to put up a hand to feel what her cousin had done with her hair, but Melit stopped her.

"Don't touch it!" she cried. "You'll wreck it."

"Lovely," Vedukha declared with approval. "Even the color. Melit has managed to feature the highlights, so your hair looks like red and gold flame. Wailos won't be able to help but admire it." Maqā nodded in agreement, her black eyes bright.

"Do you think so?" Naya sounded unconvinced. Melit and her mother both seemed to assume that attracting their visitor's attention was an integral part of the plan to please her father. Naya had thought a lot about what Melit had said on the way back from the blufftop the day after she'd returned, about Wailos and the advantages of a match. She had to admit, he did seem interested. And while Papa hadn't said anything to her yet about a possible marriage, he hadn't given any indication that he *disapproved*.

"Let's see how Wailos reacts at supper tonight," Vedukha suggested with a smile. "Between the dress and the hair, my guess is that he won't be able to take his eyes of you. Now girls, come help me get started with the cooking. We'll have to eat early so that Melit and Naya aren't late to their first evening of training. Maqā – you go for more water while the older girls fetch the ingredients for the fish stew. The vegetables will need to be put on to roast right away if they're to be ready in time."

Later that evening…

Naya and Melit hurried through supper and were excused from helping to clean-up. Even so, they were almost the last to arrive outside the women's tent, reaching the entrance just ahead of the priest's wife. She wagged a finger at them. Trying to be polite, Naya held back the entrance flap so that Uksor could proceed them into the tent, then nearly choked trying not to laugh when Melit pulled a face behind the old woman's back.

Inside, three other young women who were to be presented were already settled on cushions forming a semi-circle around the central hearth. Only the places on either end were unoccupied. One open spot was next to Naya's cousin Elēn, Swesor's daughter. She and Naya were not as good friends as Naya and Melit, but the two got along, mostly because Elēn was kind to everyone. Next to Elēn on the other side, sitting beside one another, were the twins, Petsna and Perom. Despite being part of the same clan, Naya had spent very little time with either of them. Their father was Papa's cousin, which made the twins Naya's second cousins, like Melit, but he was one of Skelos's followers, while the twins' mother had never liked Naya's mother and disapproved of Naya.

Seeing that the other unoccupied place was next to Perom, Naya hesitated. She'd been teased by the bolder of the twins on more than one occasion when they were younger – nothing as mean as the taunts

Krnos tossed her way, but bad enough that Naya didn't want to have to sit beside her. Melit had already claimed the cushion on the opposite end next to Elēn, however, so Naya had to settle for shooting her friend an accusatory glare.

You did that on purpose, she mouthed, taking the empty seat. Melit responded with a shrug. Naya tried to remember her advice when they found out that Perom and Petsna, along with Elēn, would also be taking part in the training. *Keep an open mind*, Melit had advised her. *They're actually really nice.* Naya wasn't so sure. She and the twins exchanged awkward smiles.

"Nice dress," Perom said. Naya couldn't tell if she meant the compliment or was being snide.

"And I like your hair," offered Petsna. She seemed more sincere compared to her sister. Naya gave her a more genuine smile in return.

"Girls," called Awija, clapping her hands for attention. "Time to get started."

She and Uksor were seated on cushions across the hearth from the Naya and the others. The priest's wife scanned them with a sanctimonious frown. Her gaze lingered on Naya, making Naya want to squirm. Just then Amu snuck into the tent, along with Elēn's dog Mashu. The two lay down companionably off to one side and both began chewing on strips of rawhide they'd carried in with them. Naya hoped the dogs' presence wouldn't get her and Elēn into trouble. So far, neither her grandmother nor Uksor seemed to be paying them any heed.

"We have a lot to accomplish," Awija began. "We'll be meeting almost every evening after supper, from now until the start of your three-day vigil. The vigil itself will begin two nights before the official commencement of the Gathering, just prior to the dark period of the next moon cycle. After three nights spent in seclusion, you will emerge at sunrise on the morning of the summer solstice and be presented to the entire tribe as newly recognized young women."

Naya and the other girls exchanged excited looks and might have started to whisper among themselves had Uksor not interrupted.

"It is of the *utmost* importance that you perform *impeccably* during the presentation," she warned. "Your personal reputations, and more importantly the reputations of your family and of our clan, depend upon your correct behavior. Do you understand?" She looked down her nose at them. Naya and her fellow trainees nodded in cowed silence.

"Don't worry," interjected Awija with a reassuring smile. "As the wife of our esteemed senior priest, Uksor will be in charge of instructing you in all the necessary protocol. As long as you follow her directions, you'll do fine." Uksor continued to glare at the girls, her humorless features unchanged.

"This period of training prior to your presentation is meant to be special for you," Awija went on, looking at each of the girls in turn, her own expression growing more serious. "We've set aside this time so that you may prepare to move into new roles as adults – and more particularly as *women*. Do you understand?"

Each girl nodded again, solemnly this time, although Naya wasn't certain that she and her fellow trainees fully grasped Awija's meaning. As far as Naya knew, the clan's rite of passage for females – three days of seclusion followed by presentation to the entire tribe assembled for the Gathering – was intended to serve primarily as a public recognition of a young woman's eligibility for marriage. The whole exercise came under the authority of the senior priest and took place at his behest. Yet Naya knew her grandmother well enough to guess that with Awija involved in their preparation for the ritual, she and the other girls would not merely be studying how to make someone a good wife.

"Alright then," Awija said briskly, sitting up a little straighter. "The Gathering is a month and a half away and we have much to teach you. Before the start of your vigil, you'll receive instruction on a wide variety of topics – some more interesting than others – but all of them important."

Naya stole a glance at Uksor, wondering how often the priest's wife would be leading their discussions – presumably the ones on the less interesting subjects.

"Regretfully," Awija went on as though in response, "due to her many important responsibilities leading up to the Gathering, Uksor will only be able to join us when we talk specifically about the presentation ceremony and about the day-to-day conduct that will be expected once you've been recognized as young women of the clan. The rest of the time, you'll be with me."

Naya dropped her eyes to her lap, disguising her relief. When she looked up a moment later, her grandmother had turned to Uksor.

"Of course, you are always welcome whenever your duties allow," she added tactfully. Awija and the priest's wife exchanged ostensively cordial smiles before Awija turned back to survey her audience. "Are there any questions so far?"

Melit put up a hand.

"Yes, my dear?"

"Can you tell us more about the vigil?" Melit looked around at the other girls. "We're all so curious."

Naya saw her grandmother give the priest's wife a swift sideways glance, as though considering what to say in front of her, before shifting her attention back to the trainees.

"In essence," Awija began, "the vigil is meant to provide you with an opportunity for solitude – time alone in the sanctuary of a shelter you will have built for yourself, to mark your transition from one stage of life to the next. When you emerge at the conclusion of your vigil, you will have crossed a threshold. As young women, you will be bound by a new set of roles and responsibilities, constrained by expectations and standards of conduct dictated by others."

She looked grave. Naya noted that her grandmother made no mention of gaining additional freedoms and privileges, such as was the case for young men upon entering adulthood. Instead, she spoke of limits and obligations. Uksor nodded in evident approval.

"However," Awija went on, "for the days while you are in seclusion – for those three days at least – you will have the luxury of belonging to no one but yourselves."

The priest's wife frowned. Although Naya had a notion of what her grandmother meant, the other girls' faces looked blank. Awija gave a small sigh and continued.

"For some of you," she observed, "having only yourselves for company for three days will be the hardest part."

She raised an eyebrow at Melit, who everyone knew was too social to ever voluntarily spend any length of time alone if she could help it. The twins stifled a giggle.

"For others, it may be your last opportunity for the solitude you've come to value as essential."

This time, Awija's green-flecked gaze settled on Naya with a familiar expression of compassion and concern. Naya recognized the look. Awija had always encouraged her solitary roaming. Last fall, in particular, she'd been adamant that Naya be allowed to go on her own to search for the red filly and her herd, in pursuit of her quest to tame them.

Would her grandmother understand why she had to give up on the whole idea? Naya worried she wouldn't approve. Worse, she feared Awija would be disappointed in her.

Unable to bear her grandmother's regard, Naya dropped her eyes once more to her lap. *I can't please everyone*, she thought. *Doing what Papa expects of me and making him proud are more important than what I want, or what Awija wants for me. Besides, I mustn't do anything to endanger the horses any more than I have already.*

"Alright," Awija said after a pause. "That's enough about the vigil for now. In fact, I think that's plenty of talk for our first evening together. We'll meet after supper again tomorrow and you'll receive your first assignment."

The other girls looked surprised. Preoccupied with her own thoughts, Naya almost missed what her grandmother said.

"I'm afraid so," Awija verified. "You will have tasks to complete."

The girls groaned in unison.

"We'll also be required to leave the comfort of the women's tent from time to time, in order study the night sky," Awija warned. "In a few evenings, when the moon is full, we will gather outside, down at the stone circle. I'll say no more at the moment, other than be prepared for some late nights and early dawns. For now, you are all dismissed." She waved a hand, indicating the girls could be on their way. "Pile your cushions next to the door when you leave."

Speculating to herself about the nature of their first assignment, Naya rose with the other girls and started toward the tent's entrance, cushion in hand. Just as she was about to add it to the stack, Awija called out.

"You two," she said, indicating Naya and her cousin Elēn, who were the last in line by the door. "Before you leave, make sure you take your dogs with you. I don't want them in here all night, keeping me awake with their snoring."

Naya and Elēn traded grins, well aware that their grandmother was the one who snored. Uksor, getting up from her seat to follow the girls out of the tent, raised her eyes disdainfully as Awija chuckled at her own joke.

Elēn called to Mashu and together they disappeared through the door flap. Before Naya could do the same, Awija motioned to her without getting up. "A goodnight hug for my favorite grandchild?"

Acceding to her grandmother's request, Naya returned to her side and leaned down to receive her grandmother's embrace. Reaching up, Awija wrapped an arm around Naya's shoulders and drew her close, careful not to disturb her elaborate braid.

Cheek to cheek for the space of two shared heartbeats, Naya rested in the familiar comfort of her grandmother's love. Then swallowing hard, she straightened and stepped back. Gesturing for Amu to follow her, she hurried out after the others, glad to escape into the darkness before Awija could notice her tears.

Chapter Eight

Four nights later…

"You and Wailos seemed pretty friendly at dinner," Melit commented.

Naya made a noncommittal noise in reply. They were down by the river, lying on their backs within the stone circle, waiting for Awija and the other girls to arrive. Felt blankets kept off the nighttime chill. The orange glow of a huge full moon rising in the eastern sky dimmed all but the brightest stars.

"Has he asked you to go exploring with him yet?" Melit was not to be put off.

"Tomorrow," Naya answered. "I'm a little nervous," she confessed.

"Why?" Melit asked in surprise. "It's just a walk. You could show him the ravine south of where the horses are, the one with the cave."

"No!" Naya exclaimed, more emphatically than she intended. Melit turned her head to look sideways at her. "I'd rather stay away from the bluffs," Naya offered by way of explanation. In truth, she didn't want to risk stumbling on the red filly. If she and the gray stallion and the mare were still nearby, they could easily be in one of the many ravines like the one that held the captured herd.

"What worries me is finding anything to talk about," she went on, steering the conversation away from any mention of the horses. "I know *you* can't imagine having difficulty, but for me, knowing what to say can be really awkward."

"Talking to boys is easy," replied Melit, turning back to look up at the night sky. "You spent all winter talking to what's-his-name – Aytal – right?" Naya didn't reply. She remembered *not* talking to Aytal – the silence between them so comfortable they didn't need words.

"I'm sure Wailos will be no different," Melit went on, "even if he is a handsome warrior and the son of a clan chief and Aytal is only a scruffy trader with terrible aim. Just ask Wailos questions about himself and pretend to be interested in the answers." She pointed upward, excited. "Look! A shooting star. Make a wish."

You're not helping, Naya wanted to retort. What should she wish for? To be as confident and unself-conscious as her friend?

"Just be yourself," Melit said, as if Naya had spoken aloud. "You are the daughter of a clan chief, don't forget. You and Wailos are equals."

That's the problem, Naya thought. She couldn't imagine herself and Wailos as equals. He was a warrior, and she was… Truthfully, Naya wasn't sure *who* she was these days. She knew she no longer wanted to be her old self, but she hadn't had much practice at being her new self – the daughter who would finally make her father proud. She sighed and looked up at the radiant disk of the moon above. If the moon could start off as a mere sliver and grow into all her resplendent glory, then perhaps she could as well.

Yesterday evening, Awija had asked the girls to consider what lessons the moon might have for them as young women. Tonight, once everyone arrived at the stone circle, they would be discussing the subject. Naya could hear voices approaching along the path and soon Petsna and Perom appeared, arms laden with blankets. They were followed more slowly by Elēn, carrying a cushion in one arm and supporting Awija with the other as she helped guide the old woman's steps. Naya silently berated herself for not offering to assist her grandmother in making the trek down to the stone circle in the dark. Although the moon was bright, the track was somewhat steep and rough in places. Of course, Elēn, who was always considerate, would have offered to accompany their grandmother, Naya thought. She sighed, vowing to do better.

Once everyone was settled – the girls lying side-by-side under their blankets, face-up to the night sky and Awija seated on her cushion behind them, wrapped in her shawl – a natural quiet descended. Directly overhead, a river of stars washed against the black void of the heavens, while to the east, the full moon hung above the horizon, turning the surrounding sky a deep indigo. In the stillness, sounds and scents began to materialize. Nearby, the great river flowed with quiet purpose, wafting aloft the faint odor of fish. Further away to the south, carried on a gentle breeze, came the *hoot, hoot* of an owl perched among the poplars lining the riverbank. The breeze also brought the pungent smell of garlic and leeks, growing at the forest's edge. Naya reminded herself to go in search of them tomorrow.

Awija's voice, emerging from the darkness, was low but distinct. "When you look at the moon," she asked quietly, "what do you see?"

For a long moment, no one replied.

"Remember what I suggested yesterday, about how the moon can show us something about our lives?" Awija prompted. "Come now, speak up, be brave!"

"Right now," Elēn began tentatively, "the moon looks full enough to burst."

"Like a ripe plum," added Melit. The other girls giggled.

"Very good," Awija said with approval. "What else?"

"When the moon shines, the darkness seems softer, somehow," offered Petsna. "Less frightening."

"Very good," Awija repeated. "What else?"

"It's the opposite when there's no moon," Perom observed. "When the moon disappears, the dark seems even more mysterious."

"Quite true," Awija agreed. "Nothing wrong with a little mystery," she added, a hint of mischief in her voice. She waited for someone else to speak. "Naya," she asked after a moment, "what about you? What can you tell us about the moon?"

Naya should have known her grandmother would not let her get away with not contributing. "Change," she answered, offering the first observation that came to her. "The moon is never the same two nights in a row. Moonrise happens at a different time and in a different place in the sky, depending on the phase and the season. But if you pay attention, there's a pattern – a cycle – that eventually repeats. Much more complicated than the sun, but more interesting, I think."

Silence ensued. Naya felt mortified. Why did she have to go and give a speech on something so obvious? Why couldn't she keep it simple, like the other girls?

Eventually, Melit spoke up, coming to her rescue. "Naya's right," she said. "The best thing is that the moon is never the same. I love the new moon, the full moon, *and* the old moon too. Every phase is beautiful." The other girls murmured in agreement. It sounded better when Melit said it, thought Naya.

"You've all made good points," Awija said. "One important aspect you left out is the moon's influence on your monthly flow. Perhaps none of you is regular enough yet to notice, but the moon's cycle is as much a part of your natural rhythm as your heartbeat."

"Petsna's hasn't started yet," revealed Perom. Her sister squeaked, pulling her blanket over her head to hide her embarrassment. The twins' mother had insisted both girls be allowed to participate in their training together, so that Petsna wouldn't feel left out, even if she might have to wait until the following year to be presented.

"Not to worry," soothed Awija. "All in good time. The important point is that the moon tracks not only a woman's monthly flow, but also the larger cycle of her life. You girls are at the new crescent stage, just moving into the promise of young womanhood. As the moon ripens to fullness, likewise you will enter your most fertile, creative years – whether or not you are blessed with children. As the moon wanes, so too will your bodily strength, replaced by the hard-won wisdom of age. When you're ancient, like me, you'll know better than to try to come down that hill in the dark." Awija chuckled. "In the final stage," she continued, "just as the three nights of utter darkness each month conceal the miracle of the moon's rebirth, death for each of us will bring both an end and a new beginning."

The girls absorbed Awija's words. Above them, the moon, hanging suspended from the heavens, gradually turned from glowing orange to a luminescent white.

"Let me tell you a story," Awija said after a moment. "An ancient tale from a far-away land."

The girls exchanged glances in the dark; they'd been anticipating hearing such tales.

"As you know," Awija went on, "I grew up in a place a long way from here, a place with different customs – and different stories. Rather than following herds of cattle, sheep and goats, my people live in large villages and plant crops of grain and vegetables. Instead of moving away to get married, girls like you stay with their mothers and grandmothers for their whole lives, eventually becoming mothers and grandmothers themselves. Instead of priests worshipping the gods, we have priestesses devoted to *Cita-Amsus*, the Great Goddess. Only the Goddess isn't a personage like Sky-Father, so much as a presence. She is the sacred creative force infusing life into every aspect of the world – plants and animals, rocks and trees, mountains and rivers, sun, moon and stars.

Among other duties, priestesses of the Great Goddess are responsible for overseeing girls' rite of passage into womanhood. The story I want to tell you is one I learned when I was your age, going through my own training – only for reasons we won't go into, my people referred to it as an initiation."

Sitting up, Perom raised her hand to interrupt.

"Yes, my dear?"

"Why did you leave?"

"Because of a handsome herder," Awija replied laughing. "But that's a story for another evening."

Petsna sat up as well.

"Yes?"

"What was your training – your initiation – like?" she inquired.

"Very different from your experience being prepared to be presented, or even what the young men of the clan go through," Awija answered. "Our initiate training lasted for an entire year." This caused the other girls to sit up as well, so that they were all facing Awija, grouped in a semi-circle.

"A whole year!" Melit exclaimed in dismay. "That must have been hard work."

"It must have been wonderful," said Elēn dreamily.

"Who taught you?" Naya asked.

"The head priestess," Awija answered, "who in those days happened to be *my* grandmother, making her your and Elēn's great-great grand-mother. The other priestesses took turns helping, of course. Training each year's group of initiates was considered an important duty."

"How many girls went through training with you?" Perom wanted to know.

"Seven groups of ten, altogether," Awija answered. The girls gasped.

"Your village must have had more people than our whole tribe!" Petsna said with awe.

"Yes," agreed Awija. "Certainly, more people than you've ever seen in one place. And our training culminated in a sacred ritual far more daunting, not to say life-changing, than anything you are being asked to face, no matter how much you might be dreading three days spent in seclusion. But we are getting off topic."

"The story," Naya prompted. "About the moon." She loved her grandmother's stories, and this was one she hadn't heard before.

"That's right," Awija smiled at her. "Now lie down again and get comfortable while I tell it to you." The girls snuggled back under their blankets.

"Among my people," Awija began, "we trace our ancestors from daughter to mother to grandmother to great grandmother to great-great grandmother, all the way back to one of the Seven Sisters. In case you've never heard of them, the Seven Sisters are the foremothers of all the peoples who walk the earth, and *their* mother is First Mother. She, in turn, is the daughter of *Cita-Amsus*, the Great Goddess. This story takes place in the time before the ancestors, before the Seven Sisters." Awija's voice took on the sing-song quality of the practiced storyteller. "In those days," she continued, "First Mother had only two children: Mehnot, who was a girl, and her twin brother, whose name was Sāwel…

…The world was young then, and disordered, like a tent that had just been set-up, and its contents had still to be put to rights. Tasks needed to be assigned. First Mother inquired of her two children, Mehnot and Sāwel, as to who wanted to be in charge of illuminating the sky during the day versus during the night. Mehnot, who was a kind sister, offered her brother first choice. Sāwel chose the day, leaving Mehnot with responsibility for the night.

At first, their partnership went very well. Each was well suited to their roles. Sāwel was a cheerful boy who liked predictability. Having a single job to perform, which involved traveling more or less the same path across the heavens each day, fit his energetic, straightforward nature. He was proud of bringing heat and light to all the plants and other beings who inhabited the land, helping the Earth and all her creatures to grow and flourish. His role made him feel useful, which was important to him.

Although different from her twin brother, Mehnot, likewise, possessed a character well-matched to her assignment. Her nighttime duties were both more varied than Sāwel's, and considerably more complicated. For while Sāwel provided heat and light during the day, Mehnot assisted First Mother with everything else necessary to keep creation alive. One of her most important tasks, for example, was to direct the waters of the land. This included sending rain and snow to where they were needed, as well as controlling the flow of streams and rivers and governing the rising and falling tides of the seas. She also kept track of the seasons, so that all living beings knew when to give birth and begin to grow, when to mature, and when to die and be reborn. By overseeing each being's fertility and life span as decreed by the will of the Great Goddess, Mehnot helped the world to remain in balance.

Awija paused, reaching for the water skin she'd brought with her. "As you can see," she remarked between sips, "whereas Sāwel had to focus on only one thing at a time, Mehnot needed the ability to accomplish many things at once." She gave a rye laugh. "You girls will appreciate that aspect of the story even more as you get older. Now, where was I? Ah yes…

… As part of regulating the Earth's annual cycle, First Mother gave her son very clear instructions about when to rise and when to set, which arc to travel in the sky and how brightly to shine during each of the four seasons. At first, Sāwel was happy to follow First Mother's direction. As he grew into a young man, however, he became frustrated with doing as he was told. He also began to wonder if perhaps he was not as important as his sister Mehnot. He felt jealous toward her, whereas she was too busy to care, which only made things worse.

Awija broke off again. "You girls who have brothers know how they can be. No doubt twin sisters can be just as troublesome," she added, giving Petsna and Perom a wink.

"My boy cousins are like that," put in Elēn, who, like Naya, was an only child. "They refuse to listen to anything I say. Then when they don't do as I tell them, I end up being the one to get in trouble."

"Precisely," agreed Awija. "Just listen to what happens to Mehnot…

…One day in early spring, Sāwel decided not to follow First Mother's carefully crafted plan. Instead of setting when he was supposed to, so that his sister had equal time to accomplish her tasks that night, he lingered in the sky. The next day, when he was supposed to set a little later, he set earlier. The day after that, he refused to come up at all. On some days, even if he rose and set on time, he didn't offer the Earth enough warmth. On other days, his rays were scorching hot.

Chaos resulted. Great ice sheets appeared, then melted, flooding the land. Storms raged and fires burned. Parts of the land were parched with drought, others inundated with mud, so that no plants could grow and the animals and people suffered. Far from being dismayed, Sāwel was rather impressed at his power to wreak havoc. Meanwhile, Mehnot ran here and there, trying her best to undo the damage caused by her brother's recklessness. Sometimes only part of her could be seen in the sky at night because she had to be in so many places at once, trying to clean-up the mess. At other times, she could be glimpsed in the day-time sky, keeping an eye on her twin.

Awija paused. When she didn't continue right away, Perom spoke up. "What was their plan?" she asked, eager to hear more of the story.

"For the moment, you will have to wait and be patient," she replied. "This is not a tale that can be told all in one evening. By and by, you shall hear more."

As the other girls groaned in protest at the delay, a memory flashed into Naya's mind of the image from her journey on the night of the winter solstice, of the sun and the moon conjoined. Before she had time to wonder if the otherworldly vision might somehow figure in her grandmother's ancient story, Awija changed the subject.

"We need to talk about another assignment," she announced, ignoring the girls' disappointment. "This one is quite important. Sit up and turn around please." Everyone complied, curious as to what Awija had in store for them now.

Once they were settled facing her and she had their attention, Awija resumed. "How many of you recall what you dreamed last night?" she asked. "Raise your hands." Perom and Elēn's hands went up. The other girls looked at one another. Melit shrugged as if to say, *not me, what about you?*

"Perom." Awija singled her out. "Care to share your dream with the rest of us?"

"Well," Perom began, closing her eyes to help her remember, "Petsna and I were beside a creek. It must have been summer, because the water was low enough to walk along the edge without getting our feet wet. I wanted to wade in but Petsna kept refusing to come with me."

"Anything more?" Awija asked.

"There was an *empis*," Perom added, referring to a dragonfly. "I just remembered that part. But that's all I can recall." She gave an awkward laugh. "Does that count?"

"Yes, yes, that's fine. How did you feel in the dream?" Awija inquired.

"Frustrated." Perom looked at her sister. "Like I always am when Petsna won't go along with my ideas."

"But sometimes your ideas aren't safe!" Petsna protested.

"You think everything is too dangerous," Perom rejoined. "If it were up to you, we'd never do anything the least bit daring – or fun!"

"Girls," Awija interjected. "Let's see what might be learned from the dream. Perom, tell us more about the *empis*."

"It was beautiful – shining green and blue – it skimmed the water, and its wings flashed in the sunlight. I wanted to follow it but Petsna wouldn't come with me. That's when I woke up."

"Maybe that's why you were so grumpy this morning," Petsna suggested.

"Maybe," Perom agreed matter-of-factly. "I didn't think about it until just now. Your fault." She gave her sister's shoulder a playful shove.

"Don't blame me!" Petsna objected, shoving her back.

"Girls!" Awija interrupted again. "Let's see what we can learn from the dream. Perom, does the dream remind you of anything that's actually happened in the past, or might happen in the future? It could involve wading into the creek, but maybe not. It could be something else that brings up a similar feeling of fascination with the *empis* or frustration about Petsna cautioning you, or both."

Perom thought. "Well, I've always loved *empis*," she said after a moment.

"Why?" Awija prompted.

"The way they zip around and seem to change colors," she answered. "Once, one landed on the back of my hand. In the dream, I really wanted to follow the *empis* across the creek."

"Alright," said Awija. "Since *empis* seem quite important to you, and one is showing up in your dreams, perhaps you should spend some time observing them. See if there is anything else that you can learn from them. You might try to imagine what it would be like to *be* an *empis*. And also you might try to guess what might be on the other side of the creek. We'll check back with you after a few days."

Elēn put up her hand.

"Yes, my dear?" Awija asked.

"Last night I dreamed about a tent. It wasn't our family tent, but it still seemed familiar. I was looking for something that was lost – I'm not sure what – but I was searching and searching. I knew whatever it was that I couldn't find was in that tent, if only I could remember where. I woke up before I found what I was looking for." Elēn looked at Awija. "What was the dream about," she asked, as though hoping her grandmother might have the answer. Naya and the other girls turned to Awija as well.

"How did the dream make you feel?" Awija asked.

"A little desperate," Elēn replied. "Whatever I was searching for was really important."

"Anything else?" Awija asked.

"Curious too, I guess, to know what it was," Elēn said. "I wish I could go back into the dream and find out," she added.

"You can, you know," Awija pointed out. This got everyone's attention. "It takes practice," she explained, "but it's possible to re-enter a dream you've already had, or to ask for a new dream as an answer to a question."

"How?" Perom asked, intrigued. The other girls leaned in, obviously interested. Only Naya hung back. All this discussion of dreams was making her uncomfortable.

"You must set an intention before you go to sleep – ask to have your questions answered," Awija explained. "And you must also be ready to be surprised. Sometimes the answers you receive in a dream are not what you might expect. The dream might require some investigation for its meaning to be revealed."

"So, I can try to revisit the same tent while I'm asleep, and figure out what I'm looking for?" Elēn asked.

"Yes, my dear. In fact, that's your assignment. We'll check back after a few nights. Don't be disappointed if you don't succeed, however. That sometimes means that finding out what you were searching for isn't the important aspect of the dream." Awija paused for another drink from her waterskin.

"Naya, Melit, Petsna, you three have been very quiet," she went on, looking at each of the girls in turn. "Any questions?"

"Yes," Melit responded. "Why are we spending time on dreams?"

"I'm glad someone asked that," Awija replied. "The dreams that Perom and Elēn shared with us are *ónerjos* – ordinary nighttime dreams. You've all had similar ones, I'm sure, even if you haven't paid much attention. Not all *ónerjos* dreams are of much consequence – although sometimes they can be very amusing. On occasion, they can bring useful insights into daily life."

"You mean, the *empis* could be a messenger?" Perom inquired.

"Yes, exactly," Awija confirmed. "The thing is, remembering your dreams and learning to interpret them takes practice. This training period before your vigils is a perfect opportunity." Awija surveyed her audience. Naya was careful not to meet her grandmother's eye.

"There is an additional reason for us to talk about dreams," Awija went on. "While *ónerjos* are common, every now and again, you might be visited by a *swopnjājō* – a 'big' dream." Naya could feel Awija's gaze lingering on her.

"What's that?" Perom wanted to know.

"As explained to me when I was your age, a *swopnjājō* is a dream sent by the ancestors for a special purpose. Like an ordinary dream, a *swopnjājō* might relive the memory of an event from the past or offer warning of something that might happen in the future. It might bring knowledge, the answer to a problem or some other insight." Awija paused.

"But that sounds just like the dreams we've been talking about," Melit objected.

"The difference," Awija emphasized, "is that big dreams are much more vivid and can be disturbing. They also tend to reoccur. Most important to remember is that ignoring a *swopnjājō* can be dangerous. You could be putting yourself, your family – maybe even the entire clan – in peril. Or, you might miss out on a life-changing opportunity." She looked at the girls down the length of her nose. "Understand?" she inquired. Everyone nodded. Naya kept her gaze downcast, continuing to avoid eye contact with her grandmother.

"The reason I'm telling you this," Awija explained, "is that there is the possibility that you will experience a *swopnjājō* as part of your vigil." This produced a frisson of excitement. "Not always," she cautioned, "but it's important to be prepared. That's why we practice remembering and interpreting our ordinary dreams, so that you'll know what to do if you receive a big one. Between now and the time of your vigils, you must all pay attention to your dreams and be prepared to share them, so that we can all gain experience with understanding the ancestors' messages."

Naya thought of the nightmares she'd had following her injury last winter, and again at the beginning of the trip back to the clan's winter settlement. She'd never shared the details of her dark visions with anyone, although her mother knew she'd suffered from them and Oyuun had seemed to guess something of their contents. Unlike the exhilarating visions of galloping with the red filly in a world where the sun and the moon were as one, the images from her nightmares were terrifying – filled with desolation, toil, fear and agonizing death; she had no wish to revisit them.

"Dreams have power," Awija observed, as if following Naya's thoughts. "Especially big dreams. They can disturb not only our sleep, but our waking thoughts as well. It's important to talk about them – not with just anyone, mind, but with someone whom you trust – in order to grasp their meaning while taking away their ability to overwhelm us."

No one said anything. Naya risked a glance at the other girls. Their eyes were round, whites reflecting the light of the full moon above. She thought of the first time, last fall, when she'd encountered the spirit of the red filly as though in a dream. An *etmn itājō*, her grandmother had explained when she'd told her about it – a spirit journey. Afterwards, everything in her world had changed. Were her journeys the same as big dreams? She didn't want to ask. More important, she didn't want to journey again, or dream, not at the risk of inviting more nightmares like she'd had last winter. She squeezed her eyes shut.

"You can't stop big dreams from coming," Awija said after a moment, again as if she'd followed Naya's thoughts. "Any more than you can force them to visit you. It's up to the ancestors. In my experience, even if you try to fight against a *swopnjājō*, the dream will still find a way, and you may not like it."

Naya felt as though her grandmother was speaking to her directly. She looked up – and was relieved to see Awija looking not at her but at Petsna, who had raised her hand.

"Yes, dear. What is it?"

"I think I've had a big dream," Petsna offered, voice timid. "Should I share it now?"

Awija glanced upwards, as if to track the progress of the moon.

"Not tonight," she answered. "We've gone on late enough. Come to me tomorrow, and we'll talk in private. We can decide together about sharing with the group, if it's appropriate and you feel comfortable." She gave Petsna a kind smile. "The thing to remember, girls," she added, addressing them all, "is that big dreams are sacred gifts and should be handled accordingly." Awija pulled her shawl up around her shoulders. "Mehnot is well on her way across the heavens and it's getting cold – time for us to be finished for tonight. Who wants to lead the closing prayer?"

Melit volunteered. In a clear, high voice, she spoke the words of blessing that she and the other girls had memorized over the previous four days. Hands joined to form a circle, they repeated after her:

"For love of the Goddess, may we be strong in body and mind."

"For love of the Goddess, may we be kind in thought and act."

"For love of the Goddess, may we be whole in heart and spirit."

"For love of the Goddess, may we know that we are one with all Creation."

Then together, they recited:

"May we be strong, may we be kind, may we be whole, may we be one."

After a moment of collective silence, still seated, each girl brought her palms together and bowed, first to Awija, then to one another. "Peace, protection, and blessing," they echoed each time, offering one another the concluding words of the prayer. Finally, heads tilted back, eyes uplifted toward the heavens, palms open and raised, they gestured in honor of Mehnot, just as Awija had taught them.

Afterwards, while Melit and the twins gathered blankets and cushions, Elēn moved to help Awija to her feet. Not to be outdone this time, Naya came and took her grandmother's other arm, so that she and her cousin could together escort her up the trail. The other girls went on ahead, their murmured conversation drifting back on the night air. Elēn, Naya and Awija walked in silence, footsteps crunching on the dry gravel of the path.

PART TWO

Chapter Nine

One month later…

Over the course of the next moon, Naya's life settled into a new routine. Before being away last winter, she'd often sought the solitude of the steppe, especially once the clan left the settlement to follow their herds to summer pastures. These days, she spent most of her time within sight of the tents along the river, almost always in the company of Melit and their fellow trainees under Awija's supervision, or else doing chores at Vedukha's behest. She rarely saw her father, other than for the evening meal. He was busy hunting, helping to train the younger warriors, or overseeing Wailos's work with the captured horses, all activities from which Naya was excluded for one reason or another. Wailos did make time for her, inviting her to accompany him on short forays, but otherwise, her world was circumscribed by the boundaries of the settlement and its immediate surroundings, and by the expectations of her anticipated role as a young woman of the clan. And not just any young woman, Naya reminded herself whenever the sense of confinement started to feel stifling. She was the clan chief's daughter and must do her best to act as such and bring credit to her father.

Some days and tasks were easier to bear than others. She didn't mind foraging with Melit or collecting fish from the weirs. Even walks with Wailos, although awkward, were usually bearable, but Naya hated anything to do with needle work, spinning, or twisting fibers into cordage. The dexterity required did not come naturally to her, nor the patience. Besides, the work reminded her of her mother, whose skills were renown, which just added to Naya's frustration when whatever project she'd undertaken ended up in a hopeless tangle of knots.

Training took up a lot of time as well. Sessions with Uksor were inevitably tedious, but if her grandmother was in charge, the subjects they discussed were generally much more engaging. Naya especially looked forward to the evenings when they gathered under the stars in the stone circle, as they'd first done on the night of the full moon, so that Awija could tell them stories, listen to their dreams, and instruct them in identifying the constellations.

On the night of the next full moon, a startling phenomenon occurred. Once again, Awija and the other trainees were gathered at the stone circle, watching the sky. Although the weather had been overcast earlier in the day, the clouds had departed, and the night was clear. The girls were stretched out on their backs under light blankets. Awija sat behind them on her cushion, shawl wrapped around her shoulders. She had warned them of a surprise but would not tell them anything else. They began the evening as usual, with a discussion of any dreams that the girls might care to share, after which Elēn had offered to tell them a version of the ending of the story of Mehnot and Sāwel which she'd made up herself.

As expected, the full moon came up round and glowing orange beyond the river, then paled as it climbed. Petsna was in the midst of describing an ordinary dream she'd had involving two goats when Melit interrupted, pointing upward.

"Look!" she exclaimed. "What's happening to the moon?"

"It looks like a dark stain is seeping across part of it," Elēn said with wonder.

"Almost like it's had a bite taken out of it," Perom suggested.

"Is the moon going to die?" asked Petsna fearfully.

Naya, who had spent more nights under an open sky than the other girls, said nothing. Normally young children were sheltered from viewing such strange celestial occurrences, for fear of attracting the potential harm they portended, but she'd seen something similar over two and half years earlier, while on a hunting expedition with her father. Fingering her bear tooth necklace, she remembered: she and Papa and the other men had surprised an enormous female bear outside a cave where she'd hidden her two cubs. Naya had seen the bear first and warned the others but not soon enough to save the life of Bhermi, her father's best friend and Skelos's older brother. Skelos had never forgiven either Naya or her father, both of whom he blamed for Bhermi's death. The night before the attack, Naya recalled, the full moon had first gradually become completely shrouded, then turned an eerie blood red, then gone dark once more before eventually emerging from the shadow. A bad omen, the hunters had agreed, especially considering what happened to Bhermi the next day. Although Naya's father had given her the necklace with the bear's tooth to commemorate her bravery, he'd never allowed her to accompany him and the other hunters again.

Tonight, only part of the moon was obscured, but it was beginning to turn the same ominous color. Naya stared along with the other girls, too fascinated to look away.

"Do not fear." Awija's soothing voice came out of the darkness. "The moon is not going to die. She reminds us, however, not to take her for granted. We must not forget that while usually a wise and benevolent force, she can also be moved to anger. Perhaps tonight Mehnot does battle with some evil in the world. For all we often refer to her as a gentle soul, she is a warrior as well, especially when called upon to defend those she loves."

An image flashed into Naya's mind of a woman straightening to her full height, staff in hand, eyes flashing sparks, as intimidating as an enraged mother bear, determined to protect her family. She wondered if the vision could be from the past, evoked by the stories her grandmother told, or somehow a premonition of the future. Naya immediately dismissed both notions; she was finished with such things.

After a while, as the red glow faded and the partial shadow no longer obscured the moon's surface, the girls began to stir.

"Did you know that was going to happen?" asked Melit over her shoulder.

"Yes, my dear. Long ago, I was taught how to keep track of such events. Among the women in my family, the knowledge is passed down from mother to daughter, or granddaughter, depending on who has an aptitude for detailed calculations."

Naya guessed Awija was referring to Elēn. Her cousin had been spending extra time with their grandmother, learning the secrets of plant medicine. Moon lore must also be part of what Awija was teaching her. Naya did not begrudge Elēn the additional attention. She only wished she had a better idea of where her own gifts might lie. Other than being able to tame and ride a wild horse, which had all been a big mistake, she had yet to discover any special talent or ability.

"Alright girls," Awija said once the moon had returned to its normal state. "Let's get back to what we were doing. Who besides Petsna has a dream they'd like to share, before Elēn tells us her story?" None of the girls raised a hand.

Naya, still on her back looking up at the night sky, felt her grandmother's eyes on her. She had yet to share even a single ordinary dream during their evening gatherings. She realized that at some point, she was going to have to make something up, except that she was sure Awija would know if she wasn't telling the truth. And the truth was that she hadn't been sleeping well since returning to the settlement. Dreams disturbed her rest, she was sure, but when she awoke, she remembered nothing. Instead, she started each day feeling physically and emotionally spent. She managed to carry on – she was just as happy to have no memory of whatever might be haunting her in the dark – but the lack of rest was having an impact. She didn't feel like herself.

"Alright," Awija said after a moment. "If no one has anything else to share, let's hear from Elēn. Come sit beside me, my dear. The rest of you can stay as you are."

Rising, Elēn brought her cushion and settled next to her grandmother. Taking a deep breath, she picked up the tale of Mehnot and Sāwel where Awija had left off.

"…and so, First Mother and her daughter came up with a plan…"

The following day…

Naya was still thinking about Elēn's rendition of the story the following day. She'd drifted off in places and missed some of it, but somehow Mehnot found a special plant whose leaves, when dried and burned, produced a smoke which gave Sāwel the ability to envision the future. When he'd witnessed the extent of the destruction and misery that would result if his capriciousness continued, he relented, agreeing to return to his duties with a new appreciation for the importance of exercising his power responsibly. Walking back up the path in the dark afterward, the girls agreed that Elēn had come up with a better ending than Perom, who'd taken a turn as storyteller a few nights earlier, but later, as Naya thought more about it, she realized that both accounts had left her dissatisfied. Something important was missing. In Elēn's version, as well as Perom's, the defiant twin brother's capacity to cause destruction was eventually brought under control, but his fears, which had led to his rebellion in the first place, were never addressed, nor his apparent inability to understand or appreciate his sister and value their partnership. There had to be more to the story.

Perplexed, Naya pondered the question as she went about her daily tasks. At one point she was so preoccupied that she almost cut herself with her flint knife while helping Vedukha to debone the fish for that evening's stew. She speculated as well about what had happened to the moon the previous night. Her grandmother hadn't been surprised or frightened by the event, but neither had Awija dismissed it as unimportant. Might the moon's mysterious transformation somehow figure into her grandmother's story? And what about Naya's own remembered vision of the sun and the moon joined together in the same sky, inexplicably suspended between day and night? She couldn't help imagining that the strange apparition from her winter solstice journey might have something to do with her grandmother's story as well. Perhaps, she mused, she would try incorporating the sun-moon image into her own version of the story's ending, without telling anyone how she'd come up with it.

When suppertime arrived, Naya was still distracted. She and her father and Awija gathered around the family fire outside Potis's tent, along with Vedukha and Melit and Melit's siblings. As usual, Wailos joined them as well, but not his cousin, who had left that morning to return home. He'd be back in a fortnight, in time for the Gathering, along with the other members of Wailos's clan, including his father, Regos.

Once everyone had been served, Potis and Wailos began discussing arrangements for where to pitch the visitors' tents when the rest of the tribe began to arrive, a subject in which Naya was not particularly interested. Her mind wandering as it had all day, she failed to notice when a lull fell in the conversation.

"What happened this morning with the herd?" her father asked, interrupting the brief silence. He held out his trencher for Vedukha to serve him a second helping of fish stew.

Roused out of her preoccupation by her father's question, Naya looked across the fire toward Wailos, waiting for his answer. At first, whenever the topic of the horses had come up, despite her vow to distance herself from the captured herd, she'd struggled not to voice her own views about taming them but eventually, after enough disapproving head shakes from Melit and quelling looks from Vedukha, she'd succeeded in stifling the urge to interject herself into the discussion. They had no idea of the depth of Naya's experience – they just knew it was unseemly to interrupt. Still, Naya couldn't help being curious.

"The big yellow mare continues to give the most trouble," Wailos replied, holding out his trencher for seconds as well. "She's just not willing to admit who's in charge," he added, nodding his thanks to Vedukha. "She puts up a fight long after the others have given up." Glancing over at Naya, Wailos gave her a wink.

Not sure where to look, Naya dropped her eyes to her empty bowl, blushing in confusion. Although she'd become the envy of all her marriageable cousins over the past month, due to the attention Wailos paid her, Naya was often unsure about how to behave in his presence, especially when he flirted with her. She wished she were as unabashed as Skelos's sister Saurosa. Naya couldn't help but notice how Wailos's eyes seemed to linger whenever she passed nearby, hips swaying as she walked, lips wearing the knowing half-smile of a woman fully conscious of her own allure.

In private, with only Melit as a witness, Naya had tried imitating Saurosa. More often than not, her cousin ended up rolling on the ground with laughter at her efforts. Yet despite Naya's misgivings, Melit and her mother assured her that as long as she focused on being an engaging companion when she and Wailos spent time together – listening attentively and not expressing too many of her own ideas – everything would be fine. Just this morning, Vedukha had complimented Naya on her success in securing Wailos's interest. *If you manage to marry him*, she'd said, *you'll fulfill every wish your father has ever had for you.* Naya hoped Vedukha was right, and that her father had taken note and approved of her efforts.

"How about that archery lesson tomorrow?" Wailos inquired around a mouthful of stew.

"Alright," Naya replied, looking up with as bright a smile as she could muster. "That would be fun."

Naya had accompanied Wailos on several occasions to the archery range, which was still set-up near the stone circle. Normally her role was to provide an admiring audience. The day before, however, while out walking, she'd let slip that she had her own bow that she'd made herself and had been learning to shoot. Immediately Wailos had insisted on seeing what she could do, proposing they visit the archery range together the next day. In retrospect, Naya wished she'd never mentioned her efforts. Despite her boast to Melit about competing in the *Wesr-Admn* contest, she hadn't touched her bow since the morning of the colt's death and wasn't sure she wanted to ever again. Now, as a result of yesterday's conversational slip, she found herself struggling not to make a fool of herself.

Setting down his own bow, Wailos came behind Naya. "Here, let me show you one more time," he offered. Placing his hands over hers, he demonstrated the correct angle at which she should hold her drawn bow. Head tilted close to hers, left arm braced as the fingers of his right helped to pull back the taut string, he made small adjustments until satisfied with her stance, then stepped back.

Despite herself, Naya was glad when he did. His breath against her ear made her heart race, but not in the way she remembered from when Aytal had first shown her how to draw. She squelched the memory, reminding herself to concentrate instead on hitting the target. Unfortunately, it wasn't working. Whenever she was just about to release the bow string, the image of the lion lunging at the colt in the pre-dawn mist flashed into her mind. She'd lose focus, and the shot would either sail wide or land short.

"Never mind," Wailos said as another arrow buried itself harmlessly in the turf. "No one expects you to be able to handle a bow. You have better things to do. Wait here while I collect the arrows."

Grateful for the reprieve from further disgrace, Naya gave Wailos a self-deprecating smile and watched as he went off to retrieve her scattered shots.

What's the matter with me? she wondered, irritated at herself. Being distracted by her memories – whether of Aytal's arms around her or of the lion attack – was bad enough. Her reaction to Wailos was equally troubling. Why couldn't she relax and enjoy herself when she was with him? *He's both handsome and charming,* she reminded herself. *Everyone thinks so. And he's been nothing but nice to me.*

Wailos had indeed been unfailingly attentive, even if he did like to tease her, which Melit assured Naya was only further indication of his interest. He'd also been generous with his knowledge and talents, especially as a hunter and tracker. Despite appearing to find her fascination with such pursuits an amusing oddity, nevertheless he'd taken the time to show her some of his tricks for stalking larger game and he hadn't seemed in the least put off when she'd inadvertently mentioned her attempts to learn archery, insisting that he would enjoy helping her with her skills.

Granted, he'd been dismissive of her bow and arrows when she'd first shown them to him, although he'd politely tried to disguise the fact, but thereafter he'd been a remarkably patient instructor, tactfully correcting some of the more egregious habits she'd fallen into. *I don't want to criticize your previous teacher,* he'd said without mentioning Aytal by name, *but he should have shown you how to do it this way* and then proceeded to demonstrate. Although she never would have accused him of showing off, inevitably his shot hit the center of wherever he aimed. Still, she thought, something seemed to be missing from Wailos's technique – a purity and grace that she remembered Aytal possessing, the single time she'd watched him loose an arrow, that fateful day when they'd first encountered one another, out on the steppe…

As though aware of her regard, Wailos turned and gave her one of his dazzling smiles. Mortified to be caught staring – though really, she'd been daydreaming – Naya put on a bright smile of her own. She even gave a nonchalant wave for good measure, as though accustomed to having a good-looking young warrior fetch arrows for her while she waited.

"I don't know why I ever wanted to learn to shoot in the first place," she said with an awkward laugh when he handed her quiver back to her. Better to play at flirting, rather than let him see how frustrated she actually felt. Melit would have been proud of her.

"You're too pretty to have to fill your own cooking pot," Wailos agreed, teasing. "Shall we go back? They'll be expecting us for supper."

Turning, they began to make their way single file up the path back to the settlement, Wailos in the lead. The sun was just about to slip behind the bluffs above the settlement. Late afternoon summer shadows stretched across the trail. After an unusual month-long stretch with almost no rain, a storm had passed through earlier in the afternoon, soaking the parched ground. The air remained humid, fragrant with the scent of damp earth. Wailos stepped off the path to avoid a puddle.

"You should have a husband who will bring you all the meat and fish you need," he continued, looking back over his shoulder. "Along with as many cows and goats as you could wish for." He grinned at her again and winked as he'd done at supper the previous night.

"Oh really?" Naya replied, trying to match her tone to his. She skirted the puddle on the opposite side. She was determined to excel at this game of trading flirtatious comments, regardless of feeling self-conscious.

"And where might I find this paragon of manhood?" she queried once they were both back on the path. "Surely not yourself?" Naya attempted to sound appropriately scornful but then worried that she'd been too bold. They were walking side by side again, the track from the archery range having widened out.

"Well, as a matter of fact…" Wailos stopped and turned to her, his face suddenly serious. "Would it be such a bad idea?" he asked.

Caught off guard, Naya didn't know how to reply. They were half-way back to the settlement. Someone might come along and interrupt them at any moment. Could he actually be asking her such an important question, here, in the middle of the trail?

"What do you mean?" she finally ventured. Her heart raced as it had earlier when he'd put his arms around her and she had trouble getting a breath.

"I mean, silly girl, that marrying me might be the very best thing you could do for all concerned. Surely, you've thought about it?"

They stood facing one another, separated by a strip of well-trodden earth. Naya didn't know how to read Wailos. Was he sincere or was he mocking her? Too agitated to be able to give him a straight answer, she grasped the first excuse that came to her.

"As you must know," she pointed out, lifting her chin and looking down her nose in an effort to affect an air of injured dignity, "I cannot possibly consider marrying *anyone* until after my presentation." Tossing her head for good measure, she turned her back and crossed her arms, as if offended that he would suggest such a thing.

"Of course," Wailos responded with exaggerated curtesy. "Please, forgive me." Naya looked back over her shoulder in time to see him bow deeply from the waist, as though begging her pardon for a grave transgression. "But that still means you'll think about whether or not you want to marry me," he added, raising one dark brow as he straightened. He gave her his most wickedly charming smile.

"Yes," Naya replied, pretending to sound imperious. "I'll consider it." Relieved that they seemed to be back on safer footing, she made as though to continue up the path to the settlement but found her way blocked. Wailos loomed over her,

"Seal it with a kiss then?" Grasping Naya's upper arm to prevent her from moving past him, he gave her another smile, this time with a hint of menace. His grip wasn't painful, just forceful enough that she knew she would have had to struggle if she wanted to get away. He lowered his head toward hers. *Don't be ridiculous*, she told herself when she thought she saw a predatory glint in his eyes. *This is what's supposed to happen.*

The shock of Wailos's mouth meeting hers nearly caused Naya's knees to buckle. If he hadn't held her by the arm, she might have fallen. Hard, insistent lips took possession of hers, forcing them apart and allowing his tongue unimpeded access. Then as swiftly as it had begun, the encounter ended, leaving her stunned.

"Now you know what a real warrior's kiss feels like," Wailos said, grinning smugly. "More where that came from – as long as you promise not to think about marrying anyone else."

Casually releasing her, he turned and started again up the path to the settlement, clearly expecting her to follow. Not entirely certain of the ground beneath her feet, Naya fell in behind him, matching her step to his and saying little for the rest of the way back as she tried to regain control of her shattered senses.

Chapter Ten

Later that evening…

"Naya!"

Awija's voice was sharp, arresting Naya before she could follow the others out of the women's tent. Turning back, she found her grandmother's gaze intent upon her.

"You stay," she commanded. "I want to speak with you, alone."

Here we go again, thought Naya, anticipating another scolding for her inattention.

Preoccupied by what had happened with Wailos on the path back to the settlement before supper, she'd had a hard time concentrating during training that evening. Uksor had joined them to discuss the proper etiquette required for the presentation ceremony following the conclusion of their vigils. More than once, she interrupted her instructions to reprimand Naya, telling her that she would disgrace herself, her father and their entire clan if she couldn't pay heed and follow directions. Naya assumed Awija's call for her to remain behind after the other girls had been dismissed meant her grandmother had something to add to the tongue lashing she'd received already. At least Awija had waited to speak in private, rather than embarrassing her in front of her peers as Uksor had done.

"You go on," she whispered to Melit. "Awija wants something." Letting the hide flap drop back into place, Naya returned to her seat by the fire and with eyes lowered, waited for whatever her grandmother had to say to her.

Awija studied Naya's bowed head in silence, feeling sympathy rather than disapproval for her granddaughter. Who could blame the girl for letting her mind wander? Awija had stifled more than one yawn herself while Uksor went into excruciating detail about what would be expected of the trainees at their presentation ceremony. She was more than willing to let the priest's wife handle such matters of protocol. To her mind, the whole practice of *presenting* the newly recognized young women to the rest of the tribe made them seem more like valuable *lāpos* – unbred female cattle. Awija's concerns for her charges went far deeper.

So little time, she thought, waiting for Naya to look up. Less than a fortnight remained of the precious interlude allotted to her, when she had the girls more or less to herself. By sharing the old stories and teaching them to interpret their dreams, as well as talking with them about their hopes and fears for the future, Awija sought to instill in them not only a reverence for the Goddess, but also faith in her infinite love for every aspect of creation, including themselves. Likewise, she sought to help the girls to understand that their three-day vigil represented only one of many possible opportunities to discover the unique destiny intended for each of them; they would still have much to learn about themselves and the world as they experienced more of life. That was why she'd always steadfastly refused to refer to the presentation ceremony, along with the period of seclusion that preceded it, as an initiation, although that was the terminology the old priest preferred.

To Awija's mind, the whole ritual made a mockery of a true initiatory experience. As the girls in her charge contemplated being presented to the tribe as marriageable young women, she wanted them to recognize that their capacity to bring forth and nurture life represented a sacred gift from the Goddess, to be honored and celebrated, not regarded as a mere resource, to be bargained over by men.

Now, as she waited for Naya to lift her head and make eye contact, Awija wondered if her lessons were taking root. She also wondered how long her granddaughter would maintain such an uncharacteristically submissive posture. Cocking her head to one side, Awija considered. Ever since Naya's return to the settlement, the girl had not seemed herself. No doubt the ordeal she'd been through over the winter had impacted her but something else was off as well.

Awija couldn't fault her behavior – in all respects Naya seemed to have transformed herself into Uksor's idea of an exemplary young woman – but that was just the problem. Awija missed the defiant spark that used to flash so often from her granddaughter's blue eyes. These days, she seemed intent on keeping her gaze modestly downcast, careful not to draw undue attention to herself – nor reveal her true feelings. *Perhaps not even to herself*, Awija thought. Evidently the effort was taking a toll. Clearly Naya hadn't been sleeping well. Even in the dusky light from the dying fire, Awija could see dark circles tingeing the delicate skin below her lowered lashes. But *why* wasn't she sleeping? And why was she acting so unusually compliant?

Awija shifted on her cushion. Still, her granddaughter did not look up. Awija sighed. What troubled her most was Naya's lack of interest in the horses. To Awija's knowledge, she'd had made no effort to visit the corrals nor expressed any desire to go after the red filly. From talking with Sata, as well as with Oyuun on the evening before their departure, she'd learned most of what had transpired over the course of the winter and spring, highlighted by Naya's first ride on the filly and the splendid gallop across the steppe, and concluding with the disappearance of the three horses in the wake of the unfortunate attack on the colt. Sata and Oyuun both seemed to assume that Naya blamed Aytal for the little creature's death, but Awija was not so sure. In any case, she needed to speak with her granddaughter herself and find out what was going on in the girl's head – and in her heart.

"Naya," she said finally. "Look at me." Naya raised her chin but would not meet Awija's gaze for more than a moment before her eyes slid away.

"I'm concerned about you, child." Awija's voice was gentle. "The granddaughter I know would have disobeyed her father by now and gone to see those horses in the corrals. She would have made some effort to find the red filly. What's going on?"

Naya glanced up. From her expression, Awija guessed her granddaughter might have preferred anger to sympathy. Better another scolding than having to explain herself.

"Nothing," Naya muttered. "Everything's fine. I guess I'm just not that interested in the horses anymore." She looked down again.

Awija was skeptical but let the excuse go unchallenged. More interesting than the words themselves was the possibility that her granddaughter wanted to believe them.

"Your mother told me about what happened with the colt," Awija probed. "That must have been very upsetting." Watching closely, she saw Naya's jaw tighten. Still, the girl continued to avert her gaze.

"Are you upset with Aytal? Is that why you haven't gone down to the corrals?"

Naya raised her eyes for another brief instant before looking away again. "It's not that simple," she managed. "Please can I go now? Melit's waiting for me."

"Not yet," Awija replied. "You've made no mention of the task I assigned more than a month ago. What do you remember from your dreams?"

Naya knew if she looked her grandmother in the eye, she wouldn't be able to keep from blurting out the truth and they would end up in an argument. She was certain Awija would not approve of her decision to abandon her quest to tame the red filly. Nor she suspected, would her grandmother endorse the idea of marrying Wailos. At the very least, she would want to give Naya advice, which Naya did not want to hear. As for the assignment, she had nothing to report. Still, she couldn't refuse to respond to a direction question.

"No, Grandmother," she answered, eyes averted. "No dreams."

More accurate would have been to confess that she couldn't recall the details. Last night, as seemed to occur most nights, she'd awakened drenched in sweat, with a thirst so great she'd drained the full waterskin she kept beside her sleeping mat. Staring unseeing into the pre-dawn darkness, heart thumping, she'd listened for the reassuring breathing of the others with whom she shared the tent – Vedukha, Melit and her sister Maqā – and tried to go back to sleep. As happened more often than not, sleep refused to come.

Naya recognized that what she was experiencing was most likely a *swopnjājō* – exactly the kind of recurring dream Awija had taught her and the other girls not to ignore at their peril. But if she woke up with no memory, what was she supposed to do about it? She'd been determined to put her dreams and visions, along with her nightmares, behind her, and apparently she'd succeeded. But she couldn't tell her grandmother that.

"If you aren't willing or able to recall what you've dreamed recently," Awija suggested, "perhaps you can tell me about the dreams you had while you were away."

Naya kept her head down. How was it that her grandmother always seemed to know what she was thinking?

Awija sighed. "Your mother mentioned something about visions that came to you while you were battling fever. I can't help you if you won't talk to me," she added. "What are you afraid of?"

Naya's head shot up. "I'm not afraid!" she insisted, indignant. "I can't remember."

"Can't remember, or don't want to remember?"

Naya crossed her arms across her chest. Lips set in a mutinous line meant to keep them from trembling, she tried to hold her grandmother's gaze. "I know you think what happened last autumn – the visions I had – were something mystical. Some kind of visit to the spirit world. And maybe you're right. But I don't want to go there anymore. I don't want to be an *etmn itājōr*. I don't want to journey. I don't want to dream." Naya swallowed hard. "I just want to live my life."

She looked away. Yes, the visions she'd had of the red filly had been magical, as had the time she'd spent with the young horse and her herd mates, but the dark images of her nightmares had been terrifying – and she feared the nightmares might be coming true. Why had she not realized sooner the selfishness of seeking her heart's desire? For Réhda's sake, as well as the others, she no longer wanted to dream, or to journey, ever. Maybe then, the red filly, at least, would be kept safe.

Awija observed her granddaughter's profile in silence, concealing her dismay. *What about the red filly and your heart's desire?* she wanted to ask. *What about your grandfather's prophecy?* Remembering that Naya didn't know about Awos's dying words, Awija considered telling her, then decided this was not the most opportune moment.

"What about the horses in the ravine?" she asked after a moment.

"The captured herd?" Naya glanced back at her. "From what I hear, Wailos has everything under control." She feigned disinterest. Awija was not convinced.

"Ah yes, Wailos," was all she said. "You seem to be spending quite a bit of time with our guest."

Naya started to put her hands up to hide the blood rushing into her cheeks but stopped herself. "He's nice to me," she said, lifting her chin.

Hmph, Awija thought. "I'm sure he is," she replied mildly. "What about Aytal? Have you seen him since your return?"

"Of course not!" Naya sounded scandalized. "Papa told me not to go down to the corrals. Anyway, why would I want to see him?"

Awija wanted to respond with *because maybe you're in love with one another?* but kept the comment to herself. "It might be the kind thing to do," she remarked instead. "He's been doing nothing but care for those animals. He doesn't know anyone but you – he might appreciate seeing a friendly face. Besides, haven't you wanted to see what they're doing with the horses? I'm sure Wailos would be proud to show you, and if you asked for permission, your father would be unlikely to mind."

"If you think I should," Naya answered, unenthusiastic. "May I go now?" she asked, clearly hoping to escape further questioning. "I'll ask Papa about it tomorrow after breakfast."

"Yes, yes, alright," Awija replied, waving a hand in dismissal. "But I'm not finished with you. We need to have another private conversation before your vigil begins."

"Yes Grandmother," Naya agreed, evidently relieved to have gained a reprieve for the moment. Awija lifted her cheek to receive a kiss, which Naya hastily bestowed before heading for the exit. "Good night," she called over her shoulder as she lifted the door flap and stepped out into the darkness. Frowning, Awija watched her go.

Early the following morning…

Just after dawn, before most of the settlement was stirring, Awija sent Maqā, whose turn it was to check on her, with a message for Potis.

"Tell the clan chief that I need to speak with him before he starts his day. He must come to me here, in the women's tent, as soon as he can." *That way he'll know it's important.* "Build up the fire and put the pot on before you go," she added.

Although the day would warm quickly, Awija still liked to banish the morning chill with something hot to drink. Maqā complied, then hurried away on her errand. Within a short time, just as the water in the clay vessel had begun to boil, Awija heard the clearing of a masculine throat outside the doorway to the shelter. *Good*, she thought, *he hasn't wasted any time.*

"Come in," she called.

Potis entered, seeming in a hurry. Awija came straight to the point.

"You need to allow Naya to visit the corrals," she declared. Busy with making tea, she did not look up to gauge his reaction.

"I would ask why, but I suspect you'll tell me," Potis replied, sounding impatient.

"I will if you have a seat. Nothing is so pressing that you can't spare your mother a few words." Awija indicated a pile of furs opposite her place beside the hearth. Potis settled himself and she continued. "I'm worried about Naya."

She handed Potis a mug, then poured one for herself. Morning light was just beginning to filter in, softly illuminating the circular space. In contrast to the winter, when dwellings were covered in hides, during warmer seasons the tents were fashioned from felt, with sides that could be rolled up, allowing in more air and light.

"Aren't you curious as to why she's become so obedient to your orders all of a sudden?" Awija fixed her son with an inquiring look.

"The question had occurred to me," Potis admitted, returning her gaze. He wrapped his hands around the mug but made no move to drink from it. "I'd like to believe that with all that's happened, she's starting to grow up a bit and be more like the other girls. Melit seems to be having a good influence on her."

Awija lifted a skeptical brow. "Be that as it may," she said, "something isn't right. Has she mentioned anything about the red filly to you since she returned?"

"Actually, no," Potis replied. He looked down at his tea. "She seemed anxious to talk when she first got back but with *Wesr-Admn* there wasn't time and since then the subject hasn't come up." He looked back at Awija. "I'm relieved, to tell you the truth. The idea she had for taming the horses was never going to work. Better that she seems to have let it go."

Awija, who had been about to take a sip of her own tea, lowered her mug. "You do know she managed to win the trust of that filly enough to be able to ride – gallop – out on the open steppe?" she pointed out. "Just as she envisioned. And the stranger's son – Aytal – he befriended an outcast young stallion that turned up over the winter and had been hanging around with the other horses. He was able to ride as well."

Potis looked away. "I gathered as much from Sata before she left," he conceded. The admission was grudging, whether because Potis didn't want to discuss his daughter's success with the red filly or because he did not wish to dwell on the absence of his wife, Awija couldn't be certain. "Maybe she got it out of her system," he added, sounding unconvinced.

"Nonsense," Awija replied. "Did Sata tell you about the colt? The one born to the filly's mother? How he died in Naya's arms just before their return to the settlement?"

"Tausos told me." Eyes on the mug still cupped between his palms, Potis did not elaborate.

"Did he tell you it was an arrow from Naya's bow that killed the little creature?"

"No." He looked up, surprised. "How did that happen? Tausos said it was lions."

"Lions attacked, that's true," Awija remarked, "but Naya was responsible for the fatal shot."

"What was she doing fighting off lions by herself? Where was the young stranger? Isn't he supposed to be such an expert shot?"

"That's a long story. The important thing is that the girl is suffering. Aytal tried to take the blame for the colt's death – I know you don't think much of the boy – but if you ask me, he's not the one Naya's angry with. But that's not all that's going on with her." Awija leaned forward and laid a hand on Potis's forearm. "Something isn't right," she insisted. "She's not herself." Withdrawing, she shook her head. "All the time she's spending with Wailos, for example. It's not like her."

"Vedukha says everyone in the clan believes he wants to marry her." Potis glanced sideways at his mother.

"What I hear is that everyone in the clan believes *you* want her to marry him," Awija countered. "Which is it?" She gave him a sideways look of her own.

Potis waited a beat before responding. When he did, his voice had dropped. "If that's what everyone believes, including our visitor, it may not be such a bad thing," he remarked, looking past Awija. He shifted uncomfortably. "I can't tell you much more than that. You'll have to trust me." He brought his gaze back to hers. "At one time I might have considered it a good match, but now – let's just say I have doubts. The only thing is, I need more proof. Until then…" Potis trailed off. Awija saw his grip tighten around the clay mug still held in both hands.

"Until then, you're using your daughter as bait?" she queried. "That's a dangerous game."

"It can't be helped." Potis avoided looking her in the eye.

"What if she thinks she's in love with him?" Awija objected. "Worse, what if she is convinced you really do want her to marry him?" She forced Potis to meet her gaze. "She'll do anything these days that she thinks will please you. It's part of what's worrying me. It should be worrying you too."

"I won't let anything happen to her," Potis vowed.

"What makes you think you'll be able to protect her?" Awija rejoined. "She has to be able to pay attention to her own sense of when something's not right – but she can't rely on her instincts if she's too busy trying to be the perfect daughter." Awija refused to let Potis look away. "It's as if her head isn't listening to her heart," she declared. "As if she's afraid of what she might feel, if she let herself. And that's a dangerous situation. Her future is at stake."

"I won't let anything happen to her," Potis repeated, more emphatically this time, as if to persuade not only his mother but himself. "Besides, when has Naya ever been afraid of anything?"

"That's just it," Awija persisted, setting down her mug and bringing her palms together to emphasize her point. "Beyond whatever Wailos is up to, Naya should be afraid of being trapped by a future that's not right for her, but instead, the thing she seems to fear most is becoming who she's meant to be – and somehow disappointing you in the process. How are you going to protect her from that?"

Awija watched as, goaded by her words, Potis set down his own mug of tea, lukewarm and untasted, and rose as if to pace. Confined by the sloped ceiling and clutter of the women's tent, he had to settle for standing with his back to her and the hearth.

"What about your father's prophecy?" she continued, unrelenting. "From what I've heard, what's going on with the horses down in that corral is not what either Awos *or* Naya had in mind. Do you remember when we first talked about Naya's visions and taming not only the red filly but her whole herd? Only Naya had the heart for it, your father said. She has to be the one leading the rest of us into a new way of being with the horses – not some arrogant upstart son of a rival clan chief!" Awija's voice hardened with contempt. Potis's shoulders stiffened in response. *Good*, she thought. She'd finally hit a nerve.

"The priests must have their *Sāwel-Dom* sacrifice," he said tightly. "And there's Father's funeral ceremony as well," he added, still with his back to her. "Better these horses than the filly." Awija waited, giving Potis an opportunity to regain control of his fraying temper. After a moment, some of the tension drained from his stance. With a sigh, he turned to her.

"What do you want from me?" he asked, gesturing with open palms. "I'm trying to preserve what's left of our herds and flocks, along with our standing among the other clans. You have to trust me. All I can tell you is that I have a good idea of who organized the raid on our livestock. As long as I'm able to prove it, not only will our stolen animals be restored but so will our position in the tribe. I may even be able to spare the horses, but you have to appreciate how much I'm up against."

"So much that you are willing to risk your daughter's future?"

"It won't come to that."

With a raised eyebrow, Awija let the matter drop. Whatever Potis suspected, she'd find out from him eventually. She gestured for him to resume his seat. "Can you at least tell me how Wailos came up with the idea of capturing the horses? That's always seemed like too much of a coincidence – and why would he be so eager to help us recover from the raid, given that he and that ambitious father of his arguably have the most to gain from our misfortune?"

Potis lowered himself once more onto the cushions. "I'm not certain of all the answers yet," he replied, "nor would it be safe for me to say, even to you. All I can tell you is that we will get our animals back, and when we do, we'll have proof of who was responsible for the raid. Just as important, we'll know who from our clan was in on the scheme. The raiders couldn't have acted alone – they must have had help. My guess would be that whoever was involved also tipped off Wailos about the horses. They either knew about Naya's attachment to the red filly or Father's prophecy or both. There's no other explanation. I'm not clear on Wailos's motivation for helping us, but he's not to be trusted."

"So members of our own clan are implicated?"

"Are you surprised?" Potis laughed grimly. "I know I don't have to warn you to keep this to yourself," he went on. "You're the only person other than Tausos who knows anything about any of it. The whole story will all come out at the Gathering. We just have to be patient."

"You haven't spoken to Vedukha about it?"

"No." Potis's reply was terse.

"If Sata were here, you would have confided in her." It was not a question but a statement, which Potis did not bother to deny.

"But she's not here."

"And whose fault is that?"

Giving his mother a look, Potis did not answer.

"Your wife is no different from your daughter," Awija observed. "You can't keep asking either of them to be who they are not, in order to suit you. Sata tried for years but somewhere along the way, she lost heart and you never seemed to notice. Would you wish the same fate on Naya?"

Mouth drawn in a thin line, Potis remained silent.

"I'm not telling you this to be put blame on you, son," Awija continued, voice softening. "In fact, quite the opposite. If anything, you're even harder on yourself than on your wife and your daughter. Your heart could use some tending as well."

Awija paused. Another opportunity might not come. "Vedukha wants to love you the way you deserve to be loved," she said gently. Potis turned away, refusing to acknowledge her words, but Awija continued. "I'm not saying she would ever go so far as to intrude on your marriage vows or betray her cousin," she went on, "but Sata sees the situation for what it is. It's part of why she left. She had the courage to act on what she knows in her heart. Maybe you should follow her example and give yourself permission to love the woman who loves you, even if that woman is not your wife."

Potis rose abruptly. "I really don't have time for this," he managed through a clenched jaw. "Why did you call me in here?"

"Naya," Awija reminded him. "If she comes to you about seeing the horses, give her permission to visit the corrals. You've asked me to trust you. Now you must trust me. It's important. Don't ask me why. Just allow her to go."

"Fine." Potis was already circling the hearth, making for the exit, eager to get away.

"One more thing." Awija stopped him before he could lift the tent flap.

"What?" he barked before remembering his manners. "What else can I do for you, Mother?"

Choosing to overlook her son's obvious irritation, Awija voiced the other request for which she had summoned him. "Aytal – I want to speak with him. Can you arrange to relieve him from his duties long enough to visit me here? The path back and forth to the corrals is more than I care to manage these days."

"Not without raising a lot of questions," Potis protested. "It goes against his sentence. Why would you bother with him? Is there a message you can send instead?"

"No, I need to talk with him directly. If it wasn't important I wouldn't ask. Couldn't Sunus cover for him? No one else needs to know. In fact, given what you've just told me, I'm sure it would be better if he came in secret."

Awija could tell that Potis wanted to refuse but he knew, based on past experience, that continuing to argue with her was likely to be a losing battle. "Fine," he said, resigned. "I'll arrange it. It might take a couple of days before he can come." Wasting no more time, he lifted the hide flap and stepped out into the brightening day.

Chapter Eleven

Following the conversation with her grandmother, Naya waited a few days before approaching her father about visiting the corrals. She was surprised at how easily he granted his permission. Up until now she'd been relieved to have his orders as an excuse not to go near the corrals and risk the flood of remorse and regret she knew she would feel if she laid eyes again on the horses. Renouncing her attachment to Réhda had been the hardest choice she'd ever made and she wasn't sure her resolve could stand seeing the red filly's captured herd mates. But her grandmother's insinuation that she was afraid had gotten under her skin.

She and Wailos had started out early this morning, not long after breakfast. No one else was around yet – her father had said he might join them later, after he'd assigned tasks for the day. Coming down the steep trail into the ravine, she kept her eyes on the path. Once they'd reached the bottom, she focused on anything other than the animals in the pen. She looked for Aytal but if he was in his tent, pitched not far from the corrals beside the stream that ran through the ravine, he hadn't emerged. More likely he was off gathering food for the horses, a job too big for one person, although Naya was sure Aytal was doing his best. She thought of how hard the two of them had worked to cut dried grass for the gray stallion last winter. It seemed like a lifetime time ago.

Now, standing outside the corral fence in the shade of the large oak, Naya risked a glance in the horses' direction. The sight was worse than she'd feared. After nearly a month and a half in captivity, instead of displaying glossy, muscled coats nourished by rich spring grass, the mares and their offspring were coarse-haired and winter-thin. Their expressions of alert curiosity had been replaced with wary, hollow-eyed distrust. Naya's stomach felt queasy. Why had she let her grandmother provoke her into this? She looked away.

"Watch this," Wailos called over his shoulder.

Reluctantly, Naya turned back to observe as Wailos, just inside the fence, directed her attention to the band of horses who had retreated to the opposite corner of the enclosure. Held loosely in his left hand was a tall staff, its bottom end resting on the ground at his feet. Securely attached to the pole's top was a loop of rawhide, the tail end of which Wailos held in his right hand. A knot was tied such that pulling on the loose end would tighten the loop. Wailos had called it a *uurga* when he'd described it to Naya earlier, explaining that he and the other men needed a way to get a rope around the horses' necks without getting too close. Now, clearly pleased with the tool he'd invented, he offered to show her how it worked.

"I'll grab one of the youngsters," he called, voice raised so that Naya could hear him over the corral fence. "They can be tricky because they're fast and the mares tend to get in the way but once you catch them, they're easier to handle."

Wailos began moving closer to the herd standing bunched against the cliff face, eyeing him nervously. With the ravine's sheer limestone walls behind them, the horses had no way to escape. Naya wanted to tell Wailos to stop, that he didn't need to bother the frightened animals on her account, but she couldn't force the words past the constriction in her throat. Rebhjo, the biggest of the mares, stood like a shield between Wailos and the other horses. Knowing the mare as she did, Naya expected at any moment to see the defiant horse lower her head in preparation to charge.

Instead, Rebhjo's head came up, her attention drawn to movement among the bushes flanking the streambed near the mouth of the ravine. Rather than react with alarm, she nickered deeply, as though in welcome. Moments later, Aytal appeared, stripped to the waist, dark hair pulled back from his face, dragging behind him a sledge piled high with tall stalks of straw-like grass from last year's growth, the only fodder available that could be harvested and transported back to the corrals. Naya hadn't seen him since his sentencing. Her heart did an unwelcome somersault. *I should not have come*, she thought. Before Aytal could spot her, she moved out of sight behind the oak tree's broad trunk.

Emerging from the underbrush that grew along the creek, Aytal stopped to wipe the sweat from his forehead with a felted rag. His daily tasks caring for the captured herd had given him plenty of opportunity to reflect on how much less work would be involved if the horses could simply forage for themselves. Of course that wasn't possible. How could they be expected to stay around, let alone be interested in being handled, given the way they were being treated? True, some of the yearlings and one or two of the more timid adults had learned to appear docile once Wailos's rope noose landed around their necks but others, like the one Naya had named Rebhjo, continued to resist being subdued. Despite the horses' eager greetings whenever he showed up with food, Aytal had no doubt that given the first opportunity, the whole band would gallop for freedom. Alone at night, listening in the dark for anything that might threaten the herd's safety, he convinced himself that he was glad that Naya had yet to venture down to the corrals, though he yearned to see her. She would have been as distressed as he was by the horses' circumstances, not to mention the fate that awaited them.

Tucking the rag back into his belt, Aytal took up the poles of the sledge, ready to resume his task. Only then did he notice Wailos, standing just inside the corral fence. His heart sank. Like the horses, Aytal preferred the peace of the ravine when no one else was present, especially Wailos. In front of other clan members, their visitor maintained an easy, cordial demeanor, but once he no longer had an audience, the mask dropped. The horses were never fooled. The herd feared him, and Aytal bristled at Wailos' arrogant attitude when no one else was watching. He'd learned the hard way not to rise to Wailos's bait, however, and to concentrate on his job instead. His father had warned Aytal before bidding him goodbye that developing such self-control might be one of the hardest aspects of his sentence, and he'd been right.

Aytal had pulled the sled alongside the enclosure's gate and was about to open it to go inside.

"Hold on." Wailos put up a hand to stop him. "They can wait to eat until we're finished here. Naya wants to see how we catch the horses and maybe pet one of the foals. Everything needs to be under control before she gets too close – wouldn't want her to get hurt."

Confused, Aytal set down the sled poles just as Naya stepped out from the shadow of the oak. He stared at her in surprise. A flood of hope mixed with uncertainty surged through him. *Why had she come down to the corrals now, after all this time? And why wasn't she the one showing Wailos how to approach the horses, not the other way around?* As though in response to his unspoken questions, Naya gave an almost imperceptible shrug before looking away. Frowning, Aytal turned back to Wailos. "Would you like help?" he asked politely.

"No of course not," came the dismissive reply. Immediately Wailos seemed to think better of his tone. "I'm sure you have other things to do," he added solicitously. "We'll be fine here on our own and be out of your way soon."

From her post under the tree, Naya spoke up. "It's alright Wailos," she called. "You don't need to catch one for my benefit. I've seen them. Let's go back." To anyone else, she might have sounded indifferent, even bored, but Aytal caught the edge in her voice. He looked back at her, worried now. If Wailos noticed anything amiss, he paid no heed.

"I'll just show you how the *uurga* works at least," he called back. "You don't have to come in with them if you don't want to." Resuming his advance on the bunched horses, Wailos maneuvered until he'd managed to separate the small mare with the star and her tiny foal from the others.

"Watch this," he repeated, brandishing the pole in the horses' direction while continuing to dodge and weave as necessary to keep the mare and foal from rushing past him to rejoin the others. Within moments, he had snared the foal, pulling the noose tight around the little creature's neck. The foal struggled for a moment, then quieted. Skittish, the mare kept out of reach but refused to be shooed away.

Meanwhile, Aytal had taken advantage of Wailos's focus on the horses to join Naya under the oak. "Why are you letting him do this?" he whispered, having moved close enough for her to hear him. "What's wrong with you?"

"Nothing's wrong with me," she hissed back. She gave a little wave, letting Wailos know she was watching. "What do you expect me do about it?" she added in an undertone.

"Then why did you come down here?" Aytal managed to keep his voice low but couldn't disguise the hurt. For him, at least, this was about more than just the horses.

"Don't," Naya warned. "Please, don't make this any harder than it is already." She kept her eyes averted, as though focused on what was happening in the pen with the herd.

Even standing this close, Aytal couldn't decipher Naya's tone or read her expression. He did, however, notice the dark shadows beneath her eyes. "What's wrong?" he asked again, voice softening with concern. He wanted to touch her in an effort to get her to look at him but restrained himself. "Please don't shut me out." he implored. "I love you."

That got her to glance up at him, and when she did, the anguish in her blue eyes pierced Aytal's heart like an arrow. "Don't," she repeated in desperate whisper. "I can't…" Before she could say more, Wailos called out, sounding irritated.

"Hey!" His voice carried easily to where Aytal stood beside Naya under the oak. "Is he bothering you?" Slipping the noose off the foal's neck, he strode to the corral gate and let himself out, resecuring the ropes.

The horses, relieved to be left in peace for the moment, regrouped, touching noses to be sure of one another's well-being before retreating once again to the back of the enclosure.

Taking a step back, Aytal dropped his gaze to his feet. "If you're finished," he said to Wailos. "I'll just take the horses their grass."

Keeping his eyes down, he returned to where he'd left the laden sled. As he bent to picked up the poles, he looked up, hoping to catch Naya's eye, but all of her focus was on Wailos, who had taken his place at her side under the oak. They had their backs to him. From behind, Wailos's posture looked menacing. Aytal wondered if he should intervene.

Naya could feel Aytal's eyes on her but didn't turn around. "He was just asking how I've been since getting back," she said, doing her best to sound nonchalant while ignoring her thudding heart. She didn't know which was more upsetting, seeing the horses or seeing Aytal. Taking Wailos's arm, she looked up with what she hoped was an engaging smile. "Don't tell me you're jealous?" she teased, steering toward the path that led back to the settlement.

"Of course not," Wailos responded. "Why would I ever be jealous? I just wanted to be sure he wasn't bothering you." His considerate tone displayed no trace of his earlier flash of irritation. Putting his arm around her waist, he gave it a possessive squeeze. "You've made it quite clear how you feel about me," he continued playfully, voiced raised. Looking back over his shoulder as though to be sure Aytal was watching, Wailos turned Naya in his arms so they were facing one another and with a wolfish grin, began angling his head toward hers.

Naya put a hand to his chest, hoping to fend him off. She'd gotten used to having Wailos kiss her, just not in front of Aytal, at least if she could help it. "Quite clear," she confirmed, tilting back her head and offering a coy smile she hoped appeared more confident than she felt.

Pausing in his decent, Wailos lifted an eyebrow and his expression turned smug. Apparently satisfied for the moment, he turned Naya loose, motioning for her to proceed him up the narrow trail. Relieved, Naya did as she was bidden.

Women's tent, later the same night…

"Thank you, Dayan. You may wait outside. If anyone tries to enter, tell them that I am conducting a private ceremony and that I asked you to be certain that I am not disturbed." Awija waited to be sure the boy comprehended her instructions, then added another admonishment for good measure. "You mustn't tell anyone about my visitor," she warned, "Your brother's life depends on your silence. Do you understand?" Receiving a wide-eyed nod from the boy, she dismissed him with a wave of her hand.

Hurriedly, Dayan ducked out, leaving Awija with her late-night guest.

"Please," she said, indicating the same pile of furs opposite the hearth where she'd received Potis a few days earlier. "Make yourself comfortable." Awija waited as her visitor seated himself. He moved with natural grace, she observed, despite obviously feeling awkward and uncertain about why she'd summoned him to the women's tent. She decided to put him at ease as soon as possible.

"Young man," she said, smiling kindly once her visitor was settled. "I want to start by thanking you for coming. I know there is no small risk involved." Would he meet her eye, she wondered, or keep his gaze downcast? Small gestures held so many clues to a person's character.

As if in answer, Aytal lifted his head, intercepting Awija's appraising look with a forthright expression of his own. Once again, she noticed his unusual eyes, as vivid a blue as her granddaughter's. Now that she knew that both their mothers had been born into the same tribe, the strange coincidence made more sense.

"I'm honored that you would ask to speak with me," Aytal said politely. "Sunus assured me when he took my place with the horses that the clan chief himself had arranged it. I am at your service." He gave a respectful bow of his head, causing an escaped lock of dark hair to fall forward across his brow. Running a hand through the unruly tangle, he pushed it aside in an unconscious gesture. *Boyish*, Awija thought, *yet no longer a boy*. Pausing for a moment, she considered how best to proceed. As usual, she chose the direct approach, although with a slight preamble to soften the impact. She would need to judge how willing he was to confide in her.

"Still," she began, "as I said to your brother, there is a risk in bringing you here. I wouldn't have asked you to come were it not important. There is something I need to know from you. Do you think you can give me an honest answer?"

"I suppose that depends somewhat on the question," Aytal responded. "But I will do my best."

"Don't be alarmed by what I'm about to ask you," Awija warned him. "Be assured that I have your best interests at heart. You can trust me. But I have no time to waste on pleasantries. If Naya has told you anything about me, you know that I have a habit of coming straight to the point."

Awija watched closely in order to gauge Aytal's reaction to the mention of Naya's name and was gratified to see a slight flush rise in his cheeks. Although he shifted in his seat, he did not drop eye contact. *Ah, there's the answer to my question*, she thought, *and given what I've seen of him so far, he's unlikely to deny it.*

"Are you in love with my granddaughter?" she asked bluntly.

Now Aytal did look away, but only for the briefest moment. When he returned her gaze, his expression held a trace of defiance, which Awija noted with approval.

"I am," he said simply.

"Have you told her?"

"As a matter of fact, I told her today, when she came down to the corrals."

Ah good, Awija thought. At least that part of her plan had worked. Not only had he acknowledged the truth to himself, he'd been either brave or foolhardy enough to share his feelings with Naya.

"How did she react?" Awija asked. She couldn't help but be curious, although she suspected she knew the answer to this question as well.

"We didn't have much of an opportunity to talk," Aytal confessed. "I think I took her by surprise. She was upset… but I don't think so much by what I'd said as…" He trailed off, as though uncertain of how much more to say.

"The horses?" Awija finished for him. "I imagine she can't stand for them to be penned up." She knew talking about Naya's response to seeing the captured herd would be easier for the young man than discussing her granddaughter's reaction to seeing him – or his reaction to seeing her with Wailos.

"Penned up. Panicked when anyone approaches. Even when they're left alone, they rarely relax," Aytal agreed, then hesitated once more.

"It's alright," Awija reassured him. "You have nothing to fear from me – just don't let the others – especially Wailos – know how you feel. If he finds out, you have an opinion about those horses – or about Naya – he will not be pleased." She chuckled wryly. "He's not terribly interested in anyone's views other than his own."

"He acts very sure of himself with her," Aytal ventured. "Is…" He swallowed. "…is it true that he's claimed her?" he blurted.

"My granddaughter is not a possession to be *claimed*, as you put it," Awija replied sternly, then relented when she saw the look of contrition her rebuke produced. "I'm sure you would never think of her in that way," she went on, giving him a reassuring smile. "While Wailos seems quite confident of himself, nothing final has been decided about Naya's future, least of all by Naya herself, as far as I know. Her father has promised both her mother and me that she shall have a voice in what happens to her, and nothing will be formally discussed until after she is presented at the Gathering."

So don't lose hope, she wanted to add, seeing from the young man's doubtful expression that her attempt at encouragement had not provided much relief. Awija wondered if perhaps he knew more than she did about her granddaughter's intentions after his brief encounter with her down at the corrals.

"How did she seem to you when you saw her with Wailos today?" she asked.

Aytal took a moment to reply, apparently still cautious about speaking his mind. "She acted like the horses," he finally answered. "Wary but going along with him for the sake of avoiding trouble." Aytal glanced at Awija from under his brows. "There is one mare who resists," he added. "She won't let herself be tamed, at least not the way Wailos is going about it." He looked away.

Awija waited for him to elaborate. "It must have been quite different between my granddaughter and the red filly," she prompted.

Aytal looked back, visibly grateful for the invitation to talk about something other than Wailos and the captured herd. "You should have seen them together!" he replied eagerly. "They were magnificent. Did Naya tell you about galloping the filly across the open steppe? They were like one creature, skimming over the earth." He gestured, evoking a bird in flight. "Within the blink of an eye they travelled a distance that would have taken half the morning to cover on foot. But the most wonderful thing was the look on Naya's face afterwards. I've never seen anyone so filled with joy." Aytal beamed at the memory. "The filly seemed pleased with herself as well," he added.

He looked even more boyish than he had earlier, and rather handsome, Awija conceded, with those unusual eyes set-off by dark brows. His broad smile, displaying white, even teeth, was full of warmth and genuine admiration for her granddaughter. She could understand why Naya would be attracted to the young man – why she might have begun to open her heart to him – even if the girl had yet to admit as much to herself.

Momentarily distracted by her own musings, Awija brought her attention back to what Aytal was saying.

"Everything Naya and the filly accomplished together was only possible because the filly trusted her," he insisted, his voice grown earnest. "And she trusted the filly. From the beginning Naya was adamant about not restraining her, not using ropes – nothing like what's been done to the horses at the corrals." In contrast to the animated expression he'd worn a moment before, a disapproving frown now tugged at the corners of the young man's mouth. Once again, he averted his gaze. Awija took note.

"Thankfully you've been there to take care of them at least," she observed mildly, reaching behind her for another piece of kindling. "Just as you've taken care of my granddaughter," she added, turning back in time to catch the reaction her words produced. As before, a slight blush stained the young man's cheeks. He kept his eyes on his lap.

"Don't be ashamed," she went on, placing the wood on the fire. "I know that wounding Naya was an accident, and I know that you kept her alive until help arrived," she told him. "I also know something of the *etmn itājō* – the spirit journey – that you undertook on her behalf." At this, Aytal looked up, his expression a mixture of surprise and dismay. "Sata told me," Awija explained. "She's very grateful to you. But she and your father also told me of the sacrifice you made." Awija stopped, watching once more for the young man's reaction.

Aytal stared mutely into the fire. Bright orange flames, renewed by the addition of fresh fuel, leapt high, illuminating his features. The new wood, still green, crackled noisily before emitting a series of explosive pops – trapped moisture expanding in the heat. The tent remained otherwise silent as Awija, waiting for Aytal to speak, watched the firelight accentuate the planes of his face. She felt sorry for what she saw there.

At last, eyes downcast, Aytal uttered what sounded like a confession. "I failed," he said, voice just above a whisper.

"Why do you say that?" Awija asked quietly.

"Because it's the truth." He looked at her then. Bitterness, mixed with frustration and not a little despair, had darkened his eyes to slate.

"Whatever you believe to be the truth is likely to be so," Awija conceded. "But sometimes we only believe what we already assume to be true and as a result, we don't always see clearly. Perhaps you need to look again, and this time, try to see with the eyes of your heart." She held his gaze.

"You sound like my father," Aytal answered. "Or my spirit guide," he added ruefully.

"I'm flattered," Awija returned, "on both counts. Which makes paying attention to what I'm about to say to you all the more imperative, as I speak for those who care for you but are not here at the moment to advise you."

She drew herself up, expression intent.

"There are two kinds of sacrifice," she began. "The first is a false sacrifice, made upon the altar of fear, requiring us to believe that we must give up something precious – a piece of ourselves – in order to gain what we think we desire. Inevitably such a sacrifice diminishes us, making us less of who the Goddess intends for us to be. Yet always we believe more is demanded, until we have nothing left to give and must prey on others to meet the false altar's insatiable demands."

Aytal's eyes were solemn. Awija could see he was concentrating on what she was saying to him, even if he might not fully comprehend the meaning of her words. She continued. "The second type of sacrifice – true sacrifice – is made upon an altar of love, not fear. Rather than taking something from us, this second type of sacrifice asks no more than a humble outpouring of our truest selves, in gratitude for all that we've already received. Because the source of such gifts can never be depleted but instead continually renews and refills us, such unconditional sacrifice enables us to give of our whole being so that we may in return receive and give again." Awija waited a beat. "Does this make sense?" she asked.

Uncertain, Aytal nodded, then shook his head.

Awija regarded him, considering. "We have talked enough for one night," she said after a moment. "You may not fully understand what I've said but you will after giving it some thought. I will send for you again. When you return, be prepared to answer this question: on the night when you journeyed in search of my granddaughter's spirit, you made two sacrifices, one true, one false. The question you must answer is, which was which? Will you think about it?"

Still looking confused, Aytal nodded.

"Good. You may go then. We'll just have Dayan make sure no one is around to witness you leaving."

Intending to call for the boy, Awija made an effort to rise but found her joints had grown painfully stiff from too much sitting, an affliction that troubled her more and more lately. Seeing her difficulty, Aytal jumped to his feet and offered both hands to assist. With a grateful smile, Awija grasped the young man's outstretched arms and pulled herself upright. Once standing, however, she did not immediately release her hold on him.

"One more question," she said instead. "I wonder, what made you to decide to tell my granddaughter that you love her?"

Awija's query caught Aytal off guard. "I don't know exactly," he replied awkwardly, trapped by her hold on his forearms. Although the bones of her hands felt as thin as a bird's, her grip was surprisingly strong – another way in which she reminded him of his spirit guide. Like the gyrfalcon, the wisdom that Naya's grandmother sought to impart came in the form of difficult questions. Other than fearing he might not have another opportunity, he had no idea why he'd declared his feelings to

Naya. The words seemed to have uttered themselves of their own accord. He had no plan for what was supposed to happen after he'd said what was in his heart.

"I was afraid that I might never have another chance," he answered truthfully.

"It is well that you spoke when you did," replied Awija, placing one weathered hand against Aytal's cheek before releasing him. "Go now, and we will talk again soon. Remember what I have asked you to think about."

Later that night…

Lying under the faint gleam of distant stars while listening to the horses shift restlessly in the blackness of the night, Aytal considered Awija's questions and how they might be connected. What *had* made him confess his love for Naya, not only to her but to her grandmother? And what did love have to do with sacrifice?

The reality was that during the long days and nights of caring for the captured horses, Aytal had thought of little else besides his feelings for Naya, and hers for him. Reliving the details of their time together before returning to the settlement – ordinary daily interactions as well as the moments of shared awe and excitement with the red filly and the gray stallion – he'd asked himself repeatedly whether he'd been deceiving himself, daring to believe that Naya cared for him in the same way that he cared for her. Then he'd recall the scene in the little ravine – mist-shrouded and dawn-lit, Naya on her knees, soaked in mud and blood, holding the dead body of the colt in her arms, the look in her eyes piercing his heart. Had he managed, in the flash of an instant, to destroy whatever feelings she might have had for him?

Eventually, being honest with himself, he'd realized that he should have done everything in his power to help Naya to defend the horses from the lion attack. He should have used his bow. If he had, he might have stopped the female lion in her tracks. Instead, in the moment when it mattered, he'd failed to act. And then, in a desperate attempt to atone for his failure, he'd tried to rescue Naya from the truth by pretending that it had been his shot that killed the colt. Whether the look she'd given him meant that she blamed him, or herself, or both, he might never know. Either way, it hardly mattered. Either way, he bore responsibility for what had happened.

Then, just as shame threatened to overwhelm him, other recollections would surface – of holding Naya in his arms, his arrow in her back, and pledging his life to her if only she survived, of Naya and the red filly, copper hair streaming as they raced the wind, followed by the visceral sensation of the first and only time he and Naya had kissed. With the memories came the conviction that he and Naya were bound to one another with ties stronger than any rope. How could he *not* love her, regardless of whether she felt the same for him?

Through sleepless nights alone in his tent, as well as exhausting days caring for the horses, Aytal had held fast to the memories – until this morning, standing with her under the oak tree, when he'd somehow summoned the courage to speak the truth that was in his heart. Now, staring up at the stars, he wondered if his words to Naya had found their mark – or was he already too late, having mistakenly sacrificed all that he'd been given and all that was his to give?

Chapter Twelve

Five days later…

"Just out of curiosity," called Krnos, "why is it that no one ever sees you with that bow that you keep stashed in your tent?"

He leaned against the oak, chewing a grass stem and watching idly as Aytal used a pitchfork fashioned from antler tines to shovel manure onto the sledge that also served to haul hay. It was mid-day, three days before the commencement of the Gathering, and Aytal was sweating from exertion. The horses stood nearby, dozing in the early summer heat and occasionally swishing at flies.

"It's almost like you're afraid of something," Krnos added speculatively.

"I don't know what you're talking about," Aytal replied, not looking up from his chore. He would have preferred not to answer at all but knew if he ignored the other young man entirely, Krnos would report him to his father for being rude. Skelos had a cruel streak matching the jagged scar marring his face and needed little provocation before resorting to casual violence – unless the clan chief was on hand to intervene – and so Aytal was careful not to antagonize either Skelos or his son.

"If you're wondering how I know about the bow," Krnos added, "it's because I've searched your tent. On my father's orders of course. Can't be too careful with strangers." He clearly hoped this information would elicit a reaction, but Aytal was determined to disappoint him. Back turned, he concentrated on appearing fully occupied by the task at hand.

"I hear Naya finally visited the corrals," Krnos observed, trying another tack. "She and Wailos make quite a nice couple, don't you think? There's talk of marriage."

He paused, as if waiting for a response. Aytal silently fumed. He'd heard the rumors. Listened as the other young men stood around the corral teasing Wailos about the clan chief's daughter. Seen them together himself. Beyond declaring his love to Naya, and confessing as much to her grandmother, Aytal felt powerless.

Krnos pressed ahead. "Given how much Naya likes horses, I'm surprised it took her so long to come down here." Pushing off the tree, he strolled over to the corral fence and leaned his forearms against the top rail.

"That red filly, for example," he went on in a conversational tone. "I used to see Naya all the time last autumn, hanging around with that filly and the rest of this herd, although I doubt she saw me. Did she ever mention them when you two were together over the winter? Probably not. I imagine she wanted as little to do with you as possible, considering you almost killed her – although that was quite the look you two exchanged at your sentencing, not to mention her reaction to your punishment. Such a commotion she caused, fainting like that. If it didn't sound so far-fetched, I'd say she was attracted to you. Unless of course she was upset for some other reason?"

Krnos left the question hanging. Aytal kept his head down to hide his alarm. He'd seen Réhda, standing on the edge of the bluff on the day of his sentencing. Naya must have seen her too and that's why she'd called out. Aytal had searched for the filly and the mare and the gray stallion every day since, whenever he went to gather fodder, but no luck. He hadn't had time to ask Naya about them when she visited the corrals the other day. How much did Krnos know? Had he seen the red filly on the bluff top as well? Did he know where she and the others were?

"Either way," Krnos continued matter-of-factly, "it's no wonder you don't want to touch that bow of yours. Who knows what further damage you might do?" He snorted derisively. Turning, he leaned back against the fence and leisurely crossed one ankle over the other while looking off into the distance in the direction of the creek.

"What I can't understand," he went on, twirling the grass stem between his teeth, "is why your brother spent all winter bragging about what a skilled bowman you are."

Taking advantage of Krnos's back being turned, Aytal glanced up, wishing the fence would collapse under him.

"You're lucky Wailos got you out of taking part in the contest," Krnos said over his shoulder without looking around. "Personally, I was hoping to see you compete. You would either have humiliated yourself by losing or proven that you're nothing more than a coward by refusing to take part. In any case, Naya would not have been impressed."

Uncrossing his ankles and pushing off the fence, Krnos turned back to face the pen. Aytal moved closer to pick up the last pile of manure but kept his gaze averted.

"Wailos now," Krnos remarked with evident admiration, "he knows how to handle a bow." He mimicked drawing a string, then releasing an imaginary arrow. "Maybe you could get him to give you a few pointers."

Out of the corner of his eye, Aytal saw Krnos, apparently bored with the one-sided conversation, stoop and pick up a handful of pebbles and begin flicking them one at a time over the fence. Eventually one hit him in the back of the neck. He put up a hand, as though to swat away an annoying insect, but otherwise didn't react. Krnos returned to his monologue.

"Wailos tried teaching Naya to shoot," he scoffed, chuckling, "but she's pathetic, especially with the useless set of weapons she's got. Did you make those for her? I noticed you have an arrow that must be hers in your quiver. It's shorter than the others and doesn't have the same double fletching. Does she know you have it? Holding on to it as something to remember her by?"

Seething, Aytal had to muster every shred of self-control not to round on Krnos and hit him over the head with the muck rake. *He's not worth it*, he reminded himself. Gritting his teeth, mouth drawn tight, Aytal drew in a deep breath. Exhaling, he wiped all signs of emotion from his features before turning to face his tormenter.

"I'm sorry, but I have a lot of work to do," he said evenly. "If there is something you need or anything I can do for you, please let me know. Otherwise, I should take this to the dung heap."

Aytal placed the pitchfork crossways on top of the ladened sledge and, grasping the handles, began to drag it out of the enclosure. Krnos had the good grace to open the gate for him and then close it again, resecuring the stout ropes that kept the horses from escaping.

"If I were you," he called after Aytal, who was making his way along a path leading to where the manure pile lay screened behind a thicket of undergrowth some distance from the corrals, "I'd keep that bow of yours handy, even if you aren't much of a shot. You never know when something might try to get at the horses. I wouldn't want to be you if anything were to happen to them. In case no one's told you, the clan chief has a nasty temper – although he hides it well. You wouldn't want to be responsible for embarrassing him in front of the rest of the tribe at the Gathering." Laughing and obviously pleased with himself, Krnos turned and headed up the trail leading back toward the settlement.

Dropping the sledge handles, Aytal watched him go. Krnos's sole purpose was to goad him into saying or doing something he would regret, but it was hard to keep the gibes from getting under his skin. Like nettles, Krnos's words contained just enough truth to make them sting. Even had Wailos not intervened on the day of his sentencing, Aytal would have refused to participate in the archery contest. He wished he could justify the choice, if only to himself, but the reality was that the reason his bow sat unused in the corner of his tent was that he was afraid. Ever since the day with his father last winter, when he'd failed to take down both the deer and the auroch, fear had gnawed at him.

What if his inability to shoot had nothing to do with performing the sacrifice he'd thought was necessary to restore his honor and save Naya? After all, he had not actually rescued her during the drum journey on the night of the winter solstice, and yet she had survived, so it was possible that renouncing the use of his bow had meant nothing one way or the other. What if the real issue was his own recklessness and pride? What if, as punishment for all the harmed he'd inflicted with his bow, his gift had been taken from him?

How could he live the rest of his life enduring such a loss? Never had he felt more truly himself than with his quiver at his back and his bow in his hand – other than when he'd held Naya in his arms. Just as he missed her smile, he missed the feel of his bow's worn leather grip, as familiar, he imagined, as a lover's touch. He missed the sense of possibility vibrating in the bowstring held taut against his cheek. Most of all, he missed watching the arc of the arrow's flight, tracing with piercing clarity the path of his intent.

And yet, to save Naya's life – or so he believed – he'd foresworn its use. Afterwards, his gift seemed to desert him. As the fulfillment of the vow he'd made? As the price for his mistakes? Or solely as the result of his own inadequacy? He was afraid to find out. He feared the truth. *Perhaps,* whispered a voice in his head, *you truly are a coward.*

The admission left Aytal demoralized but also strangely rebellious.

Something deep inside refused to accept the voice's judgement. Standing beside the manure pile, still smarting from Krnos's taunts, his visit with Naya's grandmother came back to him. As instructed, he'd been pondering what she'd told him about the two types of sacrifice. Now, in a flash, he understood. All this time he had been allowing fear to diminish him, believing he must give up what he held most precious in order to atone for his transgressions. That was the wrong kind of sacrifice. He'd been given a gift – a power – as vital as life itself, which he'd squandered. Despite his failings, he must find the courage to reclaim the gift and, this time, use his power with wisdom and humility, in service to those he loved.

Could it really be that simple? Aytal began shoveling the contents of the sledge onto the mound of manure. He could almost hear Awija's voice in reply. *Simple,* she would agree, *but not easy.* Dumping the last of the manure, he returned with the empty sledge to the corrals, then reloaded it from the pile of hay leftover from the horses' breakfast and left it just outside the fence. The herd had everything they needed for the moment, leaving him free to explore his newfound insight. When Naya's grandmother summoned him again to speak with her, he'd ask her to confirm that he was on the right track. In the meantime, there was something he wanted to try.

The same morning, in a grove of woods not far from the settlement…

Naya and Amu stopped at the edge of a small clearing surrounded by leafy aspen and birch, with the occasional pine and oak standing sentinel. Absently reaching back to tie up her thick hair, which was sticking to the sweat on the back of her neck, Naya surveyed the area. The shade from the trees offered welcome relief from the summer sun and the opening in the underbrush felt secluded, despite the short walk from the settlement. She was still well within the designated perimeter the trainees had been told to observe when choosing a location for their shelters, but whereas the other girls had scattered toward the sparsely forested hillside beyond the settlement to the north, Naya had set-off in the opposite direction, heading toward the denser woods to the south, closer to the flood plain where she was fairly certain none of them would follow. A squirrel scolded from a nearby branch, and she could hear a woodpecker tapping not far away. Insects buzzed. Otherwise, the grassy, sun-dappled space felt peaceful and entirely private.

"This is the place," Naya said to the dog, reaching down to scratch him behind his ragged ear. The wounds from the lion attack had healed but not all the hair had grown back over the scars, giving him a rather disreputable appearance. Setting down the heavy bundle she'd brought with her, she scanned the area for saplings of the right diameter to cut and trim for tent poles. Once she constructed a simple frame, she'd be able to stretch the felted cloth from her bundle over the structure, anchoring the covering with cords tied to the wooden stakes she'd also brought along.

Uksor had warned the girls to be sure their shelters were securely built, letting them know she planned to inspect them herself. This was an essential matter of protocol, as the priest's wife had reminded them. Once their vigils began, each girl was expected to stay in seclusion for three full days and nights, with no possibility of anyone entering or leaving the shelter. To ensure their solitude remained inviolate, once each girl had entered her shelter, its opening was to be sewn shut from the outside with special twine, dyed with *miljom* – sacred red ochre. At dawn following the third night of the vigil, the fastening of each shelter would be slit open by the senior priest, using a sanctified blade. The newly initiated young women, as Uksor referred to them, were then to gather out of sight, along with other newly initiated young women from the clans who had arrived for the Gathering. Once assembled, she explained, the initiates would form a procession and be escorted with great fanfare to the stone circle, where each would be formally presented to the entire tribe.

On the evening when Uksor first went over the details, Naya got the sense that her grandmother disapproved of the priest-led rituals surrounding the period of seclusion, but Naya wasn't sure why. Uksor said the girls' emergence from their sealed and sanctified shelters was meant to symbolize their passage over the threshold into womanhood, but Awija never spoke in those terms. Perhaps, Naya speculated, there was something about the ritual that Awija wasn't allowed to discuss.

Taking out her hand ax, Naya began cutting down saplings with a diameter no larger than her thumb, pliable enough to be lashed together and bent into a frame. Although she wasn't bothered by the prospect of solitude during her vigil, she dreaded the ordeal of the presentation ceremony. She supposed she must get used to such occasions, however. As Wailos's wife, she could expect to find herself often the center of attention. She wondered when her father was going to discuss the marriage with her. Only one day remained until her vigil began. She wouldn't emerge until the second official day of the Gathering. If an announcement regarding an engagement were to be made to the assembled tribe, it would happen on the third and final day of the festivities. That didn't leave much time for a conversation. She'd tried more than once to talk with him, but he kept putting her off.

Of course, Papa is busy, she thought, stripping leaves and branches from the saplings she'd cut. Preparations for the Gathering were well underway, and a buzz of anticipation filled the settlement. Visitors from the other clans would begin arriving tomorrow, bringing with them provisions to be shared as well as animals to be sacrificed as part of the ceremonies. As host, her father was responsible for keeping everyone organized, along with settling whatever disputes arose regarding who was entitled to the best camping sites and other matters of precedence. But surely he would have to make time for her before she went into seclusion.

"Right, Amu?" she asked out loud. Amu lay in the shade, watching her work. She pushed a stray lock of hair off her face and regarded the dog. She was concerned about leaving him unsupervised during her vigil, especially with so many visitors and strange dogs arriving. "What are we going to do with you?" she asked him. Amu tilted his head in response. Naya knew the answer – the best person to leave him with – but she dreaded the awkward conversation required if she were to ask the favor.

She had not entirely forgiven Aytal for not helping her to defend the horses against the lion attack, even if she mostly blamed herself for the colt's death. But that wasn't the problem. Seeing him at the corrals the other day had stirred up other complicated feelings she'd thought buried, leaving her upset with him once more, as well as irritated at herself. *Why did Aytal have to declare his love for me?* she thought. Their friendship – the time they'd spent together and the way he'd made her feel, at least when she wasn't angry with him – were now all the harder to forget. Roughly ripping away a stubborn branch from the last of the saplings, Naya ended up splitting the trunk in the process. She threw down the useless sapling in disgust. Wiping the perspiration off her forehead with the crook of her elbow, she stood with hands on hips, looking at the pile of slim poles she'd created. They would have to do. She set about constructing the frame.

Later…

Worn out but at least calmer, Naya stood back and admired the finished shelter. Dome-shaped, with a smoke-hole in the center, it was only tall enough for her to stoop inside, not stand up right, but there was plenty of space for a small hearth and a sleeping mat and cushions, along with the provisions she would need for three days. Building the structure had given her time to decide what to do about Aytal. Talking to him couldn't be avoided if he was to take care of Amu for the next several days, and painful as it might be to discuss how things between them had to be, he deserved to hear the truth from her. Wearily, she gathered her tools.

"Come on, Amu," she called. "We're finished here for now. We have another chore to do."

They were about to emerge into the open from the stand of trees that concealed her shelter when the dog began to growl, low in his throat.

"What's the matter Amu?" Naya asked, laying a hand on his back. The hair between his shoulder blades bristled. The growl turned into a series of menacing barks.

"Your dog still hasn't learned to like me." She turned toward the voice and saw Wailos coming from the direction of the river.

"Hang on," she called back, grabbing a length of leftover cord. She knotted it around Amu's neck. Wailos, seeing the dog about to lunge, had stopped twenty paces away.

"Amu!" Naya said sternly, bringing the dog up short. "Stop it."

"Could you tie him to a tree or something. I've been looking for you, to say goodbye."

"Goodbye?" Naya echoed, doing as Wailos bid and securing the other end of Amu's rope to a sapling. Still snarling, the dog strained against the tether. "Stop it!" Naya commanded, again to little effect.

"If that were my dog…" Wailos started, then seem to think better of whatever he'd intended to say. "Never mind," he continued, giving Naya a deprecatory smile. "Come over here where we can talk without him bothering us." Holding out a hand, he beckoned, guiding Naya toward a grassy hollow in the slope leading down to the flood plain.

153

The depression offered a perfect place to sit, screened from view, with a sweeping panorama of the Rā.

"You're leaving?" asked Naya, confused. She lowered herself to a seat next to Wailos. The depression was just big enough for them to wedge together, shoulder to shoulder. Wailos was bare-chested in the summer heat, and she could feel the warmth radiating off him, as well as a masculine scent of sweat and leather. No air moved in the little hollow. For once she was grateful for the long, loose-fitting skirt of her dress, which gave her something to sit on while allowing her to draw her knees up modestly underneath. *The Gathering begins in three days*, she thought. *Where could he possibly be going?*

"To meet my father," Wailos replied, as if in answer. "He's due to arrive in two days. If I go now, I can meet him upstream in time to help with the river crossing." He put an arm around Naya's waist and gave her a squeeze. "Before I go, I wanted to share the surprise." He grinned at her.

"What surprise?" Naya looked blank. Something dropped in the pit of her stomach.

"As you may have guessed," he began, "showing up here when Unksra and I did wasn't an accident – and searching for summer pastures was mostly an excuse. Father wants closer ties with your clan, to be sealed by a marriage between myself and… a suitable bride." His arm tightened around her waist. "And while my idea of capturing the horses was meant as a real solution to the unfortunate loss of your clan's livestock, it also provided a perfect excuse for me to stay around, so that my future wife and I could become better acquainted, without the pressure of a formal announcement."

One corner of his mouth quirked up, creating a dimple in the otherwise smooth planes of his face. His teeth flashed white as he winked at her. Naya thought he looked very pleased with himself, and with her. Suddenly he was kissing her, exuberantly this time. With his avid lips pressed against hers, he seemed joyful. Or triumphant, perhaps? She should feel the same elation. Here was confirmation of everything she'd been working toward. Her father would be so proud of her. When Wailos released her, she stared at him. His black eyes glinted back at her.

Removing his arm from around her waist, he leaned forward, resting his forearms on his knees, and looked out at the river. "Of course, nothing will be official until the details are settled, but my father is coming with enough of our choicest cattle to serve as a most generous bride price." He looked sideways at her. "You realize what this means?" he continued, expression both earnest and eager. "Your father and the rest of your clan have nothing to worry about – even without the captured horses, the cattle for the bride price would be enough to fulfill your clan's obligations for the Gathering." He beamed, as though the clan's change in fortune was all because of her. Naya swallowed, unable to find her tongue.

"I'm sorry to miss the start of your vigil, but I'll be back before it's over, I promise. You'll see me before you know it, and when you do, I'll have another surprise for you. But don't let on about what I've told you – nothing is official until your father and my father and the priests have their say. Our secret, swear?" Wailos drew a finger down her cheek, ending with gentle but firm pressure against her lips.

Naya nodded.

"I'm off then," he announced, jumping to his feet and offering her a hand up. "You'll see me again before you know it," he repeated. Another flash of teeth, a raffish wink, and he was gone, disappearing over the lip of the hollow.

Chapter Thirteen

Later the same afternoon…

By the time Naya and Amu made their way down the steep trail to the corrals, shadows had started to lengthen and some of the day's heat had begun to seep out of the still air at the bottom of the narrow ravine. The corral area seemed deserted, except for the horses. Although their heads came up warily, when she did not approach the fenced enclosure, they went back to searching the bare dirt for missed wisps of hay. The smaller corral next to the horses' pen stood empty, as it had since the morning after Naya's return. The clan's remaining livestock had been driven out to pasture on the steppe under the watchful eyes of the herders. In two days, they would bring the animals down to the flood plain along the Rā, in time for the Gathering.

The horses, Naya knew, were to be saved for a grand entrance, once all the clans were assembled. It was the final element of Wailos's original plan – the spectacle of the sacrificial animals being led past the entire tribe – intended to rescue her clan's standing and, more importantly as far as Naya was concerned, preserve her father's reputation. But now, there was another option. Although Wailos hadn't said so explicitly, he'd seemed to imply the horses' lives might ultimately be spared. She could only hope. The alternative made her sick to her stomach.

Determined not to succumb, Naya barely glanced at the captured herd as she and Amu gave the corral a wide berth. They stopped under the giant oak and Naya looked around at a loss. Where was Aytal? After her conversation with Wailos, her errand was even more urgent. Aytal's tent, with the flaps tied back in order not to trap the day's heat, was clearly unoccupied. Could he be out on the steppe, gathering fodder? But no, the sledge stood near the corral entrance, piled with cut grass.

"Where is he?" she asked out loud, addressing Amu as though he might be able to tell her. The dog sat on his haunches gazing up at her, head tilted nearly sideways in an effort to understand her words. Just then, Naya heard a muffled *twang*, followed almost immediately by a dull *thwap*, coming from the direction of the manure pile. Calling to Amu to follow her, Naya headed toward the sound.

Rounding a dense thicket of undergrowth that served to screen the muck heap from the more open area in front of the corrals, Naya at first could not see what might have made the noise. The manure pile, which had grown to impressive proportions, blocked her view of the rest of the clearing. Then she heard the sounds again, louder this time. Skirting the mound, she and Amu came upon an unexpected sight.

With his back turned and his attention focused on what he was doing, Aytal did not at first notice their arrival. Stripped to the waist except for the quiver slung across his back, he stood with an arrow nocked, poised to send it toward the makeshift target he'd set-up some thirty paces distant. Naya stopped in her tracks at the sight of him – legs squared, arms raised, muscles taut with the effort required to steady and draw the powerful bow. She held her breath, waiting for the release of the bowstring. When it came, the shot sailed wide, pinging off a stray rock and skittering to rest well past the intended mark.

"*Ojt!*" Aytal swore in his own tongue, sounding like he might want to fling the bow after the errant arrow.

"Does that mean what I think it does?" Naya called.

Startled, Aytal turned, then froze. Blood rushed into his face and he looked momentarily mortified, before offering a sheepish grin.

"Probably," he admitted. "I'm sorry you had to see that." Still holding the bow in his left hand, with the fingers of his right he combed back the hair that had fallen across his brow. "I'm a little out of practice."

The confession was an understatement, but at the moment Naya didn't have much sympathy. A surge of bitterness caught her by surprise. *So whatever vow you took not to use your bow no longer applies?* She almost said as much, then swallowed back the accusation. Apparently, she wasn't as close to absolving Aytal over the colt's death as she believed. She knew he hadn't killed the poor creature – that was her fault, even if she'd never found her missing arrow. His refusal to use his bow to help fend off the lions was the part she couldn't get past, any more than she'd been able to forgive herself for her errant shot. His choices were no longer her concern, however. She just needed to get through what she'd planned to say without breaking down.

Amu barked, snapping Naya back to the present. Springing forward from her side, the dog reached Aytal in two bounds, nearly knocking him off his feet. Like Naya, Amu had been forbidden to go down to the corrals since returning to the settlement. Continuing to bark ecstatically, he spun in excited circles, clearly overjoyed at being reunited with one of his favorite people. Aytal seemed equally glad to see Amu – almost as pleased as he looked to see Naya.

"I wondered where he was the other day when you came with Wailos," he remarked, squatting down so that the dog could wriggle into his arms and try to lick him in the face. "Why didn't he come with you?" he asked, laughing while fending off Amu's attentions.

Naya, amused at the dog's antics despite herself, felt her smile fade. "Wailos doesn't like him," she answered with a shrug. "And Amu doesn't like Wailos. He growls and gets his hackles up whenever he sees him, so I have to tie him up if Wailos is around and leave him behind if we go anywhere together."

Aytal was at a loss for how to reply to this revelation, although it didn't surprise him. Amu, like the horses, was a good judge of character. Extracting himself from the dog's boisterous display of affection, he rose, then stood gazing at Naya. She returned his regard, apparently equally tongue-tied. To Aytal, the space separating them felt like a chasm.

"It's nice to see you – Amu too," he finally ventured. "I didn't know if you'd come again, after the other day."

"It was a little awkward." Looking uncomfortable, Naya did not offer to elaborate. After a moment she appeared to collect herself. "Could we go somewhere else and talk?" she asked, glancing askance at the manure pile, buzzing with flies.

"Of course," Aytal agreed. "We can go back to the corrals, if you like. It's past time to feed the horses again – you could help me or sit and watch – whichever you prefer. Just let me gather everything."

Aytal hastened to pull two arrows from the stuffed target he'd been using but had to search the surrounding underbrush for the rest. It took longer than he would have liked.

"When did you start shooting again?" Naya asked once he'd rejoined her. Her tone was carefully neutral. Aytal looked at her sideways before answering.

"Just today," he replied, uncertain where this line of discussion might lead. Motioning for Naya to proceed him up the path for the short distance back to the corrals, Aytal asked himself whether he should apologize again for not doing more to save the colt. Before he could make up his mind, Naya broke the brief silence.

"Just today?" she asked, echoing his reply to her question. As she spoke, she glanced back at him over her shoulder, eyebrow raised. The look was exactly like the one Awija had given him.

"Your grandmother sent for me several nights ago," he disclosed. "She made me think that maybe I'd been wrong to lay aside my bow when I did. She got me wondering about a lot of things."

"She has that effect on people," Naya acknowledged. "I'm supposed to meet with her once more before my vigil starts tomorrow. I'm really not looking forward to it."

They'd reached the open space in front of the corrals. Unslinging the quiver from his back, Aytal propped it, along with his bow, against the oak's sturdy trunk. "Do you want to come in with me?" he asked, indicating the sledge mounded with freshly cut hay waiting outside the fence. "I've already gathered what they need for the rest of today, so the hard work's done." Aytal felt at once tentative and full of hope. The hungry horses began to nicker and move closer to the gate.

"Maybe," Naya answered, sounding dubious at the idea of entering the enclosure. "Could we talk first? There's a favor I need to ask."

"Anything," Aytal answered quickly. "We can go over there, if you like." Motioning in the direction of his tent, he indicated a grassy patch not far from the little creek. Wishing he had his cloak to spread for them to sit on, Aytal considered ducking into the shelter for it, but decided behaving as though he expected her to share it with him might seem presumptuous. Picking a spot at random, he lowered himself to the turf and waited for Naya to do likewise.

Amu, unable to resist a perfect place to roll, was already upside down in the grass, paws in the air, happily writhing back and forth. Naya remained standing, watching the dog and looking self-conscious, as though uncertain where she should sit. Making up her mind, she picked a spot and positioned herself, arms wrapped around her bent knees, so that if she wanted to, she could gaze not at Aytal but instead at the little creek which murmured cheerfully as it flowed past.

"So what did my grandmother tell you?" she asked, resuming the conversation where it had left off.

"It was more the questions she asked." Aytal hesitated before saying more. Something at his core told him he must be honest with Naya or risk losing her forever. "You know the night of the winter solstice, when we had the big storm and you were still so sick?"

"Yes," Naya replied, sounding uncomfortable at the apparent change in topic. "I journeyed." She looked at the creek.

"We *both* journeyed," Aytal informed her, realizing she must not have known the drum's call had been meant for him, not her. "Did you ever wonder why?"

"Why?" she echoed, looking back at him, surprised.

"Why we both visited the Spirit World."

"Because… I don't know." Clearly she was struggling to absorb the news that Aytal had journeyed that night as well.

"I went because we all believed that your spirit was lost and I offered to try to find you," Aytal said quietly. "That's when I made the vow to give up what was most precious to me – my bow – because I thought that's what I needed to do to rescue you."

Naya turned to face him, looking indignant. "You didn't have to rescue me," she objected. "I never asked to be rescued!"

"I'm beginning to understand that now," Aytal admitted. "I confused finding you with saving you. And I didn't even find you – I only glimpsed you and the filly from a distance – so when I came back from the journey I was convinced that I'd failed, and I'd given up my bow in vain. Afterwards, that first time when my father and I went hunting and I missed those two shots – shots I never should have missed – I wanted to believe that maybe I'd succeeded after all – that in exchange for surrendering my prowess with the bow, maybe I *had* saved your life. After that, I told myself that if I went back on the bargain, something bad would happen to you, so that gave me an excuse."

"An excuse?" Naya's brow lifted.

"An excuse not to shoot." Aytal hesitated. Dare he confess he'd been afraid – as much for himself as for her?

"So why have you decided now, after everything that's happened, to take up your bow again?" Naya persisted, before appearing to regret that she'd asked. "Never mind," she said. "It's not important for me to know."

To Aytal, the dismissal felt like a slap in the face.

"There's something else we need to talk about," she went on, gaze shifting back to the little creek. "Something I need to ask. I came to see if you'd look after Amu for me."

"What?" Aytal exclaimed in surprise. Apprehension quickly followed. "Is something happening? Are you going somewhere?" He thought of Wailos's dislike of the dog, along with the rumors of marriage. The breath seized in his chest.

"My vigil begins tomorrow," Naya replied, eyes still averted. "I was hoping Amu could stay down here with you until it's over and you could keep him out of trouble."

Struggling to regain his composure, Aytal didn't immediately reply. By the time Naya turned to look at him, he'd at least partially succeeded. "Of course," he assured her with a smile. "Whatever would help. Is that all?" he added. "Is there anything else I can do for you?"

"No," Naya answered. "That's it for now." She returned her attention to the creek.

An awkward silence ensued. Unable to think of anything else to say, Aytal watched Naya shift her gaze to Amu. The dog lay on his back, all four paws in the air, head lolling to the side, tongue hanging out. Taking a breath, she turned to face him.

"Aytal," she began. "There is one other thing." Aytal waited with a sense of dread for what might come next. "What you said the other day, about how you feel about me? It's impossible."

"It's not impossible!" he protested. "It's how I feel."

"That's not what I mean," Naya tried to clarify. "*We* are not possible – you and me. It would never work. I'm the daughter of a clan chief." Aytal started to object but she held up a hand for him to hear her out. "You have to understand," she went on. "I have a duty – a duty to do whatever is necessary to serve the interests of my father and the clan."

Aytal, eyes now fixed on the little stream, said nothing. What *could* he say? He should have expected this, yet he felt stunned.

"Is this really what you want?" he finally managed. He turned to look at her, but she'd angled her face away. She nodded but didn't speak. He turned back to the creek, staring blindly straight ahead.

"Can we go see the horses now?" Naya eventually suggested.

"What? Yes, of course." Aytal shook himself, as though waking from a trance. Jumping up, he reached out to help Naya to her feet. As though oblivious to his offer of assistance, she rose on her own, leaving Aytal to withdraw his outstretched hand as if he'd been stung.

Naya turned and walked ahead of Aytal back toward the corrals. She'd managed what she'd come for, so why didn't she feel relieved? Instead, she felt incredibly weary. *I just need to survive until tomorrow evening*, she told herself. Once her vigil began, she'd be able to retreat to the welcome solitude of her shelter, where she could take time to adjust to the reality of how her life was about to change. In the meantime, she forced a smile and turned to face the horses. She didn't really want to linger but after what she'd said to Aytal, it was the least she could do. A moment ago, he'd been so eager for her to stay.

"Could you open the gate for me?" Aytal asked.

Silently, Naya complied.

Aytal dragged the sledge into the enclosure and waited for Naya to follow him in before resecuring the gate. "You should know," he said, head bent as he retied the ropes, "I look for the Réhda and the others whenever I go out to the steppe to gather forage. I've seen no sign of them."

Standing just inside the fence, with her back turned, Naya tried to act as though she hadn't heard him. She could feel him studying her but was determined to hide the surge of relief she felt. *Better he thinks I don't care anymore*, she thought.

"I'll toss around a few piles of hay," he continued after a moment. "That way the horses won't be so anxious about getting fed. As long as there's hay on the ground, they might allow you to get close. Rebhjo is the most suspicious, but at least around me, the others have become quite friendly again, almost like they were last winter."

Taking up several armloads of dried grass, Aytal spread them at intervals around the enclosure. Still standing by the gate, Naya watched but made no move to help. Accustomed to the mealtime routine, the horses normally would have fanned out as well, each claiming a pile. Instead, they remained huddled in a band at the back of the pen, eyeing her with evident concern.

"Maybe they don't recognize you," Aytal suggested. "Do you want to try offering them some of the hay?"

"Alright," Naya agreed but without much enthusiasm. Grabbing a handful from the sledge, she started walking slowly toward the horses, holding the grass in front of her. She'd only progressed a short distance when Rebhjo, who was closest to her, flattened her ears and lowered her head threateningly. Dismayed, Naya stopped, dropping her arm, and took a step back.

What's wrong with me? she thought crossly. She'd been staring at the horses, and not breathing. She needed to move calmly, she told herself, but with self-assurance, as though the mare's menacing behavior hadn't frightened her. Pulling herself upright and putting on a confident expression, she tried again. Aytal stood beside the sledge, watching. This time she got somewhat closer before Rebhjo glared at her, again halting Naya in her tracks. Trying once more, she had taken only two additional steps when the mare, neck snaking and teeth bared, looked as though she might attack. Leaving the handful of grass on the ground, Naya retreated to a safe distance.

"I don't think she likes me anymore," she said, looking toward Aytal with a self-conscious laugh.

"It's true, she tends to be very protective of the others, but I'm surprised she's being this hostile, particularly with you."

"Well, it doesn't really matter," Naya answered, brushing stray pieces of hay off her hands and clothing. "I should go anyway." She felt mortified.

"Are you sure? If you give her some time to get reacquainted or maybe try one of the others…" Naya could tell Aytal didn't want her to leave but she'd had enough. Coming in with the horses had been a mistake.

"What about the one over there," Aytal suggested, indicating a mare who had moved off to stand by herself near one of the smaller piles of hay. "She's the one who lost her foal."

"Lost her foal?" Naya echoed, surprised. She hadn't heard about one of the foals dying. "What happened?"

Aytal looked as though he regretted mentioning anything. "It was four or five days after they were captured," he explained. "The mare was pregnant but then when she gave birth, the foal was already dead."

Hearing the words, an image flashed into Naya's mind of MeHnd's colt on the night of his birth. He almost hadn't made it. She'd been the one pleading with the mare, his mother, not to give up. Then another image of the colt, bleeding out in her lap. This time, she hadn't been able to save him. She pushed the image away. She couldn't allow herself to feel, or to remember. "That's too bad," she said. Even to her own ears, her voice sounded oddly detached. "Well, maybe she'll want to say hello," she continued, turning in the little mare's direction.

Stooping to gather up the dropped grass stems, Naya began to approach. With each step, she felt more and more disconnected from herself and her surroundings, as though observing from a distance. Within a few paces, without quite knowing how, she had closed half the gap between herself and the lone mare, who other than lifting her head, had not stirred. Oblivious to what was happening elsewhere in the corral, Naya would have continued approaching had Aytal not called out to her.

"Watch out!" he warned. Startled, Naya turned just in time to see Rebhjo charging in her direction. Running for the fence, she vaulted up and over to safety.

"Damn you!" she swore from where she'd landed on her knees in the dirt outside the corral. Dust and sweat stained her face. Equal parts frightened and embarrassed, she didn't know who she was cursing – Aytal or the big mare – but it hardly mattered. She'd completely lost her temper. "That was *your* fault!" she lashed out at Aytal. "Were you trying to get me killed?"

Speechless in the face of her rage, Aytal, who had come running from inside the corral, gazed down at her, apparently uncertain whether he should offer a hand to help her to her feet or not. Amu, with his tail between his legs, seemed equally unsure of how to behave. Meanwhile, the horses had gone back to eating their hay, as though nothing untoward had happened.

"Were you trying to get me killed?" Naya repeated, pushing herself to her feet without assistance.

"Of course not. Maybe the mare doesn't recognize you. She doesn't know if she can trust you." He paused. "You don't seem quite like yourself," he added, as though he didn't recognize Naya either. "Maybe the horses can tell and don't like it."

"Well I don't like them either," she retorted. To her distress, she burst into tears. Without another word, she turned and fled up the path leading back to the settlement.

Amu started to follow, but Aytal called him back. "No," he commanded. "You're meant to stay here with me. Sit." Whining plaintively, Amu nonetheless obeyed, dropping to his haunches and watching as Naya's figure disappeared over the rim of the ravine. Sighing, Aytal squatted next to the dog and put his arm around him, offering what comfort he could. "She doesn't want anything to do with either of us," he said, "at least for now."

Crouched beside the dog, Aytal felt something press into the side of his hip. Reaching into his *makēn*, the pouch he kept at his waist, he pulled out the small carving he'd been working on, a gift for Naya to mark the occasion of her presentation at the Gathering. He'd been so surprised by her visit that he'd neglected to take the opportunity to give it to her in person. He'd have to find another way to get it to her before tomorrow evening, when her vigil began. More than ever, he sensed, Naya needed reminding of her true name and who she really was – *A't Munar Urug* – She-Who-Rides-Horses.

Chapter Fourteen

"Potis!"

At the sound of his mother's voice, the clan chief stopped and turned. On his way to the river with Tausos to check that the early arrivals from the visiting clans were settled in, he did not have time to be interrupted. The sun had long since disappeared behind the bluffs. Darkness would soon fall.

"What is it?" he replied, sounding short-tempered.

"A word." Inclining her head, Awija indicated that he should follow her out of earshot of the rest of the family, still lingering over supper.

"Go on without me," Potis said, waving off Tausos. "I'll be along shortly." He and Awija moved far enough away from the others to not be overheard. "What is it?" he repeated.

Awija frowned, indicating Potis should lower his voice. Even at a whisper, her tone was unequivocal. "I need to speak to Aytal again – tonight."

Potis's refusal was equally adamant. "That's not possible," he asserted. "There's no one to watch the horses."

He half-turned to go but Awija laid a hand on his arm to stop him. "Where is Sunus?" she asked. "He wasn't at supper." Tausos's oldest son had not been the only one missing from the evening meal. Vedukha had not joined them tonight – she was in her tent with a headache – and Wailos had been absent as well, having told everyone of his intention to go and meet his father, Regos, enroute to the Gathering.

"Sunus isn't here." Potis gave his mother the same stubborn look he'd adopted as a boy whenever she'd tried to pry information out of him.

"Potis?" The inflection in her voice told him he might as well give in.

"I sent him to meet Ceru," he said, lowering his voice even further.

"Ceru? He's coming here, now? Isn't that a rather bold move?" She turned her back to the collection of tents and cooking fires. "I don't need to point out to you that within a matter of days, Plānos warriors will be assembled in force." she whispered. "Given Tausos's report about the raid, surely Ceru doesn't intend to make an appearance at this juncture. He's likely to incite a war!"

Potis glanced around to be certain no one was listening. "When Tausos went looking for the raiders, he made it farther than he let on – close enough to the Dānus camp to meet secretly with Ceru," he explained. "Our animals were there, as he reported. But Ceru's warriors didn't steal them."

"Oh?" Awija didn't sound surprised. No doubt she'd been skeptical from the beginning that the Dānus were responsible for the raid. "Who then?"

Shooting his mother a warning look about the confidentiality of what he was about to tell her, Potis hastened to clarify. "According to what Ceru told Tausos, a band of young warriors – a *kóryos* – showed up with the animals, claiming them as their own. The group's leader, obviously the son of a chief, alleged that his father sought an alliance with the Dānus and offered him the livestock as the bride price in exchange for a promise of marriage between himself and Ceru's daughter."

"Who...?" Awija started to ask, but Potis cut in before she could finish.

"Ceru didn't recognize the young warrior, but he recognized my bull. Remember, I told you that Tausos and I ran into Ceru last summer, when we were out hunting? I described the bull to him then – and how I'd acquired him – which made Ceru suspicious of the young warrior's story. That, and the fact that he claimed to be *my* son."

Potis and Awija exchanged a look.

"Ceru was cunning enough to pretend to go along with the idea of arranging an alliance," he continued, "knowing sooner or later I'd send someone to look for our stolen livestock."

"So now what?" Awija asked. "Ceru might be able to provide testimony against the perpetrators, but he won't be welcome at the Gathering," she pointed out. "Not without an invitation."

"Ceru plans to request permission from the priests and the other clan chiefs to attend," Potis elaborated, "ostensibly in order to arrange a formal alliance with our tribe, to be sealed by a marriage between his oldest son, Perqos, and one of our young women, presumably Naya. He and I have talked off and on about someday arranging a marriage between our children, so the idea is not so far-fetched. He's bringing a delegation of Dānus warriors, as well as all of our livestock, including the young bull, purportedly as the bride price. Once they're here, the whole story will come out. We'll be able to prove who led the raid and what happened afterwards."

"Because Ceru can identify the young warrior who brought the animals to the Dānus in the first place?"

Potis nodded.

"And when all of this comes to light, the other clans will be so appalled at the treachery that they'll willingly name you chief of chiefs?"

Again, Potis confirmed his mother's grasp of the situation. "The only missing piece," he added, "is who from our clan aided in the operation, because the raiders must have had help, if only in subduing the herders' dogs. But even that's not much of a mystery."

Awija nodded. "So, back to my original question. Where is Sunus?"

"Ceru and his warriors and the livestock mustn't arrive too soon," Potis explained. "The timing is important. Sunus has gone to meet them. The plan is for him to guide them to one of the ravines further down the river from where the horses are – the one with the cave – so the livestock can be kept out of sight." Potis frowned. "We should have had some word by now."

"And what about the captured horses?" Awija wondered. "How do they fit into all of this?"

"I'm not sure," Potis confessed. "Our distinguished guest has been playing at something all along – he and his father have no reason to be helping us – but until we have everything in place, I obviously can't confront either of them, especially in front of the other clan chiefs. We'll have to see how things unfold."

"But at least with the return of our livestock, you'll have the cattle you need for the rites, so you won't have to sacrifice the horses?" Awija asked.

Potis nodded.

"And I assume," she went on, "you don't intend to sacrifice your daughter either?" Her voice held a bite.

Potis looked offended. "I never did!" he protested. "But now you can see why I've had to go along with and even encourage the rumors. No one could know anything about another match for Naya, let alone my other suspicions. And now I really have to go. The others will be wondering what's keeping me. I don't need to warn you not to breath a word of any of this to anyone." He started to turn away.

"There's one important detail you've left out of your plans," Awija observed, ignoring her son's attempt to end the conversation.

"What's that?" Potis replied, impatient to be off.

"Naya."

"What about Naya?" Potis turned back, perplexed. His mother said nothing, merely raised a single brow.

"Surely it's obvious," she said after a pause when he didn't reply. "You need to talk to her – give her at least some idea of what's going on – before she does something both of you regret."

Potis started to object but Awija persisted. "Did you notice how upset she seemed at dinner? Something must have happened today. Besides being even more distracted than usual, she had raw scrapes on the palms of her hands and a skinned knee." Awija gave Potis an exasperated look. "You need to talk to her," she reiterated.

"I don't want her involved – it's too risky," Potis protested. "Safer for her not to know about any of this."

"She's already involved," Awija pointed out. "What's dangerous is for her not to understand what's really happening. She shouldn't be left in the dark. All she wants is to do what she believes will make you proud – what she thinks will serve your interests as clan chief. If you never include her, how is supposed to know how to help? How is she supposed to know that you value her the way you do your nephews, or Vedukha's two boys, even Dayan for that matter? Doesn't your own daughter deserve the same? Instead, you act as though you don't trust her."

"It's not that I don't trust her," Potis prevaricated. "I'm trying to protect her."

Again, the eyebrow went up, although Awija said nothing.

"Maybe you've got a point," Potis admitted after a moment. "You really think I should talk to her?"

"The sooner, the better," Awija urged. "Preferably before she goes into seclusion prior to her presentation."

Potis looked over to where Naya, Melit and Elēn were finishing up their after-dinner chores. "I can't now," he said. "I'm expected down at the river..."

"She and the other girls have their final meeting with me this evening," Awija conceded, "but by tomorrow, before the start of her vigil."

"Alright," Potis agreed. "Now I really do have to go." Once again, he turned to leave.

"What about Aytal?"

"Does it have to be tonight?"

Awija nodded.

"The horses can't be left unattended," he reminded her. "Especially now." He was silent for a moment, thinking. "Could you make it to the top of the bluff – the trail up isn't as steep as the path down into the ravine – maybe with Dayan to guide you?"

"Is that my only choice?" Awija asked.

"Aytal can meet you up there and still keep an eye on the horses from the rim. I'll have Dayan take him a message and then come back and get you, after you're finished with the girls."

"Alright," she acquiesced. "Go on then, go do your duty as a good host... and son?" For a final time Awija laid a hand on Potis's arm to detain him.

He turned back to her, wondering what more she could possibly want from him.

"I love you."

Acknowledging her words, Potis gave his mother a half-smile, then turned away.

Later the same evening...

For one last time, the girls gathered in their familiar semi-circle around the hearth in the women's tent. Awija listened with only half an ear as Uksor finished going over instructions for the next day. In the late afternoon, the initiates, as the priest's wife insisted on calling them, were to visit a hidden cove, located a short way down-river, where they would partake in a ritual cleansing. Afterwards, clothed in fresh shifts, the girls would return to the settlement where their mothers, sisters and aunts, along with the rest of the clan's women, would gather in the women's tent to conduct a ceremony and present them with gifts before accompanying them to witness the start of their vigils. Once each girl was safely inside her shelter, Awija would offering blessings as the senior priest sewed shut the entrance, using the red twine which the girls had twisted and dyed themselves.

"There is one final imperative which I wish to emphasize," Uksor said sternly, looking at each girl in turn from her seat across the hearth. Awija watched as the girls exchanged glances. The priest's wife had already inspected their shelters. Once the three days of seclusion began, they knew no one was to enter or leave until Bhlaghmn slit the sacred cord. Awija guessed they were wondering what additional instructions Uksor could have for them.

"Once you've emerged from your shelter and been presented, you'll be recognized as newly initiated young women and will be, shall we say, *eligible*," she warned. "Young men from the other clans may try to court your interest." Awija saw the girls looked at one another again. Melit raised her eyebrows at Perom, who responded in kind, as if they shared a secret. Petsna blushed. Elēn and Naya both kept their eyes downcast. *Hmmm*, thought Awija. *Better find out what that's about.*

"Under no circumstances must you succumb to temptation," the priest's wife admonished. "Your duty, above all, is to your family and your clan. Each of you will fetch a substantial bride price when you marry. This is especially important now, when our herds are so depleted. No potential husband of any merit wants to raise a son who is not his own. To be blunt, you do not get to choose with whom you couple. Have I made myself clear?'

Impressed by the gravity of Uksor's tone, as well as her message, the girls all nodded, expressions sober. Melit raised a tentative hand.

The priest's wife did not sound disposed to answer questions. "Yes? What is it?"

"What about…"

Perom, seated next to Melit, elbowed her in the ribs, cutting off whatever she'd been about to ask. Uksor frowned at them both. "What?" she repeated, sounding suspicious this time.

"Never mind," Melit apologized. "It's not important."

The priest's wife looked down her nose, still skeptical. "Heed what I say," she cautioned. "Otherwise, you'll disgrace yourselves and your families. Worse, you'll ruin your worth to the clan." Appropriately cowed, the girls regarded her in dutiful silence. "Good," Uksor said, softening somewhat. "I'll see you tomorrow then." Her sour face twisted into the semblance of a smile. Rising, she made her way to the door. "Don't keep them too much longer," she added, addressing Awija. "They shouldn't be up late, wandering around in the dark now that guests from the other clans have begun arriving for the Gathering."

Nodding her agreement, Awija watched as the priest's wife left the tent. When she was sure Uksor was out of earshot, she turned to Melit. "What were you about to ask, my dear?"

"Well..." Melit hesitated.

"Go on. Uksor has a point, to be sure, but that needn't stop you from asking honest questions." Throughout the girls' training, Awija had worked to gain the girls' trust. Whatever Melit and Perom might be planning, she'd rather know about it ahead of time from the girls themselves.

"It's just... Saurosa..."

Melit didn't need to say more for Awija to guess what must be going through the girls' minds. "Yes, I know. Saurosa makes her own rules when it comes to coupling," she acknowledged. There was no point in mincing words; the girls were well aware of Saurosa's penchant for bedding whichever visiting warrior happened to catch her eye. Still, a bit of a reminder of clan history might be in order.

"As you've no doubt been told," Awija began, "Saurosa's father, who was a younger brother of the old clan chief, was already well into elder-hood when Saurosa was born to his third and much younger wife. He passed not long afterwards. Saurosa's mother, in turn, succumbed to a fever when Saurosa was still a little girl, leaving her to be raised by her older brother, Skelos. So even though Saurosa is Melit's aunt, she's only five winters older than you girls." The girls nodded. This was common knowledge but didn't explain how Saurosa got away with her behavior around men.

Awija continued, "when Saurosa was a newly presented young woman like you're all about to be, she defied every rule the priest and his wife and her older brother set for her. Skelos tried more than once to discipline her into obeying him, without success. Nor would she agree to marry someone not of her own choosing. At some point, Skelos gave up trying to make her submit and so did everyone else."

More likely, Saurosa and Skelos reached an agreement about how to cooperate in order to further their mutual ambitions, but this was speculation on Awija's part. All she knew was that it hadn't take long for Saurosa's reputation to be transformed into an asset, with young men and seasoned warriors alike vying to be the one to win more than her momentary regard. Saurosa had made clear, however, that not until marriage suited her purposes, would she give her assent to wed. Until then, she enjoyed herself with whomever she pleased. As far as Awija could tell, Wailos seemed to be the current recipient of her favors.

"Surely you're not aspiring to follow in Saurosa's footsteps?" she asked the girls, pretending to be shocked but knowing full well that none of this year's group, even Melit, possessed the desire, much less the audacity, to emulate Saurosa's conquests. If Melit and Perom had a dare going, it most likely involved which of them managed an innocent kiss with a handsome young visitor before the Gathering concluded.

"No!" Melit protested, looking genuinely scandalized. She glanced at the other girls and went on. "It's just… Saurosa's been hinting about something to do with… coupling… having a role in the initiation – I mean presentation – rite." Awija had admonished them not to refer to what they were about to undergo as an initiation, even if that was the word that Uksor used. "We… that is all of us… were just wondering…"

"Ah," Awija replied. "Now I think I understand."

When Saurosa went through her training, Awija had still been permitted to discuss such matters openly, including the initiation practices followed by her own people – which featured a ritualized introduction to the sexual act – along with passing on the herbal lore associated with avoiding pregnancy. Uksor had reported Awija to Bhlaghmn, blaming her in part for Saurosa's subsequent wantonness, and the old priest had henceforth forbidden explicit mention of such topics as part of the training the clan's young women underwent before being presented to the tribe as candidates eligible for marriage.

But if the girls asked questions, Awija reasoned, she was obligated to answer them. "Sexual union is a sacred act," she began. "Coupling can bring children, of course, but it's also intended to be pleasurable, for the woman as much as the man." She had the girls' full attention. "As I've stressed throughout your training, each of you represents a vessel, which the Goddess has filled with Her own power and capacity to bring forth and nurture life. This power is to be celebrated for itself, regardless of whether an actual child results from the joining of male and female. The sexual act, and the pleasure it brings, are meant to be enjoyed – whether between a man and a woman, or between partners of the same sex. That, at least, is the teaching among my people."

Perom raised a hand. "But Uksor just said…"

"And she's right," Awija affirmed. "Regardless of how I was raised, for you girls, coupling without the sanction of the clan's leaders would have serious consequences. You mustn't forget that. But it doesn't mean you should not be taught that the coming together of two people who care for one another is meant to be a sacred experience – a gift from the Goddess herself."

Elēn raised a shy hand next. "Did you say something about partners not having to be a man and a woman?" she asked.

"I did, my dear. In the community in which I grew up, a few women sometimes desired to live solely in the company of other women and the same for men. They did so without judgment. In fact, some of our most powerful healers and priestesses either chose to remain celibate throughout their lives or partnered with another similarly inclined female friend.

"Oh!" replied Elēn, a speculative look on her face. Awija smiled to herself. She would discuss the subject further in private with her granddaughter.

"Alright," said Awija briskly. "We must move on to your individual interviews if we're not to be up all night. Who would like to be the first to go?"

This time Petsna put a hand up. "What about the ending of the story about Mehnot and Sāwel?" she asked.

"Ah yes," Awija acknowledged. "Sun and moon, male and female. Much in keeping with what we've just been discussing. However, it's getting late. Hearing the ending of the story will have to wait until after your vigils." The girls groaned in unison. "Don't be disappointed," Awija reassured them. "We mustn't hinder whatever original insights about the story might come to each of you during your period of solitude. After the Gathering is over, we'll reconvene one final time as a group, and I will tell you how the tale concludes."

Looking at the girls across the embers still burning in the hearth, Awija smiled at them fondly. "Now, who's first for your final interview?" she repeated. "The rest of you, please wait your turn outside."

"If that's all, my dear, you may be dismissed. Please send Naya in."

"Yes, Grandmother." Elēn rose, bowed her head, and ducked out of the women's tent.

Shifting on her cushion, Awija straightened her shawl across her shoulders and sighed. She'd saved the most difficult conversation for last. The other four girls were more or less ready to begin their vigils the following day. Last minute questions had been answered, and nerves had been calmed. Petsna had shyly but proudly announced to Awija that her moon-flow had begun that very day, which meant that, much to her relief, she would be eligible to be presented to the tribe along with the other girls. Awija had made sure that each girl would heed Uksor's admonitions. In contrast to the freedom and prerogatives gained by the clan's newly-initiated young men, as eligible young women they would have to be guarded as carefully as the clan's most valuable livestock until suitable marriages could be arranged, lest they be captured and carried off by raiders, a danger that had increased in recent years as drought drove unfamiliar tribes into Plānos territory. Given the clan's current predicament and how high the stakes were, Uksor was not wrong to emphasize to the girls what they could expect – and what would be expected of them – following their presentation.

At least Awija had the final word. Meeting individually with the girls on the eve of their vigils offered her the opportunity to reinforce one of the primary teachings she'd tried to convey to them throughout their training: contrary to the messages received from the priest, his wife, and most likely their own families – as well as symbolized by the presentation ceremony – their value as young women consisted of more than their marriage prospects. In addition, by affording the girls a last chance this evening to share with her their deepest hopes and fears for the future, Awija hoped to be able to advocate with their fathers and the clan's other leaders on their behalf, giving them at least an indirect voice in the decisions affecting them.

The twins, she would argue, should not be separated – two brothers from another clan would be ideal. Melit deserved a young warrior who was her equal in both wit and self-assurance, as well as kindness – otherwise there would be trouble. Elēn must be given another year or two at least to further her studies as a healer. She might prefer not to marry at all, if possible, now that she'd learned another option might exist. And last but not least, Naya. As Potis's daughter, and Awos's granddaughter, she represented the greatest prize of all and thus faced the greatest risk. Like one of those captured horses down in the ravine, if tamed against her will, Naya's spirit would die as surely as if she'd been offered as a sacrifice. Awija must do everything in her power to prevent such a tragedy from occurring.

She sighed again. *Where was the girl?*

At last, the tent flap twitched aside and her granddaughter entered. Eyes downcast, she seated herself on the vacant cushion.

"Do you have any questions, my dear?" Awija began. "You were very quiet earlier."

"No, Grandmother," Naya replied, not looking up.

Awija counted three heart beats. "Enough!" she said, more abruptly than she intended. "Naya," she commanded, "look at me."

Naya raised her head. Awija glimpsed the same troubled expression she'd noticed at supper but before she could begin to decipher the meaning, Naya withdrew behind a mask of polite attentiveness. Awija pressed ahead anyway.

"If you have no questions, I have some important matters to discuss with you."

"Yes, Grandmother."

"We'll start with your grandfather's last words on the night he passed." *That got her attention*, Awija thought, seeing a spark of interest flash across her granddaughter's features. Perhaps Naya had heard rumors of Awos's deathbed utterances.

"He spoke of the horses… and you," she said. "He was certain you'd return from your winter on the steppe, and when you did, he said the horses would come with you. He predicted that with their help, our people would become more powerful than could be imagined, able to transform the world. He warned we must never forget the horses' gift. We would owe them our lives and our future."

To Awija's dismay, relaying the old chief's final prophecy failed to elicit the reaction she intended, or any reaction at all. No angry outburst, no tearful confession. Instead, although Naya did not look away again, her eyes went cold, as though she'd disappeared behind a wall of granite. She said nothing.

Awija tried again. "What about your own visions?" she prompted.

"You've been granted the gift of sight. If you close yourself off from it, as you seem intent on doing, you risk sacrificing something precious. You keep saying you don't remember, but that's what worries me. If your dreams and visions are to reveal themselves, you must have the courage to receive them. Only then can you serve your life's purpose and honor the horses' offering, as your grandfather has foreseen."

No response.

"You've been given a task, Naya," Awija admonished, losing patience. "You and the red filly have started something. You've created a bond. Even if you've decided that for her sake, you never want to see her again, the rest of the herd trapped down in that ravine can't be ignored. You're responsible for them being there. The future your grandfather foretold is happening, whether you want it to or not. Our relationship with horses will never go back to what it was before."

Naya continued to regard her in stony silence. Awija was determined to penetrate her granddaughter's defenses. "You have to show everyone what's possible, Naya!" she insisted. "Otherwise, men like Wailos will be in charge and the horses will suffer. Is that really what you want?"

"You don't know anything about Wailos or about what I want!" Naya erupted, leaping to her feet. Red hair, escaped from its braid, rioted rebelliously around her shoulders. Awija had succeeded, perhaps a little too well, in provoking a response. "You don't know anything about me," Naya continued, voice rising. "You just don't think I should marry Wailos, even though you know it's what Papa wants."

"That's not…" Awija started to object, but Naya had already turned on her heel and headed for the door. "Stop trying to ruin everything," she demanded over her shoulder. "I don't care about some supposed prophecy. I don't want anything to do with horses! I just want my father to be proud of me. Leave me alone and let me live my life!"

Before Awija could stop her, Naya yanked aside the entrance flap and disappeared, leaving her grandmother speechless – and more concerned than ever.

Chapter Fifteen

Later the same night…

Sitting alone in the darkened women's tent waiting for Dayan to fetch her, Awija reflected on the disastrous exchange with her granddaughter. The girl had her father's temper. Whatever had happened earlier in the day had frayed it to the breaking point. Mentioning Wailos had caused it to snap. Awija sighed. Although her granddaughter might brandish her assumptions about what was expected of her like a shield, Awija refused to believe that Naya's tender heart had completely turned to stone. Hopefully when Potis spoke with her tomorrow before the start of her vigil, he'd be able to get past the girl's defenses and set her straight about everything. So much depended on that conversation.

Just as Awija was beginning to wonder what was keeping Dayan, she heard running footsteps, followed by the appearance of the boy's head at the tent's entrance.

"Where is *Dukos*?" Dayan asked, breathless and clearly agitated. "He's not in his tent and my brother said not to tell anyone until I'd found him."

"Tell anyone what?" Awija demanded. "If you want me to help you find the clan chief, you'll have to tell *me* at least what all the fuss is about."

"The horses," Dayan replied. "They've escaped!"

All evening the big mare had been more restless than usual, communicating her disquiet to the others. Something in the atmosphere had changed. If she and her herd had been out on the open steppe, she would have kept them moving. Instead, trapped in the enclosure the two-leggeds had built, all the mare could do was pace the fence line, looking futilely for a way out – just as she had done ever since she and the others had first been captured. The disturbance she sensed, along with the danger it might represent, was not imminent. The mare didn't believe they were about to be attacked. But she couldn't identify the source of the mounting tension in the air, and that had her worried.

Perhaps part of what she was feeling was left over from what had happened earlier in the day. The quiet human who she and the rest of the herd had come to trust, at least a little, was bringing them food, as he did several times a day. His presence was much less upsetting than the other two-leggeds who entered the enclosure. The one who stalked like a wolf preparing to attack was especially frightening, particularly when he carried the tall stick with the rope at the end. So far, the big mare had fought hard to elude the noose settling around her neck. Not all her herd mates had been as successful. This afternoon, however, the quiet one had brought another two-legged into the pen with him. The horses recognized her from last winter – she'd been kind and trustworthy – but since the herd's capture, she'd only visited once and had kept her distance.

This time, as soon as the girl entered the enclosure, the big mare sensed something different about her – not intimidating like the wolf-man – but her presence still made the mare nervous. What little she could feel coming from the girl was scrambled and difficult to decipher. More disturbing was the blank space where her heart should have been. The mare depended on being able instantly to sense and interpret the intentions of those around her, whether the other members of her herd, or a potential predator. She didn't understand what to make of the girl, other than that she seemed to be hiding something or to be disconnected somehow. This made the mare concerned for the safety of herself and the other horses. The girl wasn't threatening – but she had no comfort to offer either, despite the food she held out at arm's length. For the sake of her herd mates, the mare had wanted the confusing two-legged to back off. Unfortunately, the girl had been oblivious to her warning signals until finally the mare resorted to chasing her out of the enclosure.

The incident stuck with the mare, adding to her sense of unease. And now the quiet one had left them alone, a strange occurrence that had not happened since the horses' capture, at least not during the night. The only other time he'd gone away after dark, another two-legged – one of the kinder ones – had stayed behind in his place. Otherwise, the quiet one had always been present, except during the day when he went to gather food for them. At night, the big mare had been aware of him, resting under the tree, or sometimes inside his shelter, but always keeping watch. Once she'd come to understand that he could be relied upon as a sentinel, looking out for the herd's safety, the mare occasionally relaxed her own vigilance.

Tonight, however, the quiet one had climbed up the trail that led out of the ravine, leaving behind only the dog. The mare didn't mind the dog – he wasn't dangerous – but she had no confidence that he would be of any use if something were to happen. And every fiber of the mare's being told her that something was about to happen.

Just then, the sound of feet sliding on loose gravel alerted her to the careless approach of at least one two-legged – no, two – coming into the ravine from the bluff top above on a path different from the one the humans normally travelled. The dog set up a deafening racket, sending all the horses, the mare included, into a frenzied gallop along the solidly built fence line.

Just as suddenly, the dog's infernal noise ceased. Coming to a stop, the big mare turned, signaling the others to stay behind her while she assessed the danger. She lifted her head. Her nostrils flared at the familiar scent of the intruders. The dog must have known them as well. One was merely annoying. The other – the wolf-man – she feared, though not enough to flee. Instead, the mare stood her ground, arching her neck and shaking her mane defiantly. She didn't need to remind the others to remain alert. Heads lifted, the herd waited.

Before long, the two-leggeds reached the place where a gap appeared in the fence whenever they wanted to enter the enclosure. The big mare had tested that part of the pen repeatedly to see if the herd could break through but without success. While the annoying one held aloft a lighted torch, the wolf-man appeared to work at untying the stout ropes that kept the gap closed. He continued for some time, longer than the mare had learned to expect. At last, he stepped back and moved away. No opening appeared. To the mare, the fence still looked solid, but she couldn't tell for sure.

As she watched, the wolf-man and the other two-legged approached another spot along the fence and climbed over. They separated and began to drive her and the other horses toward where the opening in the fence should have been, pushing them up against the barrier. With no avenue of escape, the horses began to panic. Turning to face the two-leggeds, the big mare prepared to hold them off. The other mares, along with the youngsters, pressed into a tighter knot, leaning against the fence, which groaned under the pressure of their collective weight.

The two-leggeds kept advancing, although more slowly, as though waiting for something to happen. Just as the mare made up her mind to charge, she heard snapping, like the crack of a tree branch. A gap in the fence appeared. As one, the herd wheeled. Chests crashing against the broken barrier, the adult horses fought their way clear of splintered wood and severed rope. The youngsters followed. The dog, straining against the tether that kept him tied to the big tree, barked uncontrollably, adding to the horses' determination to flee. Led by the big mare, the entire band rushed past the dog and disappeared, galloping toward the freedom of the open steppe.

Moments afterward, back at the settlement…

"Where's Aytal?" Awija demanded.

"He went back down to the corrals, to see what happened." Dayan was nearly desperate. "What should I do?" he asked, hopping from one foot to the other. "He told me to tell *Dukos*, and no one else."

"If you've already checked the clan chief's dwelling and he's not there, my guess would be the men's tent," Awija answered. "Your brother is right to alert Potis first. We must make sure he knows that Aytal didn't have anything to do with the horses' escape. Where did you say he was when it happened?"

"At the top of the trail leading down this side of the bluff," Dayan answered "He didn't want for you to have to go so far in the dark, so instead of waiting at the edge of the ravine where he could still look down and see the horses, he came most of the way back with me. We heard Amu barking, but then he stopped, and we didn't think much of it and kept going. When we got to where the trail starts down from the top of this side of the bluff, he said he'd wait there and I was just about to head down to fetch you when we heard Amu start barking again, frantically this time. We both ran back to the other side of the bluff. We could see, even in the dark, that the horses had broken through the fence. Aytal sent me to find *Dukos* while he went down after them."

The boy, anxious to carry out his brother's instructions, clearly wanted Awija's help in deciding what he should do.

"I'll go with you to find Potis," she reassured him. "You can wait outside the men's tent while I see if he's there. No sense alerting the others sooner than necessary, although of course they're bound to find out. But if we can give Potis even a little advance warning, it will help. Come with me."

Their efforts to be discreet made little difference. As Awija suspected, the men were meeting late, discussing how to make as impressive an entrance with the captured horses as possible in front of the rest of the assembled tribe. News of the horses' escape spread like wildfire and soon the entire settlement was in an uproar. Torches were lit and a contingent sent to investigate. How the herd had managed to break free was unclear; there didn't seem to be a plausible explanation for why the corral fence had given way. Several of the men, Skelos chief among them, wanted to blame Aytal for failing to secure the gate, an accusation Aytal adamantly denied. No one noticed when Tausos, inspecting the wreckage, unobtrusively extracted the frayed remnants of the stout ropes that should have held the gate closed.

Later, showing his find to Potis when the two were alone in Potis's tent, Tausos pointed out the subtle but unmistakable signs that the ropes had been partially severed with a sharp blade – just enough to weaken them, without making it obvious they'd been cut. The weight of a full-grown horse leaning against the fence in just the right place would easily have been enough to complete the job. Reaching the same conclusion, the two brothers regarded one another in grim silence. Someone had deliberately forced the horses against the weakened fence, enabling them to escape while making it look like the herd had broken free on their own.

"You know who did this," Tausos remarked quietly.

"Of course," Potis replied. "It's no coincidence that *both* Wailos and Krnos were missing tonight. I'd bet Skelos's story about them leaving together to join up with Wailos's father was nothing more than a ruse. But as usual, we can't prove anything without more evidence. As long as Ceru arrives as planned with the bull and the rest of our livestock, it doesn't matter – we don't need the horses – but we can't let on that's the case. We have to act like the loss of the captured herd is a crisis."

Tausos nodded in agreement. "Blame the young stranger," he counseled. "That's what the others will expect."

"Unfortunately, you're right," Potis concurred. "He'll have to take responsibility, at least for the time being. Is there any word from Sunus? He should be back by now. What could be keeping him?"

"I'm worried as well," Tausos confessed. "I wish we could send someone else to check. Maybe I should go myself."

"No. Your absence would be too obvious," the clan chief disagreed. "I have a better idea," he said after a moment. "Aytal can go."

Tausos looked skeptical. "In order for that to work, we'd have tell him at least some of the truth of what's happened, not to mention trusting him not to run off, given the opportunity. You believe we can rely on him?"

"We'll have to – I don't see any other way to find out what's keeping Sunus and Ceru. We'll let everyone think that after allowing the horses to get away, he's broken the terms of his sentence and left as well. That's at least plausible."

"Only if you don't know the boy." Awija voice emerged from the back of the tent where, apparently, she'd been sitting unobserved and listening.

"Mother!" Potis exclaimed. "What are you doing here?"

"Making sure you two don't decide to do something rash," Awija replied. "It's alright," she added, addressing Tausos. "Potis has told me about everything that's happened."

The clan chief shrugged. "You know how she is," he said to his brother.

"Yes, I do," Tausos agreed, giving Potis a wry smile. "Neither you nor I ever could keep secrets from her."

"I agree that Aytal is the one to send," Awija said, "Where is he at the moment?"

"With Glōs and the boys in our tent," Tausos replied. "Amu is there too. Aytal said Naya asked him to keep the dog for her until after her presentation. I told Aytal to stay put until one of us comes for him."

"You two wait here then," cautioned Awija. "Dawn isn't far off, and with all the excitement, others might also be awake and watching. I'll stop by Tausos's tent on the way back to the women's tent. Assuming it's safe, I'll send Aytal along so you can explain to him in private as much as he needs to know. He should leave as soon as possible, before anyone sees him."

Receiving nods of agreement, Awija slipped out, intent upon her errand.

Chapter Sixteen

Morning, following the night of the horses' escape…

The start of the day was hectic, with news of the escaped herd roiling the settlement. Not long after sunrise, Naya glimpsed her father outside his tent, surrounded by the other men, discussing what to do. With only two days to go before the Gathering officially commenced, not many options existed. A hunting party had already been dispatched, in the desperate hope that the horses might have remained nearby. Meanwhile, rumors had been circulating for days that Regos, expected to arrive soon, was travelling with an impressive number of livestock. A suggestion was floated that a contingent should be sent to intercept him and ask for his assistance.

Joining the crowd outside her father's tent, Naya overheard Skelos arguing in favor of the idea, declaring that, at this point, relying on Regos's generosity was the clan's only realistic option if they were to have the animals required for the sacrificial rites. Besides, Skelos pointed out, Wailos deserved to be notified as soon as possible of the loss of the captured herd. Naya heard her father reluctantly agree but he insisted on accompanying Skelos, who had volunteered for the errand. The clan's younger priest offered to go along as well, as he could speak directly to what they would need in order to meet their ritual obligations. The three men departed almost immediately. Naya exchanged no more than a few hurried words of farewell with her father. He gave her his blessing and told her that Vedukha would have his presentation gift for her. *Everything will turn out alright*, he promised. *Trust me.* Before she could reply, he was gone.

Naya thus had no opportunity to tell her father of her conversation with Wailos the day before and what it meant – that as soon as their wedding could be formally announced, Regos was prepared to pay the bride price, ensuring that her father would have the animals he needed to fulfill the clan's obligations and retain his standing in the tribe, regardless of the loss of the horses. Perhaps Papa had already known of Regos's offer, and that's why he'd made a point of going to meet with him, and of reassuring her prior to leaving. The match would soon be finalized, Naya told herself. She just needed to have faith in what Wailos had told to her. He'd been so elated yesterday, when he kissed her before saying goodbye. Surely, she could trust him, just as she trusted her father.

Turning away after he'd gone, Naya noticed her grandmother with Uksor and Bhlaghmn outside the women's tent. Approaching closer, she overheard them discussing whether or not to carry on with the commencement of the girls' vigils in light of all the turmoil over the horses' escape and the clan chief's abrupt departure. Awija evidently wanted to postpone, maybe even put off entirely both the vigil and the presentation ceremony until next year's Gathering. To Naya's relief, the priest and his wife insisted on going forward, overruling Awija's objections. For once, Naya was grateful for Uksor's intervention. She could only imagine how a delay might have impacted plans for her to marry Wailos. Now that the horses had escaped, the announcement of their engagement and payment of the bride price must take place as soon as possible. Leave it to her grandmother to try to interfere.

Throughout the remainder of the morning and early afternoon, as Naya and the other girls helped one another stock their shelters with everything they would need for their three days in seclusion, Naya was careful to avoid crossing paths with Awija. She did not want to risk a repeat of the previous evening's confrontation. She'd been unconscionably rude, losing her temper and storming out, but she hadn't been able to help herself. She'd felt jagged and on edge after her conversation with Aytal and the incident at the corrals. Her grandmother's insistence on sharing her grandfather's dying words – words that confirmed Naya's responsibility for all the harm she'd caused – had been almost more than she could bear. Listening to Awija berate her as a coward for abandoning her heart's desire, while disparaging the man she intended to marry, sent her over the edge. At least the captured herd had managed to escape, and there'd been no sign of the red filly, the gray stallion and the mare, at least according to Aytal. Hopefully all the horses were safe and far away by now.

Naya pushed the encounter with her grandmother out of her mind. By mid-afternoon, hot and sweaty from their preparations, she and the other girls were more than ready to visit the hidden cove and bathe in the cool, refreshing water. Afterwards, dressed in clean shifts, they sat on sun-warmed rocks along the bank, talking and laughing and combing out one another's damp hair until it was time to make their way back to the settlement.

The ceremony that followed was a simple one. In the presence of the clan's women, crowded together inside the women's tent, the five girls were called one by one to gather in front of the central hearth. With Uksor keeping time with a drum and Vedukha playing a bone flute while several of the other women shook rattles, Awija then ritually cleansed them with smoke from a smoldering bundle of fragrant *lubhjā* before praying for their health and good fortune in the coming years.

Afterwards, amidst warm hugs, grateful tears and admiring comments from the assembled audience, each girl received the gifts prepared for her by her closest relatives and friends, and they all shared a meal of delicious delicacies – freshly ripened berries, salty *piskis* eggs, thinly sliced smoked perch and the last of the previous season's hazelnuts. After everyone had finished eating, the girls, joined by the senior priest, were escorted to their individual shelters.

One by one, Awija gave them each a small, wrapped bundle and imparted solemn words of blessing and advice before ushering them inside. Using the *miljom*-dyed twine, Bhlaghmn then sewed the entrance to each shelter firmly shut. Naya, as the last to go, noted that her grandmother appeared to view this aspect of the ritual with considerable disapproval, judging by her expression as the other girls disappeared inside their shelters. The girls had not been told what to expect at the conclusion of their three days of seclusion – only that they would be summoned at dawn, the sealed entrances to their shelters would be cut open, and thereafter the final stage of the ritual would be completed, followed by presentation to the tribe.

Glad to finally be on her own in her shelter after all the day's excitement, Naya carefully folded the new dress that Vedukha had given her and laid it aside with her other gifts. A sturdy clay-fired cooking pot from one of her aunts and a practical woven satchel with leather carrying straps from her other aunt sat alongside her present from Melit, a capacious gathering sack made from soft deer skin. The two girls had laughed delightedly when they'd exchanged gifts – Naya had given Melit a nearly identical deer skin sack. Her father's present, a bison fur robe, lay folded next to the new clothing. Naya suspected Vedukha had made it in secret, along with the dress, from hides her father had provided. The other belongings she'd brought into the shelter with her earlier in the day – her bow and arrows, the auroch horn Aytal had fashioned for her, the horse collar her mother had woven from rawhide and the old tunic and leggings she'd worn last winter – were stowed in a corner. Naya wasn't sure why, but she'd grabbed them on impulse. More useful items which she habitually kept handy – her all-purpose knife, fire-starting kit, water skin and a coil of rope – had been tossed in a jumbled heap nearby.

Straightening, Naya looked around the small but cozy space that was hers alone for the next three days and nights and allowed herself what felt like the first breath she'd taken since learning of the horses' escape. A fire had been laid in the hearth, while several stuffed cushions, piled atop her sleeping mat, offered a comfortable place to rest. Containers of prepared food, along with jugs of water, were stored near the entrance. An old pot had been provided for waste, to be slid through a special gap under the tent wall when in need of emptying, so that she never had to leave the shelter. Indeed, she could not leave, not without slitting the cord which secured the shelter's entrance. Naya relished the prospect of solitude. Time alone might help to sort out her feelings. She might even get a good night's sleep.

First, however, she wanted to unwrap her remaining gifts – three small packages contained within the bundle her grandmother had handed her just before bestowing her final blessing. Sitting on her bed roll, Naya laid the packages out on the ground in front of her. The largest was from Awija herself but the others had been entrusted to her grandmother to give to Naya. One, Awija told her, was from her mother; the other was from Aytal. *Think about the meaning of each of these gifts,* her grandmother had counseled, *and about the love with which they have been given. Each comes with a message and a promise. Heed them.*

Naya unwrapped Awija's present first. Despite last night's argument, she felt less ambivalent about finding out what her grandmother had given her than about opening the other two packages. The gift, wrapped in a square of soft felt and tied with a thin rawhide thong, was about the diameter of her cupped hands but too insubstantial to contain anything as solid as a wooden bowl or pottery jar.

Untying the thong, she folded back the felt covering to reveal something as familiar as the stories of her childhood. It was her grandmother's *tekstlom* – her dream-web. Pliable willow fronds had been bent to form a hoop, then tightly wrapped with rawhide to serve as a frame, across which had been woven taut threads of the finest sinew. A sprinkling of tiny beads made of copper and jet adorned the crisscrossing strands like iridescent raindrops clinging to a spider's web. A single owl feather dangled from a leather loop at the top. Naya suspected her grandmother had gifted all the initiates with *tekstloms*, in keeping with the focus of their training, but Naya recognized that this one was special, as it had belonged to Awija herself.

How many times as a little girl had Naya gazed up at the fascinating object, suspended over Awija's sleeping mat, as her grandmother cuddled her under warm blankets and recounted the old tales? When she'd asked about it, twirling gently above her as though dancing with the invisible currents of air that carried smoke from the fire toward the opening at the top of the tent, her grandmother had explained that dreams came in the same way that the smoke went out, and that the *tekstlom* caught and held the dreams so they would be waiting for Awija to remember in the morning when she awoke.

Turning the *tekstlom* in her hands, Naya traced the intricate web. Could the delicate threads, interspersed with precious beads, truly capture her dreams, causing them to linger long enough for her to recall? She hadn't lied to her grandmother about lately being unable to remember whatever visited her in the night, even if she hadn't been honest about *why* she could no longer remember. The truth was she didn't *want* to remember. Awija was right. Naya was afraid – afraid that her pursuit of the red filly could cause her blackest visions to come true. And so she'd made up her mind, for the sake of Réhda and the other horses, to do everything in her power never again to follow her heart's desire – even in her dreams.

Now however, sitting with Awija's gift in her lap and her admonitions echoing in her ears, Naya allowed herself a moment of doubt about her choices. Holding the *tekstlom* aloft, she watched it slowly spin. Since her return to the settlement, she'd been visited repeatedly by a *swopnjājō* – a big dream – just as her grandmother had described to her and the other girls. Nothing else explained her disturbed sleep and the fatigue she felt. She'd been grateful not to know what was happening in the dark, but what if Awija's warnings were correct and the dream contained important information about Naya's future or the wellbeing of those she loved? Most concerning, what if her unwillingness to recall the contents of the dream resulted in further harm to the horses?

Much as she'd tried to shield herself from the truth, Awija might be right about it already being too late. Even if Réhda, Šuurgan and MeHnd were likely far away by now, and the rest of the captured herd had managed to escape, what about the future? Not the future her grandfather had foretold in his prophecy, but the future Naya had foreseen in her nightmares – a future in which more wild horses were trapped and forcibly tamed, only to be held for slaughter and sacrifice, or worse. Yet what was she supposed to do? The forces Naya had unwittingly set in motion seemed more than she could comprehend, let alone control.

On her own for the first time since her retreat from the bluff top the day after her return to the settlement, the exhaustion and despair she'd been fending off finally caught up with Naya. *I'm so tired*, she admitted. She didn't have the energy to hang the *tekstlom* above her sleeping mat and risk encountering a prophetic dream – not yet – even if she recognized that eventually, for the horses' sake, perhaps she must. Nor was she prepared to face whatever messages the gifts from her mother and Aytal might contain. She'd save them for tomorrow. Rewrapping her grandmother's gift, Naya placed all three bundles back among her other presents and instead turned her attention to the task of preparing a soothing mug of tea, hoping for the mercy of a good night's rest.

The following day…

Naya awoke feeling groggy and confused. At first she didn't remember where she was. Once she recalled, she had no idea how much time had elapsed since she'd gone to sleep. From the shadows cast by the trees against the shelter walls, she guessed with surprise that the sun must already have climbed past the zenith and started to descend. She couldn't remember ever having slept so late into the day. Unfortunately, rather than feeling restored, when she tried to rise she was overcome by a surge of dizziness. Her head throbbed, threatening to turn her stomach. Perhaps with all the excitement of the day before, she'd not had enough to drink. Reaching for her water skin, she took a sip. The contents tasted warm and stale – not particularly refreshing – but she didn't have the strength to pour a fresh cup from one of the water jars stored near the shelter's entrance.

Ah well, Naya thought, laying back against the pillows and pulling her lightweight felt blanket up to her chin. For once she didn't have to get up if she didn't feel like it. Closing her eyes again and rolling onto her side with her knees drawn up to her chest, she concentrated on breathing slowly in, then out – hoping to stop her sleeping mat from spinning.

The second night of Naya's vigil…

The next time she awoke, darkness had fallen. Again, Naya needed a moment to orient herself. With no moon to illuminate the darkness beyond the shelter's walls and the hearth within having gone cold, her surroundings were as black as the inside of a cave. She should have thought to add enough wood to keep the fire going, as much for light as for warmth, but she hadn't planned to sleep for so long. Now, if she wanted to see, she would have to search out her flint kit and go through the laborious process of reigniting the flames – unless by some chance a coal still smoldered amidst the ashes…

Sometime later, Naya sat cross-legged on her sleeping mat in front of a small blaze. She'd been lucky to find a few embers with enough spark left to catch the tufts of dried cattail fuzz she kept in her fire-starting kit. Before long, she was able to add small twigs and then larger branches from the wood pile that sat just inside the shelter's entrance. Once the rekindled flames burned strongly enough to enable her to see, she'd relieved herself, gotten water and food from her stores and then returned to her place beside the hearth. With only a glimpse of dark sky

191

visible through the smoke hole, she had no way to judge from the stars how far gone the night was or when dawn might come. At least her headache had dissipated. She now felt wide awake, with no inclination to go back to sleep. Indeed, if daybreak was not far off, more than half her vigil had already passed – only another day and night remained. She still had much to ponder.

Glancing upwards, Naya wondered what might have occurred if she'd hung her grandmother's *tekstlom* above her bed after all. Given how she'd felt when she'd awoken earlier, she must have been visited by the *swopnjājō*. Would she have remembered? She was glad she hadn't chanced finding out, whatever Awija might say to the contrary. Waking up feeling woozy and nauseous was bad enough. Even though she'd begun to accept that at some point she would have to confront whatever disturbing images and messages the dream might contain, she wanted to wait until she at least felt more rested.

Gazing into the fire in her small hearth, Naya recalled the other occasions since returning to the settlement when she'd been unwell or simply not herself: watching the captured herd from the bluff top on that first morning; later, during Aytal's sentencing, when she thought she'd seen the red filly; and then again when she'd gone down to the corrals with Wailos. Most recently had been the disconcerting incident when she'd actually gone into the horses' pen with Aytal. She'd felt so strangely detached, almost as if watching someone else from a distance – until she'd nearly gotten trampled.

Recalling the horses' reaction to her presence, Naya felt a fresh stab of pain. She'd been humiliated and angry to have been chased out of the corral – and yes, she'd taken it out on Aytal, which she regretted – but what hurt most was the horses' rejection. Naya had worked hard all fall and winter to gain the friendship not only of the red filly but of her entire band, even Rebhjo. Yet judging by the big mare's reaction, Naya had apparently thrown it all away. Did the horses somehow know their loss of freedom was ultimately Naya's fault? Did they blame her, as she blamed herself, for teaching them to trust humans? If she ever saw the red filly again, would she reject Naya too?

Naya didn't think she could bear it. She and the filly had a bond like no other human had with a horse. In renouncing her heart's desire to be with Réhda, had she given up too much? Reaching with a stick, she stirred the coals. She'd had good reasons, she reminded herself. Once she'd learned the intended fate of the captured herd, she hadn't wanted to draw attention to Réhda and the gray stallion and the mare. Better to keep her distance. And then, out of loyalty to her father, after all the disappointment and harm she'd caused, she'd made up her mind to be the best possible daughter she could be. Naya didn't want to fail her father the way she'd failed the horses. She didn't want to betray him either, not the way her mother had done.

Thinking of her mother reminded Naya of her two remaining un-opened gifts. Sliding forward on her knees, she retrieved them and re-turned to her seat in front of the hearth. She considered each in turn. In light of Aytal's feelings for her, opening whatever he'd given her would require more courage than she presently possessed. She set his gift aside.

The present from her mother, wrapped in a scrap of worn hide, the corners gathered and tied with a length of thread, lay in the palm of her hand. Naya regarded the small bundle.

She'd been so upset before her mother went away – outraged on her father's behalf and resentful on her own. Afterwards, once the hot flame of her anger had cooled, Naya made an effort to understand her moth-er's decision to leave, concluding that she must have been profoundly unhappy, and at the same time, too irresolute to resist the temptation that Oyuun offered. Perhaps her mother really had been homesick.

Still, Naya hadn't been able to bring herself to excuse her mother's behavior. Personal desires and discontent did not justify the aban-donment of duty to family. Hadn't Naya learned that lesson? After all her past mistakes, she'd given up *her* selfish longings. Why hadn't her mother been able to do the same? Naya loved her mother – missed her even – but she was determined to hold herself to a higher standard.

Disapproving of her mother's choices, however, didn't mean that Naya wasn't curious. She pulled at the ends of the thread until it came untied, then watched as the corners of the linen wrapping fell away. In her palm lay an exquisitely crafted obsidian arrowhead, fashioned into a necklace, with an intricately knotted cord wrapped around the base. Examining its unique shape, Naya realized the arrowhead could only have belonged to one person – Aytal – which meant it had come from his arrow, the one that had nearly killed her. But this was not a gift from him.

Last winter, when her mother had returned the arrowhead to Naya, she'd explained the obsidian point represented a powerful talisman, symbolic of Naya's miraculous survival and recovery. A little in awe, Naya had placed it for safekeeping in her *makēn* – the pouch she wore at her waist. Then a few days prior to arriving back at the settlement this spring, her mother had asked for the arrowhead, saying she wanted to make it into a necklace to go along with the bear's tooth her father had given her. Naya had forgotten all about her mother's promise to return it before the Gathering.

Holding the necklace up by the cord, Naya watched as the obsidian pendant slowly revolved, its myriad facets refracting the firelight. The arrowhead was beautiful – and deadly. Naya didn't want to consider how close she'd come to losing her life, nor how its course had changed afterwards. How different things might have been if she and her mother had not had to spend the long winter in the clearing with two strangers, away from her father and the rest of the clan, but surrounded by the horses.

If she'd never been injured, left hovering at the threshold between two worlds, she might never have journeyed with the drum and seen the remarkable image of the sun and moon combined, nor heard again the voice from her visions – even if she had yet to recall the words the voice had spoken to her. She might never have found the opportunity nor the courage to pursue her dream of riding the red filly. She never would have known the pure joy of galloping with her across the steppe, nor afterwards, the equally sweet exhilaration of being held within the security of Aytal's embrace – even if neither experience could ever be repeated. Nor would she and her mother have shared the miracle of assisting MeHnd to give birth. She remembered how proud they had been, watching together as the fragile but feisty colt first found his feet.

Perhaps, Naya thought, slipping the necklace's cord over her head, she'd been dwelling too much on her nightmare fears for the future, instead of treasuring all the precious memories from the past. She pulled at the knotted ends along the cord's length, shortening the necklace until the arrowhead hung just below the bear's tooth that nestled at the base of her throat. Reaching up, she pressed lightly, feeling the arrowhead's smooth, flaked surface against her skin, then used a fingertip to trace its knife-sharp edges. She liked the way the obsidian felt – the cool weight of it. Still, the necklace was a gift from her mother; she wasn't sure she wanted to wear it.

Lifting it back over her head, she carefully coiled the cord and was about to place the necklace in the *makēn* at her waist when she stopped to study the arrowhead one last time. Her mother had been the one to pull the arrow from Naya's back, saving her life. She – not Naya's father – had stayed behind when Naya was too injured and sick to travel, caring for her until they could both return home. Throughout the winter and spring, her mother's faith in Naya's quest to tame the red filly had never wavered. She'd made the rawhide collars for her and Aytal, and despite concerns for Naya's safety, cheered on each of her attempts to ride Réhda, culminating in her eventual success. Naya owed her mother more than just her life.

Naya's hand closed around the necklace as a wave of longing washed over her. She missed her mother more than she dared admit. Eyes and nose stinging, she dashed away an errant tear. *No!* she silently protested. *I will not let her make me cry!* Her fist clenched hard around the arrowhead until its sharp edges bit into her palm. The pain gave her something to focus on. *I will not cry*, she repeated to herself. After a moment the tightness in her chest eased. Uncurling her fingers, she took a deep inhale, then another, until her breathing returned to normal. Feeling for her *makēn*, she deposited the necklace without looking at it. Someday she'd be able to wear it, Naya told herself, just not yet.

Only then did she notice that the darkness outside had shifted to the gray light of dawn. Sunrise, marking the official commencement of the Gathering, was not far off. She should make herself something to eat, then decide what to do with her final day of solitude.

The third day of Naya's vigil…

Normally Naya did not mind spending time alone. Outdoors on the open steppe, with so much to observe, she rarely felt at a loss for something to hold her interest and time flowed by without her noticing. Being confined indoors with nothing to occupy her proved more difficult than Naya had anticipated. After sleeping through most of the first part of her vigil, today she felt wide awake and bored, with nothing to distract her from her own thoughts. She supposed that was the point, but recognizing the fact did little to alleviate the monotony.

The tedious passage of time – along with thoughts stirred by her mother's gift – brought back memories of her convalescence last winter.

195

Then at least she'd had company – even if she'd made a point of ignoring Aytal and his father – and once she'd recovered sufficiently, she'd kept busy, mostly at the behest of her mother, who always seemed to have some task for her to accomplish. Later, when she'd been able to venture outside on her own, the horses had been waiting for her…

At last, seeing from the shifting shadows against the shelter walls that the day was finally almost spent, Naya prepared a simple supper using the last of her stores. There was no point in conserving – sometime near dawn someone would come for her and the vigil would end.

Finished eating, she sat beside the fire sipping tea and deliberating about how much longer she should make herself wait before going to sleep. Not long, she decided, ready for the vigil to be over, but that meant she could no longer put off the one thing she'd been avoiding all day – finding out what was in her present from Aytal.

The awkwardly wrapped package still sat unopened amidst her other gifts. At one point she'd thought about getting rid of it – burying it somewhere or tossing it in the river – but she couldn't imagine actually throwing away something he'd meant for her. Still, she hadn't been able to summon the nerve to face whatever was inside. Opening the gifts from Awija and her mother had been difficult enough.

When, she wondered, had Aytal managed to give the package to Awija to pass along to her? He'd been conspicuously absent immediately after the horses had escaped and there had been talk that he had run off as well, although Naya found that hard to believe. Still, as she thought back, she realized she had not seen him – or Amu – at any point throughout the day prior to the start of her vigil. At the time, she'd been too preoccupied with preparations to give their absence much heed but now, after a long day alone with her thoughts, she'd grown worried. The worry in turn made her irritated. She didn't want to be preoccupied by anything to do with Aytal. Tomorrow she would be embarking on the next stage of her life, in which he would play no part. If he *had* left, and taken Amu with him, perhaps she should see it as a blessing.

"Coward," she said aloud to her tea. "Just get it over with!" Putting down the mug, Naya crawled over to retrieve the package, then returned to her seat before the hearth. Now that she looked closely, she recognized the scrap of felted wool, soft and pliable from years of use, in which Aytal had wrapped the gift. It was one of her mother's rags which they'd employed so often to groom the horses that Sata had not wanted it back. A rawhide thong tied the cloth closed around something that felt solid, despite its small size.

Curious now that she'd made up her mind, Naya undid the wrapping. Her breath caught in her throat. Nestled in the folds of the old rag lay the form of a horse, carved from wood and stained with red ochre and charcoal. Turning the figurine in her hands, Naya was mesmerized by the exquisite detail. Gaze forward, ears erect, the little horse stood proudly, mane and tail waving as though caught by an unseen wind – unmistakably the very image of Rédha. Naya recognized all that Aytal had put into its creation: the time, the skill, and most of all, the love.

She felt something inside her crack, like an ice dam about to give way. She tried to inhale but could barely breathe, as though she might be drowning.

But she did not drown. She refused. She would not give in to her feelings. Forcing herself, Naya took one long, shuddering breath, then another, and another, and another, until, at last, she felt reasonably calm. She'd turned back the storm of grief and regret without surrendering.

Rewrapping the figure of the little horse, Naya placed it in her *makēn* alongside the arrowhead necklace from her mother, then returned to her mat by the fire and lay down. She'd known opening these last gifts would be hard – Awija had warned her – but she'd survived. Now, perhaps, she could move on. Tomorrow would mark a new start.

Blanket pulled up to her chin, she willed herself to sleep.

Chapter Seventeen

After midnight…

That night, as on many nights since returning to the settlement, Naya dreamed. Unlike the shadowy, indistinct landscape of her old nightmares, the dreamscape in which she found herself this time was unbearably bright – a flat, featureless world scorched by the merciless rays of an unrelenting sun that seared her eyes, parched her throat and blistered her skin. She could find no relief, for nowhere was there shade, water, nor indeed any sign of life.

Wandering in this harsh, sunbaked wasteland, she heard a scream. Thinking that the cry might have come from the red filly, she turned, wanting to save the young horse from whatever threatened her. Instead, turning, she saw herself, a black-tipped arrow fletched with raven-feathers protruding from her chest. The scream had been her own.

Now I must die, she thought. Far from experiencing fear, however, she felt detached, almost numb. Instead of collapsing to the ground, she saw herself calmly grasped the arrow shaft with both hands, pulling it from her chest. Only then did she discover that the arrowhead had not imbedded itself in her beating heart, as she might have expected, but rather pierced the carved stone head of her father's ceremonial mace.

The stone throbbed, as though alive. Observing herself from a distance, Naya knew that if she wanted to survive, she must extract the arrow and place the stone heart back inside her chest. Not until she grasped the shaft, however, did Naya recognize the arrow as one of her own. Dismayed, she dropped the stone heart, at which point the arrow's shaft transformed back into the handle of her father's ceremonial mace.

Next, as Naya watched, a figure appeared with the legs, arms and torso of a man but the head of a wolf. Reaching down, the creature lifted the mace in both hands and held it out, gaze lowered, as though presenting an offering. After a moment's hesitation, Naya saw herself reach out to take the ceremonial symbol of her father's authority. In that instant, looking up, the creature smiled a wolfish smile so cruel that Naya wanted to call out a warning to herself to snatch her hand away. She had the sense that she should recognize the wolf-man, but before she could fathom his identity, another figure appeared, fully human, together with a horse. The pair paused, taking in the scene, then turned and walked away.

When Naya awoke and opened her eyes, the shelter was in utter darkness. Once again, she'd forgotten to stoke the fire. Disoriented, shaking and upset, she wondered for a moment if she might still be asleep. Had she heard something, a sound that had pulled her back to consciousness? With a shiver, she realized she was freezing. She'd kicked off her blanket at some point while she slept. Sitting up, she fumbled for it in the dark.

There it was again – a noise – sounding like it came from just outside the entrance to her shelter. Her heart pounded. Was she truly awake? The dream still felt so real, even though she recalled none of the details.

"Naya," a voice whispered.

She didn't respond.

The voice called again, more insistent this time. "Naya!"

Silence. Naya wasn't sure if the voice was human, let alone someone she knew.

"Naya, it's time," the voice said. "Your vigil has ended. Time for the final step in your initiation."

Relieved, Naya realized she must not still be dreaming after all. Locating the blanket at last, she gathered it around her shoulders before crawling toward the shelter's closed entrance.

"Will you let me out?" she asked. If she recalled the instructions correctly, whomever came for her – the priest? – was to sever the cord from the outside.

"No," the voice said. "You must cut the lacing from the inside. Remember?"

That didn't sound right, but perhaps she hadn't paid sufficient attention – and she was still groggy and disoriented. Yet it felt like the middle of the night, rather than just before dawn as she would have expected.

"Are you sure?" she asked. "That's not what I remember." But maybe she had it backwards.

"Naya!" the voice replied, sounding disapproving. "There's no time for this."

"But shouldn't I put on my new dress?"

"Naya!" Anger this time. "You'll change later. Hurry up and come along, or you'll disgrace yourself!" *That* sounded like the priest's wife.

"Alright," Naya replied, "let me get my knife."

Moments later, Naya emerged from her shelter. After three days inside, not moving much, she felt unsteady on her bare feet. With no moon to illuminate the little clearing, she struggled to get her bearings.

"Over here," she heard the voice say. Only then was Naya able to distinguish a darker form among the shadowy shapes of the surrounding trees. The figure wore a cloak with a hood.

"Who are you?" Naya asked.

"Silence!" the figure commanded in a stern whisper. Although disguised, the voice sounded like Uksor's. "Follow me."

"Where are we going?" Naya persisted.

"You will see."

Naya did as she was told, deciding this must be the part of the ritual that the priest's wife had left intentionally vague. Nervously, she followed along.

After the dark outside, Naya's eyes needed a moment to adjust to the warmly lit interior of the tent to which she'd been escorted. She'd been taken by her guide to the flood plain by the river, where the visiting clans were camped, and led to a cluster of shelters erected on a choice plot of ground a little apart from the rest. The site was usually reserved for the most distinguished guests assembled for the Gathering and sure enough, she was greeted by a voice which this time she was certain she recognized.

"Welcome!"

"Wailos," Naya replied, relieved.

"Who did you expect?" he asked, laughing. "Thank you," he added to the mysterious hooded figure. "You may go now. I'll take care of everything from here."

Once the figure bowed and left, he turned back to Naya. "Now," he inquired, "have you been looking forward to this as much as I have?"

He gestured for Naya to join him on the sheepskin rugs drawn up beside the hearth. She couldn't help but admire the tent's furnishings – in addition to the sheepskins, hides carpeted the ground, concealing the turf, while neatly arranged baskets and jars containing what must be stores of food and other essentials stood near the entrance. Several oil lamps hung from the tent poles, providing a soft glow of light. As she looked around, Naya noticed Wailos's weapons – his bow and quiver as well as several spears, leaning against one another in a corner, next to which a pile of clothing looked to have been recently discarded. Atop the pile was what appeared to be a cloak, fashioned from a wolf's pelt, the wolf's head, complete with snarling jaws, serving as a head covering. Naya shuddered.

"Oh, don't mind that," he assured her, following the direction of her gaze. "Come, sit." Once again, he patted a spot next to him near the fire. Naya did as he bid. She was aware of Wailos's scent – sweat, earth, and something underneath that was very male. She'd seen him before like this, bare-chested, wearing only a loin cloth and leggings, but she'd always been fully clad. Dressed only in her thin shift, the blanket around her shoulders offering scant protection, she wished she'd been given time to put on her new clothes before leaving her shelter.

"Why am I here?" she asked, once seated. The pit of her stomach started to flutter uncomfortably. Had he noticed her voice shaking? Hopefully not. She didn't want him to think less of her for being anxious for no reason, but she couldn't help continuing to feel unsettled.

"Didn't the old woman tell you?" Wailos replied. Naya assumed he meant the priest's wife. "Perhaps she didn't want you to anticipate. This is the last stage of your initiation – when you cross the threshold. You didn't really think that merely spending three days and nights alone would transform you into a woman, did you? Surely you must know that you need a man for that." He was grinning now.

"But," Naya responded, confused. "My grandmother didn't say anything about this. She would have told me."

"Maybe she thought if she discussed it with you ahead of time, you wouldn't go along," Wailos countered. "Or maybe she doesn't approve of me being the one. Sometimes I get the feeling your grandmother doesn't like me. But didn't the other girls talk to you about it? I'm sure they all understood what's meant to happen."

"No," Naya said. "Nobody said anything."

"Ah well," Wailos replied, voice reassuring. "They probably didn't know either. As it was explained to me, this is meant to be the culmination of your clan's sacred ritual for initiating its young women, and such things are generally kept secret, are they not? The other young men and I – the five of us who were selected to take part – we were told it was a great honor but that we must never reveal our identities. That's the reason for the disguise." Wailos nodded toward the wolf's head cloak. "But I knew you'd recognize me, so what's the point? In any case, I had to make sure I was the one. Under the circumstances, I insisted."

Naya said nothing. The fluttering in her stomach intensified, making her feel queasy. Was this why Awija looked so disapproving when the priest had sealed each of the girls into their shelters? Perhaps she'd been forbidden to speak to them about what to expect at the conclusion of their vigils. The priest's wife had been so adamant about the girls not choosing a partner for themselves after they'd been presented – but maybe Uksor knew that their partners had already been selected for them. In that light, everything Wailos was saying made sense and she was being needlessly silly and immature. She and Wailos were to be married, after all, so of course he would be the one chosen for her. It all just came as a surprise; she wished someone had warned her.

"But what about the wedding?" she asked, still uncertain.

"The wedding will take care of itself," Wailos replied. "Right now, discovering what it means to be a woman is much more important. Let me show you."

Rising, he made a circuit of the tent, extinguishing all but one of the lamps, then returned to where she waited, seated by the hearth. Despite the fire's warmth, Naya shivered. Noticing, Wailos lay back amidst the sheepskins, pulling her down beside him, then drew the nearest fur robe over them both. "Let me show you," he repeated. He began to stroke the skin of one bare shoulder, as if intent on taming a skittish horse.

In the beginning he was tender, and Naya attempted to follow along, as she'd been learning to do. She imagined he must be trying to arouse her, and she tried to copy his moves, thinking he was showing her what he liked. At first, he let her touch him, but before long, whatever she did just seemed to annoy him. He finally trapped both her wrists over her head, forcing her to stop, and she realized with despair that she must be doing it all wrong.

"Help me understand what you want," she managed to whisper. Instead, he silenced her, kissing her roughly without releasing her hands. When she rolled her head away in protest at the violence of his mouth on hers, he sank his teeth into the tender flesh at the back of her neck. The pain shocked her. She tried to tell him that he'd hurt her, that she didn't want him to be so rough, but he forced her mouth back to his, once again silencing her. Not only could she not speak, she felt like she couldn't breathe. Panic surged. She resisted in earnest then, trying to free herself, but most of his weight lay on top of her and he kept her arms pinned over her head. When she bucked to get out from under him, he used his free hand to yank her hair, twisting her head back and sideways until she thought her neck might snap.

"I had a feeling you'd be a wild one," he rasped, laughing in her ear. "*This* is what I like," he added, nuzzling her exposed neck. "Scream, if you want. Then everyone will know you're enjoying it."

But Naya was too terrified to scream. Failing to free herself, she now felt frozen, unable to move or utter a sound. Not long after, her awareness left her body, her essence no longer tethered to her earthly being. At one point there was a tearing sensation when he entered her. The agony of it almost brought her back, but then she floated away again to where she could observe what was happening from a distance. Even that proved too difficult, however, and she turned her eyes away, staring instead at the grimacing wolf's head until it was over. By the time Wailos finished and rolled off her, Naya was so absent she almost didn't notice.

That was why at first, when Wailos called to her, she didn't hear him. Still lying on her back where'd he left her, head turned to the side, she was cognizant of nothing beyond the wolf's empty eye-sockets, staring back at her. When she did finally notice his voice, she realized with a vague sense of surprise that he was now speaking to someone else, not her. There was someone else in the tent with them.

"Put her dress over there," Wailos was saying, "then alert the priest's wife. Just make sure to give us enough time to appear before the council." Closing her eyes, Naya waited until she was certain that whomever he'd been speaking to had left. Only then did she roll onto her side and sit up. Realizing when the cold air hit her bare skin that her shift was in tatters, she hastily pulled the fur robe around her naked chest and shoulders. Her tangled hair framed her face.

"You're quite beautiful, you know," Wailos said to her, apparently

admiring the sight. "You certainly look as though you've enjoyed yourself. Unfortunately, you can't go before the council of chiefs like that.
Here, put this on while I find a comb."

Mutely, Naya took the proffered clothing – the dress Vedukha had
made for her to wear at her presentation. Whoever had been in the tent
a moment ago must have brought it. What was happening? Did she
have to appear *now* before the assembled tribe? It was still dark, some
logical corner of her brain pointed out, the middle of the night.

"I don't understand," she ventured.

"You, my dear, were brilliant," Wailos replied over his shoulder with
an appreciative grin. "The next time you'll enjoy it even more." He moved
to the pile of discarded clothing and stood with his back to her, starting
to get dressed. "And now it's time to go before the council of chiefs and
attest that we've done the deed."

"What?" Naya still did not feel quite present. She felt raw between
her legs and wasn't sure she could stand, let alone walk. Why had no one
warned her about the pain?

Finished relacing his leggings, Wailos straightened and pulled a
buckskin shirt on over his broad chest. Flashing white teeth at her again,
he winked. "We'll have to do something with your hair, but if you braid
it to the side, it will cover the love bite – sorry about that." Nodding at
the dress, he added, "Hurry, though, they'll be waiting for us."

As they reached the men's tent, Naya put out a hand to stop Wailos
before he could enter.

"Are you sure about this?" she asked. "We're supposed to go in there
and tell them what just happened?"

"Yes, and you're already late." Saurosa stepped out of the shadows,
startling Naya. She wore a long cloak, which had served to hide her
presence outside the entrance to the tent.

"I don't understand," Naya said. "What are you doing here?"

"I'm the door keeper," Saurosa replied. "When each of the initiates
arrives with their escort, I announce them to the council." Naya couldn't
be sure, but she thought Saurosa flashed Wailos a look – either mocking
or mischievous. Another of their private jokes at her expense?

"You're the last couple to arrive," Saurosa went on. "The others have
already been and gone. They're waiting for you." She held aside the tent's
hide flap, bidding them enter. Not wanting to make a scene that might

embarrass her father in front of the other tribal leaders, Naya complied. She went in first, with Wailos behind her.

Inside, the large tent was crowded with male bodies, some seated around the central fire, the rest standing in a circle behind. Naya vaguely recognized most of them as the chiefs and priests from the other clans. From their expressions, none appeared friendly or welcoming. In fact, many scowled at the interruption. Where was her father? Searching, Naya spotted him across the fire from where she stood near the entrance. He'd risen and appeared to be trying to make his way toward her. The look on his face did not bode well. Before he'd taken more than a step in her direction, however, at a signal from a man seated nearby, two other men who had been standing unobtrusively behind her father each put a hand on either arm to restrain him. He tried to shake them off, but the two bystanders tightened their grip.

"Welcome," the seated man called, holding up a hand for silence. "I believe you all know my son and most of you will undoubtedly recognize the daughter of our host. Why is it that you've interrupted our meeting?"

Although the man's tone was friendly, a hint of cold mockery lurked underneath which Naya found unnervingly familiar. Of course, she realized, this was Wailos's father, Regos.

"Please, Potis," he was saying, "be seated. If your daughter wants to speak, by all means we must allow it. What have you to say, my dear?"

Overwhelmed, Naya could not open her mouth. This was all wrong. Searching out her father again, she sent him an anguished look. He tried to wrench free from the two men struggling to hold him back. He looked both angry and something else. With dismay, Naya realized that she saw fear in her father's eyes, something she'd never witnessed before. Only then did she begin to fully grasp what had happened – what she had done – but it was already too late.

Wailos stepped forward. "We've come to attest to the successful completion of this woman's initiation," he announced, gesturing in Naya's direction. "As is the custom of her clan, she has this night forsaken her maidenhood. Having lain with me, she is now, in every sense, a woman."

Instantly, a clamor erupted and many in the crowd who were not already standing rose to their feet. Above the tumult, Naya heard her father's voice.

"Is this true?"

She knew the question was meant for her and wanted to tell him

– tell them all – that she'd been tricked, but she knew none of the men, other than maybe her father, would believe her version of the story. Meeting his gaze from the far side of an uncrossable divide, she nodded miserably, then turned and fled the tent.

Naya's shelter…

"You're doing the right thing." Saurosa spoke matter-of-factly from where she crouched just inside the shelter's entrance. She'd followed Naya from the men's tent and now watched as Naya frantically stuffed her belongings into her satchel. "Would you like help packing?"

Looking up, Naya stared mutely at her cousin before returning to her task. Tears swam in her eyes, making it difficult to see what she was doing.

"Don't be mad at me," Saurosa laughed derisively. "You brought this on yourself. You're the one who's been throwing yourself at Wailos for the last two moons. No one with eyes will find it hard to believe that you intended to trap him into marrying you by pulling this stunt. The amusing thing is that you ever thought he'd be seriously interested in you, or that his father would sanction the match."

"I am the daughter of the clan chief!" Naya cried, voice shaking. Anger overlaid the humiliation. "Why shouldn't I have believed he wanted to marry me?"

"The point is, nothing has been announced – or even decided. But after what you've done, everyone will think you and your father concocted the whole scheme to force Regos's hand. He and his followers won't stand for it. Neither will the priests or the other clan leaders. You've almost certainly jeopardized your father's chance at becoming chief of chiefs. He may not even be able to hold on to his position as leader of the clan."

"But, but, but…" Naya sputtered, "it wasn't my idea… none of it was my idea… and my father would never do such a thing." Indignation began to give way to dismay.

"All the same, the evidence is pretty damning," Saurosa pointed out. "They'll be able to tell that instead of waiting to be released, you slit the sacred cord from the inside, letting yourself out before your vigil was complete. You then sought out Wailos, alone in his tent in the middle

206

of the night, so that you could seduce him. No doubt as we speak, he's proclaiming his own innocence to the rest of the men, explaining that you came to him with the story that bedding you was part of your initiation ritual – that you got the idea from listening to your grandmother's stories of her initiation. He'll say that you told him that if he refused, you'd be shamed, when really, you were trying to force him to marry you."

"But that's not what happened!" Naya protested. "And my grandmother specifically said this was all about being *presented*, not initiated!"

"Who do you think the men will believe?" Saurosa countered. "The best you can hope for is that your father is able to deny he had anything to do with it. Which is why leaving is a good idea. If you run now – far away – where no one can find you, your father might not have to take the blame for what you did. He can disavow any knowledge. You could still save his reputation."

In the act of stowing the package containing her grandmother's *tekstlom*, Naya stared at her cousin, unable to think of anything to say. Saurosa was right – the best thing that she could do under the circumstances would be to disappear – otherwise she would only bring more shame on herself and her family. When she'd run back to the shelter and blindly begun to gather her belongings, she'd had no clear intent, other than wanting to escape the mortification of standing before that assemblage of men. But now Saurosa's words gave purpose to her panicked desire to flee. She had to leave – right away – for her father's sake. Naya turned her back on her cousin and hastily resumed packing.

"You'd better hurry," warned Saurosa, urging her on. "If I were you, I'd find a way to get across the river and go north from there – they'll never think to look in that direction."

Facing her cousin again, Naya felt like a hunted animal. She'd managed to cram everything she'd brought into the shelter with her into two large bundles, one of which she'd slung across her shoulders, along with her bow and quiver. The other she held under one arm. Her knife she had fastened at her waist, along with her *makēn*, containing her smallest treasures. She stood for a moment – wordless – then ducked past her cousin and vanished into the night.

Holding open the shelter's entrance, Saurosa watched her go, lips curved in a small, triumphant smile.

Chapter Eighteen

Chaos erupted in the wake of Naya's abrupt departure. Two of Regos's followers, stationed on either side of the exit, moved to block anyone else from leaving. Potis's brother Tausos leaped to his feet. Still seated, Regos nodded to the guards and, amidst the shouting, two additional men – four in all – struggled to hold Potis back. He thrashed and roared, determined to follow his daughter. Someone from behind dumped a full waterskin over his head, enraging him further. He lunged, but Skelos came at him swinging. The last thing Potis felt was Skelos's solid right fist to his jaw, knocking him out cold.

When the clan chief regained consciousness, he found himself slumped before the central hearth, wrists bound in front, flanked by the same two guards who had moved to restrain him in the first place. Tausos, caught up in the brawl trying to defend his brother, was next to him, hands also bound. He, too, was just waking up. Regos, still seated, had been joined by Wailos, who now occupied the place to his father's right. Their clan priest, wearing the conical raven-feathered headdress that marked his status, sat to Regos's left. Otherwise, the tent was considerably less crowded; only Skelos, Krnos, and Bhlaghmn remained, the latter also attired in his priestly regalia.

"I see you've come to," remarked Regos, addressing Potis. "Please forgive the ropes but you and your brother were quite out of control. Under the circumstances, if we are to have a reasonable conversation, restraint seemed necessary."

Potis, shaking his head to clear it, could only growl in reply.

"Moreover," Regos went on, "in order to spare what's left of your daughter's reputation, I thought you might prefer a private conference, so I've sent the other tribal leaders away. They haven't gone far, though. We'll call them back, once everything is settled between us."

"There's nothing to settle," spat Potis, trying to clear his mouth of the blood from Skelos's blow. "Your depraved son will pay for what he's done to Naya."

"Now, now," Regos replied coolly. "Temper is what always gets you in trouble, my friend."

"We know what you've done." Potis ground out the words. "You and your son. And you two," he added, turning toward Skelos and Krnos. "You helped them – they couldn't have managed otherwise. You must have known as well," he continued, looking now at his uncle. "You're all part of it."

"Well, well," Regos replied, still unruffled. "Such wild allegations. Tell us more – although we all know you could not possibly have proof of any treachery. Even so, we wouldn't mind hearing a good story."

"It was him." Potis raised his bound wrists to point at Wailos. "On the night my father died. He and his cousin and the rest of their *kóryos*, dressed up in wolf skins. They raided our herds, slaughtered the newborns and took what remained of our breeding stock. But they couldn't have done it without help," he repeated, turning again to Krnos. "You must have lured the herders' dogs away, so they couldn't give the alarm."

Shifting back to Wailos, Potis addressed him directly. "From the beginning you realized the stolen animals would be too easily identified," he said, "so you drove them south, intending to pass them off to a foreign tribe."

"Go on," Regos prompted. "This is rather entertaining."

"What you all didn't know," Potis said, "is that Ceru, chief of the Dānus, is a friend, and he recognized our livestock. He's coming – and bringing back our animals – all the proof we'll need to show the rest of the tribe the truth of what you've done."

"You think so?" Regos replied, apparently unimpressed. "Kérberos," he said, turning to one of the guards. "Fetch the trophy my son and his companions returned with from their recent foray." The man obliged, leaving his post and returning with a heavy sack that had been stashed in a corner of the tent. Handing it to his chief, he remained nearby.

"Would you recognize this?" From the sack, Regos withdrew and held aloft by one of its horns the gory, severed head of Potis's prized young bull. "An unfortunate loss," he observed, "but the best way to convince you that help is not coming." Returning the bull's head to the sack and handing it back Kérberos, he said, "You can dispose of it now. Make sure no one finds it."

Potis and Tausos looked at one another, stunned. What did this mean for Ceru, his son Perqos and their men, not to mention Sunus and Aytal, who had been sent to look for them? And what about the remainder of the clan's stolen livestock?

"They're not coming," Regos reiterated. "Face it, Potis. You've lost. You have nothing left. Not even a daughter to bargain with."

At the mention of Naya, Potis made an awkward attempt to wrench his hands free and stand. He wasn't clear what he meant to do – try once more to go after her or assault someone. The remaining guard forced him down.

"Ah yes," Regos remarked, still unperturbed. "The girl. Wailos, why don't you take over the tale from here?"

"Certainly Father," Wailos answered. Facing his erstwhile host, the young warrior looked Potis up and down for half a beat before speaking. Gone was the deferential mask he'd worn for two moons.

"Really the next part was remarkably easy," he began. "Before leaving the Dānus camp, we heard a rumor that their chief intended to arrange a marriage between his son and your daughter, if she still lived. Of course, I realized that situation would never be acceptable, so I had to improvise. The plan I came up with turned out to be rather ingenious, if I do say so."

"The horses?" This from Tausos.

"Exactly," Wailos confirmed. "I needed an excuse to stick around to see if the girl had survived the winter and then court her if she showed up," he explained. "Actually, it was your sister who gave me the idea – Swesor really should learn to guard her tongue. She told Saurosa about Awos's deathbed ramblings and of course Saurosa passed the information along to her brother – who as you've figured out, has been privy to my father's scheme from the beginning." Wailos chuckled.

"Skelos sent his son to meet me on my way back from the Dānus camp," he continued, "and Krnos passed along the old chief's dying words, which got me thinking – what if we could convince the rest of your clan to capture a herd of wild horses, to take the place of the lost livestock? And you all fell for it." Again, Wailos laughed, clearly pleased with himself.

"We decided to trap the herd Krnos had seen with the girl last autumn – the band with the copper-colored filly – figuring they'd be easier to catch," he went on. "You do know, by the way, that it was Krnos – with his father's blessing – who arranged for the girl to become separated from the caravan last fall, and then followed her so that he ended up witnessing what happened? What a pity those strangers were so honorable – they might have saved themselves and everyone else quite a bit of trouble if they'd just left her where she fell."

At this revelation, Potis went very still, amber hawk's eyes staring across the fire at Skelos. Although aware of his cousin's enmity toward Naya and himself, before tonight he would not have believed Skelos or Krnos to be capable of such malice – to have lured Naya away from the clan in the hope of some accident befalling her, and then leaving her to die. He realized now that there were no limits to the harm they were willing to cause, whether on their own account or in alliance with Regos. Who else among his own clan had shifted their allegiance? What had they been promised by the rival chief? Was there anyone left whom he could trust? Had Skelos turned all the men of their clan, as well as the rest of the tribe, against him? He'd known there was a danger, especially after he'd learned the truth of what had happened to the herd, but he had not fully grasped the depths to which Skelos was willing to descend to satisfy his hatred and serve his own ambition.

From the other side of the hearth, Skelos stared back at him, silent, mocking, one corner of his mouth lifted in a wordless sneer. A muscle twitched in the clan chief's jaw.

"Anyway, where was I?" resumed Wailos. "Oh yes – the scheme to capture the horses. Your priest – Bhlaghmn here – seemed especially eager at the prospect of procuring the red filly to offer as the prime sacrifice for the solstice rites."

Potis turned a narrowed gaze on his uncle, who returned it without apology, obviously seeing no need to explain himself.

"Unfortunately," Wailos went on, "despite our best efforts, the scouts never did locate the filly. We were lucky enough to trap the rest of the band, minus the stallion, of course. And then that very day – as if willed by the gods – guess who shows up, alive?"

Leaning forward, Wailos lowered his voice conspiratorially, as though what he said next was meant for Potis's ears alone. "Everything was already going according to plan with the horses," he said with a sly wink, "so all I had to do was trick your daughter into compromising herself – a tedious undertaking, I'll admit, but not at all difficult – while at the same time making sure there was no possible way for you or your clan to meet your obligations at the Gathering. The truly surprising thing is that you didn't do a thing to stop me."

Sitting back smugly, the young warrior went on as before. "No doubt, you've figured out by now that Krnos and I were the ones who set the horses free the other night, once it was too late for them to be recaptured. Afterwards, we met up with my cousin Unksra and a few others to make sure the Dānus chief and his son would not be interfering. I got back just in time to sort out the girl once and for all – and here we are."

Wiping one hand against the other to indicate the satisfactory completion of his task, Wailos's smile was now closer to a smirk. "Ruining your standing as clan chief was the intent all along," he couldn't resist adding, "Defiling the little *skortum* was rather a bonus."

Potis nearly erupted. The word Wailos had used to refer to Naya represented one of the worst insults that could be spoken against a young woman.

"He's baiting you," Tausos whispered under his breath from his place at Potis's side. "Don't let him."

Brows lowered, mouth pressed in a tight line, Potis did his best to heed his brother's advice. Attempting a reply, whether to defend his daughter or denounce his enemies, risked the loss of what little grip he retained on his self-control.

Regos had evidently not heard the details of his son's exploits. "Well done," he commended, clapping Wailos on the shoulder. "You'll make a worthy successor."

Addressing himself once more to Potis, he returned to the matter at hand. "With the horses gone and no hope of rescue from outside allies," he pointed out, "not to mention your daughter having so thoroughly damaged her reputation, I don't see how you can possibly retain your position in your own clan, let alone be named chief of chiefs of the tribe. Your father would be so disappointed in you." Regos shook his head in feigned regret.

"At least the other members of your clan need not suffer the consequences of your failures," he went on. "As you'll hear, I've offered a solution. Fortunately, there are those with your clan's best interests in mind who are more than willing to go along with what I suggest. If you care about the future of your people, my friend, you will do the same."

Regos paused, making sure the implied threat was unmistakable. Waiting in grim silence to hear the rival chief's proposition, Potis looked across the fire at those seated opposite: Skelos, Krnos, and Bhlaghmn. No surprise that these three had betrayed *him* – but the harm they'd caused to Naya! Again, Potis fought down the visceral urge to lash out. He almost missed what Regos said next.

"In exchange for guaranteeing your clan's support for my candidacy as leader of the tribe," he announced, "I've agreed to back Skelos's bid to replace you as clan chief. He's next in line, by right of seniority, and has my full support. To seal the arrangement, Wailos is to marry Skelos's sister, Saurosa. From everything my son tells me, she will make a most satisfactory wife."

Regos offered a nod of acknowledgement to Skelos, then continued speaking to Potis. "The generous bride price which I'm prepared to pay will serve to meet your clan's obligations for the *Sāwel-Dom* sacrifices, and replace the lost livestock, preserving the clan's standing in the tribe and insuring your people's future well-being, since you have so clearly failed them."

The rival chief spoke magnanimously, as though he did not himself bear responsibility for the clan's misfortunes. Potis would have accused him of as much, but still didn't trust himself to speak.

"If you agree to these terms," Regos went on, "you and your immediate family will be allowed to go into exile. Maybe your wife's people will take you in – I hear she's already left you to return to them." He laughed derisively, then sobered. "If you don't agree," he warned, "you and your brother – and anyone else who tries to thwart me – will regret your choice. I presume I've made myself understood?"

As if on cue, Saurosa appeared for the second time that night at the entrance to the men's tent, interrupting whatever answer Potis might have offered. Holding aside the door flap, she ushered in another woman, who turned out to be the priest's wife. In her arms, she bore a heavy bundle, swathed in deer skin.

"More surprises," remarked Regos, greeting Uksor as though he had not been expecting her imminent arrival. "What is it that you've brought us?"

"Forgive the intrusion," Uksor simpered, inclining her head in Regos's direction before addressing her husband. "I have the items you requested." She stayed by the entrance, not daring to advance any further into the men's private sanctum.

"Thank you my dear," Bhlaghmn replied as he rose to take the bundle from her. Returning to his seat next to Skelos, he placed the hastily wrapped package on the ground in front of them. "You may stay for the moment," he said, still speaking to Uksor. "You may remain as well," the priest added to Saurosa. "This concerns you, after all."

Turning back to the others assembled around the fire, Bhlaghmn reached forward and pulled aside the bundle's covering, displaying its contents for all to see. "These," he said, "are our clan's symbols of leadership, which my wife has kindly fetched at my request."

Laid out before Skelos and the priest were the heavy stone mace and the copper torque, last worn by Potis at *Wesr-Admn*. In addition, resting alongside was an elaborately fashioned chest plate featuring rows of curved boars' tusks laced together and adorned with shell and copper beads.

"As you can all see," Bhlaghmn continued, "my wife has also brought another sacred item which by rights belongs to the Plānos tribe's chief of chiefs."

The chest plate had not been displayed since Awos's final ceremonial appearance at the previous year's Gathering, when in front of the assembled tribe he had formally relinquished his position as clan leader, naming Potis as his successor. Custom held that while such an action was within the prerogative of a retiring clan chief, whose wishes would normally be respected, choosing a new chief of chiefs for the tribe could only take place following the old chief's death and required the unanimous consent of all the tribe's leaders, including the priests.

"My nephew has had custody of these items since the passing of his father," Bhlaghmn went on, glossing over the fact that the mace and the torque, at least, were in Potis's possession because, in accordance with his father's recommendation, he'd already been officially recognized as clan chief, and had the line of tattoo-marks across his cheeks to prove it.

"The time has now come," he announced, "to decide who is in fact worthy to claim these symbols, along with the power and authority they represent." The priest leveled an imperious look at Potis, seated across the fire. "While you may be my elder brother's son," he declared, "you are not – and never have been – fit to succeed him, not as clan chief, and certainly not as leader of the tribe.”

Potis, hands tied, surrounded by foes, glared back at his uncle. How dare Uksor enter his dwelling and rummage among his things! What did the priest’s wife know of the full plot against him – and against his daughter? Had she sanctioned beforehand what Wailos had done to Naya or was she only just finding out the adulterated version of what had happened? Unfortunately, news of Naya’s incriminating admission before the chiefs’ council was likely to have spread throughout the whole tribe by now.

“Where is Naya?” he demanded, speaking to the women.

“She appears to have run off,” Saurosa answered serenely. “As far as I know, no one saw her go.”

“Yes, it’s quite shocking, even for her,” Uksor put in. “I could scarcely believe what Saurosa told me just now when she came to find me – that Naya was not in her shelter – but having checked for myself, I can attest that she did indeed break her vigil. The proof is there for anyone to see – the sacred cord, slit from the inside.” Clearly outraged, the priest’s wife seemed rather titillated as well. “Who knows what she’s gotten up to now, or why she’s run off, but I wouldn’t put anything past the girl.”

So, Potis thought, either Uksor was very good at pretending ignorance, or she honestly did not yet know what had happened. His guards tightened their grip on his shoulders.

Bhlaghmn answered his wife, wasting no time in enlightening her. “What she’s done,” he said, “is to seduce our guest – son of the tribe’s most powerful chief – so that he would be trapped into marrying her.” Potis started to shout a denial when his guards’ fingers bit into the flesh around his collar bones, nearly causing him to pass out again.

At her husband’s revelation, Uksor looked appropriately shocked. “What about the rumors?” she asked. “Everyone has assumed she and Wailos were to wed.”

“Apparently, the girl decided to take matters into her own hands.” Bhlaghmn looked down the length of his nose at Potis. “What we don’t know,” he went on for his wife’s benefit, “is to what extent her father put her up to it in order to secure his own hold on power. Regardless, the girl’s actions have served not only to bring shame upon herself but to thoroughly disqualify her father from any role in the leadership of this clan, let alone the tribe.”

Looking across the fire to where Potis sat, with Tausos next to him, Uksor appeared to notice for the first time that both men had their hands bound in front of them, with guards stationed behind. She looked back at her husband for an explanation.

"You know what a temper my nephew has," the priest said dismissively. "He's already lost it once this evening."

"So true," concurred Regos, resuming charge of the conversation. "But the night is almost spent. I believe it's time to call back the other leaders. Bhlaghmn, would you ask your wife to be so kind as to request their return? Some of them are probably waiting in Skelos's tent and they'll know where to find the others. Saurosa, my dear, you will stay so that you may be presented as my son's intended bride. No point in waiting on the announcement, now that we've sorted everything out."

"But Naya?" Uksor asked, voice uncertain. "Shouldn't we try to find her?"

Before either Regos or Bhlaghmn could answer, Skelos spoke up. "Good riddance," he sneered. "With any luck, she's thrown herself in the river. Wailos is right, I've always known she'd turn out to be a *skortum*.

This time, the words were more than Potis's overstretched temper could withstand. Something inside snapped. Hands still tied, with a roar he threw off his guards and lunged across the fire, trying to reach his cousin.

Grabbing the first weapon that came to hand to defend himself, Skelos's fist closed around the handle of the ceremonial mace, resting on the deerskin in front of him. Emitting a roar of his own, in one smooth motion he came to his feet and swung. The blow contacted the side of Potis's head with a sickening thud, felling the clan chief like a tree. Narrowly missing the flames, he landed face down beside the hearth and lay motionless, blood already beginning to seep from his left ear.

Tausos's tent…

"What if he never wakes up?" The question came from Vedukha, who was distraught. She and Tausos's wife, Glōs, along with Tausos and Awija were gathered around Potis's prostrate form.

Awija was grateful that when Tausos had shown up at his tent with the body of his brother, his wife had the presence of mind to come herself to fetch her, rather than sending someone. "There's a good chance he might not," she said, her voice tight with concern. "The blow has broken his skull. Still, there could be hope. Fetch me water and clean rags. Tell Elēn to bring the medicines I'll need from the women's tent. She'll know which ones… Oh never mind – she's still in seclusion. You'll have to go instead. Just bring my entire kit."

Relieved to have something to do, Vedukha hurried out. Dawn was just beginning to light the eastern sky.

"Build up the fire," Awija continued, speaking now to Glōs.

The younger boys had been sent to their aunt Swesor with instructions that everyone, including Swesor herself, should stay put. The fewer bodies crowding Tausos's tent the better. Only Awija, Tausos and Glōs remained.

"Later, I want to know everything that happened," Awija said, "but right now…"

Before she could finish, the tent flap was pushed aside and two figures entered. Tausos, unable to see clearly in the darkened interior of the tent, rose to challenge them.

"It's us, Father," said the one who had entered first. "We just made it back to the settlement and came straight here. What's happened?"

Recognizing the voice of his oldest son, Tausos relaxed but only slightly. "Who's with you?" he asked.

"It's me," came the voice of the other figure. "Aytal."

As he and Sunus stepped into the firelight. Awija, still at Potis's side, could see that both young men were disheveled – clothes torn, faces covered in dirt and dried blood. No wonder they hadn't been recognized.

"Aytal?" The question came in a hoarse whisper.

"Potis?" Beckoning, Awija gestured for Aytal to move closer. "He's awake. He wants to say something to you."

"I'm here," Aytal answered, coming to crouch at Potis's side. Shock registered on the young man's face as he saw for the first time how badly the clan chief was injured. A garish bruise was beginning to bloom at his left temple. Obviously alarmed, Aytal looked to Awija, who shook her head, silently telling him that now was not the time to ask.

"I'm here," he repeated.

Potis's eyes were closed and the skin of his cheeks looked hollow beneath his tattoos. Blood continued to leak from his ear, and from his nose as well. Aytal laid a hand on the clan chief's arm, letting him know of his presence by his side.

"Go… after… her…" Struggling for breath, Potis's words were difficult to hear.

"After Naya?" Aytal asked, wanting to be sure he understood.

"My… daughter…" the clan chief murmured. He was losing consciousness again. "Find… her…"

Chapter Nineteen

Emerging from the woods surrounding her shelter, Naya paused, unsure which way to go. Her heart pounded in her chest. She knew she must head away from the settlement and the flood plain crowded with visitors. She couldn't risk running into anyone who might try to stop her. Maybe Saurosa was right – she should cross the river, follow the path northward through the marshes to higher ground and continue north from there. But she didn't trust Saurosa. Even in her panic to get away, Naya felt certain she must not do as Saurosa suggested.

South. She needed to go south. But not along the riverbank. On this side, the undergrowth was too dense. Anyone following her could track her and quickly catch up. On the river's east side, no paths led southward, making travel on foot through the marshes in that direction impossible. A boat. She needed a boat. Floating downstream, carried by the Rā's swift current, she would leave no trace. But where to procure one? Her clan rarely crossed the river at this time of year, when the central channel still flowed fast and deep from the spring melt. Various vessels belonging to visitors were currently beached below the stone circle but if she took one, it would be missed.

If not a boat, Naya decided, she'd make do with something else that would float. Stumbling in the dark, she made her way through the woods, following the faint path leading to the hidden cove where she and the other initiates had bathed. She remembered seeing a disused raft, half-buried in vegetation at the water's edge.

Birds had begun to call to one another in the darkness, signaling that dawn was not far off. Reaching the cove, she set down her bundles beside one of the rocks where she and the other girls had dried their hair only a few days before. To Naya, a lifetime seemed to have passed.

She couldn't let herself think about what had happened – not now – she needed to keep moving. Searching the undergrowth close to the water's edge, she found the raft. Made of once-sturdy logs bound together with stout rope, it had long since been reclaimed by the forest. Naya feared that even if she managed to drag the raft into the water, the logs would prove to be rotten, or the ropes would give way. But this was her only option.

Struggling to grip the mossy length of line once used for tying up the raft, Naya dug in her heels and pulled. The line held but the logs refused to budge. Moving around to the far side, she sat facing the raft, placed both feet against it with her arms braced behind her and shoved. This time, the raft shifted. Pulling and pushing, she coaxed it toward the water's edge, until, with one final effort, the logs slid into the water. To Naya's relief, they floated. Grabbing her belongings, she piled everything on top and, propelling the raft in front of her, waded out of the cove toward the central channel of the river. At some point she'd need to fashion a rudder to steer, but for now, she planned to guide the raft into the main current, climb aboard, and trust to the Rā to carry her downstream.

Moving tendrils of water curled around her bare legs, so cold after the protected shallows of the cove that they stole her breath. Hidden rocks stubbed her toes. Naya's new dress quickly became soaked to the waist. Overhead, the sky had begun to lighten. She glimpsed the eastern marshes across the rippled surface of the river's broad expanse. The sun would be up soon.

Caught by the strengthening current, the raft began to tug against Naya's hold. She tried to hoist herself aboard, but her weight tipped the logs, nearly submerging the raft and sending her belongings into the water. Three attempts later, her forearms and the palms of her hands scraped raw by the effort, she managed to shimmy aboard and collapse onto her stomach. Never had she felt so cold, wet and exhausted. With one arm wrapped around her sodden bundles, the other hand holding tight to her bow, head resting on the makeshift pillow of her belongings, she closed her eyes and surrendered to the mercy of the Rā.

When Naya awoke, dazed and disoriented, she needed a moment to remember where she was. Her whole body felt numb, except for a dull throb in her temples. Lifting her head, she squinted into the sun.

Mid-morning. She'd fallen asleep. The raft was afloat in the middle of the Rā, drifting downstream with the current. The river's western bank, clad in dense woods, towered above the water. Tall cattails and marsh grasses blocked her view to the east.

Naya knew she was lucky not to have run aground. This stretch of the river contained numerous sandbars, as well as debris piles closer to shore. She needed a way to steer, as well as a chance to dry her clothes and other belongings, not to mention finding something to eat. But not until she'd put more distance between herself and the settlement.

Naya maneuvered herself into a sitting position aboard the unsteady raft, causing it to spin in a slow circle. In that moment she noticed a subtle shift in the light, as though a thin cloud had passed over the sun. She risked an upward glance, eyes widening before she quickly squeezed them shut. A crescent appeared to be missing from the sun, reminding Naya of the night when she and the other girls had witnessed the moon's strange transformation – except she'd never heard of such a thing happening in broad daylight, to the sun.

Not daring to look up again, Naya watched with growing unease as color gradually seeped out of the surrounding landscape, as though heralding the arrival of twilight. She thought of Awija's story about Mehnot and Sāwel. Was this First Mother's solution for Sāwel's misbehavior, to slowly extinguish his light from the sky? But that didn't make sense. Her grandmother's story was old, far older than her grandmother, and this strange phenomenon was happening before Naya's eyes.

The solstice! She'd almost forgotten. Today marked *Sāwel-Dom*, the celebration of the sun reaching its zenith. Naya pictured the ceremony that would have occurred at dawn at the stone circle – the priests leading the assembled tribe in observing the sacred rites meant to elicit Sky Father's ongoing favor, even as the sun commenced its descent into the dark half of the year. She could hear the chanting, see the knives poised for the sacrifice, then the blood spilling crimson over the rough surface of the altar, dripping down its granite sides, staining the earth, as the people looked on, mesmerized.

Naya shuddered. Surely the sun's strange appearance, occurring just after the completion of the ritual, must be interpreted as a bad omen. *Or worse, what if the required rites hadn't taken place?* she thought with sudden horror. What if the disruption she'd caused had delayed the ceremony and Sky Father was angry? She would be blamed and her father subjected to further condemnation. All the more reason to run.

Light-headed, Naya lay down again on the raft's rough surface, shutting her eyes and hugging her belongings to her for security. She felt as though she were continuing to spin, even as the current carried her steadily southwards. Mouth dry, she was unable to recall the last time she'd had anything to drink, yet she couldn't summon the energy to sit up and fill her waterskin from the river. Afraid she might pass out, she tried to ignore the waves of dizziness washing over her.

Visions, unbidden, invaded her imagination. She was in the midst of a parched landscape, scorched by blinding sunlight. A figure appeared, dressed in wolf skins, a leering grin visible below the lifeless eyes of the wolf's head mask he wore to disguise his face. But she knew who he was. She tried to cry out but had no voice. Chest pounding, she wanted to turn and run but found herself rooted to the spot. The wolf-man held something out to her – an offering. She recognized her father's ceremonial mace. The image shifted. She was in the men's tent and her father was reaching for her, wearing the same look of fear and dismay as when Naya had last seen him. Before she could fling herself into the safety of his arms, a menacing figure stepped between them, brandishing the ceremonial mace as the wolf-man looked on. With horror, Naya watched the figure swing the mace in an arc, striking her father a sickening blow to the head. He collapsed, crumpling at her feet.

Naya's scream tore at her throat. Sitting up aboard the raft, she opened her eyes to a world drained of light. A chill breeze prickled her skin, while a cacophony of bird calls filled the air. Above the clamor, she heard voices shouting from the woods lining the river's western bank. Men had come for her, baying like a pack of hunting dogs on the trail of their quarry. When they emerged from the trees, their triumph turned to panic. Naya looked up. Above, an enormous black disk encircled by flames blotted out the sun. Behind the flaming disk, stars shone from a night sky.

Blinded, Naya squeezed her eyes shut. From behind closed lids, the image burned – not her vision of the sun and the moon conjoined, coexisting in miraculous symmetry, but rather the terrifying aspect of the sun's brilliance eclipsed, turning day to night. Opening her eyes again, all Naya could see was a fathomless void, fire licking at its circular edges, surrounded by darkness. She could still hear the men yelling to one another, their voices growing fainter as they retreated into the forest, back the way they had come. With a whimper, Naya cowered on her knees aboard the raft and buried her head in her arms, afraid the world must be ending.

Undisturbed, the Rā flowed southward, carrying Naya and the raft with it.

Sometime later…

Naya raised her head. The dizziness had abated. Her body ached, but her mind and vision had cleared. She wasn't sure how much time had passed, and she didn't dare look up at the sun to check, but the daylight appeared normal. Still, the river no longer felt safe. Men were looking for her and they'd spotted the raft, which meant they would be back. She had to find a place to hide, at least until she succeeded in throwing her pursuers off her trail. Only then could she stop to consider the disturbing omen she had witnessed, and the terrible vision that had accompanied it.

That's when Naya remembered the cave. Toward the end of the chain of bluffs flanking the Rā's western bank, one of the limestone cliffs came all the way down to the water's edge. The river had carved out a low-ceilinged cavity in the rock that extended well under the bluff face. She had found the entrance during one of her solitary explorations years earlier but hadn't told anyone of her discovery. Others must have known of the cavity, however, because inside she'd found a stash of dry firewood and an abandoned *plowós* – a boat made from a hollowed-out log.

Naya scanned the riverbank, looking for landmarks to judge how far the current had taken her. Had she already passed the cave's entrance? She didn't think so. Around the next bend she spotted what she was looking for – a sheer rock wall dropping all the way into the water, with no sign of an opening. The first time Naya had been here, the Rā's level had been much lower. Now, just as she hoped, the river was high enough to hide the cave's entrance. Even if someone pursuing her knew of the cavity's existence, they would be unlikely to think she'd taken refuge in it.

Naya slid into the water, gasping at the cold. Towing the raft, she swam toward the towering bluff face until her bare feet found purchase on the sandy, rock-strewn river bottom, then waded until the water was just below her waist. If she remembered correctly, the cave's location was marked by a twisted juniper clinging to a crevice high above. She spotted the juniper but was unable to see the cavity's entrance beneath the river's murky surface. Instead, she felt it – a warmer flow of water past her bare calves, mixing with the cooler current of the river.

Keeping one hand on the raft, Naya ran her other hand down the bluff face beneath the water's surface, looking for the lip of the cave. She found it at a depth level with the middle of her thigh. She tried to remember the height of the opening once past the entrance. Would the river have flooded the entire cavity? *Only one way to find out*, she told herself. Looping the line attached to the raft around a protruding rock, Naya filled her lungs and dove. Eyes closed against the silt-filled water, she felt with outstretched hands for the rim of the entrance, then groped her way past the threshold. Almost immediately, the passage opened into the larger cavity. Clinging with one hand to the interior lip of the entrance, Naya maneuvered her feet underneath her and with her free hand reaching above, cautiously attempted to stand. To her relief, her head broke the water's surface without hitting the ceiling. She could breathe.

She could not see, however. Although a small amount of daylight filtered through the cave's underwater entrance, giving her confidence that she could find the way out, the cave's interior was as black as pine tar. Naya tried to recall the cavity's dimensions. When she'd been here before, the river had been low and there had been no subterranean lake. She remembered both the floor and the ceiling sloping upwards toward a broad shelf of rock at the back, with enough room to sit. The *plowós* and the firewood had been resting on the ledge against the cave's back wall.

Hunched over, with hands outstretched, Naya began to wade. At first, the water dragged at her legs but gradually the lake became shallower, and she gained more overhead clearance. Soon the water was only up to her ankles, and she could stand almost upright. Getting down on hands and knees, she located the base of the rock shelf rising from the cave floor, rough and chalky to the touch. Reaching toward the back of the ledge, she found both the pile of firewood and one end of the log boat. Even better, she could feel the movement of air against her cheeks. There must be at least one cleft in the rock that led to the surface, thus enabling an exchange of air in the cave despite its flooded state. The limestone bluffs flanking the river were riddled with such fissures. She would be able to breathe and also keep a fire going to banish some of the darkness.

Satisfied she'd found a safe place to hide, Naya retraced her steps toward the entrance, took a deep breath and dove back through the opening. Outside, the raft tugged at its hastily secured line. Thankful the logs hadn't already floated away, Naya gathered her belongings in one arm, awkwardly holding everything aloft while releasing the line with her free hand. Giving the raft a firm shove, she sent it into the middle of the river, where the current could carry it downstream until it ran aground. Hopefully if her pursuers found the raft, they would assume she'd beached it in order to continue inland, and they'd be thrown off her trail. Meanwhile she would take refuge in the cave and then tonight, under cover of darkness, she would continue her journey down the Rā aboard the more river-worthy *plowós*.

Watching the logs float downstream without her, Naya mentally ran through the contents of her bundles. Other than her fire-starting kit and her bow string, both stored in the water-proof *makēn* strapped to her waist, nothing inside either bundle would be permanently harmed by being submerged long enough for her to enter the cave. With luck, the bison hide robe her father had given her, folded fur-side in inside her water-resistant leather satchel, would stay dry enough to wrap-up in while she waited for nightfall. Just to be safe, she took off her belt along with her *makēn* and shoved them both inside the satchel as well. Slinging the satchel and her quiver crossways across her shoulders and clutching her other bundle to her chest, along with her bow, Naya felt with her free hand for the cave entrance, took a breath, and once more dove inside.

This time, less cautious, she reached the middle of the lake before surfacing, just as her knees started to scrape the bottom. Staggering to her feet, still burdened by her dripping belongings, Naya took a step at a time, one hand outstretched in the dark, until she came to the water's edge. Placing her bundles on the ledge, she felt for the wood pile and began blindly gathering enough kindling to start a fire.

Sometime later, after fumbling in the dark and many unsuccessful attempts with her flint, Naya sparked a small blaze. As it flared, she heard a voice.

"Perqos? Are you in here?" The tone was deep and male, and although emanating from overhead, sounded close by. Kindling in hand, Naya froze.

"Yes Father," came another voice. "At the back."

Naya heard the second voice even more clearly. Her heart hammered in her chest. The two men must be somewhere above her, perhaps in another cave, their voices amplified by a fissure in the limestone. Naya thought of the large cavern accessed from the upper reaches of one of the ravines south of the settlement – Melit had suggested she show it to Wailos during their exploratory rambles. The location seemed about right. Her hiding place must be connected to the cavern by an air shaft, perhaps the same one serving as a chimney for her nascent fire.

"Thank the gods you've come, Father." The younger man sounded relieved.

"What happened? Where are the others? What about the livestock?" The older man was evidently alarmed.

"We were attacked last night, not long after dark," his son replied. "A small raiding party, dressed up like wolves."

Naya sucked in her breath. *Wailos. Who else could it be?*

"Wolves, eh?" the older man responded. "That sounds familiar. How many of the livestock did they take?"

"They were only interested in Potis's bull. They made off with him just as the sentries sounded the alarm. We tried to stop them, but they were more intent on leaving with their prize than engaging in a fight and had the advantage of being on familiar ground. Later we discovered they'd slaughtered the poor beast – severed his head."

Naya stifled a gasp. Such a valuable animal! How could anyone, even Wailos, do anything so senseless? And who were these men? She didn't recognize their voices, but apparently they knew her father and had been in possession of his prize bull.

"Were any of our warriors hurt?" the older man wanted to know. "Did you send anyone after the raiders?"

"No one was seriously injured," his son assured him, "although Potis's nephew Sunus and a companion were on hand when the raid occurred. They got a bit banged up. As soon as they recovered, they went back to the settlement to tell Potis what happened. Since we had a good idea of the raiders' identity, we didn't think it wise to pursue them, given our presence in the area is supposed to be a secret. Instead, our warriors took the rest of the livestock out to the open steppe, where they'll be less vulnerable to another surprise attack. I waited behind for you, knowing you'd look for us here first."

"You did well, son."

Naya heard a clap on the shoulder.

"I'm sorry I wasn't on hand when the raid occurred," the older man apologized. "The delay to check on the horses was unavoidable."

Naya's ears pricked. *Horses?*

"Any sign of the three who were with Potis's wife when she and the trader passed through?" his son inquired.

Excitement rising, Naya held her breath.

"Yes," the older man replied. "I saw them myself, in the same area as one of the herds we've been following. I gave orders that they not be harmed. I wanted to let Potis know and tell him I'd spoken with Sata as well."

Naya felt a rush of relief. The red filly, the gray stallion and the mare must have followed her mother and Oyuun when they left, which would explain why there'd been no sign of them in the vicinity of the settlement. Apparently all three horses were safe, at least for the time being, as was her mother.

"What do we do now?" the younger man asked.

"Potis will send word. Maybe he'll come up with another plan. In the meantime, you and I should stay here, out of sight, at least for another day. If we don't hear anything by tomorrow, we'll rejoin our men and head back to our own territory. What a disaster."

Naya imagined the older man shaking his head in dismay. Based on everything she'd overheard, she guessed he must be her father's friend Ceru, chief of the powerful Dānus tribe whose territory lay to the south. And the son's name… Naya tried to remember what Ceru had call him a moment ago. Perqos? But what were they doing *here*, with the clan's missing livestock? And if Wailos had indeed led the raid, why? What was the point of beheading her father's prize bull?

After a pause, Perqos spoke. "He's even worse than we thought, isn't he?"

"As is his father," Ceru agreed. "There's no limit to their ambitions."

The two men must be discussing Wailos. Then a terrible thought hit Naya. What if Wailos and his companions had been responsible not only for last night's attack, but for the original raid, back in the spring? Animals had been senselessly slaughtered then as well, by men disguised as wolves. But if that were the case, her father couldn't possibly have known, or he never would have welcomed Wailos as a guest of the clan. Still, why was her father's friend here – seemingly with her father's knowledge – and in possession of the clan's stolen animals, now minus the young bull? Had the unknown raiders who'd been marauding in the area last spring delivered the livestock to Ceru's tribe without being aware of his friendship with her father and Ceru had come to return them? But that still didn't explain why Wailos would mount a surprise attack targeting the bull – nor how Perqos would have known it was him. Nothing made sense.

Naya shivered in her wet clothes but didn't dare add too much wood to the fire, for fear the men in the cavern above would smell the smoke and discover her hiding place. Friend of her father's or not, she wasn't certain yet that Ceru could be trusted. Besides, if she wanted the light to last, she had to eke out the meager supply of wood. Quietly pulling her bison hide robe from her satchel, Naya was relieved to find the fur was still reasonably dry. Stripping out of her sopping dress, she wrapped the robe around her shoulders.

A third man's voice called in a loud whisper, evidently from the cavern's entrance.

"Perqos? Are you still here?"

"Sunus?" Perqos answered. "Is that you?"

Naya recognized her cousin's voice as well.

"We're at the back," Perqos continued. "My father's arrived – we didn't expect you to return so soon."

Naya heard the crunch of approaching footsteps.

"What did Potis say when he found out about the bull?" Ceru demanded without preliminary.

"We didn't get a chance to tell him," Sunus replied. "Wailos and his men made it back to the settlement well before we did – they must have taken a short cut. According to my father, Regus showed Potis the severed head in private, then disposed of it, in order to demonstrate that the plan to expose Wailos's treachery wasn't going to work."

Brow wrinkled, Naya tried to puzzle out the implications of what she'd just overheard.

"*Skerdā!*" Ceru swore. "Now what? Does Potis want us to come anyway?"

"Our men with the rest of the livestock haven't gone far," Perqos put in. "We could still show up with them before the Gathering concludes."

"It may already be too late." Sunus's voice was sober.

A chill of premonition ran down Naya's spine.

"What do you mean, too late?" Ceru demanded.

"The clan chief is gravely injured," Sunus explained. "When I left, he was fighting for his life."

Nooooo! Naya's hand flew to her mouth, smothering the sound of her outburst. The image of her father collapsing at her feet flashed before her eyes.

Ceru gasped in disbelief. "What happened?"

Clutching the edges of the bison robe to her chest, Naya held her breath, trying to stop shaking so she could listen.

"You'd have to ask my father for the full story – he was there – but from the brief version he shared with me, after the matter with the bull, Potis and Skelos got into an argument, Potis lost his temper, and Skelos struck him in the head with the clan's ceremonial mace."

Again, Naya stifled a gasp. Just as in her vision!

"He was unconscious when I left," Sunus went on. "Alive, but barely. My grandmother is caring for him."

"I don't understand," Ceru spoke, obviously distressed. "I can believe Potis lost his temper over the bull," he conceded. "But getting into a fight with weapons, and coming out the worst?" He sounded incredulous.

"Actually, his hands were already tied," Sunus clarified. "And losing his temper wasn't about the bull. It was over what Skelos said about Potis's daughter, Naya."

"What did Skelos say?" Perqos asked.

"He called her a *skortum* – a whore."

Naya couldn't listen any longer. Heedless of whether Ceru and his son might hear her, she dropped the robe and splashed into the lake until the water was deep enough for her to plunge headfirst beneath the surface, drowning out their voices. The shock of the water, warm compared to the river yet still frigid against her naked skin, barely registered.

Skortum. The awful word rang in Naya's ears. *My fault!* she silently cried. *Papa is going to die – may already be dead – and it's my fault.*

Gasping, she came up for air, then submerged again. *Think!* she told herself. *You can't fall apart now."* Breath held, eyes squeezed shut, with her arms wrapped around her knees, Naya forced herself to the sandy bottom of the subterranean lake. *What am I going to do?* With her father grievously injured, returning to the settlement wouldn't be safe and could only make things worse. Keep running? But where should she go? She'd had no clear idea of a destination when she left – only a determination not to be caught.

Surfacing, Naya gulped in air, then made herself take a slow breath, willing herself to calm down. She couldn't think about Papa – not now. It was too late for her to do anything to save him. She needed a plan. Listening for the men's voices, she made her way back to the stone ledge, trying not to make noise this time. She was numb with cold, and shock.

The fire still burned, a small beacon in the dark, its smoke wafting gently upward before disappearing into the unseen crevice above. Crawling back onto the ledge, she wrapped herself in the bison robe and tried once more to distinguish what the men in the cavern above were saying. After a moment, she realized they were still talking about her.

"She disappeared," Sunus was explaining to the others. "A group of the tribal leaders insisted Wailos go after her."

"On what grounds?" Ceru wondered. "I would have thought, after ruining her reputation, Wailos would have felt fortunate to be rid of her."

"That's just it," Sunus replied. "My father thinks that injuring my uncle – likely fatally – was a big miscalculation on Skelos's part. Potis is popular and some of the other chiefs were suspicious of Wailos's story about Naya seducing him, especially after she ran off. As a condition of granting Regos their support, they insist that Wailos find Naya and bring her home safely. There was even talk that if Potis dies, Wailos should be obligated to marry her and be responsible for her keep."

"I certainly wouldn't wish that fate on the girl," Ceru observed. "Wherever she's gone, let's hope Wailos doesn't catch up with her – although he's not likely to give up easily. Has anyone else been dispatched to find her?"

"Aytal," Sunus replied. "He was with us last night. Perqos met him."

Naya's heart skipped a beat. Aytal had been sent to look for her?

"Tell me about him," Ceru inquired. "He's not part of your clan, is he?"

"No," Sunus confirmed. "But he's trustworthy and proved he can hold his own in a fight. I like him. He and his father rescued Naya and her mother last winter. They're strangers – traders from the north."

"I thought so," Ceru replied. "We met Oyuun, Aytal's father, when he and Sata passed through earlier this spring on the way to Sata's homeland in the mountains. I meant to tell Potis when I saw him…" Ceru's voice trailed off.

"I can't believe my uncle might not survive," Sunus lamented, sounding stunned. "He's like a second father to me." The others were silent. Naya bit down hard on her lower lip. She could not allow herself to break down.

"What was the state of things at the settlement when you left?" Ceru asked. "Aside from what happened to Potis."

"Not good," came Sunus's terse reply. "My father warns that you and your men should take the livestock and head back to your own territory with as much speed as you can manage."

"That bad, hmmm?" Ceru didn't sound surprised.

"That's not all of it. My father is certain that Skelos will take over as clan chief without opposition, despite what he did to my uncle. His first act will be to decree that as Potis's brother, my father is no longer welcome in the clan." Sunus paused.

Naya heard the scrape of gravel and guessed her cousin must have gotten down on one knee. He cleared his throat and continued. "On behalf of my parents, my grandmother and my younger brothers – and my uncle, if he lives – I am to make a formal request for sanctuary."

Naya pictured Sunus bowing his head in supplication.

"Of course," Ceru replied, his deep voice generous. "Although your appeal is not mine alone to grant. Your father – and your uncle, should he be spared – will have to appear before our tribe's council of chiefs. We'll be convening at summer's end, near the time of the autumn *Aiqos*. Provided Potis recovers, that should give your family more than enough time to make the journey. Tausos knows where to find us, near the confluence of the two rivers, the Dān and the Lik."

Sunus must have nodded silently in acknowledgement, then stood. Naya again heard the crunch of gravel. Perqos spoke next.

"We should hurry, Father," he urged, "if we're to protect the remainder of the livestock and not risk another confrontation."

"My son has a point," Ceru agreed, addressing Sunus. "We will keep the animals safe on your family's behalf," he promised. "No point letting them fall into Wailos's hands, although I've no doubt he'll harass us along the trail if our paths cross, especially if he believes Naya might be with us."

A generalized shuffling ensued. Naya guessed packs were being shouldered in preparation for departure. She noted the sound of fore-arms being clasped.

"Please convey my prayers for your uncle's recovery," Ceru was saying. "And tell him and your father that we'll look for them and the rest of your family around the time of our Autumn Festival."

"I will," Sunus answered.

Footsteps retreated from the cavern, followed by silence.

For the first time since entering the cave, Naya felt truly alone. Mercifully, exhaustion finally caught up with her. Too tired to think beyond adding enough wood to her fire to ensure the feeble glow remained alight, she curled beneath her robe and fell into an unsettled sleep.

When Naya awoke and opened her eyes, her first sensation was relief. She could see, at least a little. The fire burned low, hardly more than coals, but hadn't gone out. She couldn't judge how long she'd been asleep. Glancing toward the cave entrance, she detected watery green sunlight. How much of the day remained, she had no idea. Reaching for the wood pile, she felt for what kindling remained. Not a lot, but hopefully enough to last until nightfall, when she could safely leave the cave under cover of darkness.

Placing a few sticks atop the embers, Naya crouched, and holding her hair back from her face, blew gently, coaxing the flames to life. She sat back. Although it was summer outside, the air in the cave was bone-chillingly cold, prickling her bare skin. Pulling her robe up around her shoulders and holding it closed with one hand, she groped about with the other until she found her discarded dress – still damp but no longer soaked. One-handed, she spread it out on the ledge to dry. Rummaging inside her satchel, she found her old tunic and leggings. She wasn't sure why she'd brought them – they no longer fit – but until her new dress dried, they were all Naya had. In her haste to leave, she'd left behind the dress Vedukha had made over for her. Shivering, she pulled on the tunic and laced up the leggings, which tied around her waist. Although tight across her chest, the tunic at least came down to mid-thigh, if not all the way to her knees. The leggings, which had once brushed her ankles, reached to mid-calf. Despite being outgrown, the familiar garments felt more comfortable than either her new presentation dress or Veduhka's cast-off that she'd been wearing all spring.

Thinking of Veduhka brought Melit and her sister and brothers to mind. What would the family do, now that Skelos was in charge, *especially if Papa...?* Naya stopped short of imagining the worst. But even if Veduhka and her children wanted to leave along with the rest of Naya's extended family, Skelos was Veduhka's brother-in-law; he might not allow it. What would become of Melit in that case? Would Skelos marry her off to someone from Wailos's clan – his cousin, Unksra, for example? Naya couldn't imagine a less compatible match. She wondered if she would ever see her friend again. And what about her grandmother? Would Awija be strong enough to make the journey south to join Ceru's tribe? Knowing Awija, she would insist on trying. *But what if...?*

Staring unseeing into the flames of her small fire, for the first time since her panicked flight from the settlement, Naya confronted the enormity of what she'd done by running away. Even aside from her father, there were others whom she loved whom she might never see again. A wave of desolation threatened to overwhelm her.

Be practical! she admonished herself. She needed a place to go and people willing to help her. Her first thought was of Ceru. Traveling with him now might be too dangerous, because of Wailos, but perhaps she could make her way on her own to the meeting place he'd mentioned at the confluence of the two rivers. Surely Wailos would give up long before going *that* far in search of her. Then she could at least learn the whereabouts of the red filly. She might be able to reunite with the remnants of her family, including her father if he somehow managed to survive, and possibly even intercept her mother and Oyuun on their return journey from her mother's homeland. From there, she could decide what to do next.

Naya glanced toward the cave entrance, trying to judge how much daylight remained. By now, the mid-summer sun must surely have dropped behind the bluffs and twilight would soon descend. Full dark could not be far off. Certainly she felt hungry enough for a full day to have passed since her last meal. Thirsty as well, Naya wondered if she could find a source of water that would be cleaner than the somewhat stagnant lake. Caves such as this often featured underground springs. She didn't remember any from her previous visit, but perhaps she'd missed something.

As she considered exploring further along the rock shelf, she heard voices again, coming from the cavern above.

"They've been in here, recently. The ashes from their fire are warm and the smell of smoke lingers. At most they have half-a-day's start."

Naya breath caught. She recognized Unksra, Wailos's cousin.

"*Skerdā!*" Wailos himself swore.

At the sound of his voice, Naya's heart pounded as though it might beat out of her chest. What if he found her hiding place?

"Any evidence of her being with them? Footprints?"

"No sign," Unksra replied.

"We'll have to split up. You take a couple of the other men and shadow the Dānus…"

Wailos's voice became muffled. He must have turned away. Naya strained to catch whatever words she could hear.

"…check the river again…"

The raft! Had Wailos found it? Naya held her breath.

More discussion followed, only snatches of which she understood.

"*Dōsos*… infernal dog… lead me straight to her."

Aytal! Wailos must know he'd been sent to search for her. The derogatory term he'd used referred to a slave following orders. And of course Amu was with him. With the dog's help, Aytal was sure to find her. All Wailos needed to do was follow their trail.

Terrified of alerting Wailos to her presence, Naya waited for the sound of footsteps on gravel, indicating he and his cousin had left the cavern. Silence followed. Only then did she dare exhale and consider her options.

Piecing together what she'd heard, Naya concluded that travel by boat still made the most sense, as long as she waited in the cave until long after dark. By then, Wailos would have given up on finding her along the river and she'd have a good chance of eluding him. Assuming she'd gone inland, Wailos would hopefully set-off after Aytal and Amu instead, expecting them to locate her for him. With luck, Aytal would realize he and the dog were being followed and he'd be clever enough to lead Wailos astray. Meanwhile, the Rā would carry Naya a good way south into Dānus territory before turning east, at which point, in order to meet up with Ceru, she would have to abandon the river and continue on foot, but by then she'd be well out of Wailos's grasp.

Having settled on a plan, Naya made herself comfortable beside her small fire, intending to wait until the darkest part of the moonless night before venturing out. So much depended on chance and luck, but at least she was prepared to *do* something, rather than letting everyone else make decisions for her. When the time came, she would maneuver the *plowós* off the rock ledge into the lake, pile her belongings inside, and after wading to the cave's entrance, force the log underwater and out into the Rā's main channel. From there, her true journey would begin.

PART THREE

Chapter Twenty

During Naya's first days on the river, time seemed to flow with the pace of the Rā – swiftly on occasion, as when the banks narrowed and the current took hold, but more often with lazy indifference as the waterway meandered past sandbars and islands, oblivious to Naya's fears of pursuit as well as her impatience to make progress toward her objective. Thankfully the *plowós*, equipped with its own paddle, proved a steady, well-balanced craft, streamlined and low to the water. Naya soon learned to handle the log boat with reasonable competence. Still, despite paddling to hurry time and the *plowós* along, the days passed at the river's measured pace, affording Naya more opportunity for reflection than she welcomed.

The basic requirements for survival did not occupy her unduly. She kept hunger at bay by catching fish with a line and hook discovered amidst her fire-starting kit, and river water was plentiful, if not as sweet as the spring water she preferred. After setting off in the dark the first night and nearly running aground repeatedly, she elected to travel during the day, even if that meant keeping a constant eye on the river's west bank to be sure she wasn't being followed. Eventually, with no sign of pursuit, she eased her vigilance. Nevertheless, when not traveling downstream, she tried to stay hidden, usually along the Rā's eastern shore. At the end of most days, she tied up among the cattails, exhausted enough from paddling to fall into a deep slumber.

On some nights however, despite her fatigue, Naya still slept fitfully, her rest troubled by inchoate dreams – disturbed memories entwined with lurid nightmares – none of which she could recall with any clarity when she awoke. Her grandmother's *tekstlom* remained buried in her pack. Despite the chastening lesson she'd received about the dire consequences of rejecting the prophetic power of her visions, Naya didn't dare allow Awija's dream web to guard her sleep, lest whatever visited her in the night be caught in its strands and cause her to falter in her journey. She must continue down river in search of Ceru. Afterwards – someday – she could think about learning to harness what her grandmother called her gift of sight.

On her fourteenth day on the river, after paddling since sunrise, Naya came to a place where the Rā split in two, flowing on either side of what appeared to be an island of impenetrable matted tussocks threaded through with smaller water channels. Considering which branch of the main river to follow, she chose the western side, where the current seemed stronger. Unfortunately, she ended up trapped behind a series of fish weirs, the first sign of other humans that she'd encountered on her journey.

Leaving the *plowós* jammed against the wooden traps, Naya waded ashore to a strip of beach. Sitting on the sunbaked sand with her knees drawn up, her belongings beside her, she looked across the water toward the island and considered her options. It was midday, a half-moon since fleeing the settlement. A slight breeze carried a marshy smell of rotting vegetation. Overhead, a bird wheeled – an osprey perhaps – but otherwise the sky stretched empty and silent. Naya's stomach rumbled. Her old tunic and leggings, soaked through, stuck to her skin. Wet hair hung in tangles down her back. Had she dared, she would have dropped her head onto her folded arms and closed her eyes against the headache that plagued her most days, a result of sun glaring off the water. But she couldn't let her guard down. The fish weirs indicated a village was nearby.

Beyond the weirs, the branch of the river she'd chosen to follow appeared to skirt the island's southern tip and turn back toward the east, suggesting she may have reached the major bend in the river where she intended to abandon the Rā and turn inland. After growing accustomed to traveling by boat, however, Naya found herself reluctant to leave the relative security of the river, especially without a clear idea of where she was going. Perhaps she should risk approaching the village and asking for directions. She could investigate first, before revealing herself, but the *plowós* would give her presence away. She'd have to hide it before someone came to check on the fish traps.

As if on cue, Naya heard voices approaching in her direction from the embankment above the beach. She scrambled to her feet, prepared to flee. Moments later, three figures appeared, still some distance away. Seeing Naya, they halted.

"Look, Mamma!" two girlish silhouettes exclaimed in unison. "Who's that on the beach?"

The pair of figures broke away and began to hurry down from the embankment. Naya held her ground, right hand wrapped around the hilt of the flint knife tucked into her belt. Two dark-haired girls, one slightly taller than the other, stopped a few paces away. Naya loosened her hold on her knife.

"*Ala*," the younger girl said in greeting. A broad smile dimpled both cheeks. "What's your name?" Her tone was friendly and inquisitive, as though finding a bedraggled stranger washed up on shore was cause for curiosity rather than alarm. The taller girl, whom Naya took to be her older sister, eyed Naya with a scowl but said nothing. Before Naya could answer, the girls' mother joined them.

"*Ala*," she said. "May we assist you?" The expression in her dark eyes was guarded but not hostile. Behind the polite inquiry lay other questions: *Who are you? What are you doing here? Where did you come from? Are you alone?*

Not wanting to seem ill-mannered, Naya hastened to respond. "I am Naya," she said, straightening her spine and squaring her shoulders. "I've come down river from the north." She didn't want to say more until she knew whether the woman and her daughters could be trusted. But she did need help. "May I impose on your hospitality for a meal, and perhaps some guidance about journeying inland from here?"

The woman scanned her from head to toe. "Naya," she repeated. "The red hair and blue eyes… are you Naya, child of Potis, leader among the Plānos?"

"I am." Naya lifted her chin. Denying her identity was pointless – despite her disheveled state, her unusual looks had given her away – and her father would have wanted her to behave with pride in her status as the daughter of a clan chief.

To Naya's surprise, the woman opened outstretched arms. "Welcome!" she exclaimed, inviting Naya into her embrace. "I am Elōr, wife of Ceru, chief of the Dānus. Your father and my husband are good friends." Stunned, Naya hesitated, then stepped forward and allowed herself to be hugged. To refuse would have been awkward – rude, even – yet she could hardly comprehend her good fortune. Of all the people she might have encountered, how was it possible she'd stumbled upon the wife of her father's friend?

"But what are you doing here, and in such a condition?" Elōr asked, as though she too had trouble grasping the situation. Releasing Naya from her embrace, she continued to rest her hands on Naya's shoulders, regarding her with an air of maternal warmth and concern. She was tall – as tall as Naya's mother – with a kind smile. Naya's reserve melted a little under her scrutiny. Still, standing bedraggled under the hot sun beside the river, she was not prepared to confess she'd run away, nor speak of anything else that had happened,

Naya's wretched appearance must have spoken for her, however, for Elōr pulled her into another hug. "Never mind," she said soothingly. "You can tell us your story when you're ready. First, let's get you into some clean, dry clothes and find you something to eat." She put her arm around Naya's waist, drawing her away from the beach. "Girls," she called over her shoulder. "Fetch Naya's boat and pull it up on the sand before it damages the fish traps. Then bring along her things. We'll meet you back at the village."

"Yes, Mamma," they replied, hurrying to do their mother's bidding.

Elōr's tent, later the same day…

After changing into borrowed clothing and eating a light meal, Naya gratefully followed Elōr's suggestion that she retire to her shelter for a nap. When she awoke, she could tell by the golden light filtering through the door flap that the sun had already begun to lower in the west. She'd spent most of the afternoon in blissful slumber. Just as she sat up, Elōr entered, carrying a stack of folded felt blankets.

"Ah, wonderful, you're awake!" she remarked pleasantly. "I was afraid I might disturb you." She crossed the circular space, moving with a grace that again reminded Naya of her mother.

"Did you have a good rest?" Elōr asked over her shoulder, setting down the blankets beside a pile of clothing.

"Yes," Naya replied. "I do feel much better. Thank you." She ran a hand over her tangled hair, wishing she had a comb to make herself more presentable. As if guessing her mind, Elōr rummaged in a corner and handed her one. "Thank you," Naya said again with an embarrassed laugh. "I must be a dreadful sight."

"Nothing that can't be remedied, my dear," Elōr replied cheerfully. Stooping to put her head out of the tent's entrance, she called out, "Rei! Our guest is awake." She turned back to Naya. "My oldest daughter," she explained. "Rei is short for Reiwos. You met her younger sisters, Swelā and Aknā, on the beach. Rei's about your age, maybe a year or two older. She was off gathering provisions when you arrived. She's been waiting to be introduced to you. She can help with your hair, if you like."

The door flap lifted, and a young woman entered. Tall, like her mother, with dark hair pulled back in a braid, in the dim light of the tent she seemed to Naya to be a younger, slimmer version of Elōr.

"Rei," Elōr greeted her daughter. "Naya might like help sorting out her hair. Would you mind?"

The young woman replied with a smile in her voice. "If you'd like me to," she addressed Naya.

Naya smiled back. Having someone to untangle her hair would be a welcome relief. With a pang she thought of Melit. "Please," she responded, holding out the comb. Rei took a seat behind her and lifting Naya's heavy mane off the back of her neck, began to work the comb through the knots.

"We're packing," Elōr remarked, making conversation as she worked. She was folding more clothing, adding to the stack beside the pile of blankets. "It's time for us to move south and find the herds. We can't wait any longer. My husband and his men will have to catch up."

"Find the herds?" Naya asked, attention alerted.

"Yes," Elōr replied. "Earlier in the spring, our herders moved our livestock to pastures near the river Lik. It's the southern-most left bank tributary of the Dān and flows near the border of the Dānus tribe's territory. After escorting them most of the way, my husband and his warriors turned back north to take care of some unfinished business. Meanwhile, the girls and I, along with the other women and children, spent much of the spring and early summer here, at the river camp along the Rā. We're to rejoin the herders a month from now, in anticipation of convening for our tribe's annual autumn festival. We must start back tomorrow to arrive at the designated meeting place on time. Ceru was going to accompany us, but he's obviously been delayed. Or perhaps he decided to go straight there."

"Maybe Naya can tell us when Papa might return," Rei put in.

"Hush Rei, let her be." Elōr spoke in a low voice before Naya could say anything. "Isn't her hair a stunning color?" she remarked brightly in a louder tone. "Like flame."

"It's beautiful," Rei agreed, following her mother's lead. "But so thick, it must be hard to manage without another pair of hands." Her deft fingers brushed lightly against Naya's scalp as she coaxed out the snarls. Naya closed her eyes and felt the tension in her neck and shoulders begin to unwind under the young woman's gentle touch. She decided to let pass for now the mystery of how Rei might suppose that Naya herself would have information regarding her father Ceru's whereabouts and instead allowed herself the simple luxury of being able to relax.

After a moment, Elōr resumed discussion of their imminent departure. "You're welcome to come with us," she offered casually. "As long as you don't mind leaving behind your boat."

Naya opened her eyes. Elōr's back was turned. The older woman's tone had been sincere but not insistent. No pressure, only a genuine gesture of hospitality. Had she been adamant that Naya accompany them, Naya might have felt cornered and balked. Instead, for the first time since fleeing the settlement, she felt… safe.

"If you wouldn't mind," she agreed.

"That's settled then." Elōr sounded relieved. "We'll leave together at first light."

Chapter Twenty-One

Naya traveled with Elōr and her daughters and the other members of their clan for a full moon cycle. They headed away from the Rā, following a well-worn trail leading to the south and west through a mix of open, rolling grasslands interspersed with lightly forested water courses. For the most part, the Dānus clanspeople were friendly and welcoming without being intrusive and, after a few days, appeared to take Naya's presence among them for granted. She suspected she had Elōr to thank for the others' discretion, for which she was grateful. Only Elōr's middle daughter, Aknā, acted resentful, speaking to Naya in monosyllables and otherwise keeping her distance. In contrast, Elōr's youngest child, Swelā, with her sunny disposition, more than made up for her older sister's prickly demeanor. Swelā's favorite pastime was to hold Naya's hand as they walked and chatter away about the puppy her father had promised her.

"Did you ever have a dog?" she asked Naya one day.

"Yes, once," Naya answered.

"What did you call him?" Swelā couldn't make up her mind what to name her new pet.

"Amu," Naya replied, trying not to think about how much she missed him.

"Did he die?" the little girl asked softly. She must have sensed something amiss in Naya's tone.

"No," Naya reassured her. "I had to give him away."

"Oh, but that's sad too!" Swelā exclaimed. "Would it be alright to name my new puppy Amu? Then we can both be reminded of your dog." She looked up at Naya, her smile hopeful.

"I'd like that," Naya answered, doing her best to smile back.

Rei also stayed close by Naya's side, keeping up friendly conversation as they traveled. Naya soon learned all about what it had been like to grow up with two older brothers, as well as two younger sisters, and found herself laughing out loud as Rei recounted all their various childhood escapades. In addition, her vivacious new friend described for Naya the place where they were going – a wide, fertile plain bounded by two rivers, the mighty Dān and its smaller tributary to the south, the Lik. Rei assured her that when they arrived, the normally lush pastureland between the confluence of the rivers would be teeming with the Dānus tribe's vast herds of cattle, sheep and goats.

"Of course, it's been drier than usual so far this summer. There's hardly been any rain," Rei remarked as they approached the end of their journey. "Not as much grass for the livestock to eat. But the number of animals will still be impressive."

"Do you ever see herds of horses?" Naya inquired as nonchalantly as she could manage. Keeping her relationship with the red filly secret had become so ingrained, Naya didn't dare risk seeming too curious. Yet Rei's father and oldest brother had spoken of horses when Naya overheard them in the cave.

"Sometimes," Rei replied. "Especially near the place where we're going. Papa and Perqos are experimenting with taming them."

"Oh? How do you mean, *taming* them?"

"Well, the horses aren't docile, like our cattle, but there are several small bands who have become accustomed to people and even our dogs. Under my father's direction, my brother and some of the other young men take turns guarding them, coaxing the lead mares to move to new pastures along with our other herds of livestock, that sort of thing. The horses are hardier than the cattle, especially with the winters we've been having lately. When we need to, we cull the surplus males for meat, or for the priests' sacrifices."

Naya was astounded by what she was hearing. "Have *you* seen the horses lately?"

"No – not since early spring, when my mother and sisters and I moved to the river camp with the other women. Why?"

"No reason," Naya answered, swallowing her excitement. "Just wondering."

On the second-to-last day of their trek, the group pushed ahead, eager to cover as much distance as possible before dark. They hoped to reach their destination by noon the following day. As the summer sun began to drop behind a distant line of trees, the travelers, satisfied with their progress, agreed to stop for the night. Two boys, not yet old enough to have joined the ranks of the herders, were sent ahead to alert the rest of the tribe of their proximity. Aknā and Swelā begged to go as well and eventually wore their mother down.

"Fine," Elōr said, looking up from the fire she was attempting to start. "But mind you find Árdejā when you get to camp. She'll look after you."

The girls scampered off after the boys, eager, even after the long, dusty day of travel, to be the first to reach camp with news of the larger group's imminent arrival.

"Árdejā?" Naya asked, overhearing the exchange. About to fetch water from a nearby stream, she held a large waxed-leather pouch in one hand. Rei had gone to collect additional wood.

"Ceru's great-aunt," Elōr explained, returning to her fire-starting task. "She is a medicine woman, as is your grandmother Awija, from what I understand?" Elōr did not look up, but Naya heard in her voice the invitation to speak more about her grandmother.

"Yes," Naya replied. "She's a gifted healer and very wise. She's always looked out for me and believed in me, even when I've made mistakes and I… I…"

And I might never see her again. Suddenly, Naya's heart felt like a stone in her chest. She wanted to cry. "I'll go for the water," she managed instead. Turning away, she went in search of the stream.

After supper, gathered around their small fire a little distance from the rest of the group, Elōr, Rei and Naya laid out their bedrolls in companionable silence. Hushed voices, along with smoke from the other campfires, wafted toward them on the night air. Eventually, all grew quiet. Curled on her side on her bison robe, her light blanket pulled up to her chin against the mild chill of the summer night, Naya worried about what the next day would bring. She was bound to be introduced to the rest of the tribe and could no longer avoid the inevitable questions.

Nearly a full moon cycle and a half had elapsed since she had fled her clan's settlement. With no one, including Elōr, pressing her for her reasons for leaving home, Naya had managed, most of the time, not to dwell on what had driven her away. Soon, though, they would encounter Ceru and the rest of the Dānus and explanations would be necessary.

On the one hand, Naya anticipated the moment with dread. More than once she'd almost confessed everything to Elōr, but she always stopped herself, unable to put into words the enormity of what she'd been through. Confronting a group of strangers with her story might require more bravery than she could muster.

On the other hand, she'd come this far to find Ceru. She had questions that only he could answer: Was Wailos still searching for her? Was her father still alive? Could Ceru arrange for Naya to be reunited with her uncle's family? Maybe even with her mother? Last but not least, did he know the whereabouts of the red filly?

But first, she would have to explain what she was doing by herself so far from home. And to do that, she would need to face what had happened.

Rolling onto her back, Naya gazed up into the enormous dome of the night sky. Usually, she loved watching the infinite field of stars circle the heavens. When she was a little girl, Awija had told her to imagine each glimmer as the spirit of an ancestor, shining down on her with love and protection, but tonight's passing clouds obscured all but the brightest stars. Still, the full moon rode high, giving Naya some comfort – until she thought of her grandmother's story. Would she ever hear the ending and learn what happened to Mehnot and Sāwel – the Moon and the Sun? With a heavy sigh, she rolled back onto her side.

"Naya?" Elōr's low voice broke the stillness. Naya didn't answer. "We need to talk," Elōr went on, not waiting for a response. "Before tomorrow, it's important that Rei and I understand more of what's brought you to us. If we're to protect you from gossip and misjudgment, you must share with us what drove you away from your own people. We want to help you, but we can't unless we understand what happened. Will you trust us with your story?"

Yet again, Naya hesitated. Revealing the truth was hard.

"Please? Whatever it is, we only want to help." Rei's soft entreaty echoed her mother's concern.

Tears stung Naya's eyelids and burned in her nostrils. *I have to tell them,* she realized. *Otherwise, how can I expect to face Ceru and everyone else tomorrow?* She inhaled a ragged breath, not trusting herself to speak. Rei shifted on the bedroll beside her and Naya felt a hand reach for hers, giving it a squeeze. Drawing courage from the gesture, Naya found her voice.

"It's all my fault," she began.

Naya did not tell Elōr and Rei everything. She did not mention the red filly, the accident that almost killed her, and the winter spent with her mother and two strangers while she recovered from her wound. She revealed nothing of her otherworldly journeys, her old nightmares, nor the terrors that stalked her more recent dreams and visions. Instead, she started with the springtime raid on her clan's livestock, followed by the fortuitous arrival of a young warrior, son of one of the Plānos tribe's most powerful chiefs, with a plan for how to restore her clan's standing, along with her father's honor, in time for the tribe's annual *Sāwel-Dom* Gathering.

"I believed him," she said, without going into the details of Wailos's scheme involving the captured band of horses. "And so did everyone else, including my father. We all thought he wanted to help us. I believed everything he said to me, and everything everyone said about him. Most importantly, I believed that I was helping my father. But I was wrong."

Haltingly, but without interruption, Naya described how Wailos had courted her, convincing her that the rumors were true, about her father and his father wanting them to marry to strengthen the ties between their two clans. Given Wailos's apparent willingness to assist her clan with recovering from the raid, his interest in her had seemed legitimate. But then everything had gone horribly wrong, starting with the mysterious cloaked figure who had summoned her to leave her shelter before the conclusion of her vigil, and ending with her humiliation in the men's tent, in front of her father and all the other male leaders of the tribe.

"I believed him," Naya concluded, her voice barely above a whisper. "I never should have believed him." Still curled on her side with her hand in Rei's, she turned her head back toward the cavernous expanse of the night sky, her vision obscured. A single unshed tear escaped, sliding past her ear. Furtively she brushed it away.

After a moment, Elōr inquired gently, "When did you realize Wailos's true intent in seducing you was to harm your father?"

Naya had referred only elliptically to what Wailos had done to her in his tent. Her mind shied from reliving the details, while she lacked the words to name the assault for what it was.

"As soon as I saw the look on my father's face in the men's tent afterwards," she confessed, gazing upward into the darkness, seeing again the crowd of male faces, mocking and predatory except for her father's. "I was still confused enough to think that maybe Wailos was telling the truth – but I could see my father was horrified."

Closing her eyes, Naya wished she could blot out the memory of his expression. "I never should have assumed that Wailos could ever truly have been interested in me," she berated herself. "Instead of helping my father, I let Wailos use me to bring shame upon him. Now you see why I thought I needed to leave. Everyone would have accepted Wailos's story, that I tried to entrap him. At least with me gone, I believed my father could disavow any involvement."

"Are those your words, or someone else's?" Elōr asked.

"My cousin, Saurosa," Naya admitted. "I realized later that she must have been in on Wailos's plan all along. She was the cloaked figure who called me out of my shelter and led me to him, and then she ushered us into the men's tent afterwards. When I ran back to my shelter, she followed me and told me the best thing I could do would be to leave. Only..."

Naya's voice caught and Rei squeezed her hand again.

"...only there's more."

"Go on," Elōr prompted.

Freeing her hand from Rei's, Naya rolled to her side and sat up. Pulling the blanket around her shoulders and hugging her knees to her chest, she rested her forehead on her crossed forearms and willed herself not to cry. "It wouldn't have mattered if I'd stayed," she managed, voice muffled. "My father... he's... he might be..." She struggled to continue.

Elōr must have guessed what Naya couldn't bring herself to say. After a moment, she asked quietly, "How do you know?"

Naya swallowed without looking up. "Ceru," she began, then stopped, still striving to compose herself. She lifted her head. "I was in a cave... along the river, hiding from the men who were searching for me. I overheard my cousin Sunus... talking to Ceru and Perqos."

Naya tried to draw breath. She'd managed through sheer determination to recount the story so far but now had to force herself to go on.

"Sunus told them what happened after… in the men's tent. My father… an argument… angry… lost his temper…" Naya hiccupped. "Skelos… mace…"

At last she broke down entirely, sobbing in earnest. "I saw it," she wailed. "In a vision… it's my fault."

"Oh Naya," Rei exclaimed, sitting up and putting her arms around Naya's shoulders. "I'm so sorry! But surely it's not your fault. How could it be?"

Turning into Rei's embrace and laying her head on her shoulder, Naya surrendered, allowing the tears to flow unchecked – tears she'd been keeping at bay ever since learning in the cave that her vision on the river had come to pass and her father could well be dead. At some point, Elōr rose and came to sit on Naya's other side, wrapping her arms around both girls. Only after the storm subsided did anyone speak.

"It's not your fault," Rei repeated.

Head still buried in Rei's shoulder, Naya waited for similar words of reassurance from Elōr, but the older woman remained silent. Instead, withdrawing her embrace, she returned to her place by the fire.

Through the remnants of her tears, Naya wondered if she'd been wrong to reveal so much. She imagined Elōr must be weighing everything she'd confessed and considering the ramifications. Did Elōr condemn her for her credulity where Wailos was concerned? For her failure to obey the firm instructions she and the other girls had been given to remain in their shelters? For embarrassing her father and causing him to lose his temper? Did Elōr blame Naya for her father's likely death, just as Naya blamed herself? Wishing she hadn't said anything, she forced down a fresh outburst of grief. Rei's arms tightened around her.

At last, Elōr spoke. "I'm very sorry for all you've been through, and that you've carried this burden by yourself, for all the time that you've been with us," she said. "You obviously didn't wish to speak of it, and I had to honor that. Rei and I wanted to allow you to come to know us before asking you to trust us with your secrets."

But do you blame me? Naya wanted to ask. Beneath the genuine sympathy and concern, there was a hard edge to the older woman's voice. Naya looked up, trying to discern her expression, but Elōr's face was hidden in the darkness.

"Thank you for finding the courage to share your story," she continued. "I know it was difficult, but now that we understand what you've been through, we'll know better how to shield you going forward. I'm sure your mother would do the same for Rei, were your situations reversed."

There it was again, the controlled tightness behind the kind words. Anger, yes, but perhaps not aimed at her? Summoning the last of her nerve, Naya spoke up. "You're not upset with me?"

"With you?" Elōr sounded surprised. "No, my dear, of course not! As Rei said, none of this is your fault. If I'm upset with anyone, it's with those who failed to protect you."

Relief flooded Naya. Far from condemning her, Elōr was furious on her behalf.

Elōr shifted, adding wood to the fire before settling her hide robe around her shoulders. "Where *was* your mother in all this, by the way?" she asked.

"You didn't meet her?" Now it was Naya's turn to be surprised. She pulled away from Rei and sat straighter, hitching up her own blanket. "I overheard Ceru mention that he'd run into her when she and a companion passed through Dānus territory, earlier in the spring. I assumed you would have been present as well."

"That must have been after we set out for the river camp," Elōr replied. "We haven't seen my husband since then. How did your mother come to be so far from your settlement?"

"She was traveling," Naya hedged, stating no more than the obvious. Casting about for an explanation that would not place her mother in too unfair a light, she settled on the briefest possible version of the truth. "She was homesick and had an opportunity to return to where she grew up, in the mountains south of here, for a visit. A trader we knew was going that way, and so she… she went with him."

It sounded simple, Naya thought. Perhaps it *was* that simple. Ceru hadn't seemed scandalized when he'd mentioned Sata and Oyuun traveling together, nor, for that matter, had her father seemed to mind that much when her mother had left, nor missed her after she'd gone. He'd been too busy. Why had Naya been so hard on her?

"Ah," remarked Elōr. "I thought as much. Your father may not have realized what Wailos was up to — men can be rather obtuse sometimes — but your mother never would have allowed things to get so dangerously out of hand."

"Mamma," Rei's voice broke in. She sat up straight. "We have to tell Naya — now — tonight. Before she hears it from someone else."

"What?" Naya demanded, alarmed. Shadows hid Rei's expression despite the rekindled fire. Did she and Elōr know something about her mother after all? Had something happened to her? Fear clutched her heart. "My mother?" she asked anxiously.

"No, my dear. As far as we know, your mother is fine," Elōr replied. "But Rei is right – you have been brave enough to trust us with your story – now we must disclose a painful truth to you. First, you mustn't blame yourself for what has happened. You cannot be held responsible for believing Wailos. You are young and inexperienced, while Wailos is charming and a practiced deceiver. You had no idea the extent of his scheming. Your father, however, cannot make the same excuse."

"What do you mean?" Naya asked, confused. The edge had returned to Elōr's voice and she spoke of Wailos as though through personal experience.

"No doubt your father had his reasons for not sharing with you what he knew," Elōr continued, leaning forward once more to poke at the fire. "I'm sure he thought he was keeping you safe." The disapproval in her tone was unmistakable.

"What?" demanded Naya, increasingly bewildered. "What did my father know?"

Elōr sat back. "The raid on your clan's livestock last spring?" she began. "That was Wailos. He and his *kóryos* made off with the prime animals, but not with the intent of keeping them. No, his aim was solely to weaken your clan's standing within the tribe and, in the process, destroy your father's reputation so that his own father would be named chief of chiefs following the death of your grandfather."

"And my father knew?" Naya was incredulous. "How?"

"Because," Elōr answered, "Wailos brought the animals to us." Across the fire, she held Naya's eyes with hers.

Naya's head was spinning. Her supposition about Wailos's involvement in the original raid was correct, but it still didn't seem possible, nor could she grasp Elōr's revelation about her father. "I don't understand," she stammered. "Why would Wailos… My father never…" She trailed off, unable to make sense what she was hearing.

Elōr hastened to explain. "Early last spring, when the raid occurred, a portion of our herds were grazing north of here, about halfway between your settlement and where we are now, an area we often frequent. Wailos must have known where to find us. He claimed to be the son of your father and to have been sent to arrange a marriage alliance between himself and our oldest daughter – Rei."

"He made my skin crawl," Rei remarked, shuddering, "although lots of the other girls thought he was *so* good-looking."

"Before you claim too much credit, my dear, remember that you had the advantage of being taken into *your* father's confidence from the beginning," Elōr observed. "Wailos offered the stolen livestock as the bride price," she went on. "What he didn't count on was that Ceru would recognize the animals, and to whom they belonged. In particular, that handsome young bull gave Wailos away – when Potis and Ceru ran into each other last summer, your father bragged about acquiring him."

"But how did my father learn of all this?" Naya's blanket had slipped, unnoticed, from around her shoulders.

"The search party, led by your uncle. Although they stopped short of entering our camp, Tausos and Ceru met secretly and reasoned out the gist of Wailos's plot. They agreed that Ceru would keep the animals safe and then bring them to the Gathering, so that your father could demonstrate Regos's treachery to the Plānos tribe's other leaders."

Naya stared into the flames as the pieces began to fall into place. She could feel Elōr's gaze on her from across the fire.

"Among the Dānus," Rei put in, "only my father and my oldest brother – plus Momma and I – know about the raid and that the animals really belong to your clan. Everyone else thinks my father and his warriors took the young bull and the rest of the animals to your tribe's Gathering in order to arrange a marriage for his eldest son."

Naya was only half listening. "Another marriage?" she managed, then realized Rei was referring to Perqos, the young man whose voice she'd heard in the cave. "Who is *he* supposed to marry?" she asked, looking up.

"You!" Rei answered.

"Me?!" Naya stared at Rei, incredulous.

"It's not such a far-fetched idea," Elōr pointed out. "My husband and your father have discussed the possibility more than once since you and Perqos were small. But that's why Aknā has been so unfriendly. She's naturally suspicious of strangers, and when she found out you're the young woman her beloved oldest brother is supposed to marry, she made up her mind to dislike you."

"But why did Wailos come back to our settlement after the raid?" Naya asked Elōr. "And why didn't my father denounce him when he did?" Her first night home, Wailos had been the center of attention, and she hadn't been able to get her father to speak to her. Why hadn't he told her what he knew?

"Those are very good questions, my dear," Elōr replied, the now-familiar edge returning once more to her voice. "As far as Wailos showing up, I suspect he wanted to keep an eye on things. He may even have gotten wind of the possibility of a marriage involving you and Perqos and decided to ruin any chance of such an advantageous alliance compromising his plans to weaken your father's standing.

"As for your father, he already knew Wailos was behind the raid and likely up to further mischief but couldn't accuse him without proof. Regos is too powerful. In the meantime, he must have decided to keep an eye on Wailos as well, without tipping him off. Obviously, your father didn't watch Wailos closely enough."

Staring into the fire, Naya said nothing. From all the overwhelming truths, one fact stood out. Her father had known all along – and told her nothing. He hadn't believed her worthy of his confidence, even when knowing the truth would have protected her. A log shifted, sending a shower of sparks skyward. Something inside Naya cracked, then shattered into a thousand pieces. Her body shook, but no sound emerged. Rei tried to put her arms around her again, but Naya ducked away.

"Let her be," Elōr admonished her daughter gently. Rising, she draped her own blanket around Naya's shoulders before returning to her seat by the fire. "Both of you, try to get some rest," she added. "We'll decide how to handle all of this in the morning."

Chapter Twenty-Two

"Pssst!" A man's voiced hissed near Naya's ear, waking her. Startled, she sat up, still clutching Elōr's blanket around her shoulders. The fire was out.

"Shhh!" warned the man. His voice seemed familiar. "Where's Elōr?"

"I don't know," Naya whispered back, glancing toward Elōr's empty place beside the cold fire. "She and Rei were here when I fell asleep." The full moon, not yet set, cast enough light that she could tell that Rei's bedroll was deserted as well. Where could they have gone?

"Who are you?" The man was insistent.

"Naya," she answered, too surprised to think of whether she should tell the truth or not.

"Ah, thank the gods!" declared the man, evidently relieved. "But where's Elōr?"

"Here," Elōr's tall figure emerged from the shadows. "Ceru? Is that you?"

"Yes. Where's Rei?"

"I'm here too, Papa." Rei stepped from behind her mother.

Ceru? Naya was stunned.

"Quickly." Ceru's voice was low and urgent. "All of you, gather your things and come with me. Be as quiet as you can. I'll explain when we get where we're going. It's not far."

Light was beginning to creep into the eastern sky as they neared their destination. At the top of a low rise, Ceru stopped and pointed. Naya could make out a line of darker shadows cast by a stand of trees – poplars, she guessed – marking a waterway. Despite Ceru's assurance that they didn't have far to go, he'd set a brisk pace and by Naya's reckoning, they were now a good distance southwest of where they'd started, which must mean they weren't far from the main Dānus encampment. With no discernible path to follow, she'd been grateful for Rei's hand linked with hers as they'd hurried after Ceru and Elōr in the pre-dawn darkness. They'd traveled in silence, only the crunch of dry grass, brittle from lack of rain, marking their passage. Naya had been too busy concentrating on keeping up to give much thought to the previous night's devastating revelations, nor to speculate about where they were going. She'd felt nauseous when she'd gotten up and wished they'd been able to eat something before setting out.

Now, as they approached the line of trees, figures began to materialize – some crouched, others standing – evidently awaiting their arrival. Naya counted five silhouettes. Just as she wondered who they might be, a shape burst from the shadows and came streaking toward them. Moments later, Naya was flat on her back, a warm, wet tongue frantically licking her face.

"Amu!" she gasped, trying unsuccessfully to fend off the dog. She was as surprised as he was overjoyed by their reunion.

"Is he yours?" Rei asked, unnecessarily. She put out a hand as Naya struggled to regain her feet.

"Hush girls," Elōr cautioned, but with a hint of humor in her voice. Amu, managing not to bark, wagged his tail ecstatically.

"Come along," Ceru added, less obviously amused at the dog's exuberance. "We don't have time to waste."

Before Naya could ask if Aytal was among the waiting group, they reached the shelter of the trees and she found herself being introduced to Ceru and Elōr's two sons, Perqos and Weri, as well as Ceru's brother Awontlos and Awontlos's two grown sons, Merkō and Mikāmi. All the men were dark-haired, tan-skinned and of medium height and imposing build, like Ceru himself. She saw no sign of Aytal's taller, less burly form. Wriggling with excitement, Amu circled her legs, threatening to trip and knock her over again.

"Naya." Ceru beckoned to her. "Come and meet my great-aunt, Árdejā. She insisted on accompanying us to find you, so that she might speak with you."

Stepping aside, Ceru gestured toward a hunched form, seated at a distance from the others, whom Naya had not noticed when they arrived. Wrapped in a generous shawl against the dawn chill, the figure pushed back her head covering as they approached, revealing a glimpse of snow-white hair. Naya couldn't make out the old woman's features, beyond an impression of brown skin as deeply furrowed as the bark of an ancient tree.

"Welcome, my dear." The withered voice sounded like the croaking of a heron.

"Thank you," Naya stammered, wondering why Ceru's great-aunt, who must be even older than Awija, would want to come out to the woods before sun-up to meet her. "I'm honored," she added, remembering her manners.

"You may call me Árdejā," the old woman replied, inclining her head. "You have questions," she went on, looking up at Naya and appraising her with a shrewd, bird-like eye. "My nephew will answer them," she continued. "I only have breath for what's important. Listen carefully."

Gesturing, she indicated Naya was to sit across from her. Naya hastened to comply. As soon as she was seated, Amu climbed into her lap and leaned into her chest. Naya put her arms around him.

"Ceru, Elōr – you must listen as well," Árdejā pronounced. "Sit," she ordered, pointing to either side of Naya. "The rest of you…" She gave a glance back over her shoulder, accompanied by a dismissive flick of the wrist. "Go away." Obediently, the others faded into the shadows to wait at a respectful distance, well out of ear shot. Ceru and Elōr took their places as instructed. Naya was impressed. She'd never encountered anyone quite so imperious, even Awija.

"Your grandmother is a wise woman," Árdejā began, as if in response to Naya's unspoken thoughts. "No doubt she has done her best to counsel you. Your grandfather, too, possessed much foresight. You must take all they have said to you to heart. Do you understand?"

"Yes, Árdejā," Naya answered, baffled by the old woman's knowledge of her family.

"Of course I know who you are, and who your grandparents are!" Árdejā remonstrated impatiently. "They have spoken to you, as do I, with the voice of the Ancestors. You would be wise to listen."

Chastened, Naya bowed her head.

"You have been called, more than once, to see with the eyes of your heart, have you not?" Naya looked up, startled, and encountered the intensity of the old woman's gaze. She nodded. The words were those spoken by the voice in her visions – the words that, up until this moment, Naya had never been fully able to recall. *How does she know?* she thought.

"I know because I know," Árdejā assured her. "Your spirit feels a deep yearning – one you cannot deny, although you have tried. Am I right?" She held Naya's eyes with hers.

Naya stared back, her heartbeat quickening. *Who is this person?* On either side of her, Ceru and Elōr exchanged glances.

Árdejā turned her gaze on Ceru. "This girl – Naya – she is sought by the enemies of her father, who is your friend, yes?"

Ceru nodded.

"You must protect her. Do you understand?"

Ceru nodded again. "Of course," he said. "For her own sake, as well as the sake of her father."

"This is for the girl's sake," Árdejā agreed. "And also for the sake of the horses."

Naya sucked in her breath. *She knows about the horses?*

"Yes, I know about the horses," Árdejā replied, looking at Naya. "You have been called," she repeated. "You accepted the call and undertook a task – and you have accomplished much – but the covenant to which you agreed remains unfulfilled. Abandoning the task now would be worse than never having begun. You know this in your heart, do you not? Answer me!"

"Yes," Naya whispered. She thought of her confrontation with Awija, before the start of her vigil, when her grandmother had lectured her about the horses and the future that she and the red filly might already have been set in motion. Her grandmother had said much the same thing as Árdejā, but Naya had not wanted to listen.

"This time, you *must* listen," Árdejā reproved. "For your own sake, and the sake of the horses. My nephew can explain when I'm finished." She turned back to Ceru. "The cave," she said. "You know the one I mean?"

Ceru nodded. "Perqos and I had the same thought," he told her.

"The dark will keep her safe," Árdejā went on. "The dark will restore her heart. She may be guided as far as the cave's entrance by someone you trust with her life, but she must be left to journey into the darkness alone. No one else can know where she's gone, if she is to be safe, and no one may accompany her into the darkness, if she is to be healed."

Naya's arms tightened around Amu, still snuggled in her lap.

"She may keep the dog with her," Árdejā conceded, without taking her eyes from Ceru.

"How long must she remain hidden in the cave?" he asked.

"Until the next full moon," she answered. "Someone may look after her well-being but there must be no contact. Do you understand?"

"Yes, Árdejā." Ceru's voice was grave.

"Is this really necessary, Árdejā?" Elōr spoke for the first time. "Such a long time to remain hidden…"

"For her safety, yes," the old woman replied. "Her pursuers will not leave her in peace, otherwise. But also, she must be given time to begin to heal and to learn to see – alone, and in the darkness. It is the only way. Do I have your agreement?" Her voice was sharp.

"Yes, Árdejā," Elōr acquiesced, still sounding reluctant. "We will see to it," she promised.

"Good. That's settled then. Awontlos and his sons may take me back to the encampment now."

"Wait!" Naya protested, finding her voice. She addressed the old woman. "I don't understand any of this."

"My nephew will explain," Árdejā repeated.

"But…" Naya objected.

Árdejā held up a stern hand, silencing her. "I've said all that I came to say," she declared. "Except for this. Remember, Naya, that you have been wounded and wandered in the dark before. You have lost courage, only to rediscover it. You would not have been called were you not capable of fulfilling the covenant. Trust your heart. Do not be afraid of what it knows and feels. In the darkness, you will discover an important ally, someone who has been with you all along, and you will learn to see." Pulling her shawl back over her head, the old woman turned away, signaling the audience was at an end.

Ceru had already risen, clearly eager to get moving. "Perqos," he called softly, beckoning to his son to approach ahead of Awontlos and the others. "You are to escort Naya to the cave, as we discussed." Perqos nodded and Ceru turned back to Árdejā. "His absence will be the easiest to explain and there is no one I trust more with her life." The old woman nodded her agreement. "Awontlos!" Ceru called more loudly, waving to his brother.

"Stop!" Naya felt as though she was waking up from a trance. Pushing

Amu off her lap, she came to her feet. "I'm not going anywhere with anyone until I understand what's going on. How do you know so much about me?" she asked Árdejā, looking down at the old woman, who was still seated. "And how did my dog get here?" she added, turning to Ceru. "Where's Aytal?"

"Shhh!" Ceru warned, glancing toward his brother and nephews, who were now almost close enough to overhear. "Naya," he said in an undertone, "Elōr and I will remain behind with you and Perqos. After the others have gone, we can talk."

He turned as Awontlos drew near. "Árdejā is ready to return," he announced. "Please take Rei and Weri back with you as well. Elōr and I will follow as soon as we can, while Perqos takes Naya, here, to catch-up with the visitor who was in camp yesterday."

Awontlos gave his brother a look but then bowed his head in assent. "As you wish."

Naya watched as he and his sons, along with Weri, took hold of the ends of the poles of the makeshift litter upon which Árdejā was seated. Lifting the old woman between them, they set off through the trees. After giving Naya a quick hug and a glance back over her shoulder, Rei followed.

"Now will you answer my questions?" Naya demanded as soon as the group was out of earshot. "I don't understand any of this." She and Elōr stood facing Ceru under the shelter of the trees. Amu paced a circle in the space between them. Perqos waited off to one side, as though unsure whether he was meant to be included in the conversation.

Ceru gestured for him to join them, then spoke to Elōr. "Does she know about her father?"

"What about my father?" Naya interjected, suddenly apprehensive. Despite everything, she'd been holding onto a slender thread of hope that he'd survived. She couldn't decipher Ceru's expression, only the grim set of his shoulders.

"Yes, what about her father?" echoed Elōr, stepping closer and putting an arm around Naya. "She knows that Potis learned the truth early on about Wailos and the raid, if that's what you mean, but only because Rei and I had the decency to tell her. And she knows about the prize bull being slaughtered, and Potis having been gravely injured – news *she* shared with *us*. Is there more?"

"But how..?" Ceru and Perqos chorused.

"She overheard you talking with her cousin in the cavern near her clan's settlement …" Elōr began.

"…but when Sunus came to you, he wasn't sure if my father was going to survive or not," Naya finished. "What more have you found out?"

When neither Ceru nor Perqos replied immediately, Elōr spoke up. "Just be honest," she chided. "That isn't like you, Ceru. The young woman is strong enough to bear the truth. Stop treating her like a child. That was her father's mistake. If he'd trusted her enough to bring her into his confidence from the beginning, this all might have turned out differently."

"You're right." Ceru acknowledged, addressing his wife. He turned to Naya. "He's gone, Naya. He died from the blow to his head."

Despite the blunt words, Ceru's voice was filled with compassion. Naya stared at him blankly. The slender thread of hope she'd clung to snapped, and with a moan, she buried her head in Elōr's breast. Amu whined, pressing himself against her legs.

"When did you find out?" Elōr asked Ceru, wrapping her arms around Naya's shoulders.

"We only found out for certain yesterday, when the young man sent to look for Naya showed up at our encampment near the meeting place."

"Aytal?" Wiping away tears, Naya turned back to Ceru. Elōr kept an arm around her waist.

"Yes," Ceru confirmed. "Apparently, Naya, your father's spirit left this world on the morning of the solstice, just as the sun darkened. A more ominous omen has never been seen in my lifetime."

"But how could Aytal know for sure?" Naya protested, still grasping for the thread. "Didn't he set out sooner than that to look for me?" *Papa. Dead.* She couldn't stand to think about it.

"He did – at your father's command. They were his last words. Aytal is a very brave and determined young man. He and the dog have been on your trail for well over a moon." Ceru gestured with his chin toward Amu.

"But if they've been following her for that long," Elōr asked, "how did Aytal have confirmation of Potis's death?"

Naya stood frozen, arms crossed tight against her chest, grateful for Elōr's questions so that she didn't have to speak. She concentrated instead on what the others were saying.

"Why didn't Aytal catch up to her?" Elōr wondered. "Did he know she was on the river?"

"Yes, he quickly figured out the way Naya must have gone but he also discovered that he wasn't the only one trying to find her. Not long after he set out, Aytal became aware that Wailos and his men were following *him*. At first he wasn't sure why, but by eavesdropping on their camp he learned not only that Potis had succumbed to his injuries – a scout from the settlement had just brought Wailos the news – but also that Wailos and his men were tracking him in order to find Naya. As soon as Aytal realized the danger Naya was in from Wailos, he had the good sense to lure Wailos and his companions away from the Rā." Ceru turned to Naya. "Without Aytal, you might never have made it safely as far as you did."

"But I don't understand." Elōr still spoke, her arm tightening around Naya's waist. "Why is Wailos so determined to find her?

"He needs me." Voice flat, Naya answered before Ceru could reply. "I'm valuable to him. Otherwise, the other tribal leaders won't support Regos as chief of chiefs." She met Ceru's gaze, daring him to contradict her.

"You overheard that part too?" Perqos asked.

Naya nodded without taking her eyes from the Dānus chief. "With Papa gone, Wailos will never give up, will he?" She knew the answer. The realization landed with a sickening thud in the pit of her stomach.

"Unfortunately, I'm afraid that's the case," Ceru agreed, returning Naya's regard. Árdejā is right to insist that you stay well-hidden, at least long enough to throw him off track."

"And Aytal," Elōr asked. "Why did he end up at our encampment? Shouldn't he have led Wailos off into the steppe somewhere?"

"He did," Ceru explained, "but then he doubled back and picked up our trail. Tausos told him before he left the settlement how to find me if he needed help. Perqos and I and the rest of the men arrived back at the encampment the day before yesterday, only a day ahead of him."

Pausing, Ceru took half a step toward Naya. "Are you alright?" he asked. To Naya, his voice sounded strangely muffled. "Perqos," he directed, closing the distance, "fetch a waterskin from my pack. Naya looks like she could use something to drink."

Before Perqos could comply, Naya's knees started to buckle. With Elōr and Ceru supporting her from either side, she slid to the ground.

"She's about to faint." Worried, Elōr knelt beside her.

"I'm okay," Naya mumbled, putting her head between her knees.

Elōr shifted to support Naya's forehead with the palm of her hand. "See if you can find something to eat as well," she called to Perqos.

"There should be some leftover seedcake," Ceru added, moving back to give Naya air. He crouched in front of her, collaring Amu to keep him out of the way. Elōr stayed at her side.

Closing her eyes, Naya took a deep breath in through her nostrils. "Aytal?" she prompted. She wanted Ceru to keep talking, so that she had something to distract her from the images invading her mind – of her father, struck down, dying at her feet, and Wailos, garbed in his wolf pelt, chasing after her.

Ceru, sitting back on his heels, obliged. "Aytal showed up in camp yesterday afternoon," he told her. "Thankfully, he had the good sense to wait to relay his story until we could talk in private – we don't need the whole tribe knowing all the details. Last night, after most of the camp had gone to sleep, he and Perqos and I were in my tent, debating what to do about Wailos, when Aknā and Swelā appeared with news of finding a bedraggled young woman on the beach near the river camp. They obviously knew who you were, Naya, and informed us you'd be arriving with Elōr the next day. You should have seen the relief on that young man's face when he heard you were safe!"

"Where is he?" Naya asked, lifting her head and sitting back. Still queasy, she no longer felt in imminent danger of passing out. With as much of a smile as she could muster, she accepted the wrapped packet Perqos handed her, along with a waterskin. Perqos smiled back, then moved to squat beside his father and took over the job of restraining Amu. "Why didn't Aytal come with you?" Naya persisted.

"He left," Ceru replied. "He couldn't afford to wait around for you to arrive in camp."

Naya's heart sank. *He never wants to see me again,* she thought, re-membering the unkind words she'd spoken the last time she'd seen him, even before she'd lost her temper.

"But why go in such a hurry, without waiting to see her?" Elōr pressed, as though sensing Naya's disappointment.

"It's part of the plan we came up with," Ceru replied. He turned to Naya. "Before Aknā and Swelā arrived, rumors were already spreading in camp about Aytal and who he was looking for – so we sent him to find you. At least that's what we're telling everyone."

"But she's here," Elōr objected.

"And she's still being followed," Ceru countered. "Wailos is bound to show up before too long. We couldn't risk having Naya come into camp and be seen by the entire tribe – as you know, not everyone can be trusted. We must heed what Árdejā told us and hide Naya in the cave as soon as possible – it's the safest place for her. Meanwhile, Aytal will continue to lead Naya's pursuers off-track. He's headed further up into the mountains, where supposedly Naya has gone to find her mother – at least that's the story we're spreading." Placing his hands on his knees, Ceru prepared to stand. "If you're feeling up to it," he said to Naya, "you and Perqos should get moving."

"No, wait." Naya finished the last bite of seed cake. "At least tell me what you know about the horses," she insisted.

"Yes, Ceru," Elōr spoke as well. "What did Árdejā mean, *for Naya's sake, and the sake of the horses*? Surely she wasn't referring to the ones you and Perqos have been trying to tame – how would Naya even have heard about them? I know for a fact you never revealed to Potis what you've been up to."

Naya interjected. "Rei told me," she confessed, "but only because I asked her. Also, I heard you and Perqos talking about horses in the cave," she went on, addressing Ceru, "in particular, the ones who may have been following my mother and Oyuun…?"

Naya left the question hanging. She didn't want to be the first to mention Réhda and the others, but now was her chance to find out.

"The ones…?" Elōr started to ask.

Ceru interrupted. "I know all about the red filly, if that's what you're wondering," he said, speaking to Naya. "Your mother told me."

Naya's eyes widened. "Everything?" she asked.

"Maybe not everything," Ceru conceded, "but enough."

"Explain," Elōr demanded, looking between her husband and Naya.

"Did Naya mention that last spring, her mother passed through with Aytal's father, on their way to Sata's homeland?" Ceru asked.

"She did," Elōr confirmed.

"And did she mention the horses who accompanied them?"

"No, she left that part out."

"It was after you and the other women left for the river camp," Ceru clarified. "We haven't seen each other since then," he explained to Naya. "Your mother wanted me and my men to be on the look-out for the red filly and the others – the gray stallion and the mare. She told me what you accomplished, Naya, but made me promise to be discreet, lest either you or the filly be put in danger. Your mother is very proud of you, and with reason.”

Naya dropped her eyes, embarrassed.

Ceru turned to Elōr. “This young woman managed to not only tame but *ride* on the back of a wild horse – a stunning copper-coated three-year-old filly.” He was clearly impressed. “I can understand why Árdejā believes you’ve been called to a special purpose,” he continued, addressing Naya again. “I’ve seen young warriors attempt to mount a trapped horse on a dare, but no one has ever succeeded in staying on, at least to my knowledge. I hope someday when we have more time together, you’ll share your secret.” Ceru inclined his head in respect, followed by one of his most charming smiles.

Feeling self-conscious, Naya blushed. “Aytal rode as well,” she protested. “I couldn’t have done it without him.”

“Be that as it may, Árdejā was clear about your special destiny,” Ceru reproved her. “Aytal, too, spoke of it when Perqos and I talked to him last night. He calls you *She-Who-Rides-Horses* in his language. Did you know that?’

Discomfited, Naya shook her head. She didn’t know whether to be irritated or pleased. Perhaps Aytal wasn’t as angry with her as she thought.

“Your mother also told me about the rest of the herd you befriended – and that they were captured, thanks to Wailos,” Ceru went on, “although later we heard from Sunus that those horses managed to escape. In any case, Sata and Oyuun reported sighting the filly and the mare and the stallion repeatedly on their journey south through our territory. Sata made me promise not to let anything happen to them, if I could prevent it. After she and Oyuun continued on their way, I had several reports of the three horses being spotted – always at a distance. Before I left to travel north, I tracked them down for myself. They appear to have been accepted into one of the bands we monitor – at least the mare and the filly. The young stallion was hanging around on the outskirts. I’ve given orders they are not to be hunted, nor harassed. As far as I know, they’re still together and unharmed.”

Naya felt faint again, this time with relief. Her mother was safe, and so was the red filly. Elōr, who’d been holding the waterskin, passed it to her with a smile and she took a drink as Ceru looked on. Perqos, his pack slung over his back, stood off to one side, waiting.

"Feeling better?" Ceru asked as soon as Naya had finished and handed the water skin back to Elōr.

"Yes," Naya replied, wiping her mouth with the back of her hand.

"Good." Ceru stood. "We can't delay any longer." Indeed, the sun was now well up, casting east-to-west shadows amongst the small grove of trees, and the air was already warm.

"Gather your things," Ceru prompted. "Perqos will see you safely to where you're going and remain close by to bring provisions and keep watch. Otherwise, I advise you to abide by Árdejā's instructions to avoid contact and stay hidden by yourself in the cave. Even if you did not need to disappear for your own protection, you would be wise to do as she commands. Knowing Árdejā, a treasure beyond worth awaits, if you but have the courage to go alone into the darkness in search of it."

A short while later…

Walking side by side, Elōr and Ceru set out along an open track that skirted the woods lining the water course leading back to the encampment. The day promised to be hot and Elōr was glad they did not have too far to travel.

"I'm still not sure I understand how we're going to keep Naya's whereabouts a secret," she commented. "Or why we need to. Árdejā was certainly insistent, and Naya seemed to understand, but I'm not sure I do – why exactly is Wailos so set on finding her?"

Ceru glanced at Elōr. "Did Naya tell you what happened – the reason Potis and Skelos came to blows?"

"If you mean what Wailos did to her, yes, although she didn't seem to know how to speak of it," Elōr answered. "Rather than being outraged at having been violated, she blames herself. She's consumed with regret for bringing shame on her father. His death only makes it worse – now that she knows that he's gone, she's bound to hold herself responsible, even as she's upset at not being taken into his confidence."

Elōr didn't bother disguising her frustration. "She needs to take some anger into that cave with her, rather than just the guilt," she said, turning to Ceru. "Anger at Wailos, and anger at her father as well." Ceru didn't respond and Elōr returned to her original question. "But why is hiding her whereabouts necessary in the first place?" she asked. "And for an entire moon! Is she really that important to Wailos?"

"She is now. Tausos's theory is that Regos didn't fully account for the degree of enmity between Potis and Skelos," Ceru replied, "and I think he's probably right. Wailos's performance with Naya in front of the other clan leaders – the whole scheme to use her to discredit her father – might have worked were it not for Skelos striking Potis and…."

"… and causing his death?"

Stopping, Ceru nodded, staring straight ahead without speaking. Halting beside him, Elōr searched his profile, then laid a hand on his arm. "You miss him." Ceru nodded again, not looking at her, his mouth a tight line. After a moment, he released an audible breath, Elōr withdrew her hand and they resumed walking.

Ceru continued with his explanation. "Whether or not it was an accident," he said to Elōr, "it all looks too suspicious, especially followed by Naya's disappearance. Afterwards, Wailos had to make a show of good faith. He had to demonstrate that he didn't intend to harm Naya, any more than Skelos intended to eliminate Regos's chief rival, in order to prevent the other clan leaders from turning against all three of them and upending Regos's ambitions."

Elōr wanted to be sure that she understood. "So, by going after Naya and bringing her home safely, Wailos can at least attest to his own innocence in what happened on the last night of her vigil?"

"That's right," Ceru agreed. "By herself, Naya may not be that important to the other clan leaders, but she *is* Potis's only child. As such, she's worth a lot – both as a hostage to Wailos's reputation and as surety for Regos's quest to become chief of chiefs. In fact…" Ceru glanced at Elōr as they walked, "I wouldn't be surprised if Wailos now *does* intend to marry her, as further evidence of his integrity and to secure alliances within the tribe." He shook his head. "At least she's not pregnant. If Wailos thought there was any chance she was carrying his son, he'd never stop looking for her."

"As far as we know," Elōr replied.

"As far as we know, what?" Ceru turned to her.

"As far as we know, she's not pregnant." Ceru gave her a look, eyebrows raised. She raised hers in reply. "You saw how she almost fainted this morning. The timing is about right."

"That would certainly complicate things," he acknowledged. "We'd better hope Aytal finds her mother, in that case."

"Oh?"

"With Potis gone and Tausos's whereabouts unknown, only Sata, as Potis's wife, has a legitimate say over what happens to Naya. If Naya is carrying Wailos's child and Wailos finds out, he has an unconditional right to the child – there's nothing to be done about that – but he could demand custody of Naya as well, as the child's mother."

Ceru's tone was grim. "He wouldn't even have to marry her, necessarily. Other than Tausos, Sata is the only one with a right to object – unless in the meantime Naya is married to someone else – and even then, she could still be expected to relinquish the child, especially if it's a boy."

"It wasn't always thus," Elōr observed quietly. She stopped again and turned to Ceru. "Árdejā speaks of the time of the Ancestors, when children belonged to their mothers, and young women chose their own partners, without so much interference. What happened?"

"Cattle," Ceru replied. "When our people – the Plānos as well as the Dānus – left off following the wild herds and started raising our own animals instead, everything changed. Cattle can be stolen, which means men have become warriors, following the example of the gods who bestowed the cattle upon us in the first place. Nothing has been the same since – at least that's what Árdejā explained to me when I was a boy." He sighed. "She always swore that cattle were less a gift from the gods than a curse."

Elōr looked away, gazing into the distance across the open grasslands. She worried about what the future held for her own children and wished for a moment that Rei were not also, like Naya, the daughter of a clan chief.

Ceru must have guessed her thoughts. Reaching out, he took Elōr's pack from her, slung it over his shoulder, and putting his free arm around her waist, drew her to his side. "Don't worry, my love. I was raised to play this game of men vying for dominion over other men – it's no different from when we competed as boys."

"Except that now you have sharper weapons – and deadlier," Elōr pointed out, not mollified. Arms about one another's waists, they started walking again.

"True," Ceru conceded. "But Wailos and Regos, for all their bravado, are not the masters of the steppe. I will keep our children safe – daughters as well as sons – and I will do whatever I can to keep Naya safe as well, for the sake of her father, who was a good man, and my friend." He kissed Elōr's temple, then released her. "Look," he said, stopping to point as they crested the top of a small rise. "The herds!"

Elōr stood at Ceru's side to take in the sight. Cattle grazed as far as the eye could see, as well as smaller flocks of sheep and goats. In the far distance, she made out the outline of tents.

"Ceru," Elōr mused, gazing out on the Dānus tribe's combined wealth, "what if a herder – or a warrior – instead of walking on foot, could ride on horseback?"

"What if?" Ceru replied. He turned to his wife and smiled. "What if?"

Chapter Twenty-Three

Ceru warned Naya before she and Perqos set out that their journey to the cave would require three days and the crossing of one major river – the Lik – followed by countless smaller streams. That said, it was not an arduous trip.

"The path begins as a wide course traversing a shallow valley," he told her, "then narrows and climbs toward the forested foothills of the southern mountains, before dwindling to little more than a deer trail. Only toward the end does the way become especially steep and difficult. Otherwise, with Perqos to guide you, you should have little difficulty in making the trek."

Such assurances to the contrary, Naya found the first day to be more challenging than predicted. While the initial river crossing proved uneventful, and the terrain of the valley beyond was not particularly rough, the wide-open plain offered little respite from the summer sun. With the quick pace Perqos set to avoid pursuit, Naya struggled to keep up. Worse, she couldn't overcome her awkwardness in the company of the young man whom she hardly knew, but who was now serving as her guardian and protector. Perqos seemed equally nonplussed at being thrown together. The fact that their fathers had once intended for them to marry didn't help. Only Amu was completely at ease, running ahead to scout the trail, then doubling back to check on them, pink tongue lolling.

The first evening, after they stopped to camp, was little better – an exchange of polite words and diffident smiles while eating the cold provisions that Perqos produced from his pack. Fortunately, the decision to forego a fire removed any expectation of post-meal conversation. Instead, Perqos insisted that he and Amu would keep watch overnight while Naya rested. Needing no further excuse, she rolled herself into her blanket and pretended to sleep. More exhausted than she realized, she dropped almost immediately into a deep if restless slumber.

The second day passed more easily. Somewhat revived even after her disturbed night's sleep, Naya took a greater interest in the landscape and asked questions about unfamiliar plants and birds. Perqos, less tongue-tied, gladly answered her queries. Having spent much of his boyhood wandering the foothills beyond the boundary of the Lik, he proved a fount of information.

"Whenever I could, I'd sneak away by myself and explore," he explained as they approached the threshold where the open valley they'd been traversing gave way to a more thickly wooded hillside. "If I came across anything I couldn't identify, I'd remember every detail and ask my grandfather about it afterwards. He always had an answer and never scolded me for going off on my own and being curious. He called me his spy and made me observe everything I could and report back to him."

"He sounds like my grandmother," Naya remarked. "Maybe I'll meet him someday."

"He's not with us anymore," Perqos replied, sobering. "An old injury left him crippled, which was why he relied on me to be his eyes and ears, and three winters ago, he finally passed."

"I'm sorry," Naya said, feeling self-conscious once more. She shifted her pack, trying to relieve the ache in her shoulder. Her old scar from the arrow wound had begun to nag at her. "My grandfather died last winter," she added after a moment. "I didn't get to say goodbye."

Now it was Perqos's turn to express his regret. "You must miss him," he sympathized, but without asking for further details, for which Naya was grateful. They were both quiet for a long time afterward, but today the silence was less uncomfortable. Naya suspected Perqos was taking care not to stray too close to the subject of her father's death which, again, she appreciated. In truth, Naya was doing her best not to let herself dwell on *any* of what had happened. Once alone, she would have to make sense of everything. For now, it was enough to keep moving, following Perqos's lead.

On the third day, they talked about the horses. Naya had been want-ing to learn more about the whereabouts of the red filly but hadn't found the right moment to broach the subject. Perqos saved her the trouble.

"Can I ask you a question?" he inquired.

It was late morning, and they had just emerged from a stand of larch and alder into a sunny meadow where they could walk side by side at a slower pace. After two days with no sign of anything larger than a fox, they were feeling less cautious about being pursued. Amu, setting off to explore the furthest edges of the meadow, seemed unconcerned as well. Perqos glanced at Naya, his warm brown eyes the color of ripe acorns. Indeed, with his solid presence, he reminded her of a sturdy oak.

"I suppose," she replied, returning his gaze.

His angular features – well-defined jaw, straight brows and wide-set cheekbones – were offset by a generously curved mouth. A crooked nose, looking as though it had been broken, made his otherwise symmetrical face all the more interesting. Coarse black hair, pulled back from his square forehead, was secured with a thong at the nape of his neck. He was not much taller than Naya, nor – at nineteen summers – that much older, but his broad shoulders, thick chest and muscled arms, along with the broken nose, gave him the intimidating look of a seasoned warrior. Until he smiled. Then, he seemed boyish. He was smiling now, his expression open and unguarded.

"What is it like to ride a horse?" he asked. "How did you manage it?"

"Well…" Naya hesitated, not sure how to answer.

She'd never described or even discussed the feeling of riding before, except with the three people who were there – Aytal, her mother, and Oyuun. Not even Awija had heard the full tale in Naya's own words – although her grandmother had asked. Nor had her father, despite how much she'd wanted to tell him. Her mother may have provided Ceru with the broad outlines to convince him to keep the filly and the other horses safe, but Naya doubted she would have risked disclosing more than necessary. As for the more mystical elements of her relationship with the red filly, Naya herself wasn't certain of the details. To this day, she'd never been able to remember all that had been said by the voice from her visions. And yet Árdejā had seemed to know…

"Only share as much as feels comfortable," Perqos offered, as though intuiting the reason for Naya's lack of response to his question. "And I won't tell anyone. It's just…" Halting midstride, he turned to her. "…it's just that I've dreamt of it – of riding." The words tumbled out. Stopping as well, Naya stared back at him. She didn't know what to say.

Perqos tried to decipher the expression in the blue eyes that held his.

Surprise? Uncertainty? He could understand both, especially if Naya's feat with the red filly had been inspired by anything like his own recurring dreams. In them, he galloped astride a golden stallion, dappled coat flashing in the sun, both horse and human reveling in the shared joy of racing the steppe wind. He'd never told anyone about the dreams, except Árdejā.

How could such a thing even be possible? he'd asked her. Árdejā had offered no explanation, just nodded sagely. *Keep the dreams to yourself, for now,* she'd advised him. *You and your father continue with this plan of yours, with the horses. Then you'll see.*

That had been nearly a year ago. Yet despite all the progress he and his father had made in persuading several bands of wild horses to remain in the vicinity of their cattle herds, Perqos had never been able to come near enough to touch one of the creatures, let alone climb astride and ride. There seemed no way to approach that didn't risk frightening the horses away.

And then to learn that the daughter of his father's friend had achieved the seemingly impossible! Perqos had been speechless a few nights ago at the encampment, listening to Aytal refer reverently to Naya as *She-Who-Rides-Horses*, with no mention, incidentally, of his own accomplishment. Perqos's father hadn't seemed surprised by Aytal's revelation. He must have heard the whole story from Naya's mother. Apparently Árdejā knew about Naya as well, hence the old woman's insistence on speaking to her. No need to guess whether Árdejā thought Naya's connection to the horses was important. Perhaps that was why, even though she had cautioned Perqos a year ago against mentioning his own dreams, in talking with Naya just now he'd felt emboldened to let the truth slip.

"How did you get close to them?" he continued, wanting to understand what she'd done to overcome the wild horses' shyness. Naya looked back at him, still without answering. She had the most striking appearance – all that flaming gold-streaked hair framing strong yet feminine features newly emerged from the softness of childhood – and those eyes!

Realizing he'd been staring, Perqos looked away and resumed walking. "We don't plan on harming them, at least no more than our cattle, if that's what concerns you," he added, wanting to reassure her.

Naya still seemed reluctant to satisfy his curiosity. "How many horses are there, in the herds that you look after?" she deflected, falling in step beside him.

"The biggest band includes eight mares and their offspring, plus a senior stallion and a younger stallion who serves as his deputy," Perqos replied. "There are also four other smaller bands." He glanced at Naya, guessing what she really wanted to know. "My father thinks the red filly and the mare who followed your mother may have been accepted into one of those smaller groups." Naya's face lit up, even though she'd heard the news earlier from his father himself. "He said the filly is beautiful," Perqos went on. "He described her coat as being an unusual copper color." *Like your hair*, he stopped himself from adding.

"So you think they're still safe?" Naya's voice was eager.

"As far as I know, they're fine," Perqos assured her.

"And the gray stallion? He's a bit of a misfit." Naya smiled ruefully.

"That's true," Perqos agreed with a laugh. "According to Father, even the other bachelors kept chasing him away, but he seemed pretty determined to stay with the mare and the filly. The stallion of the band they joined is tolerant though – I wouldn't be surprised if he allows the gray to remain, at least on the fringes."

"So, you've tamed them?" Naya inquired.

Perqos couldn't quite interpret her tone. "I wouldn't say we've tamed them," he demurred, "but we get along. The horses have figured out that humans and our dogs will keep other predators away. In return, now and then we'll cull a few – but only occasionally. Otherwise, we mostly leave them alone." He caught himself before admitting that last winter, when food stores ran low, they'd taken down several of the bachelor stallions; he didn't want her to worry about the gray.

"Why bother with wild horses at all, then?" Naya persisted. "Aren't the cattle enough to manage?"

She probed without saying what was really on her mind. Perqos decided to be honest. "We do still hunt some of them," he conceded, "but it's more than that. The horses are much hardier than the cattle. They can fend for themselves. They handle the cold and snow in the winter better, and the poor-quality forage during the dry, hot periods in the summer. They know where to find water. Their adaptability makes it easier for the other livestock to survive as well. It's worth the extra effort required to supervise them if it means having a more reliable source of meat in an emergency."

"That's what Rei said," Naya acknowledged. She glanced at him sideways. "And you don't use ropes?"

"Do you mean to capture them? Is that how you…?"

"No!" Naya's reply was emphatic. "But Wailos…" She didn't elaborate.

"What would be the point?" Perqos wondered. "Wouldn't ropes just frighten them? That doesn't seem like a very useful strategy to gain their cooperation, at least not at the beginning."

"It depends on your intentions," Naya replied.

He looked at her, one eyebrow raised.

"Wailos wasn't interested in riding." she said. "I don't think the idea even occurred to him. The horses were merely another part of his plan to…" Again she stopped, this time turning her face away, but not before Perqos saw the cloud pass over her features.

"What is it Naya? I know Wailos was a *sterkos* – pardon my language. I don't blame you for not wanting to talk about what he did to you – and to your father – but why won't you tell me about riding the red filly? It's as if you're keeping a secret, although I'm not sure why. I've dreamed about it, the same way you must have. Doesn't that count for something?"

She turned to him, her forehead furrowed. "I did have dreams – or visions – but I've also had nightmares."

Perqos waited for her to say more. They'd entered a glade of trees on the far side of the meadow they'd been traversing. The path narrowed, requiring them to walk one behind the other. Perqos gestured for Naya to precede him.

"Please go on," he requested.

Naya walked ahead. After the warmth of the sun-filled meadow, the shade provided by the towering oaks, beeches and chestnuts came as a welcome relief. The path they were following, now hardly more than a narrow track, wound through a relatively dense understory, featuring smaller bushes and moss-covered fallen logs, interspersed with the occasional pine or fir. A soft matting of fallen leaves cushioned their footsteps. Birds flitted among the branches overhead, while squirrels scolded their passing.

Naya knew Perqos wanted her to explain herself. "It's complicated," she began, looking back at him. How did she describe the ambivalence she felt about everything having to do with the horses – the longing and the joy, coupled with the sickening dread of what the future might hold? "How much further do we have to go?' she asked.

"It's almost midday," he replied. "If we push on, we should reach the cave by late afternoon. Why? Do you want to stop for a rest now? The going does get steeper towards the end."

Naya didn't want to delay their arrival but she was also tired. Despite sleeping soundly, at the start of the day she'd still felt somewhat unwell. A chance to have something to eat and drink was appealing. If they took a break, however, she would have no excuse not to answer Perqos's questions.

"If we could stop for a bit…" she relented, reaching for her water skin. "Maybe we could sit?" She pointed to a fallen log lying alongside the path.

Unslinging his pack, Perqos waited for her to get settled before handing her one of the seemingly limitless supply of seedcakes he carried, then seated himself on the ground opposite her. His handsome face was open and expectant.

"I love her," Naya began. "The red filly I mean. That's the heart of it. Everything else comes from that place."

She surprised herself with the confession, but it was the first thing to come out of her mouth. Perqos looked as though what she'd said made perfect sense.

"I started out hoping she'd allow me to touch her," Naya continued. "I had this crazy idea that I could somehow catch her with a rope. And then I had a vision – more real than a waking dream. I don't recall all of it, but the filly seemed to speak to me."

She shot Perqos a look from under her lashes. His brows were drawn together in concentration as he listened, but she saw neither disbelief nor derision in his expression.

Reassured, Naya went on. "We must have made some kind of promise to one another," she said. "Somehow Árdejā knew – she called it a covenant. That's the part I can't quite remember. Afterwards, I realized that what I wanted – with all my heart – was to ride Réhda – that's what I started calling her. But to get to that point, I had to earn her trust, and the trust of the other horses in her band. That took a lot of time, and patience. I made mistakes. Mostly what I learned was to pay attention, and to let her know that I was aware of her and how she was feeling, moment to moment. It's the way the horses are with one other."

Perqos nodded. Naya guessed that he, too, had spent countless days observing how the horses behaved, learning their ways, picking out their individual traits and characteristics, noting the relationships that bound them as a herd.

"And what about when you finally rode her?" he asked.

"You mean after I got bucked off?" Naya laughed. "Once I made sure that she was more comfortable with the idea, it was magical."

She closed her eyes, reliving the moment, then opened them again. "Strange, at first, to feel how much her skin and muscles slid around, but then both of us got used to the feeling and figured out how to move together. After that, we gained more and more confidence, until finally, one day, we took off for the horizon, just as I'd imagined."

She looked into the distance, her heart quickening at the memory.

"But you said you had nightmares too?" Perqos prompted after a moment. "Is that why…?"

"In part," Naya answered, bringing her gaze back to the young man seated before her. His forearms were crossed, elbows resting atop drawn-up knees, a rapt look on his face. "From the beginning, although my parents and grandparents encouraged me, they were also worried about what might happen if the rest of the clan – the priests, in particular – found out about my visions. We kept the project of taming the horses a secret. And then, last spring, when we returned to the settlement…"

Naya paused to be sure Perqos was aware of the winter she and her mother had spent on the steppe with Oyuun and Aytal. He nodded. "When we got back, before I had a chance to tell my father about riding the filly, I saw for myself what had happened to the rest of her band." She looked away, swallowing hard. "Witnessing the mares and foals trapped in that corral made me physically sick," she said. "When I found out they were going to be sacrificed, as part of the *Sāwel-Dom* rites… I knew it was all my fault."

Naya turned back to Perqos, whose brows were furrowed in sympathy. "I was upset anyway about… about a lot of things," she went on. "Seeing the captured herd and how they were being treated – as if my nightmares were already coming true. I didn't know how to stop it. By then, the red filly and her mother and the gray stallion had disappeared, so I just… I just…"

"You don't have to explain," Perqos interjected. "Of course you couldn't stand what was happening." He paused, looking down. "What my father and I have been doing with the horses is… different." He plucked a withered oak leaf from the ground, twirling it by the stem.

"We do have ulterior motives in trying to gain their trust," he admitted, returning his gaze to Naya. "But we've never intended to take away their freedom. In exchange for safety and protection, we're hoping they let us work with them, same as the cattle."

He hesitated. "There's something else we can offer the horses, though. They're more curious and social than the cows, or even the goats. You can see what strong bonds they form with one another, how connected they are. I want to be part of that – crazy as that sounds. For me, taming the horses is about… I don't know…" He seemed at a loss for how to articulate what he meant.

"Friendship?" Naya suggested.

"Yes, that's it," he replied. He looked a bit sheepish, more like an enthusiastic boy than a seasoned warrior. Naya noticed the flash of a dimple and how the corners of his eyes crinkled when he smiled. She smiled back, then sobered.

"Before my grandfather died, he said that if we didn't tame the wild horses instead of continuing to hunt them, the horses would die out," she said, "so what you and your father are doing – it's important."

"But you have reservations?"

Naya shifted on the log. "My grandfather also predicted that with the horses' help, we would become more powerful than could be imagined," she said. "But power can be dangerous," she added, frowning. "That's where the nightmares come in. In my darkest dreams, I've seen and felt what could happen – what I fear *will* happen – and it's far worse than anything you could envision."

She shuddered. "My grandfather insisted that we must never forget the horses' gift to us – that we would owe them our lives and our future – but what about *their* future? If we tame them, we're responsible for them, forever."

"You're worried that if we succeed in befriending more horses, and demonstrating that they can be ridden, men like Wailos will take over – with ropes?"

"And you're not concerned?"

"But if it's going to happen anyway, shouldn't people like us set the example? People committed to putting the horses' freedom and welfare first?"

Naya didn't respond. She'd gone round in circles in her own mind. "I don't know," she finally answered. "Ask me again after I've had time by myself in the cave to think about it." She gave him a crooked smile.

"Speaking of which – we should get going, if you're ready." Perqos rose, offering Naya a hand. Accepting, she stood as well, then swayed as a wave of dizziness overtook her.

"You okay?" Perqos tightened his grip on Naya's hand while reaching for her other elbow to steady her.

"I got up too fast, that's all," she apologized, grasping his forearm for support.

As soon as the world righted itself, she let go and would have stepped back, but the log blocked her. They stood for a moment, self-consciously close to one another, Perqos still with one hand under Naya's elbow before he released her.

He bowed, arms outstretched, laughter in his brown eyes. "At your service," he smiled. Naya inclined her head, smiling as well, and the awkwardness vanished, carried away on the summer breeze that rustled the forest leaves.

As soon as they'd each shouldered their packs, Perqos gestured for Naya to take the lead and once more they set-off up the track.

Later that afternoon...

Naya stopped to catch her breath near a dense stand of spruce. Perqos and Amu halted behind her. The going had become rocky and steep in places, with no room to stand abreast on the narrow trail. Their view to the south was blocked by the forested slope they'd been ascending for most of the afternoon, but the vistas to the east, west and north were stunning. The afternoon sun, preparing to set in the west, tinged the eastern clouds a faint pink.

"I recognize this place," Naya remarked with surprise. "I've travelled this way before."

Perqos was incredulous. "How is that possible?"

"One summer, two, no three years ago, my father took me along on a hunting expedition into the foothills of the mountains. I had no idea we were so close to the place." Showing Perqos her necklace, Naya told him the story of the bear attack, resulting in the death of her father's friend. "The mother bear was only protecting her cubs," she concluded. "She'd hidden them in a cave nearby..."

Perqos pointed. "There, just on the other side of that rock tower." A massive balsalt pillar stood guard over a bend in the trail ahead of them.

"It must be the same cave!" Naya exclaimed.

Rounding the bend, they came upon a cavity dug into the hillside. The trail came to a dead end in front of it, the way forward blocked by a precipitous drop-off. The exposed roots of a gnarled pine overhung the opening, which looked like it had been enlarged by a set of sharp claws. Naya found it hard to imagine that the space inside was large enough to accommodate a family of bears, let alone serve as an adequate place for her to take up residence for the next moon.

"This can't be right," she exclaimed. "It's not even dark inside!"

"This is just the entrance," Perqos explained. "Where the bear likely had her den. The real cave is accessed through a tunnel hidden at the back."

"Oh," Naya said, hardly reassured. As though sensing her consternation, Amu looked up and whined, then gave a short bark. "He wants to investigate. Is there room enough?"

"Plenty of room, once you reach the actual cave," Perqos promised. "Wait until you see."

Leaving their packs outside the entrance to the bear's den, they crawled in one after the other, Perqos leading the way and Amu bringing up the rear. Once inside the shallow cavity, they barely had space to turn around.

"Shouldn't we have a light?" Naya belatedly thought to ask. The bear's den may not have been pitch dark inside, but a tunnel and whatever waited beyond certainly would be.

"No need, as long as there's daylight," Perqos replied, running his hand along a cleft between a pair of rocks buried in the rear wall of the earthen den. "Here – squeeze through after me," he instructed. Twisting himself sideways, he raised his hands above his head, then thrust his shoulders, followed by his torso, hips and legs, through what turned out to be a narrow slot. After his feet disappeared, Naya could hear scraping and grunting, along with what sounded like a shower of pebbles.

"Perqos?" Naya called.

"It's a little tighter than I remember from the last time I was here," she heard him call back, his voice muffled. "You'll fit more easily than me, though, don't worry. Once you're through the opening, just crawl forward on your stomach."

Naya looked over her shoulder at Amu, crouched in the den behind her. He looked back, curiosity in his intelligent amber eyes. "I don't know what's on the other side," she told him. "You wait here, Amu. I'll call for you." Taking a deep breath, as though preparing to dive under water, Naya copied Perqos, clasping her hands above her head, twisting on her side and pushing herself through the gap between the rocks with her feet.

Almost immediately, the space widened into a tunnel roomy enough to accommodate Naya's shoulders and hips. Head down, she shimmied forward on her belly, pulling herself with her elbows for the length of a tent pole, at which point the passage bent to the left and widened enough for her to come to all-fours. She could now see light ahead. Calling to Amu to follow her, she crawled onward, shards of sharp rock biting into her knees and the palms of her hands. The acrid tang of damp limestone filled her nostrils.

Reaching the end of the passage Naya, followed by Amu, emerged into a surprisingly spacious cavern, its ceiling high enough for a tall man to stand upright, with an opening like a huge window that spanned the width of the cavity, admitting plenty of fresh air and daylight. Perqos stood with his back to her, silhouetted against a golden orange glow. Coming to her feet, Naya joined him. Together, they gazed out over the edge of a sheer cliff. The view to the southwest was breathtaking – far below, a canopy of leafy green treetops stretched toward an exposed limestone escarpment, beyond which rose a range of snow-capped peaks. The sun going down behind them turned the late afternoon sky into a fiery blaze of color.

"Oh my!" she exclaimed, otherwise rendered speechless.

"Worth the effort to get here," Perqos observed.

"I'll say," Naya agreed. "This is *the* cave?"

"This is it," he confirmed. "At least the main chamber. There are two smaller chambers, and a couple alcoves, plus another tunnel that leads deeper into the hillside. The way we came in, though, is the only entrance. Scaling the cliff from below is impossible. You'll be safe here – and probably more comfortable than you expected." He turned to her and grinned.

"You kept this a secret on purpose!" she accused, socking his shoulder with her fist in mock irritation.

Perqos took a step back, hands raised in self-defense. "You didn't ask," he pointed out, laughing. "But it was worth it to see the look on your face."

Naya scowled good-humoredly, then turned serious. "This is truly where I'm meant to stay?" she asked, spinning a slow circle to take in her surroundings. The cave was nothing as she'd imagined.

"Yes indeed," Perqos replied, obviously pleased with her surprised reaction. "I'll stay close by to keep an eye out for intruders, and to supply firewood and provisions as required. Water from a natural spring accumulates in a stone basin over there." He gestured toward an alcove to the left of the entrance tunnel. "And you'll find some useful items in there." He indicated the other alcove to the right of the entrance tunnel. "Help yourself to whatever you find. The other openings lead to the smaller chambers I mentioned. Not luxurious, but you should have everything you'll need."

Truthfully, Naya had avoided thinking in detail about what awaited her once they reached their destination, assuming she had little to look forward to beyond cramped darkness, nagging hunger and enforced solitude. The reality was very different from what she'd expected, and she needed a moment to adjust.

"Does Árdejā know what this cave is actually like?" she asked. "She seemed quite adamant about me being alone in the dark."

"Did she say that?" Perqos inquired. Naya was reminded that he'd only heard Árdejā's instructions second-hand, from his father. "My guess is she wanted you to think we were dragging you off to a hole in the ground. Her sense of humor is like that. Even so, you will have plenty of time by yourself over the next moon – and sometimes, for me anyway, being alone with my own thoughts can feel like wandering in the dark." He glanced sideways at her. "That's not always a bad thing," he continued. "As my father likes to point out, treasures await those with the courage to go looking."

"I suppose," Naya replied. She didn't have the energy to think about it. More than anything, she just wanted to rest.

"Let's get you settled," Perqos suggested, as though guessing her thoughts. "I'll fetch your belongings, make sure you have wood to last for a day or two, and enough food for tonight and the morning at least – we're down to the last of what I brought along. First thing tomorrow, I'll lay some snares and scout for whatever I can gather in the area. Rations won't be generous, but I should be able to keep us both fed – and Amu as well."

"But Árdejā said no contact," Naya reminded him.

"I know," Perqos replied. "I'll set-up camp for myself in the bear's den – that way I can keep watch without disregarding orders – and I'll leave provisions and firewood just inside the entrance to the tunnel. You can collect what you need while I'm out during the day."

"What about Amu?" Naya asked. "He might be happier if he went with you while you're out and about, and then he can spend the nights with me."

"I *could* use his help hunting," Perqos agreed. "And you won't miss him as much during the day." He winked at her. "You'll see," he said. "There's plenty to investigate. This cave holds some surprises – almost as though the walls could talk."

"You seem to know a lot about it," Naya observed, brow raised. "As though you've spent time here yourself."

"I have indeed," Perqos confirmed. "As have many others." His voice grew serious. "Generations of my people have come to this place, seeking to understand the past or gain insight into the future. It's a place of sacred vision, as well as healing. Some call it *Antrom-Chelo*, the Cave of Desires."

A chill ran through Naya, prickling her skin. Perqos's words, like Árdejā's, seemed to hold the echo of something she couldn't quite recall.

"You'll see," he repeated. "You'll see."

Chapter Twenty-Four

The first night in the cave, Naya slept close to the central hearth, a ring of blackened stones in the center of the oval-shaped main chamber. A safe distance from the cliff's edge, she could still look out and see the stars in the western sky. The hearth was cold – Perqos had warned her not to keep a fire going unless necessary – but until she had an opportunity to investigate all the cavern's dark crevices in the daylight, she felt more secure near the central ring. Before Perqos departed, they divided the last of the provisions. He bid her and Amu good night, promising to leave food and firewood inside the tunnel entrance the following day.

Needing only her light blanket against the summer night air, Naya piled the rest of her belongings beside her bison fur robe, which served as her sleeping mat. She'd decided to wait until tomorrow to unpack, after she'd explored the cave's other chambers. With Amu beside her keeping watch, she curled on her side and fell into a restless sleep.

When she awoke, judging by the angle of the sunlight, half the morning had already passed. Yawning, Naya stretched and sat up. The dog stretched as well, forward and back, then rolled over, wriggling to scratch his back on the gravel-strewn floor of the cave. Naya reached for the portion of seedcake she'd saved from the night before and took a bite, hoping to settle the queasiness of an empty stomach. After days of meager rations, she looked forward to whatever fresh fare Perqos was able to find. In the meantime, the last of the trail food would have to do.

"What about you, Amu?" she asked. "Are you hungry?"

Coming to his feet, tail wagging, torn ears erect, the dog barked to let her know he was ready for the day's adventures. Just then a friendly whistle signaled Perqos was up as well – perhaps he'd even been out foraging already. Amu looked at her, expression eager.

"Go on," she said, giving him permission. "Have fun. I'll see you at the end of the day." The dog bounded off, disappearing through the tunnel leading back toward the cave entrance.

Naya watched him go with a pensive smile. Much better for Amu to be out exploring with Perqos during the day but with him gone, time lengthened before her with nothing in particular to do and no one to distract her. Circumstances could certainly have been worse, she told herself. The cavern, with its spacious main chamber and stunning view, wasn't a bad place to remain hidden while eluding Wailos. Even so, alone with her thoughts for the next moon, she'd be hard pressed to avoid confronting the past and considering the future – just as Árdejā had foreseen.

First things first, however; she needed to relieve herself.

Naya surveyed the cavern in the day light, more critically this time. The likeliest location for a *moighos* would be near the cliff's edge, where the ground sloped away, allowing waste to be disposed of over the rim. Standing, she made her way to a spot at the south side of the cave mouth that looked as though it had been used previously – she even found an ancient-looking twig broom tucked behind a rock.

Necessary business accomplished, Naya set about replenishing her water skin. The location of the spring Perqos had pointed out was on the opposite side of the cave from the *moighos*. Ducking, she entered the alcove beneath an overhanging archway and discovered a deep recess, its back wall slick with moisture. A steady trickle ran down the rock face, collecting in a natural stone basin. The overflow disappeared through invisible cracks at the wall's base. Sinking to her knees in front of the basin, Naya reached behind one shoulder to re-braid her hair, then bent, cupping her hands, and took a long, refreshing drink. The water, filtered through layers of limestone, imparted a sweet aftertaste. She drank again, then submerged her water skin, filling it.

Emerging from the alcove, Naya returned to the cave's main chamber. With her back to the view, she considered the cavern's rear wall. The alcove on her far left contained the spring. The next opening led out to the cave entrance in the bear's den. To the right, Naya counted three additional recesses. *No reason not to investigate*, she thought.

The first opening, just to the right of the entrance tunnel, concealed another recessed alcove, like the one containing the spring. Inside, Naya was delighted to find three rows of deep shelves carved into the malleable limestone. The bottom shelf held a selection of empty pottery containers, including a large cooking pot, a couple of medium-sized bowls, a mug and several cups, along with a carved wooden spoon – everything she'd need to make a meal of whatever Perqos provided. The middle shelf held several baskets filled with aromatic dried herbs for seasoning stews and making tea, as well as various medicinal uses. On the top shelf, she found several clay vessels of varying shapes and sizes, some with handles, all with sealed lids.

Naya hesitated. Perqos had urged her to make use of anything she found in the cave – she hoped this included whatever was in the sealed vessels. Taking one down, she broke open the lid, recoiling as the distinctive odor of beef tallow assailed her nostrils. The solidified tallow surrounded a wick of dried moss. *This will come in handy*, she thought. After replacing the lid, she put the lamp back on the top shelf and opened another of the sealed vessels, this one without a handle. It, too, contained tallow, but no wick. She guessed the same was true of the other vessels – those with handles could be employed as lamps, whereas the others contained plain tallow, suitable for cooking, making soap, and as a skin salve, along with myriad other uses. A rich trove, indeed!

Pleased with what she'd discovered so far, Naya continued her explorations. The next recess she entered sloped gradually upwards for a short distance. Inside, she had to proceed on hands and knees until the tunnel widened into a burrow-like space. Enough daylight entered for her to see that the ground was smooth and free of protruding rocks – an ideal spot to retreat if she wanted more protection from the weather, or simply a cozy place to sleep. Various niches had been carved into the walls, suitable for holding a lamp and storing small belongings.

The final opening off the central chamber began as a narrow passage through which, once again, Naya had to crawl on hands and knees. Almost immediately the tunnel opened into a small, low-ceilinged room. In the dim light, she could make out scratch marks along the walls and a fine coating of dust covering the floor. *Ochre!* she realized with excitement. The valuable mineral came in a range of shades, from yellow to brown to sacred red *miljom,* and was used for a variety of applications, including artwork.

Crouching just to the side of the entryway so as not to block the light, Naya scanned the walls more carefully for paintings but could see only signs of the different colors of ochre having been flaked from the surface of the rock. In addition, she spotted several shallow clay bowls on the ground near the chamber's back wall. Although empty, each dish was stained a different hue. She could also make out what looked like some kind of stone tool – perhaps a hand-held scraper – resting beside one of the dishes. There were no paintings, however; if the cave's previous visitors had left behind any lasting images, they must be located elsewhere.

About to back out of the chamber, Naya hesitated. A rock outcropping at the rear caught her eye. Might it conceal the opening to a secondary tunnel, much as the rocks at the back of the bear's den hide the passage leading to the main cavern? Perqos had mentioned another tunnel heading deeper into the hillside. Stooping, she made her way to the back of the chamber, bypassing the empty collection dishes.

As she suspected, behind the rocks, Naya discovered a small opening, barely large enough for her to squeeze through. Once past the rock outcropping, she shimmied on her stomach, as she'd done when entering the cavern from the bear's den the day before. This time, though, she wasn't following Perqos and no daylight beckoned from ahead.

After propelling herself no more than a couple of body-lengths along the down-sloping passage, Naya stopped, not daring to go further. Currents of cooler air moved past her bare skin, suggesting an open chamber existed deeper in the cave complex, but without a means to illuminate the pitch darkness, she was reluctant to proceed.

With no space to maneuver in the cramped tunnel, Naya had to wiggle backwards until she re-emerged feet first into the ochre room. From there she returned on hands and knees to the spaciousness of the main cavern. Relieved to be back out in the sunlight, she brushed pebbles from her arms and torso while considering her next move. Despite Árdejā's admonitions about spending time alone in the dark, and Ceru and Perqos both referring to hidden treasures awaiting discovery, Naya did not care to explore further without a source of light. One of the lamps might do, but a torch would be less likely to be extinguished accidentally. Would she be able to make one, using the materials at hand?

Naya was puzzling through the question when Amu emerged unannounced from the entrance tunnel. "What are you doing back?" she greeted the dog.

With a bark and wag of his tail, Amu turned back toward the bear's den, indicating that Naya should follow him. Perqos must have returned with supplies. Naya's stomach gave a loud rumble and she suddenly realized she was famished.

Amu barked again. "Alright!" she replied, not sure whether to be amused or irritated by the dog's insistence. "I'm coming." She followed the dog back through the entrance tunnel, eager to discover what awaited her at the other end.

Later that evening, Naya sat beside the central hearth looking out at the view. After what had seemed like an endlessly long day, punctuated by a satisfying meal of herb-seasoned broiled rabbit, the sun had finally slipped beyond the distant mountains, leaving streamers of yellow and orange to accent the darkening sky. Soon, the first stars would emerge.

As she'd done more than once since building her cooking fire, Naya considered using it to light one of several sturdy pine torches she'd found among the items Perqos had left for her in the entrance tunnel. He seemed to have thought of everything. Along with the rabbit, there'd been a sack full of mountain spinach, garlic and onions, plus several days' supply of firewood – and the torches. Now, if she so desired, she had everything necessary to go and investigate the remaining tunnel whenever she wanted.

Yet gazing out into the gathering twilight, Naya hesitated. After all, she told herself, she'd only spent one day in the cave. Plenty of time remained to learn the rest of its secrets. Instead, she retrieved one of the tallow lamps, lighting the wick with a stick from the fire. Heaping ash on the remaining coals, she made her way, lamp in hand, inside the burrow-like cavity she'd discovered earlier. Amu followed her. Placing the lamp in one of the convenient niches that pock-marked the cavity's walls, Naya surveyed the space.

"Shall we make ourselves comfortable?" she asked the dog. He cocked his head in reply. Shooing him aside, she exited the burrow to retrieve her bison fur robe. Returning with the hide in tow, she'd soon made a cozy nest for them both.

"Tomorrow, while you and Perqos are out hunting, I'll finish exploring," she told Amu, snuggling in next to him. *Plenty of time*, she repeated to herself, before blowing out the lamp.

Yet, Naya did not venture into the tunnel beyond the ochre room the next day, nor the next, nor the day after that, until almost a fortnight had passed since she and Perqos and Amu had first arrived at the cavern. Despite her curiosity, an uncertain reluctance held her back. In part, she feared re-entering the tunnel's cramped confines, even with one of the torches Perqos had provided, worried the passage might lead nowhere and she'd end up trapped. In part, she felt ambivalent about what she might discover at the other end. Either way, Naya put off further exploration.

She came up with excuses instead, starting with unpacking and putting away her belongings. With the exception of the cooking pot from her aunt, which she left in the storage alcove, she moved everything she'd brought with her into the burrow. Regardless of the small space, she felt better having all she possessed in one place, within easy reach. This included her bow and quiver of arrows, the auroch horn from Aytal and the horse collar her mother had made for her last winter, along with the satchel from her other aunt and the gathering sack from Melit, as well as her extra clothing.

That left only her grandmother's *tekstlom*. Still as hesitant to venture into the realm of her dreams as she was to descend into the depths of the cave, Naya held off even unwrapping Awija's gift, let alone finding a way of suspending it above where she slept. Instead, she tucked the bundle containing the *tekstlom* into one of the burrow's many niches. As always, her knife, fire-starting kit and the *makēn* containing her smallest treasures, including the arrowhead necklace from her mother and the carved horse from Aytal, remained belted at her waist. Her father's beartooth necklace encircled her throat.

Once settled, Naya searched for other activities to keep herself busy. Having discovered a batch of tallow soap tucked behind the sealed vessels on the top shelf in the storage alcove, she spent a whole day bathing, washing her hair and rinsing out her clothing, proceeding in stages while waiting for the water in the stone basin to replenish. Several additional days were taken up with flaking useable amounts of precious pigment from the rock surface of the ochre room, which Naya thought she might use to create a painting on one of the cave walls, although she would want it to be somewhere inconspicuous, where no one would notice, in case it turned out badly. In the meantime, she practiced drawing the symbols her grandmother had shown her and the other girls during their training, using a stick on the gravel floor of the main cavern. Circles, spirals, zigzags, arrows and wavy lines – each shape held meaning, often connected to one of the ancient stories Awija had shared with them. Naya found herself particularly fascinated with depicting the sun and the moon. Over and over she etched their images in the dirt – sometimes separate, sometimes conjoined – before erasing the designs and starting over.

Yet no matter how many distractions she devised to occupy her time, Naya was also forced to spend part of almost every day doing nothing. At first she found these periods of inactivity difficult to endure, recalling the worst stretches of boredom during her vigil. Unable to sit quietly, she would pace the length of the main chamber, back and forth, counting her steps, until she thought she might wear a trench in the floor of the cavern. On some days, with nothing better to do, she took long afternoon naps in the burrow but then had trouble falling asleep at night. More often than not, her slumber continued to be disturbed by unrecalled dreams, leaving her days as weary as they were restless.

Eventually, she had to surrender and just *be*. With her back resting against the cave wall nearest the cliff's edge, she gazed out at the view and allowed her mind to wander. Occasionally something in the landscape caught her attention – a hawk or golden eagle soaring on an updraft, the movement of clouds across the vista, the play of a breeze in the leaves of the tree tops in the valley below – but often the world beyond the cavern seemed impossibly empty and still.

In such moments, memories of the past and fears for the future would inevitably intrude. As yet unwilling to truly confront either, Naya instead began to imagine her thoughts like the passing clouds – drifting by, separate from her observing awareness. She could follow them… or not. The choice was hers. With practice, she learned to let her thoughts go on without her, enabling her mind to rest in silence for longer and longer stretches. The only thing to observe was her breath – chest and belly rising and falling – and underneath, the steady beat of her own heart. In such moments, she found peace.

Today, however, Naya couldn't seem to allow her mind to drift. Contemplating the view from her usual vantage point, she felt unsettled. The afternoon sky, too, was restless. Heavy clouds gathered in the distance, heralding the prospect of a storm. Naya welcomed the possibility. The air in the cavern felt stagnant and oppressive. There'd been no breeze for days, and no rain since she arrived. The water draining into the basin in the alcove had dwindled to a mere trickle, causing Naya to worry that the spring might run dry. A good dousing was overdue.

At her side, Amu whined. Perqos had not called for him this morning, and he'd left several days' worth of supplies at the cave entrance the evening before, suggesting he intended to go further afield to forage and had purposefully left the dog behind to keep watch in his absence.

With one hand, Naya fingered a rough greenish-blue crystal that fit easily in her palm. The stone was one of many small tokens she'd discovered among the more practical items Perqos left for her at the tunnel entrance. Often there'd be a bouquet of wildflowers, sometimes a particularly pretty feather or a perfectly formed pinecone. Once she'd found the exquisite skeleton of an *empis*, its iridescent wings outstretched. Yesterday, alongside the extra firewood and food, she'd discovered the unusual crystal, its translucent depths evoking the aquamarine tint of a mountain lake – or the eerie cast of a tempest-laden sky.

Amu whined again. "You feel the storm too, don't you?" Naya gave the dog a reassuring rub behind his ragged ears with her free hand. "It'll be okay," she told him. "We need the rain."

Watching the approaching weather, Naya recalled another storm – last spring, just before her return to the settlement, when she'd witnessed her mother and Oyuun in what had seemed to be a moment of intimacy. In a temper, she'd ridden off blindly into the steppe on the back of the red filly, only to be caught in a raging downpour, along with Aytal and the gray stallion, who'd come looking for her and Réhda. She remembered being *so* angry at her mother, and perversely at Aytal as well, over his father's role in what she believed to be her mother's infidelity. The next day had been the morning of the lion attack. Already upset, the colt's death devastated Naya. Consumed with grief and guilt, she'd been upset with everyone – her mother, Oyuun, Aytal, and most of all, herself.

Now, watching the darkening clouds mass in the west, Naya's fist closed hard around the sharp-edged crystal. She tasted bile at the back of her throat. It all seemed as fresh as though it had happened yesterday.

Why? Even if her anger had been legitimate, hadn't she since gained some perspective? A better understanding? Enough grace to forgive her mother and Oyuun, Aytal, and even herself, at least for the death of the colt? Why, with the approaching storm, did she feel this sense of fury about to crash over her like a raging torrent? She wanted to scream, but she feared if she did, she might fracture into a thousand pieces.

And then it hit her. Her father. She felt the same as the night she'd learned from Elōr the truth of his betrayal. Everything had been on *his* behalf – her outrage regarding her mother's supposed indiscretion, but especially the shame and disappointment she'd borne for all the times she'd let him down. For her entire life, she'd sought to gain her father's approval, striving to make-up for the loss of her twin brother. Always, she'd fallen short.

After returning to the settlement, she'd given up attempting to be the son her father never had, determined instead to live up to his ideal of a chief's daughter. She'd gone along with Wailos's plan, not realizing he only meant to embarrass her father. Afterwards, she'd run away to save her father from further humiliation. She'd blamed herself for his death. And for what? *He'd known!* All along, her father had known about Wailos and done nothing. He'd not confided in her, nor protected her. He hadn't trusted her. Worse, he'd betrayed *her* trust in him. And now, thanks to Ceru, she knew for certain that her father was gone.

Distractedly, Naya returned the storm-hued crystal to the *makēn* at her waist as she rose and moved to stand at the edge of the precipice. Amu joined her. Together, they watched the clouds close in, their roiling mass darkening the already leaden sky. A rising wind whipped strands from Naya's braid. In the next moment, waves of sheet lightning flashed, followed by rolling growls of thunder. The rumbling reverberated through Naya's chest. *He knew – and did nothing to protect me. He's gone – and it's all my fault.* The grief and guilt, the anger and shame – all the feelings she'd avoided were out there, part of the impending storm.

Around her the air crackled. She could feel the pressure mounting, ready to explode. Huge drops of rain began to leave craters in the cavern's dirt floor. Across the valley, lightning forked down, striking the exposed limestone of the escarpment. A moment later came a deafening crack and with the sound, Naya's self-possession shattered. She screamed into the shrieking wind until her throat was raw. Falling to her knees, doubled over, fists clenched, body wracked by ferocious sobs, she pounded the earth, even as rain pummeled the ground in drenching sheets. Next to her, Amu lifted his muzzle skyward, howling into the abyss, while around them, the storm raged.

Engulfed by tempestuous elemental fury, Naya lost all sense of identity and time. Eventually, once the lightning and thunder abated and the wind began to calm, she returned to her senses. A steady rain continued to fall. Sitting back on folded knees, wet hair plastered to her head, she took a ragged breath and made a futile attempt to wipe rainwater and tears from her eyes. Amu, still by her side, gray coat wet to the skin, tried to lick her face. One-handed, she pushed him away. The other hand closed around the bear's tooth necklace at her throat. With a violent tug, Naya ripped it free. Using all her strength, she flung the necklace into the void. In the next instant, Amu launched himself after it. Before she could stop him or call him back, he'd disappeared over the cliff's edge and been swallowed by the emptiness beyond.

Later that evening, in the burrow…

Naya called and called for Amu. She didn't dare go after him; the cliff was nearly vertical and the ground treacherously slick from the storm. Eventually, the rain had stopped, revealing an infinite expanse of star-studded night sky, but no moonlight illuminated the valley below and starlight alone was not enough to penetrate the dense foliage. Naya finally had to give up trying to see where the dog had gone. Perhaps in the daylight, with a clear view over the cliff's edge, she might be able to spot him. Maybe, if he wasn't injured, or worse, he'd find his own way back. Otherwise, unless Perqos returned, in the morning she would have to risk going herself to search for him.

Chilled, Naya retreated to the burrow to dry off. Sitting with her knees drawn up to her chest, wearing dry clothes, she did her best to comb and rebraid her damp hair. Her stomach ached with hunger, but she didn't have the energy to make herself something to eat. She felt drained – worn-out by the storm and despondent over Amu's disappearance. She didn't regret tearing her father's necklace from around her throat, only the heedless impulse to be rid of it without realizing that Amu might hurl himself over the cliff's edge to retrieve it.

Still, the act had felt cathartic, a step toward freeing herself from the power of her father's expectations. But only a step. Despite the truths her grandmother and Árdejā had spoken to her, the facts she'd learned from Elōr and Ceru, and everything Wailos had put her through, she was only beginning to comprehend how much the effort to live up to the ideal of a clan chief's daughter had cost her. She'd sacrificed so much – and was so tired. All she wanted was to sleep, her rest untroubled by dreams she couldn't recall when she awoke.

Couldn't… or wouldn't?

Light from the tallow lamp cast a soft glow. She held it aloft, scanning the various niches until she found the bundle containing her grandmother's *tekstlom*. Returning to her nest, she unwrapped the dream-web. Suspending it by the cord, she watched as it slowly spun, beads of jet and amber catching the lamplight.

She'd argued with Awija about her dreams. Her grandmother had accused her of being afraid, and she'd been right. Fear had led her to renounce her visionary gifts, along with her heart's desire. Instead, she'd devoted herself to serving her father, turning away from her own dreams and desires to be who he wanted her to be – and it hadn't been enough. Naya knew her father loved her, but he hadn't trusted her, or protected her, or even allowed her the knowledge she'd needed to protect herself.

Enough! She softened, took a breath. *Enough*, she repeated, less impatiently this time. Crouching, she searched with her fingers above the burrow's entrance until she located a protruding notch of stone from which she could suspend the *tekstlom*. "Awija was right," she said aloud. Enough of rejecting what made her who she was. Tonight, she would dream, and in the morning, she would remember.

After midnight…

At first, Naya wasn't sure whether she was still asleep. She thought she recalled blowing out the lamp before crawling beneath her blanket and falling into exhausted oblivion. But when she awoke, roused by a noise, the lamp still burned. She'd been dreaming of an intruder – someone entering the cave looking for her. A guardian had blocked the way, protecting her from harm.

In the dream, the female bear had been enormous, standing on her hindlegs with her back to Naya, shielding her. Outlined against the moonlight, the towering bear roared in anger before dropping to all fours and making a mock charge toward the intruder, who turned to flee by way of the tunnel leading out to the cave's main entrance. After two loping strides she stopped, lowered her massive head and swung it threateningly, shifting her weight from side to side, then lifted her nose to the air and let out another bellow. After huffing several times while bouncing on her front feet, she waited motionless for a long moment before exhaling and turning her back on the opening to the entrance tunnel, apparently satisfied she'd routed her adversary.

There it is again! Naya thought she heard the noise that must have roused her from the dream – footsteps, padding outside her hiding place in the burrow. Naya's heart leapt. *The bear!?* No, she told herself, that hadn't been real. A bear that size couldn't fit through the opening at the entrance to the cave. Naya shook her head as though to clear it, then scrubbed her hands over her face for good measure. Could it be Amu? She was about to call out to him when caution stopped her. *What if it's not Amu?* What if the noise had been made by an intruder, as in her dream – not a bear, but whatever the bear had chased off? *What if…?*

Naya's pulse raced. Before she could douse the light, a shadow darkened the opening to the burrow. She held her breath.

"Naya?" a male voice asked. She didn't recognize it. The voice didn't belong to anyone she knew – not Perqos and, thankfully, not Wailos. "It's me, Brathir," the voice continued, as though she *should* know him. Naya was baffled. The only person by that name had been…

"It's me," the voice repeated. "Is there room for both of us in there?"

Naya was too stunned to answer.

A young man clad in deerskin crawled through the burrow's entrance. Naya pressed herself against the back wall of the cramped chamber, eyeing the stranger with a combination of astonishment and disbelief. He looked uncannily like her. Blue eyes, perhaps a shade darker than hers, gazed out from under a shock of tousled hair that, although closer in hue to her mother's auburn than Naya's fiery copper, was nonetheless distinctively red. While the stranger's hawked nose resembled her father's, his high cheek bones, expressive russet brows and obstinate jaw mirrored Naya's own features. His mouth – with the same curved shape as hers – quirked upward at one corner, as though amused by her scrutiny.

"Who… who are you?" she managed.

"Exactly who you think I am," the apparition replied, his expression transformed into a lop-sided grin. "Did you really believe I'd never be a part of your life? That we'd never see or speak to one another? You may not have noticed, but I've been with you all along."

The young man laughed, a deep chuckle that reminded Naya of her grandfather. "Sister," he said, fixing her with a serious gaze. "We don't have much time. I'm here to tell you that all your life, you've been captive to a misunderstanding. You must let it go."

Naya, still pressed up against the back wall of the burrow, let her guard down enough to respond. "I don't know what you're talking about," she said, trying to keep her voice from shaking. "I don't understand. Who are you?"

"I know it's confusing, *dlkus*," the young man replied, using a term of familial affection. "I've come," he teased, "to help you learn to see." The bantering tone certainly made him *sound* like he could be… but that was impossible.

"You don't need to fear me," he added, shifting from a crouch into a more comfortable seated position, crossed forearms resting atop drawn-up knees. "We've known one another since before we were born. In fact, I'm pretty sure I know you better than you know yourself."

Naya eyed him dubiously. Sliding down the wall until she too was more comfortably seated, she maintained as much distance between herself and the apparition as possible, given the burrow's tight confines. Who was this stranger, claiming to be her twin who had died at birth? She pulled her blanket around her shoulders against the sudden chill that prickled her skin. "I don't understand," she repeated. "How can you be who you say you are?"

"How can you hear the voice of the red filly?" he countered. "She spoke to you in a vision – more than once – did she not? This is no different. To experience such visions is your gift. Stop denying it."

"But…" Naya objected. The person across from her seemed so… *real*. Composed of flesh and blood. And her brother was… *not*. At least not in this world.

"Your gift is becoming stronger," the young man explained, as though he could hear her thoughts. "All the more reason for you to grow up and be serious about using it responsibly. It's time, Naya."

Now he sounded like their grandmother – or Árdejā. Could this be the ally of whom the old woman had hinted? Naya regarded him but said nothing.

"The misunderstanding I mentioned?" he went on. "It has to do with our father."

She stiffened.

"No, hear me out. He loves you Naya, for who you are. He always has."

"But…" *I'm not you.* Naya choked on the words. If this person – Brathir – was who he said he was, she could never be him – the son their father had always wanted – the son she'd always believed he deserved. Tears welled, threatening to spill over and trail down her cheeks. She didn't want him to see her brush them away.

"Did he ever say that he wished I'd survived instead of you?" Brathir asked, voice gentle. "Or did you just assume?"

Laying her forehead on her folded arms, Naya hiding her face to avoid answering.

"It's true, he would have liked to have had a son," Brathir continued. "Our mother mourned my loss as well. But neither of them ever desired for *you* to be anyone other than who you are. Certainly, Father never expected you to be some imaginary paragon of a clan chief's daughter, not at the cost of your genuine self."

Naya looked up. How did he know? Blue eyes met her own – their expression filled with warmth and compassion, and a hint of amusement.

"You are precious to them both," Brathir reassured her. "Yes, you may have exasperated them at times. I'm not saying you're perfect – but just so you know, I would have been far worse, had I survived. Nor has our father been without fault. He should have brought you into his confidence. You are right to be angry with him for that. He was often too preoccupied. But those were his choices. They don't reflect on you, or your worth."

Naya wanted to believe him, but if what he told her was true, how was she supposed to feel? Was she even more at fault, for getting it all wrong from the beginning?

"Listen to me, Naya," Brathir responded. "First, while you don't need to apologize for being angry, you mustn't cling to it either. Ultimately, Father *was* trying to protect you, even if his methods were misguided. For your own sake, try to forgive him. Do you understand?"

He waited for a sign from her. Naya nodded, not entirely convinced.

"As for *your* choices," Brathir continued, "no doubt you'll admit that you, too, have made some mistakes – mostly the result of denying your heart's wisdom and trying to be someone other than yourself. Even so, you are NOT responsible for what happened to Father, any more than for what that *sterkos* Wailos did to you. *Stop. Blaming. Yourself.*" He spoke sternly, then softened. "Father has always loved you, Naya, just as much as you love him. Forgive him. More importantly, forgive yourself."

Words came back to her, spoken by the voice in her vision on the night of the winter solstice. Something about fear and bravery, trust and forgiveness. Suddenly, it was all too much. Squeezing her eyes shut, Naya pressed the heels of her hands hard against the sockets. When she opened them again, Brathir was still there, seated across from her in the burrow. The lamp still burned.

"Who *are* you?" she asked again. "How do you know all of this?"

Brathir rolled his eyes. "You," he said, "are stubborn. But it's a family trait – you come by it honestly." He paused, as though searching for another way to explain. "Think of me as your masculine half," he finally answered. "I'm the part of you who has always known that you are a warrior – the part of you brave enough to do whatever's necessary to protect the ones you love – *to take the shot* and live with the consequences."

Naya looked at him sharply. His words called to mind her actions with both the red filly *and* the colt, and she wondered at their double meaning. Brathir raised one brow and gave Naya a look she couldn't help but recognize. He was the exact image of their grandmother.

"Hear me, sister," he continued, insistent now. "A willingness to act is only part of the whole. Bravery untethered from compassion is folly – or worse. That is the way of men like Wailos and his father. Compassion devoid of bravery, likewise, lacks merit. Indeed, true compassion *demands* bravery. You are abundantly brave, my sister, but you must wield it wisely. Wisdom, in turn, comes only from the counsel of a compassionate heart."

Brathir paused, as though to be sure Naya understood. Her features must have betrayed her uncertainty, for he continued. "You can't keep pretending that your heart is made of stone, Naya. Up until today's storm breached your defenses, you've been afraid to experience your true feelings. In avoiding the pain, you've also denied yourself the joy. More importantly, by not embracing *all* your gifts – feminine as well as masculine – you've cut yourself off from your greatest source of wisdom and compassion. Sometimes, it takes a warrior's strength to acknowledge the heart's insight and be guided by its promptings. Like the moon and the sun conjoined, you must possess both the courage to feel *and* the willingness to act."

"The courage to feel…?" Naya repeated tentatively.

"…and the willingness to act," Brathir finished. "Close your eyes and say it again – three times, so you'll remember."

As instructed, Naya closed her eyes and uttered the words aloud: "The courage to feel, and the willingness to act. The courage to feel, and the willingness to act. The courage to feel, and the willingness to act." As she spoke, the image from her solstice journey – of the moon and the sun as one – flashed in her memory, giving form to the words. With each repetition, her voice grew stronger, more certain.

Naya opened her eyes to find the burrow dark. No lamp burned, and she was alone.

Chapter Twenty-Five

The following morning, Naya awoke early, feeling more rested than she'd been in ages – no queasiness, no headache. From the opalescent dawn light filtering into the burrow, she guessed sunrise was not far off. Her first thought was of Amu. Throwing aside her blanket, she crawled out the burrow's entrance, hardly noticing her grandmother's *tekstlom* as she ducked past. She also wanted to check for evidence of her late-night visitor – or visitors.

She found nothing. Although there were plenty of footprints on the floor of the cavern, all of them were old, belonging to her, or to Amu. No bear prints, and no evidence of another human – or humans. She checked the tunnel entrance leading to the bear's den, just to be certain.

Next, Naya went to the edge of the precipice and looked over, scanning for any sign of the dog. Again, nothing. *Do I go after him?* she asked herself, trying in vain to see beneath the thick forest canopy. In the storm's wake, curls of mist wafted through the valley, carried on invisible currents of air rising from below. The early morning breeze smelled fresh, with just a hint of autumn. Summer still held sway, however, and Naya knew that before long, the sun would turn everything hot and sticky. If she was going in search of Amu, she'd better get started.

Just as she turned, Naya heard scrabbling coming from the entrance tunnel and a moment later, to her immense relief, a muddy and disheveled bundle of fur emerged.

"Amu!" she cried, rushing over to him. Other than being filthy and smelling like a swamp, the dog appeared none the worse for his adventure. "What's this?" Naya asked, noticing he carried something in his mouth.

Into her outstretch palm, Amu deposited the bear's tooth necklace.

Stunned, Naya stared at it for a long moment in silence. Aside from the bison robe, the necklace was all she had left of her father – the bear's tooth a precious reminder of his love for her. She must treasure it as such. *The courage to feel,* Naya reminded herself, looking down at the necklace, her vision blurred. She would have been sorry to have lost it forever. Why did it have to be so hard?

Beside her, Amu nudged her with his nose, rousing her from her thoughts. Using a corner of her dress, Naya wiped away dirt from the tooth, then coiled the damaged cord before placing the necklace in her *makēn*. She'd repair it later. "Thank you!" she whispered, wrapping the dog in her arms, heedless of his bedraggled state. "But don't do anything like that again!" she scolded, pulling away. "Ugh," she added, looking down at her dress and her bare arms, now likewise caked with malodorous dirt. "You and I could both use a bath!"

Later, once they were both in a less objectionable state, Naya and Amu shared a breakfast of leftovers. As they ate, Naya wondered if Perqos would return by the end of the day or be away for another night or more. They had provisions enough to last for a few more days, but she hoped he wouldn't be gone too long.

The events of the previous night had unnerved her, although not because of her other-worldly visitor. That part, while discomfiting, no longer frightened her. Naya recognized that by hanging her grandmother's *tekstlom* at the entrance to the burrow, she'd opened herself once more to her visionary gifts. As a result, she'd experienced something similar to her first *etmn itājō*, when she'd communed with the red filly, only this time, she'd met the spirit of her twin. Once she'd gotten over the shock, she'd found her brother's presence, along with his words, to be comforting. Perhaps she was not quite so alone in the world as she sometimes felt – as Árdejā had promised, she'd found an ally – one who had given her much to consider.

What concerned Naya far more was the dream she'd been having *before* she'd awoken to find the lamp burning in the burrow. She remembered that she'd felt terrified – not so much of the bear in her dream, as of the possibility that the intruder she thought she'd heard was Wailos – that somehow he'd found her. Facing down an actual bear would have been far preferable. In any case, Naya told herself, she should pay attention to the dream's warning, as Awija had taught her.

"We need to be more careful, Amu," she said to the dog. "Maybe we should see if there's a safer place to hide, at least while Perqos is away."

Deciding that she could no longer put off exploring the lower level of the cave complex, Naya rose from her seat near the hearth and went to the storage alcove, returning with one of the torches. Scraping aside the old ashes that had been soaked by the storm, she laid a small fire, using only enough kindling to ignite the torch. Extinguishing the flame, she held the lighted brand aloft and called for Amu to accompany her to the ochre room.

The tunnel entrance concealed behind the protruding rocks was even narrower than Naya recalled. She was barely able to squeeze through. With the torch extended in front of her, she shimmied forward on her stomach. Amu crawled after her.

Almost immediately the tunnel began to slope downwards, gradually descending. Gravel bit into Naya's forearms, hips and thighs. Light flickered against the walls, now and then revealing evidence of where the passage had been widened. At one point the tunnel leveled out and turned to the right, before continuing its downward grade. Reminded of the cave she'd entered in her solstice journey, she wondered how much further she might have to proceed before reaching a dead-end, or if there'd be room enough to turn around. Even with the torch outstretched, she could see no more than an additional arm's length ahead and felt increasingly suffocated. She had to force herself to keep going.

Finally, as she considered giving up and edging her way backwards out of the tunnel, a gust of air caused the torch to flare and then sputter. Guessing there must be a void ahead and frantic not to be trapped in the cramped passage in the dark, Naya thrust herself forward. To her relief, he head and shoulders emerged from the tunnel into an open cavity. Pulling herself the rest of the way inside, Naya sat up. Holding the torch aloft, she looked around.

Her first impression was of a chamber larger even than the main cavern. Looking up, she realized she couldn't see the ceiling. Instead, the chamber's sides tapered gradually inward toward some point too distant overhead to make out in the dark. Moving the light in a slow semi-circle, Naya scanned the walls – and gasped.

Colorful images leapt out at her, each one outlined in charcoal and rendered in earthy tones of red, brown and yellow, accented by flashes of white. Deer, antelope, auroch and bison danced before her – and horses

– so many horses! Naya could hardly believe her eyes. Herds of individuals, each one unique, ranged over the cave's chalky limestone surface as though traversing the open steppe. Most of the horses were painted in shades of yellow or brown, with darker legs, charcoal-tipped ears, and thick manes and tails. Some were mouse-gray or nearly black. Many had a variety of white markings, achieved by allowing the underlying limestone to show through.

None was the glorious shining copper of the red filly.

Still, one figure in particular arrested Naya's gaze. Opposite where she sat at the chamber's entrance, located a little above ground level, was a golden-hued, white-bellied stallion, captured by the artist in mid-gallop, brown mane and tail streaming in an unseen wind. The colors were brilliant, as though more recently applied. *Perqos*, Naya thought. Somehow she knew this was his creation – the horse he'd told her about – the one he'd envisioned in his dreams – the stallion he wanted to ride.

Behind her, Amu whined. Realizing she was blocking him from entering the chamber, Naya scrambled aside. "Oh my!" she said to the dog. "I'm glad we didn't miss this."

Later the same day…

After several trips, Naya managed to shift all of her belongings from the burrow down to the lower cave, along with two of the unused lamps, extra torches, the remaining firewood and what was left of the food from the storage alcove. She also brought down the dishes of raw ochre she'd collected, as well as a container of plain tallow and a couple of empty bowls. On her last visit to the surface, having given Amu strict instructions to wait below, she used the small broom to erase footprints and other signs of recent habitation from the main cavern and upper chambers. She and Amu could go back up for water and provisions and Amu could leave each day to forage with Perqos. Otherwise, Naya planned to retreat to the lower level, each time following the same procedure of obscuring footprints and thereby leaving as little evidence as possible of her presence.

As soon as she'd moved everything, Naya set about laying a fire in the lower chamber's central hearth, a ring of stones smaller in circumference than the one in the main cavern. Evidently an opening existed overhead, serving to draw smoke upward, like a chimney. Otherwise spending any length of time with a fire burning in the lower chamber would have been impossible. Satisfied that a small blaze would enable her to see without having to use up either the lamps or the torches, Naya sat back, observing the play of light and shadow against the chamber walls.

Illuminated by the flickering glow, first one group of animals and then another came to life, painted figures moving to the rhythm of the crackling flames. The effect was hypnotic. For an instant, Perqos's golden horse shone bright as the sun, then vanished into darkness, only to reappear, flashing in and out of sight like a figment of her imagination. Naya envisaged adding her own contribution to the spectacle, if she dared, only instead of golden yellow, the horse of her dreams would be a fiery red.

After only a second night away, Perqos returned and their former routine resumed, with Amu departing in the morning and reappearing before sundown to summon Naya from the cave's lower reaches to the entrance of the bear's den, where a fresh supply of food and firewood waited. As before, Naya spent her days alone. Unlike earlier, however, she was now so absorbed in what she was doing, she hardly noticed the passage of time. She resolved to create a painting of the red filly worthy of its real-life subject, but artists of great ability had preceded her. If she wanted her rendering to match their example, she needed to practice.

She began by drawing with a charred stick, much as she'd done earlier when tracing symbols in the dirt of the cavern floor, but this time with greater purpose. Choosing an unobtrusive corner so that her initial efforts would not be seen by future visitors, she sketched repeatedly, erasing and starting again, until gradually her rough attempts started to resemble an actual horse. She also studied the other images adorning the chamber walls, noticing the details that had enabled previous artists to produce such life-like images and doing her best to copy them.

When she needed a break, Naya turned to learning how to make and apply paint. Using a mortar and pestle she found abandoned in a corner, she ground flakes of ochre into powder, then experimented with blending the powder with plain tallow to make a viscous paste. Next, she investigated how to apply the mixture with one of the boar bristle brushes she'd discovered discarded on the cave floor. Her first attempts amounted to no more than crude blotches, but eventually she discovered how to blend different pigments to vary the paint's shade and add more or less tallow to change its intensity and consistency, allowing her to produce the more subtle nuances the other artists had depicted in their images.

Still, despite her patience and determination, Naya sometimes despaired of ever understanding the alchemy of brush, paint and limestone canvas. One afternoon, feeling frustrated that her attempts to capture the filly's spirit were never going to live up to her expectations, Naya decided she needed inspiration. Reaching into her *makēn*, she extracted the exquisite carving of Réhda that Aytal had made for her. Holding the little figurine in the palm of one hand, she traced its smooth contours with a finger, marveling again at the detail and recalling her first mysterious encounter with the red filly in the moonlit grove. At the time, the young horse seemed to speak directly to Naya's heart – words that afterwards she never been able to fully recall.

"Will I ever see you again?" she wondered aloud, looking down at the carving that rested in her palm. *Do I want to?*

Since moving down to the lower chamber and spending day and night surrounded by life-like images of horses roaming freely across an invisible plain, Naya recognized she must confront, once and for all, the problem that had plagued her since her return to the settlement last spring. What was she to do about the red filly? Was she right to search for Réhda, if finding her meant risking a future as bleak as Naya's worst nightmares – a terrifying world filled with shadowy scenes of horrific violence and soul-crushing exploitation? Had she been justified in turning away, hoping that without her intervention or involvement, the red filly, at least, might be spared? But even then, what about the others?

Sitting in the dark depths of the cave, surrounded by a circle of firelight and holding Aytal's carving in her hand, Naya still didn't have an answer. Turning the figure over, she studied it from the other side. The carving was so realistic, she could see the steppe wind at play within the strands of the little horse's mane and banner-like tail. Had Aytal meant to capture the exhilaration she and the red filly shared after their first headlong gallop across the grasslands? If so, he had succeeded. But how could the memory of such untrammeled joy be reconciled with the misery of the red filly's captured herd mates? When she'd returned to the settlement last spring, Naya had been sickened by what she'd observed from the blufftop, and later down at the corrals. She'd felt responsible – as though what was happening to the trapped horses was all her fault.

She thought of her conversation with Perqos. He, at least, seemed to be drawn to the horses for the same reasons that she was, and to feel the same accountability for what might happen to them. If he and his father really meant to protect the wild herds while preserving their essential freedom, perhaps her nightmares did not have to become reality. Perhaps another way for humans to be with horses *was* still possible, instead of what she'd witnessed with men like Wailos in charge. For the horses' sake, Naya hoped so.

Still, she felt ambivalent about her own role. Finding Réhda probably wouldn't be too difficult, with Ceru and Perqos's help, but would she be seeking the filly for the right reasons? What if, in following her heart's desire, she was just being selfish, or worse, wanting to be admired? If Naya were honest, part of her had been pleased and rather proud to learn of Aytal's name for her – *She-Who Rides-Horses*. There'd been a time, after all, when she'd relished the idea of returning to the clan's settlement on horseback, impressing those who, like Krnos, had once teased her.

Admiration aside, though, did she *want* to be known as *She-Who-Rides-Horses*? Her more self-deprecatory side worried whether she could live up to the title and the expectations that might come with it. Yet could she justify walking away, turning her back on the role – the responsibility – that had been laid out for her in her grandfather's prophecy? Árdejā had said she'd made a promise – a covenant. Awija would agree. Her brother, too, would counsel her that she must summon both the courage to feel and the willingness to act. *But feel what, and act how?*

Sighing, Naya reached for her *makēn*, intending to tuck the figure of the little horse away again for safe keeping. *And what of Aytal?* she wondered, giving the carving one last look. He was part of this too – along Šuurgan, the gray stallion. As with so many things, since fleeing the settlement, Naya had mostly avoided thinking about Aytal and the declaration of love he'd made before she left. Yes, she'd experienced that stab of disappointment that he hadn't waited to see her before setting off for the mountains, but otherwise, she wasn't sure how she felt about him. And really, unless she saw him again, she had no way to find out. She sighed. If their paths crossed, it would have to be because Aytal came looking for her, not the other way around. At least he'd managed to return her dog.

"Where is Amu anyway?" Naya said aloud. He ought to have been back by now. Perhaps she should go up to check whether the sun had set. Putting the carving away, Naya fingers grazed the jagged edge of the blue-green crystal Perqos had left for her, resting in the bottom of her *makēn*. Removing it, she held the crystal in one palm, Aytal's gift in the other, as though weighing and comparing the two. Did the tokens Perqos left for her indicate he felt something for her in the same way as Aytal? She and Perqos hadn't actually spent that much time together, but their fathers *had* intended for them to marry…

Abruptly, Naya thrust Perqos's crystal back in her *makēn*, along with Aytal's carving of the little horse. She didn't want to be distracted by such thoughts. Nor, she decided, did she want to stop what she'd been doing. Eventually Amu would return. Until then, she'd refrain from pondering difficult questions. Better to focus instead on the project she'd set herself. Only a few nights remained before the next full moon, which meant her sojourn in the cave was almost at an end – not much time to finish what she'd only barely begun.

Gathering her supplies, along with one of the lamps, Naya knelt upright before the patch of blank wall where she intended to create the final version of her painting of the red filly. Situated to the right and a little above Perqos's golden stallion, the location was more prominent than the hidden space where she'd been practicing. Anyone entering the cavern would notice it immediately – Réhda deserved no less. Brush in hand, Naya took a deep breath, poised to begin. "Here goes," she said, and set to work.

Sometime later, Naya sat back on her heels, feeling as though she were awakening from a trance. The image before her took her breath away. There was no mistaking its subject. Neck arched, copper coat shining in the firelight, cleared-eyed gaze scanning an invisible horizon – the painting captured the filly's very essence. Naya had no memory of how it got there. Overcome, she began to weep.

"Oh Réhda," she whispered, tears falling unchecked as she beheld the vibrant portrait. Her heart swelled with love for the young horse, and fear for her future. "I wish you could tell me what I'm meant to do," she whispered.

As if in response, from out of the darkness a voice spoke: *See with the eyes of your heart. Create ties without the use of a rope. And when you have succeeded in granting my heart's desire, then shall yours be granted also.* Like the notes of a song, the words echoed off the walls – words Naya had been trying in vain to recall ever since first hearing them. How could she have forgotten? And how could she not have understood?

For the first time, with utter clarity, she grasped the true nature of the mission she'd been given, all those moons ago, when she and the filly first encountered one another in that otherworldly ravine. Learning to see with the eyes of her heart and create ties without the use of a rope was not about attaining *her* heart's desire. That was not the task. The real question Naya had been sent into the cave to unearth was not about whether or not to pursue her own dreams, with all the potential consequences, but rather just the opposite. Gazing at the life-like image before her, Naya spoke the words aloud: "What is *your* heart's desire?" Breath held, she waited for the voice to reply.

This time… silence. Neither the painting nor the surrounding darkness offered an answer. All Naya sensed was her own familiar longing. She wanted to be with the red filly. Just like on that late summer afternoon when she'd first spotted the young horse, coat ablaze in the last rays of the setting sun, Naya wanted to stroke the filly's red-gold fur. She wanted to savor the gentle touch of her soft muzzle, inhale her sweet grass-scented breath. She wanted to hear the filly nicker at her approach and come trotting to meet her as she'd done nearly every day for much of the winter and early spring. And yes, she wanted to ride.

But now, even more, Naya wanted to learn what the red filly desired in return. Why had the young horse been open to Naya's advances in the first place? What had drawn them together? Yes, she needed to understand whether she and the red filly were truly linked by a shared destiny, as her grandparents had been the first to insist. She also needed to try to grasp the larger forces at play – what was at stake for humans and horses alike – so that she could interpret her grandfather's prophecy, as well as the warnings of her own dark visions. But first, and above all, she needed to understand what the filly wanted of her.

"I need to find Réhda," Naya said aloud. The filly alone held the answers, that much was clear.

Chapter Twenty-Six

Naya stood in the dark, hands on hips, and sighed in exasperation. After finishing the portrait of Réhda, she'd come up looking for Amu but found no sign of him. Her stomach rumbled. She hadn't eaten since breakfast and now, judging by the waxing moon riding high in the night sky, it was after midnight – well past when the dog normally returned to remind her to eat supper. She'd completely lost track of time.

Naya's frustration turned to worry. On the last occasion when Perqos intended to be away, even though he'd been gone for no more than a night or two, he'd left the dog behind. Had something unexpected happened? Remembering her dream of the intruder, she decided to wait until daylight to investigate. The safest choice for now was to return underground, fix herself something to eat from what remained of the provisions, and hope Amu reappeared by morning.

Later, Naya lay on her back under her blanket, staring upward into the darkness while trying to ignore the persistent pangs of unsatisfied hunger. Upon returning to the lower chamber, she'd consumed the last of her food stores, which hadn't been enough to fill her empty stomach. If Perqos didn't return soon, she'd be forced to leave the safety of the cave to find something more to eat. Besides, her prescribed time in hiding was nearly up. She and Perqos were due to start their return trip to the Dānus encampment in order to arrive in time for the start of the tribe's upcoming celebration. And now that she'd made up her mind to go in search of the red filly, she was eager to get started. If Perqos wasn't back in a day or two, she'd consider setting off without him. She just wished Amu wasn't missing as well.

Naya let her mind wander, imagining what the Dānus Autumn Festival would be like. As always, she dreaded the prospect of meeting strangers, but Elōr and Rei would be there to welcome her and perhaps shield her from too many uncomfortable questions. She'd be able to talk to Ceru about how to find Réhda and perhaps speak with Árdejā regarding the words of instruction she'd finally remembered. If she dared, Naya might even ask the old woman about the encounter she'd had with the spirit of her twin.

Other familiar faces might be present as well. If Naya's uncle and the rest of her extended family had accepted Ceru's invitation, they could have arrived at the Dānus encampment by now, along with Melit and her family – although their presence was less likely. Perhaps her mother and Oyuun would be there – maybe even Aytal – if they'd begun their return journey from the mountains in time.

Gazing into the blackness overhead, Naya started to count on her fingers. How long had it been since she'd seen her mother? Four moons? Could that be right? So much had happened, as though a lifetime had passed. She'd fled her home nearly two and a half months ago.

Naya sat up. When had she last had her moon flow? Before leaving the settlement, she realized. *Was it possible?* She dismissed the thought. Her moon flow was often irregular. Besides, she'd have had other signs by now…

She lay down again, curled on her side this time, hoping to rest, but her mind churned. She thought of all the mornings when she'd awakened not feeling well. Always she'd attributed the nausea to sleeping poorly, or to an empty stomach, or both. She often hadn't felt like herself since returning to the settlement last spring, long before… Rolling onto her back, Naya placed both hands on her lower abdomen, imagining the unimaginable. Why hadn't it occurred to her before?

Because, she admitted, up until this moment, she'd shuddered away from recalling what had happened in Wailos's tent that night, let alone considering the consequences. Despite Elōr and Rei's kindness, it had taken Naya nearly a month to confess even the abridged version of the story. They'd insisted that what happened had not been her doing, but Naya hadn't believed them. Even after learning of her father's betrayal, the self-blame had been overwhelming. And now?

Curling once more onto her side under her blanket, Naya wrapped her arms around her knees and pulled them into her chest. Head pillowed on her extra clothing, she stared sideways into the glowing embers of her small fire. The time had come. Much as she didn't want to, she had to force herself to face what had happened that night, moment by moment, if only to prove to herself that none of it was her fault. She had to free herself from the burden of fear and shame she'd carried with her every step of her exile. If not, she'd end up paralyzed by the new realization that she might be pregnant. For her own sake, for the sake of the child she might be carrying, and for the sake of her promise to the red filly, Naya had to deal with the reality of what Wailos had done to her.

Concentrating, she thought back to the last night of her vigil. She recalled being awakened from a dream that she'd been unable to re-member – a dream she had to admit could have forewarned her. Instead, dazed and uncertain, she'd responded to the urgent summons issued by a mysterious cloaked figure, whom she'd assumed to be the priest's wife. She might have known better, but with no memory of the dream, what reason had she to be suspicious?

Upon entering Wailos's tent, she'd been relieved at first, but also awkward and nervous. In hindsight, she admitted that she'd never been comfortable around him, but she'd lacked the self-confidence to give credence to her feelings of unease. Instead, she'd been intent on trying to help her father, heeding Vedukha's advice and Melit's encouragement while ignoring her grandmother's warnings and her own misgivings. Yet had it been so wrong to want to please her father? Shouldn't *he* have warned her?

This isn't helping, Naya admonished herself. She sat up, letting the blanket fall from her shoulders, and shook out her wrists as though rid-ding herself of distracting thoughts. She'd need to take her time, remind herself that she was safe. She lay down again on her side, pulling the blanket around her once more. Eyelids squeezed shut, she made herself experience again the sensations of Wailos touching her, her efforts to please him, his increasing violence. Tears leaked unnoticed from the corners of her eyes as she hugged her knees tighter, wanting to shield herself from what she knew was coming. She had tried to resist, she remembered now. She'd fought back with all her strength. But she'd been trapped – helpless – prey at the mercy of a predator. Her efforts to free herself had only made Wailos laugh.

The cruelty of his laughter returned to Naya, along with the panicked feeling of being immobilized, unable to escape. Not knowing what else to do, she'd abandoned her body. Afterwards, stunned, she wasn't even sure how to name what had happened – wondering if, out of inexperience, she'd overreacted. She hadn't trusted herself. And then, the utter humiliation of appearing before her father and the other men… no wonder she'd run.

But Naya was stronger now – more herself. This time, she *could* fight back, if only through the sheer act of remaining present to the memory of what Wailos had done. No averting her eyes, no doubting her own truth. Like a warrior, she would stare down the wolf, with his mocking gaze, with every brutal, tearing thrust. Otherwise, she'd never be free of the fear and the shame that had driven her from her home and into hiding, nor the terror of being found that haunted her dreams. If she wanted to be released from Wailos's hold, she had to summon every shred of courage she possessed.

In that moment, huddled under her blanket in the lower cavern, Naya became aware of someone with her. Her brother. She felt his strong arms wrap around her, holding her, sharing his strength, letting her know she was secure. She would not go through the next part alone.

When it was over, Naya opened her eyes. Sitting up, still shaking, she wiped away tears. She was in the lower cavern. Reaching for the wood pile, she added the last of the kindling to the embers in the hearth, blowing gently to revive the flames. She sat back, took a long breath – and let it out. She was alright. She'd survived. She felt drained – but no longer afraid, at least not of encountering Wailos and this time standing up to him. Unquestionably he was still dangerous, but no more so than any man who posed such a threat. If he did succeed in hunting her down, she wouldn't allow him – or anyone else – to intimidate nor humiliate her. She had nothing of which to be ashamed. And she certainly wouldn't fall for his charm – no disguise could hide from her the truth of who he was.

Placing a hand on her belly, Naya wondered once more if a new life stirred inside. How did she feel about the possibility, especially with Wailos as the father? *Defiant* was her first answer. She'd be willing to die before allowing him to regain control over her, or her child. Given what she knew of such matters, she would soon be too far along to safely end a pregnancy, even if she wanted to – and she wasn't sure that's what she wanted. But If Wailos found out he would undoubtedly try to exert his rights, especially if she carried his son.

Turning from where she sat by the fire, Naya shifted sideways, so that the light from the flames shone on Réhda's portrait. All she knew for certain was that she must find the red filly. Out of food and low on fuel, she could not afford to wait much longer. Exhausted as she felt, she decided to pack-up her belongings, set the lower chamber in order, and return to the surface. The sun might well be up by now. Even if Amu hadn't returned, she could at least assess the situation by daylight.

Coming to her hands and knees, Naya began to push herself to her feet when a wave of dizziness overwhelmed her. She hung her head between her elbows, eyes closed and waited for the world to stop spinning. She hadn't slept, and she'd had very little to eat or drink. Maybe she should rest first, then pack. Reaching for her water skin, she took a long pull. Emptying it, she lay down again in her place by the hearth, and covering herself once more with her blanket, sank into a dreamless sleep.

Late afternoon the following day…

Naya emerged confounded from the cave's lower level. Instead of heralding the start of a new day, the sun had already begun to descend toward the western horizon. She'd slept much longer than she'd intended – and there was still no sign of Amu. She'd left a small fire burning in the lower cavern, but otherwise she'd run out of firewood. If she waited in the main cavern for Amu's return, she'd either have to sit under the stars or use up the last of the lamps from the storage alcove. All but one of the torches were spent and she'd need the remaining one to retrieve her belongings from the lower level.

The bigger issue was lack of food. Naya had eaten the last of the provisions in the middle of the night. She could check the entrance tunnel to see if Perqos had left fresh supplies and for some reason hadn't sent the dog to alert her, but with darkness descending, it was too late to go out to forage on her own. If Perqos and Amu didn't show up by morning, she'd have to risk leaving the cave by herself – that was clear. If she discovered no sign of them in the vicinity of the cave, she'd have to set-off for the Dānus encampment on her own.

In the meantime, she could at least be packed and ready to go at a moment's notice. In a hurry now to bring her things up before nightfall, Naya turned to head back down to the lower chamber.

"Where is Perqos?" Naya fretted aloud. Setting down her bundles beside the opening to the entrance tunnel, she stood for a moment, considering the wisdom of going down to the other end while the last of the light remained, just in case he'd left supplies for her without sending Amu to fetch her. Making up her mind, she pulled her flint knife from her belt, placed it between her teeth, and entering the tunnel, crawled on her belly toward the bear's den. Half-way through she stopped, listening intently. The crunch of dead leaves reached her ears, accompanied by snuffling and the occasional grunt – the sounds of large bodies making themselves comfortable. *Bears.* Naya could smell the reek of them, likely more than one. Perhaps a sow and her half-grown cubs. *That* would explain why Perqos and Amu hadn't been able to reach her. The season was early for a family of bears to take up winter residence, but they could easily be laying claim to the den.

Cautiously, Naya backed up the way she'd come. The opening behind the rocks in the den was too narrow for a full-grown bear to fit through, but she didn't want to attract the attention of a curious youngster. If she could smell them, they could smell her. Emerging feet first into the cave's main chamber, she considered her options. Clearly, she'd have to wait for the bears to leave. Hopefully they would rouse themselves in the morning to go foraging so that she could slip out of the den. With luck, Perqos and Amu would be waiting at a safe distance nearby. If not, she'd start out and hope they caught up with her. Everything was in order, her bundles packed and ready. She could seize her opportunity in the morning.

Empty water skin slung over one shoulder, Naya ducked into the alcove to replenish her supply from the spring. She took time to sluice water over her face, neck and arms as well, washing away traces of paint from her hands and scrubbing under her nails. If she could find her comb, she would detangle and re-braid her hair.

Emerging from the alcove, Naya stopped in her tracks, arrested by the most glorious sunset she'd ever beheld. Bands of crimson, orange and gold glowed above distant snow-capped peaks, while a layer of clouds refracted the sun's last rays, sending flames shooting skyward like beacons. Awestruck, Naya found her way to a seat near the edge of the cliff and watched until the last glow faded, leaving only the mountains, outlined in shadow, against the indigo curtain of the evening sky.

With no wood for a fire, nor food to eat, nor desire to sleep, Naya stayed where she was, comb forgotten, as the oncoming night began to unfold. One by one, stars shone out, gradually joining together to create the constellations. She named each as it appeared, just as her grandmother had taught her. Eventually, she could see the full figure of the Great Bear, mightiest of all the heavenly beings, with its brightest stars aligned to point north, to the Guide Star, around which all the other constellations revolved. Reminded once more of her dream of the giant she-bear confronting the intruder, this time instead of fear, Naya felt relief. The bear family ensconced in the outer den for the night might be blocking her departure from the cave but no one could get past them. The bears would keep her safe.

The irony did not escape her. Reaching into the *makēn* at her waist, Naya drew out the bear's tooth from her father and, in the dark, ran a finger over the yellowed canine. Perhaps if the hunting party she'd been with on that day three years ago had never encountered the she-bear, desperate to defend her cubs, much of what happened afterwards might have turned out differently. If her father's best friend, Bhermi, had not been fatally wounded, would Skelos, Bhermi's brother, have struck the blow that ended her father' life? And had Naya not been blamed for the party's bad luck and ostracized as a result, would she have spent so much time by herself on the steppe? If not, she might never have encountered the red filly. Who could say?

Naya sighed. She had yet to repair the bear's tooth necklace, but it was too dark to attempt the task now. She returned it to her *makēn* and pulled out her mother's gift instead. Suspending the arrowhead necklace from its cord, Naya watched as starlight flashed faintly from the obsidian's translucent black depths. She could imagine the precious stone having begun its journey as volcanic rock, deposited on one of the distant slopes visible from the cave. The raw material would have been collected from a mountain side, then entrusted into the care of an expert napper from among her mother's people – Aytal's people, as it turned out – who, at some personal risk – obsidian being notoriously dangerous to work with – had transformed the stone into a deadly weapon, before passing the distinctively-shaped point along to a trader. Eventually, the arrowhead had found its way to a young man with a bow – and thence to within a hair's breadth of Naya's heart.

Was it random chance that had led Aytal's path to cross with hers?

All she knew was that out of recklessness, he'd nearly ended her life, and such actions held consequences. On some level, the arrowhead bound them to one another forever. Aytal believed as much. Holding the necklace aloft, Naya twisted the cord, setting the point spinning once more. *Will I see him again?* she wondered, watching the obsidian flash in the starlight. It was the same question she'd asked earlier about the red filly. To her surprise, she realized that contrary to her assurances to herself from a day or two ago, where Aytal was concerned, she cared far more than she'd been willing to admit.

And yet, she reminded herself, catching the arrowhead in her palm and slackening the cord, Aytal's gift to her had been the carved figure of Réhda. The necklace with the arrowhead had come from her mother. When Naya had first unwrapped it, during her initiation vigil, she hadn't felt ready to wear it, nor had she been certain of how she felt toward her mother, any more than she'd known how she felt about Aytal. And now?

Sliding the necklace over her head, Naya shortened the cord until the arrowhead rested in the hollow of her throat, where the bear's tooth from her father had hung. In that moment, alone in the dark, beneath the silence of the stars, the truth came to Naya like a blow to the chest. She missed her mother desperately.

"Oh Mama," she whispered aloud, one hand on her heart as the other slid unnoticed to shield her belly. "I need you!" She longed for the familiarity of her mother's voice, the security of her embrace. For once, she would even welcome her mother's wisdom and advice. Above all, Naya yearned for the reassurance of her unconditional love.

Overwhelmed, Naya wept. She'd behaved hatefully toward her mother. Her judgments against her, their disagreements – none of it had been her mother's fault. All Naya wanted now was to see her again and beg her forgiveness, and in return receive the consolation that only her mother could give. "I'm so sorry," she murmured, setting off a fresh outpouring of desolation and regret.

Eventually, once the tightness in her chest had eased, Naya took a steadying breath. She brushed her tears away, then laughed ruefully at herself. Ever since the night of the storm, she'd cried more often and more easily than ever before in her life. Surely by now, she'd wrung herself dry. With luck, her mother and Oyuun and perhaps Aytal would be waiting for her when she returned to the Dānus encampment. If not, with Ceru's help, she would come up with a plan to be reunited – and she would go in search of the red filly.

Chapter Twenty-Seven

Naya waited until the sun was well up before venturing through the entrance tunnel to check on the bears. She brought her belongings, hoping to make a quick exit. To her relief, the family had vacated the den. Peeking out of the earthen opening, she held her breath, scanning the immediate vicinity for any sign of the mother bear and her cubs. Satisfied that she could make her escape, she crawled out, came to her feet, and set off up the trail at a brisk walk, glancing over her shoulder as she went. Her father had often warned her not to run from a bear, or any large predator, and never to turn her back.

After a month confined to the cavern, Naya felt disoriented to be out in the world again. The path leading away from the bear's den seemed more exposed than she remembered, and more perilous to navigate. She didn't recall the trail being so rocky, nor the sparse trees offering so little protection. Her heart beat harder than it should have against her ribs, and her legs wobbled – the result of lack of food but also lack of exercise. She paused frequently to steady herself, and to check her surroundings and get her bearings. Becoming lost was the last thing she could afford.

Only after she'd gone a good way downhill in what she thought was the right direction, did she take a full breath and relax her vigilance. Ahead, the deer trail faded into the woods. Once within the shelter of the trees, she'd consider how to find something to eat.

Naya paused. She wasn't alone. There, below the trail, ambling among the bushes lining a creek, she spotted a mother bear and twin cubs – likely the same family that had occupied the den. As Naya watched, the she-bear paused and lifted her head, sniffing the air before rising on her hind-legs. Naya froze. The she-bear seemed to look directly at her. In the next moment, she realized the sow was focused not on her, but on the hillside above. Turning, Naya saw another bear, an enormous male, moving in the opposite direction along a ridge higher up from where she stood. No doubt the female would be anxious for the safety of her cubs if the male changed course and headed in their direction. Naya did not want to be caught in between. Without taking her eyes off the two adults, she edged backwards along the trail toward the woods. If necessary, once she reached the shelter of the trees, she could locate an evergreen with low-hanging limbs and climb to safety.

"Naya!" A voice called to her from the direction of the trees, distinct enough to be heard but not so loud as to alert the bears. Naya's first reaction was relief. Perqos must have returned. But where was Amu? Restrained to keep him out of trouble? She couldn't risk looking over her shoulder into the woods without losing track of what the bears were doing.

"Don't turn around," the voice advised. The hairs on the back of Naya's neck stood on end. "Keep moving slowly, with your back to me," the voice went on. "I have an arrow knocked and a spear to hand."

Naya hesitated. The male bear had spotted the female and her cubs, and was heading downhill toward them. If Naya didn't keep retreating in the direction of the woods, the male would cross the deer trail only a short distance from her. He'd spot her for sure. She backed up slowly, wondering if she dared glance over her shoulder to confirm whether indeed it was Perqos who had spoken. His voice hadn't sounded quite right, but who else could it be? Unless...

The male bear drew closer, moving in the direction of the female and her cubs. Naya pulled her knife from her belt, letting her bundles slide to the ground along with her bow and quiver – she didn't trust herself to use them. Her *makēn* and the auroch horn remained at her waist, along with her water skin slung over a shoulder. As she watched, the mother bear sent the cubs scurrying to the safety of the woods close to the creek. They were still small enough to shimmy up one of the birches. Satisfied they'd obeyed her, the she-bear turned and started up the hill toward Naya, evidently intent on confronting the big male.

With the two adult bears focused on one another, Naya seized the opportunity to follow the cubs' example. Knife in hand she turned, sprinting for the nearest tree – and ran smack into a broad, deerskin-clad male chest. A hand grabbed her wrist, wresting the knife from her grasp and spinning her back around to face the bears. A muscled arm clamped around her shoulders, pinning her arms at her sides. She started to scream, but the hand with her knife was at her throat. A voice she now recognized hissed in her ear.

"Be quiet, you little *skortum*. Do you want to get us both killed?"

Wailos. For an instant Naya's vision swam with shock before her head cleared. Heedless of the risk from the knife, she tucked her chin and bit down hard. Surprised, Wailos loosened his hold just enough for Naya to wrench free. Half twisting, she aimed a knee at his groin and took off running into the woods.

Despite the brief head start, within no more than a few strides Naya realized she'd never outrun him. Even with the surge of panic, she was too out of condition and weak from hunger. Abruptly, she turned aside, leaving the path to plunge into the densest part of the woods.

There! Straight ahead was a tall, densely limbed spruce whose lower boughs were within reach. Naya swung herself up, thankful she'd dropped her bundles and could climb unincumbered. Hand over hand, desperate to escape, she clambered blindly upward into the spruce's topmost branches, her palms raked by the tree's rough bark, her face lacerated by needles as her feet frantically sought purchase.

Just as she reached the limit of how high she could safely climb, Wailos arrived at the tree's base. Looking down, Naya saw him lean over to catch his breath, one hand supporting himself against the trunk.

"You're making this too easy," he called up.

While the remark may or may not have been ironic, his posture at least afforded Naya the brief satisfaction of knowing she'd landed her earlier blow. A moment later, composure restored, Wailos straightened and continued.

"Of course, there's always the possibility that I've misjudged your motives," he offered, adopting the falsely conversational tone with which Naya was all-to-familiar. "If it's actually the bears you're worried about, as long as the male doesn't know you're here, once the female succeeds in discouraging him from bothering her cubs, he'll lose interest and move on. Same with the female. Keep quiet, and you're probably relatively safe up there. If, by contrast, you're trying to escape *me*, you'll find you've miscalculated." He laughed. "Unlike those bears, now that I know you're within reach, all I need is patience. Whenever you decide to come down, I'll be waiting. Meanwhile, we have things to discuss."

Naya wanted to scream.

"Don't!" Wailos warned, as though guessing her mind. Lowering his voice, he went on. "Safe as you may think you are, at least from the bears, even you aren't stupid enough to risk deliberately drawing their attention." His amiable tone carried a distinct undercurrent of menace. "If the male *does* change his mind about the prey he's after, he'll have you down from your perch far quicker than he'd manage to dislodge those cubs. Shall I demonstrate?"

Reaching up, he pulled hard with both hands against the spruce's slender trunk, causing it to sway. Taken by surprise, Naya nearly lost her balance.

"For now, perhaps we can both agree that you're better off up there, where I can keep an eye on you – and of course *protect* you."

The sarcasm wasn't lost on Naya. As if on cue, the angry bellowing of the two adult bears reached her ears. Wailos didn't miss a beat. "Don't do anything foolish to attract their notice, and when they've finished hurling threats at one another, they'll most likely go their separate ways," he assured her. "By then, I'll have explained how it's going to be for you and me. You'll agree to my very generous conditions regarding our future life together, after which you can climb down from up there and we can start our return journey north, during which you'll promise to be on your best behavior. In exchange, I'll make a sincere effort to forget that you were ever so silly as to run away in the first place and put me to all the time and trouble of tracking you down."

Naya couldn't believe her ears. Was Wailos seriously suggesting she go with him as though nothing had happened? "I'll never consent to marry you!" she flung down.

"Not my first choice, either," Wailos countered pleasantly. "But the tribal elders are insisting – particularly in light of the loss of your father – a rather unfortunate complication. In his absence, I've been made responsible for your well-being. That is, unless – or until – something unfortunate befalls *you* as well." Despite Wailos's cordial delivery, the implication of his words was unmistakable.

"Now that I think about it," he continued, "a bear attack might suit my purposes rather well – there would even be a certain elegant symmetry – if only I had a witness to testify to the cause of your demise. Oh wait, I almost forgot." Cupping his hands to his mouth, he produced a distinctive bird call. Moments later, a figure emerged from the surrounding woods to join Wailos beneath the tree.

Krnos. Naya's childhood tormentor, recognizable even from the height of her tree-top perch with branches obscuring her view. She should have guessed Wailos would not have pursued her alone. Krnos saluted her from the base of the spruce but said nothing.

Meanwhile, Wailos leaned his back against the tree and kept talking. "That's right," he confirmed. "Like you, Krnos has been here before – on that same ill-fated hunting trip, when his uncle Bhermi was killed. Your fault, wasn't it, for crying out and alerting the bear?" He didn't wait for a reply. "My advice would be, don't make the same mistake again," he said with a nasty chuckle. "Once we learned from our spies among the Dānus where you'd gone, with his excellent memory, Krnos was able to guide us to your hiding place. Since then, we've merely been biding our time."

Naya's stomach dropped. How long had the pair been stalking her? What had happened to Perqos?

Again, Wailos seemed to guess her mind. "It took some perseverance, but eventually your guardian left for long enough for us to flush you out. You were lucky with the she-bear taking shelter in the cave during the big storm, or I would have gotten to you sooner."

Naya thought of her dream. She'd been right to heed its warning that Wailos was after her, but something was off. Wailos spoke as though the bears had been in the den on the night of the storm, when she'd had the dream, but that had been days before the family had first shown up, or so she assumed. Unless… Naya thought of another mother bear – the one who had died defending her innocent cubs, the one whose tooth she'd worn as a necklace at her throat. The dream on the night of the storm had seemed so real, more like one of her visions. Was it possible? Had the spirit-bear been protecting her all along, even as she hid in the lower chamber, intent on completing Réhda's portrait? Dizzy, Naya wrapped an arm even more tightly around the spruce's trunk.

Wailos was still speaking. "If your guardian and that odious dog of yours do manage to reappear before we're well on our way north, it won't matter. In the absence of your father, I am your rightful protector, duly designated by our tribe's elders, and that's the end of it."

Other than Wailos's voice, the woods had gone silent. Straining her ears, Naya listened for the bears but heard nothing. There was no sign of Perqos. The sky had gone from partial clouds to overcast and sullen. The spruce began to sway in the rising wind, adding to Naya's vertigo. She must not lose her grip. Could she use her leather belt to lash herself to the trunk?

And then she remembered the auroch horn. Letting go with one hand, Naya fumbled at her waist, trying to undo the thong securing the horn. She didn't know what hope it gave her – perhaps Perqos, wherever he was, would hear it – but she had to *do* something. Besides, if the bears were still in the vicinity, attracting their attention might not be the worst idea, regardless of Wailos's dire warnings. By Naya's estimation, he and Krnos on the ground had more to worry about than she did from her perch up in the tree.

Moments later, Naya had freed the auroch horn and bound herself to the trunk as securely as she could manage with her belt. Wailos, apparently satisfied that he'd intimidated Naya into submission, ignored her while instructing Krnos to collect wood for a fire. Naya put the horn to her lips and blew a simple two-toned call, ending on a single continuous note – the distinctive signal she and Aytal had agreed meant *Danger, come!*

"What in the gods' sight do you think you're doing?!" Wailos shouted up at her. "Stop!"

Naya filled her lungs and repeated the call. The horn rang out again, louder this time, its tone pure and piercing. Naya sustained the second note until her breath failed. As the sound faded, she looked down through the branches. Below her, Wailos glared back, his normally controlled features distorted with rage, so angry, he couldn't speak. Locking eyes with him, Naya for a third time raised the horn, giving it all she had. For a third time, the call rang out.

The noise of something large crashing through the underbrush reached Naya's ears. *The bears!* she exulted. She saw Wailos's face go white. After that, her world went black.

Slipping in and out of consciousness, Naya wasn't sure what was real and what was her imagination. At first, the mother bear had been there, pacing beneath the spruce and occasionally standing on her hind legs, as though determined to defend the tree against anyone attempting to approach. Later, strong arms had seemed to support her as a familiar voice spoke, urging her to hang on, help was coming. Later still, she thought she'd briefly opened her eyes and found herself looking into another pair of eyes as blue as her own. *Brathir?* She'd tried to speak but her lips wouldn't form the name. At last, quite distinctly, Naya recognized her mother's voice, calling to her.

"Mama?" she answered.

"She's coming around." Another familiar voice spoke, sounding relieved.

"Naya?" Her mother's voice again. "Here, hand me the waterskin."

Naya opened her eyes, then quickly closed them against the light. Breathing carefully, she took stock of her situation. She was no longer in the tree. Instead, she was being supported diagonally in a partially upright position across someone's lap. She opened her eyes again, this time searching for a face. Blue eyes like the ones she'd seen earlier smiled back at her, framed by dark brows and an escaped lock of raven-black hair.

Aytal? Naya was too stunned to say his name aloud.

"I told you that if you blew the horn, I'd come." He grinned. Naya's heart did a flip. Fully alert now, she pushed herself upright, out of Aytal's grasp. He didn't try to stop her, merely shifted aside so that she could sit up on the ground beside him. He kept an arm behind her until he was sure she was steady on her own.

Swiveling to stare at him, Naya found her voice. "What are *you* doing here?" she asked, still not certain she could believe her eyes. And then she remembered. She'd heard her mother's voice. "Mama?"

"Here, sweetheart." The answer came from behind her. Naya turned to look over her other shoulder. A moment later, she was in her mother's arms. She didn't even try to stem the tears.

A short while later…

"Better?" her mother asked.

Naya nodded, wiping crumbs from her mouth with the back of her hand. From her mother's right, Oyuun reached out, offering the waterskin. Naya took a swig to wash down the seedcake. Despite being stale, it tasted heavenly. Oyuun smiled fondly at her and she smiled back, returning the water skin.

He'd been the one who'd found the seed cake for her, buried at the bottom of his pack. Apologizing for its condition, he promised fresher fare soon. Assured Naya was alright, Aytal had gone on a brief foraging expedition and should be back momentarily. Handing the waterskin to Sata, Oyuun went to crouch beside a bare patch of dirt in the clearing beneath the spruce and began laying kindling for a fire.

"We shouldn't tarry too long," he commented as he worked. "These woods aren't safe at the moment."

Naya wondered how much Oyuun knew of the dangers. What had become of Wailos? She was just about to ask when the sound of pounding footsteps and branches snapping reached them. Sata, crouching over her pack, looked up in surprise. Oyuun rose to his feet, hand on the hilt of the knife at his belt. Before Naya could scramble upright, a shaggy gray shape bounded out of the woods, followed closely by a dark-haired figure clad in deerskin. The figure skidded to a halt in the center of the clearing just as the four-legged creature launched itself into the air.

"Amu!" the newcomer shouted in a futile attempt to call off the dog.

"Amu!" Naya managed at the same instant, just before being knocked flat.

"Naya!" Sata cried, reaching for her.

"Off!" Cutting through the chaos, Oyuun delivered the order in a tone that brooked no disobedience. Recognizing a familiar voice of authority, Amu ceased his assault but continued to stand over Naya's prostrate form, grinning happily, tongue lolling, tail wagging vigorously.

"Some things never change." Oyuun remarked.

As Naya struggled to shove the dog aside and sit upright, the newcomer turned to her. "You're alright!" he exclaimed in obvious relief.

"Perqos?" Naya wondered who else was going to appear.

"You're alright?" Sata echoed. "Amu didn't hurt you?" She reached to help Naya to her feet. "What took so long?" she inquired, addressing Perqos this time.

Taking her mother's hand, Naya pulled herself to standing. "Wait," she said, confused. "You're with them?" she demanded, looking between Perqos and her mother and Oyuun. "But you and Amu disappeared. Where have you been?"

"I can explain," Perqos assured her, "but where's Aytal?"

"Here I am," a voice answered. Emerging from the opposite side of the woods, Aytal stepped into the clearing, a load of firewood in his arms and a brace of rabbits slung over one shoulder. He stopped midstride, narrowly avoiding being upended by Amu, who was delighted to see him. "About time you showed up," he said, greeting Perqos. "You missed all the fun."

They were seated around the fire, the remains of a hasty meal tossed back into the coals. Along with Naya, her mother, Oyuun, Aytal and Perqos, they'd been joined by Perqos's two cousins, who'd arrived in Perqos's wake, laden with extra provisions. For Naya's benefit, the group were taking turns telling the story of what had happened, starting from when Aytal left the Dānus encampment at more or less the same time as she and Perqos had set off for the cave nearly a full month earlier.

"So let me be sure I have this straight," Naya interjected, wanting to summarize what she'd heard so far. "Aytal and Rei, disguised to look like me, headed into the mountains toward Mama's homeland with the intention of tricking Wailos and Krnos into following them. The plan worked until Wailos and Krnos figured out about the cave and changed course. Aytal, suspecting something amiss, tracked them here, and met up with Perqos, who went back to the Dānus encampment with Amu for help."

She glanced at Perqos, who nodded. Naya went on. "That left Aytal behind to guard the cave while also trying to stay out of sight of Wailos and Krnos." She looked at Aytal.

"That's right," he confirmed.

"But not long after Perqos left, the bears took up residence in the den, blocking the entrance. Wailos couldn't get in, but neither could you."

"And I was sure you must be running low on food and firewood," Aytal apologized. "Good thing you took the chance to leave the cave when you did." He smiled at Naya and for an instant everyone else disappeared.

Her mother interrupted. "Oyuun and I would have come with Aytal, but we didn't want to take the chance of alerting Wailos that he was being followed."

"Instead, we returned with Rei to the Dānus encampment," Oyuun explained.

"But when Perqos arrived to get help, we set off for the cave immediately," Sata finished.

"My cousins and I and Amu were close behind," put in Perqos.

Naya looked around the circle. "So then, after I sounded the horn, Aytal arrived first. Mama and Oyuun showed up soon after, followed by Perqos and Amu. You two," she indicated the cousins, "were hunting rabbits and caught up later." The young men grinned and nodded.

"That's pretty much the gist of it." Perqos spoke for the group.

"And Wailos?" Naya had been afraid to ask.

"He and Krnos disappeared," Aytal replied. "I think he was pretty badly injured by the bear."

"The bear?" She'd been in and out of consciousness. What had she imagined and what had been real?

Aytal elaborated. "I came running as soon as I heard the horn. When I arrived, Wailos and the female bear were at the base of the spruce, circling each other. The male was still out in the open, in a stand-off with Krnos. Somehow both Wailos and Krnos had lost their weapons. The cubs were nowhere in sight, although they must have been nearby, or the female wouldn't have been so agitated. At one point, she charged Wailos and took a swipe at him, raking her claws across his chest. After that, he and Krnos took off. I waited upwind until both bears left, then brought you down from your perch. You must have fainted at some point. Thank goodness you thought to tie yourself to the tree." He smiled at her again. This time she managed to smile back.

"He won't give up, though," Perqos observed. "Injured or not. He's come too far." Naya surveyed the circle once more. Several faces mirrored Perqos's concern.

"My guess would be that Wailos will show up at the encampment," he speculated. "Since capturing Naya has failed, he'll try going before the Dānus council of elders to assert his claim as her rightful guardian, counting on the tribal leaders' reluctance to create an incident over the matter. After all, as far as Wailos knows, Naya shouldn't matter to the Dānus all that much, except perhaps as a bargaining token."

Naya noted that in front of his cousins, Perqos did not mention Ceru's friendship with her father. She gave her mother, seated beside her, a troubled look.

Putting an arm around Naya's shoulders, Sata leaned in and whispered in her ear. "Don't worry," she assured her. "Wailos has no claim on you."

Naya, a hand on her belly, wasn't so sure.

Chapter Twenty-Eight

The Dānus encampment, early morning, four days later...

Ceru's tent was crowded. After her time alone in the cave, Naya was unused to being surrounded by so many people and found it difficult to breathe. No fire burned in the hearth, which was a blessing, but the air was dense with assembled bodies. Lamps hung from the tent staves, providing light. Naya was seated at the Dānus chief's right, in the place of an honored guest. Her mother, positioned behind Naya, rested a hand on her daughter's shoulder and gave it a squeeze. They were the only two women present. As Elōr had explained when she'd brought them something to eat at daybreak, normally she and Árdejā might have been included in the meeting, but the tent was already too small to accommodate a large gathering and since Naya's situation was primarily a matter of external tribal diplomacy, priority had been given to the leaders of the other Dānus clans. *Don't worry, though,* Elōr had reassured Naya and her mother. *Everything will be alright. Ceru will see to it.* Naya could only hope.

Several older men, some clad as priests, occupied seats around the hearth facing herself and Ceru, forming a circle of unfamiliar faces. Others, including Ceru's brother Awontlos and his sons, stood or crouched behind those who were seated, finding room amongst the tent's domestic clutter. Oyuun was next to Naya's mother, but Aytal had stationed himself opposite Naya, near the entrance, where he could send her encouraging looks. He smiled at her now. Perqos sat in the place to Ceru's left, out of Naya's line of sight. He and Naya had exchanged a silent greeting when he'd entered the tent moments ago, but once he'd taken his seat next to his father, they could no longer make eye contact.

The door flap stirred and Wailos entered, followed by Krnos. Naya kept her eyes lowered. Space had been left for the newcomers near the entrance, directly across the hearth circle from where she sat beside Ceru. The Dānus chief motioned for them to be seated, then cleared his throat.

"Welcome to our visitors," he said, inclining his head slightly. "Please forgive the cramped quarters, but our communal shelter is being prepared for our seasonal rituals, so it seemed best to convene here instead. I hope you've been adequately looked after during your overnight stay?"

Although the Dānus chief's words were polite, Naya noted that Ceru referred to Wailos and Krnos as visitors rather than guests, a significant distinction. If Wailos bristled at the slight, he hid it well.

Addressing his fellow tribal leaders, Ceru continued. "May I present Wailos, son of Regos, along with Krnos, son of Skelos, both of the Plānos tribe. As some of you will recall, this is the second time this year that we've received Wailos – he paid us a visit last spring, accompanied by a sizable herd of cattle, sheep and goats, which he offered to us as the bride price for my eldest daughter."

Ceru regarded Wailos, one brow raised. Wailos in turn acknowledged the chief's introduction with a nod and the twist of a half-smile. Naya surmised from the unspoken exchange that while Ceru may not have mentioned Wailos's role in stealing the livestock, each recognized their mutual awareness of the unstated facts of the situation.

"I gather circumstances have changed since that previous visit?" Ceru observed dryly. "Perhaps you'd care to enlighten us and explain what new errand brings you once more within the borders of our territory?"

As Ceru spoke, Naya noticed Awontlos's two sons shift to stand behind Wailos and Krnos, on either side of the exit.

"Indeed," Wailos answered pleasantly. "Although you'll forgive me if the explanation initially appears a bit convoluted." He offered an apologetic expression to the assembly before bringing his attention back to Ceru. "First, you are correct. Due to an alteration in circumstances, I am here to petition the Dānus chief to be released from the marriage contract involving myself and his daughter. At the time of my visit last spring, when the arrangement was proposed, my father and I were under the misapprehension that a prior agreement had been nullified through the disappearance and presumed demise of the daughter of one of our own tribe's clan chiefs, to whom I had been previously committed. Happily… she lives!"

Wailos gestured toward Naya, bestowing on her one of his sincerest, most captivating smiles. Naya did not return it. Stone-faced, she stared back, determined to betray nothing of what she felt toward Wailos – neither the fear nor the loathing. *He lies through his teeth*, she thought. *How did I ever believe anything he said?*

Wailos went on. "Unfortunately, at the time of our tribe's *Sāwel-Dom* Gathering, just before our engagement was to be made official, a small misunderstanding occurred which caused my betrothed to run-off. You know how young women can be." Wailos directed the aside to the circle of tribal leaders, soliciting their sympathy. "Subsequently, her father perished in a tragic accident, leaving her without a guardian. I set out immediately to find her and bring her back to her people, where she belongs." Wailos gave Naya an indulgent look. "She's proven herself quite elusive, leading my companion and myself on quite the chase, but at last we were able to catch-up with her just a few days ago, in the foothills south of here."

Naya met the well-disguised mockery behind Wailos's eyes, refusing to look away. Inside, her stomach churned. "You've made things much harder than they needed to be, my dear," Wailos scolded good-naturedly before turning once more to speak to the assembly.

"Despite her recalcitrance, and as a tribute to her father, my father and I intend to abide by our original commitment. As soon as we return home together, we shall be married." He held out a magnanimous hand, as though inviting Naya to rise from her place across the hearth, clasp it and set out with him immediately.

An awkward silence ensued. Naya straightened her back and lifted her chin but otherwise sat unmoved. After a moment, Wailos withdrew his hand. Adopting an expression of forbearance, he sent a look around the circle as if to ask those who were gathered to witness how trouble-some and unreasonable the young woman could be. Judging by their expressions, a few of the assembly appeared to commiserate. The others remained inscrutable.

Attention turned once more to the Dānus chief. Ceru studied Wailos for a long moment without speaking, seeming to weigh his words while allowing the silence to grow. Naya wondered how he would respond. So many elements of Wailos's version of events were untrue, but how could

Ceru challenge the facts as presented without revealing his clandestine friendship with Naya's father, of which the other Dānus leaders were not only unaware, but also unlikely to approve? At one point, Ceru's friendship with Potis might have been an asset, but now, revealing what amounted to a secret alliance with the deceased and discredited rival of another tribe's most powerful chief would not enhance Ceru's standing among his own people. Nor could he risk too egregious an insult toward Wailos without creating an inter-tribal incident.

At last, Ceru spoke. "There appears to be one rather important point of confusion," he observed, his tone thoughtful. "If our arrangement is to be annulled so that your prior commitment to marry may be honored, then someone other than yourself must act as a representative of the young woman's interests, at least for the purposes of affirming the existence and the continuance of the earlier agreement. You cannot act as both her appointed guardian and as an interested party in the contract."

Heads nodded around the circle, signaling agreement with Ceru's reasoning.

"Fortunately," Ceru continued, "we have a suitable spokesperson available. First, though, I have been remiss in my introductions." Ceru half-turned to gesture past Naya's shoulder toward her mother, standing behind her. "For those among the Dānus who have not already been made acquainted, may I present Satanaya, widow of Potis, chief among the Plānos, himself the son of Awos, the tribe's esteemed former leader."

Craning her neck, Naya saw Sata gravely incline her head in acknowledgement of Ceru's introduction. She was the image of elegance and self-possession.

"And this," Ceru went on, turning to face the circle again, "is Potis and Sata's daughter, named for her mother, and known as Naya."

Imitating her mother, Naya bowed her head to the assembly. When she looked up, Aytal's eyes were on her. He offered the hint of a nod. *You are brave*, his look said, *every bit as courageous as your mother*. Returning his regard, Naya's fingers strayed unconsciously to the arrowhead at her throat.

Wailos interrupted. "Please forgive me," he began, addressing Ceru. "But you must be aware that, after our long absence from home, now that we've succeeded in our search, my companion and I would prefer to commence our return journey without delay. Who is this spokesman, to whom you refer? We know of no one to whom our tribe, the Plānos, would grant such standing, other than myself, and I've testified before you as to the situation. Surely this young woman's future is not a matter of concern to the Dānus. Under the circumstances, to continue these proceedings would seem to constitute a waste of everyone's valuable time."

Ceru's reply was measured. "Is it not the case," he queried, "that among the Plānos, as among the Dānus, in the absence of a young woman's father, her mother should be considered her guardian and be empowered to speak on her behalf?"

"Possibly," Wailos conceded. "However…" He tented his fingertips and raised his eyes to the smoke hole, as though pondering the discretion of what he meant to say next. After a moment, he lowered his gaze, leveling it at Sata. "…I would argue that in abandoning her husband and family last spring, Potis's wife surrendered any claim she might have to direct her daughter's future." He paused, arching a single censorious brow. "Or is that not what happened when you left home in the company of the individual who still finds himself at your side?"

All eyes turned to Sata, with Oyuun standing next to her. Muttering broke out around the circle. Glancing back, Naya saw her mother's lips tighten into a thin line but otherwise she did not dignify Wailos's insinuations with a response.

Neither did Ceru betray any hint of concern. "My goodness," he remarked, mildly. "Such potentially slanderous allegations. One would almost think you have something to fear from what Sata might have to say in regard to the matter before us – which, by the way, has nothing to do with her reasons for journeying to visit her homeland, nor her husband's choice of a trusted travel companion to guide her, given that the responsibilities of his position prevented him from accompanying her himself."

Looks were exchanged around the circle, and the murmuring increased. Naya could see that the Dānus leader's characterization of her mother's situation had the intended effect of calling Wailos's credibility into question, as well as serving to remind those listening that Sata was the wife – and Naya the daughter – of a fellow clan chief. Respect was warranted.

"Still," Ceru went on, raising a hand for silence, "perhaps we might avoid controversy by inviting a close *male* relative to speak on Naya's behalf. Would that suit?" He directed the question to Wailos.

Possibly regretting his strategy of attempting to cast aspersions on Naya's mother but obviously still confident in his advantage, Wailos seized on Ceru's offer. After all, as far as he was aware, Naya had no male relative available. "Of course," he replied amicably. "Just so long as the matter is decided here and now. Who did you have in mind?"

On cue, one of Ceru's nephews pulled aside the tent flap, allowing a tall shape to enter. For an instant, with the light from behind, Naya's chest seized, and she believed the impossible – that her father had somehow appeared. Only when the flap dropped did she recognize the familiar silhouette belonged to her uncle. All eyes turned to him.

"Please welcome Tausos, son of Awos." Ceru held out an arm. "Come," he motioned. "Join us." Recovering from her astonishment and disappointment, Naya watched as Perqos moved aside to offer her uncle his seat. She glanced back at her mother, who looked as surprised as Naya by her uncle's appearance. If Tausos was here, did that mean the rest of the family had made the trip as well? Was it possible they waited outside, even Awija? What about Melit and her family? It was all Naya could do not to dart out of the tent. Catching her eye, her uncle frowned a warning. *Later*, his look communicated. *Be patient*. His eyes shifted to Wailos, whom he acknowledged with an icy nod. Wailos tried but failed to hide his discomfiture at Tausos's unexpected arrival.

"Before we hear from Tausos," Ceru began, "I'd like to acknowledge before my fellow tribesmen, as well as our visitors, that I've been made aware of some rather delicate, shall we say, *negotiations* among the Plānos leaders in regard to who is to succeed Awos as the tribe's chief of chiefs. The Plānos would no doubt prefer these negotiations remain private, however certain *extenuating circumstances* are bound to come up in our discussion today in connection with whether our visitor…" Ceru indicated Wailos, "…recognizes Naya's uncle as having authority to speak on her behalf regarding the marriage contract allegedly agreed to by her father before his, *ah-hem*, death."

This was a long speech. Ceru kept his eyes on Wailos, waiting as the latter digested the gist of it. Basically, Naya realized, Ceru had threatened Wailos with exposing the whole scheme that he and his father Regos and their allies had executed in their quest for power. It was a gamble. On the one hand, Wailos might not care if the truth were revealed. Indeed, he and his father might find some advantage in the Dānus chiefs recognizing how ruthless they could be. On the other, there was little honor in Regos's naked grab for influence and authority. Rumors were one thing, but formal testimony from her uncle as to the extent of their perfidy was another. Regos's reputation among the other tribes, about which he cared immensely, would suffer.

Wailos appeared to have reached the latter conclusion. "Perhaps there is an alternative," he offered.

"Oh?" Ceru replied. "What would that be?"

"Our tribal elders' primary concern is for this young woman's wellbeing," Wailos began. "As long as they can be assured of her future welfare, perhaps they will not insist that she return to her people, if such is not her wish." He gave Naya a look of sorrowful resignation. "Much as it pains me, my dear, I am willing to sacrifice my own happiness in order to settle this matter without causing you further distress."

Naya wanted to retch.

"So she is to be allowed to remain with us?" Ceru sought to confirm. "You are authorized to speak for your tribal elders?"

A small flame of hope ignited in Naya's chest.

"As long as the proper conditions are met," Wailos agreed.

The flame sputtered. *Now what?* she wondered.

"And what would those be?" Ceru wanted to know, echoing Naya's thought.

"First, the livestock we delivered to you last spring must be returned to us – including appropriate compensation for any, ah, missing individuals."

Wailos obviously referred to the young bull, slaughtered by Wailos himself. The audacity was breath-taking. Naya wondered if Ceru would agree. The Dānus chief appeared unperturbed.

"And your other stipulations?" he prompted.

"Naya must be married." Wailos looked smug.

"I'm sure that can be arranged," Ceru replied.

"Not to just anyone." Wailos clarified. "We require a match commensurate with her status. She is the granddaughter of one of our tribe's most revered leaders, after all." Wailos scanned the circle, as though searching for a candidate. His gaze came to rest on Perqos. "Your eldest son, perhaps?"

Silence spread through the tent. Marriage to the Dānus chief's oldest son represented a significant diplomatic prize, warranting careful consideration. Everyone appeared to be evaluating Wailos's suggestion.

Scanning the faces around the circle, Naya made her own calculation. Wailos's claims regarding her standing to the contrary, with her father gone she now held little worth in terms of creating a true alliance between the Dānus and the Plānos.

Indeed, given that Ceru knew full well that neither Wailos nor his father, Regos, could be trusted, any alliance between the tribes would be meaningless. The Dānus would gain nothing from the marriage and in fact would forfeit whatever advantages might have accrued from Perqos wedding a young woman of high standing from some other tribal confederation. All of this would be obvious to Ceru, but Naya wondered if the same could be said of the other Dānus leaders, with less knowledge of the whole situation. If nothing else, Wailos's move was a clever ploy to weaken Ceru personally. She wished she could catch her uncle's eye. She was sure that, knowing as much as he did, Tausos would have reached the same conclusions.

Perqos chose that moment to clear his throat, breaking the silence. "I will marry her," he declared, addressing Wailos. "If Naya will have me," he added, turning to her with a shy smile. Naya gazed back at him, speechless.

Wailos seemed equally nonplussed but recovered quickly. "Wonderful!" he replied. "Assuming your father agrees?" All eyes turned to Ceru.

"It's certainly not outside the realm of possibility," the Dānus chief replied smoothly. "Although of course such a proposal will require a private consultation between myself and my fellow clan chiefs."

Naya stole a sideways glance at him, seated next to her. If Ceru disapproved of his son's impetuous outburst, he showed no sign.

"Is there anything else?" he inquired.

Naya didn't know what to think or where to look. Perqos kept trying to catch her eye. It seemed rude not to at least acknowledge his gallant gesture but she didn't know how without sending the wrong message. Avoiding him, she risked a scan of the circle and saw Aytal staring at Perqos with a mixture of confusion and disbelief. Only after he'd regained control of his features did he return Naya's regard. Behind the mask of composure, Naya could see his distress. She tried silently to let him know that none of this was her idea, but before she could, he turned away.

"We will need some form of proof to take back to the tribal elders,"

Wailos replied in answer to Ceru's question, "demonstrating beyond doubt that Naya has been found safe, and that her future is assured. The livestock will go a long way, of course – we can consider them as her bride price and call things even – but a personal token of some kind might also be appreciated, as evidence that she's alive and well." Wailos paused, considering.

"May I make a suggestion?" Krnos put in. "What about the bear's tooth necklace Naya usually wears? It was a gift from her father and everyone will recognize it. It would be an appropriate talisman – assuming it's still in your possession?" Krnos turned a sardonic eye toward Naya. He knew the necklace's history, and how much it meant to her. He knew the pain it would cause her to surrender it.

"That's not initially what I had in mind," Wailos remarked. "I was thinking of her bow and quiver, or perhaps that auroch horn she now carries, but yes, the bear's tooth would do nicely." He motioned for Krnos to take it from Naya.

All eyes turned to her. Naya looked to Ceru, who gave an almost imperceptible nod, indicating she should comply. Recognizing she had not choice, Naya reached into the *makēn* at her waist and pulled out the necklace, holding it up by its damaged cord. Looking Krnos straight in the eye, without a word but with no effort to disguise her hatred, she dropped the necklace into his outstretched hand.

"If there's nothing else, then we are in agreement." Ceru, his tone business-like, didn't wait for Wailos to reply. "Merkō, Mikāmi," he went on, speaking to his nephews, "go alert the herders who've been minding the Plānos flocks. The animals are to be surrendered into our visitors' custody immediately. They'll want to get underway as soon as possible. Send along a couple of dogs as well, to help them manage." The two young men ducked outside.

"But the wedding," Wailos objected. "We won't leave until it takes place."

"Oh," Ceru demurred. "I'm afraid that won't be possible." He'd come to his feet, signaling the end of the meeting. Following his lead, the other tribal elders had risen and begun making their way out of the tent, talking amongst themselves. Wailos had to push past them to reach Ceru. Naya, who'd pivoted to her mother, froze with her back turned, listening.

"You agreed to our terms," Wailos protested, "including Naya's marriage to your son. You can't back out now – unless you want us to take the girl with us after all."

He must have made a threatening move in Naya's direction. Out of the corner of her eye, she saw Ceru shift sideways, blocking him. Naya looked to her mother. Sata shook her head, telling her to stay as she was with her back turned. *Let Ceru deal with Wailos.* Oyuun moved to stand behind Naya, providing an added buffer. Tausos and Aytal had made their way over to her as well.

Perqos must have joined his father in confronting Wailos. "Don't worry," Naya heard him say. "You have my word that I intend to marry Naya." Several tribal leaders who had not yet exited the tent stopped to listen.

"All in good time, son," Ceru said calmly, in a voice meant to carry. "You know the custom." For Wailos's benefit, and the ears of anyone else who cared to hear, he explained. "Among the Dānus, once a marriage is arranged, the couple live together for a year, in order to be sure they are compatible, before the final ceremony is performed. So you see, unless you intend to return in time for our Autumn Festival next year, you will have to trust that a wedding has taken place."

He continued in a quieter tone, altogether more menacing, meant for Wailos's ears alone. "You have your proof – more than you need to accomplish your ends and certainly more than you have cause to expect. Leave her with us and be gone, before I change my mind."

"The bull?" Wailos pressed.

Whatever look Ceru gave him quelled any further attempt to bargain. "It's been a pleasure," Naya heard Wailos say instead. "Naya," he called, "I wish you nothing but happiness in your new life." She turned her head in time to see Wailos sweep her a bow. "Krnos," he said, straightening, "we should be on our way."

The latter was waiting by the entrance. Wailos crossed the tent and one after the other, they stooped and disappeared through the door flap.

Chapter Twenty-Nine

Ceru's tent, a short while later…

"I can't believe he's gone," Naya repeated, accepting a mug of steaming tea from Elōr. She'd been uttering the same remark periodically ever since Wailos left, as though to convince herself of the truth.

"Good riddance," Rei pronounced cheerfully. "Now neither one of us has to marry him!" She laughed, then changed the subject. "How long did your uncle say it would take for the rest of your family to arrive?"

Tausos, notified by one of Ceru's runners to hurry ahead in order to be present for the meeting with Wailos, had left the other travelers on the far side of the river Dān, near a seldom-used ford. He'd departed immediately after the assembly to return and fetch them – ideally without the risk of crossing paths with Wailos.

"It will take him the rest of the day to get back, and then at least two days, maybe three for all of them to make their way here," Naya replied. "My grandmother is with them, and she can't travel as far in a day as she once did." Naya was amazed Awija had been able to make the long journey at all. She couldn't wait to see her again.

"I wonder what will happen when we introduce your grandmother to Árdejā," Rei pondered, sipping her tea.

"They'll either get on like old friends, or despise one another," Sata speculated.

"My guess would be they are already acquainted," observed Elōr, looking over her shoulder from the baskets she was rearranging. While the other three enjoyed their tea around the small fire now burning in the hearth, she puttered around the tent, straightening up after the press of people who'd crowded in for the meeting.

"Who were Árdejā's people before she married Ceru's great-uncle?" Sata asked.

"The Talianki," Elōr replied.

"You're right," Sata remarked in surprise. "That's the same village Awija is from."

"Hardly a village," Elōr amended. "When Árdejā was young, more people lived there than there are cattle in all the herds of all the tribes of the steppe – or so she always claimed. Still, given that she and Awija are both descended from priestess families and married into steppe clans, I would guess they at least know of one another." Finishing with the baskets, Elōr joined the others around the hearth. "Tell me more about how the meeting played out," she said, pouring herself a mug of tea.

Naya and her mother looked at one another. "As well as could be expected," Sata replied. "The primary objective was accomplished. Ceru really is quite masterful."

"He and I debated about giving Naya the opportunity to speak," Elōr commented. "It bothers me that she wasn't able to confront Wailos and denounce him, but we agreed it would be too dangerous." She looked from Naya to Sata and back again. "I gather that was the right decision?"

"Under the circumstances," Sata agreed. "She's been through enough." Reaching out, she rubbed a hand on Naya's knee.

Naya gave her mother a grateful smile, then turned to Elōr. "I was glad Ceru let me know beforehand that I wouldn't have to say anything," she assured her. "Not in front of all those strangers. It's enough that I never have to see Wailos again."

"But you've told your mother what happened?" Elōr's voice was both gentle and insistent. Meeting her eyes, Naya nodded, then shifted her attention to her half-empty mug of tea.

"Last night," Sata filled in. "After you left us." Glancing up, Naya saw her mother and Elōr share a look. "There's more," Sata went on. She turned to Naya. "Do you want to tell them, or…"

"I'm pregnant." Before her mother could finish, the words were out of Naya's mouth. Her announcement was met with silence. Elōr and Rei regarded her gravely. Neither seemed surprised.

"You knew?" Sata asked.

"We thought it might be a possibility," Elōr admitted. Reaching out, she took Naya's hands in hers. "But don't worry. It's not obvious – not yet." She gave a reassuring squeeze.

"Ceru?" Sata questioned.

Releasing Naya's hands, Elōr sat back and nodded. "It's why he wanted to steer clear of any discussion of what happened between Naya and Wailos. Under the circumstances, no good could come of revealing what he did to her. Questions would have been raised, and if Wailos found out about Naya's condition, he would never have left without her."

"What happens now?" Rei asked.

Again, Naya looked to her mother. They'd discussed the question the night before, without reaching an answer. They'd been more worried about Wailos. Now, with Wailos gone, the reality of her pregnancy seemed suddenly overwhelming. "Awija will know best what options Naya has," Sata replied to Rei, "but if she's too far along…"

"A decision will have to be made soon," Elōr agreed. "Of course, the Goddess herself might have a say in the matter…" Naya glanced between Elōr and her mother, wondering if Elōr knew of all the pregnancies Sata had lost. "In any case," Elōr continued, "we should consult Árdejā as well – both she and Awija will have wise advice to offer, as well as practical solutions, if required. And Ceru will want to weigh in." Elōr turned to Naya. "Forgive me, my dear. Your choice is what matters, but there are many factors to consider."

"Speaking of which," Rei interrupted her mother, "did you hear what Perqos did?" Lifting the tea pot from the hearth, she offered it to the others before pouring more for herself. "I don't think it was part of Papa's plan." She sounded grave.

"Oh?" Elōr asked. "What now?"

"In front of everyone, he pledged himself to marry Naya."

"Oh?" Elōr remarked again. When the older woman's eyes turned to her, Naya didn't know where to look.

"Wailos brought it up," Sata clarified. "As a condition for surrendering his claim over Naya."

"But Perqos certainly didn't object. In fact, I'd say he's enthusiastic about the idea." Rei stopped when she saw the dismay on Naya's face. "Don't worry," she offered reassuringly. "I'm sure Papa won't hold him to it."

"Hold your tongue, Rei," Elōr warned. "This is serious."

"No, it's just…" Naya wasn't necessarily opposed to the idea either, but how could she agree to the arrangement when she hardly knew Perqos? *And what about…* She recalled the look she'd witnessed on

Aytal's face from across the council circle. She hadn't seen him since the assembly disbanded.

"Ceru did mention the Dānus custom of a one-year trial arrangement," Sata pointed out. "And he managed to evade making an explicit commitment."

Naya had a sudden thought. "Does Perqos know I'm pregnant?" she asked. "He might feel differently about marrying me if he finds out I'm carrying Wailos's child."

"Unless you told him, I doubt he knows," Elōr answered. "Ceru and I didn't mention our suspicions to him." They all looked at one another and again; no one said anything. Agreeing to accept another man's offspring as one's own was not unusual, but in this case the circumstances were complicated. If the child Naya carried was a boy, and Wailos ever found out and believed he'd been deliberately deceived, he'd come after Perqos personally, with a vengeance.

After a moment, Elōr spoke. "You have a lot to think about, my dear, and some big decisions to make," Her expression was full of sympathy. "At least no one here will force you into anything against your will – of that you can be assured."

Elōr's kindness, on top of the relief of escaping Wailos's grasp, was more than Naya could bear. Why, all of a sudden, did she feel so emotional all the time? "Thank you," she managed, tears wanting to course down her cheeks. The next moment, she found herself surrounded and embraced.

"We're all here for you," her mother whispered in her ear.

"We love you," Rei added.

"We will protect you and take care of you," Elōr promised. "And your grandmother will be here soon. No matter what, you don't have to go through any of this alone."

Naya knew deep inside it was the truth. With this circle of strong women surrounding her, she would be safe. Whatever the future held, with their support, she would survive. With their love to strengthen her, and their wisdom to guide her, she would find the courage to follow her path.

"Thank you," she repeated, meaning it with all her heart.

A low wooded rise, with a view of the Dānus encampment…

Naya sat with her back against a sturdy oak, looking out at the mass of tents arranged in interlocking circles stretching in all directions. A faint breeze, warm from the midday sun, brought the fragrance of cookfires and roasting meat. The encampment was a hive of activity, with people scurrying about in preparation for the evening's festivities. Beyond the tents, autumn-hued pastures, grazed by the Dānus tribe's bountiful herds, extended into the distance. To the north, the vista was bounded by the wide, winding ribbon of the river *Dān*, shimmering brightly in the sunlight. The sky above was a brilliant cerulean blue.

Lying next to Naya, paws crossed, head lifted, Amu likewise surveyed the scene. They'd been up here for a while. After the events of the morning, Naya had needed an interlude, away from everyone else, in order to begin to come to terms with all that had happened.

Wailos was out of her life. That, above all, was to be celebrated. Her mother was right; Ceru had managed the proceedings with consummate skill. Naya regretted being forced to surrender her father's bear tooth necklace – its loss would haunt her – but the price was worth paying. Her father was gone, yes, but with him went the necessity of living up to her role as the daughter of a clan chief. She was free. And while Naya still faced difficult choices, nothing had to be decided immediately – at least not until after Awija arrived.

Meanwhile, for the first time since leaving the cave, she had an opportunity to ponder the treasures she'd uncovered during her sojourn – the dreams and visitations she'd experienced, the memories that had come back to her, the insights she'd gleaned, and above all, the sacred vow she'd renewed. No matter what other challenges the future held, Naya did not intend to give up on her determination to find Réhda and discover how to grant the filly's deepest wish.

Leaning her head back against the oak's variegated trunk, Naya closed her eyes, conjuring the painting in the cave and remembering the voice that had spoken to her out of the darkness: *See with the eyes of your heart; create ties without the use of a rope, and when you have succeeded in granting my heart's desire, then shall yours be granted also.* Finally, so long after first hearing the words, they'd become etched in her memory, never to be forgotten.

Before she could consider once more the true nature of the words' meaning, the crunch of footsteps amidst dead leaves interrupted her thoughts. Naya's eyelids snapped open. Someone was approaching from the far side of the small copse of trees. Amu jumped up, tail wagging joyfully. *Not a stranger, then*, Naya thought with relief. A moment later Aytal stepped out from behind the massive oak. Naya's heart leapt, then sank in dismay at his appearance. Pack slung across his shoulders, bow in hand, he was obviously about to set off on a journey.

"Sorry if I startled you," he apologized, misinterpreting the look on her face. He bent down to greet the dog, then straightened. "Your mother told me where I might find you." He met Naya's eyes. "I've come to say goodbye."

"You're leaving? So soon?" She felt stunned.

"No sense in delaying," Aytal countered. "Especially while the good weather holds." His tone was carefully matter of fact.

"But where are you going?" Naya demanded, coming to her feet. "We all just got here. The celebration is this evening…"

She trailed off, realizing she sounded as frantic as she suddenly felt. Even though they'd travelled back together from the cave, others had always been around. There'd been no opportunity to talk – to dispel the awkwardness between them – let alone find their way back to being friends. And then there'd been that moment this morning in Ceru's tent – the look on his face when Perqos said he would marry her.

"Home," Aytal answered, "or at least what I'm hoping might someday feel like home. I'm going back to my mother's people, in the mountains."

"But… but…" Naya sputtered. She didn't know what to say. "What about your sentence?" In her confusion, it was the only question she could think to ask. As far as she knew, he was still required to pay his debt for nearly ending her life.

"It's been commuted," Aytal informed her. "Just this morning. Before Tausos left to fetch the rest of your family, he released me from any further obligation. Under the circumstances…"

He paused, seeming to think better of what he was going to say, and instead half-turned to look at the view. After a moment he continued. "I've come all this way," he explained, "but I've barely had a chance to meet my mother's family – just the few days while I was there before setting off again to intercept Wailos at the cave – and after this morning.…" He glanced back at Naya. "After this morning, there doesn't seem much reason to… I mean, there's no reason *not* to…" He trailed off.

"But you'll be back," Naya insisted, "once you've had a longer visit?"

"I don't know," Aytal answered, looking away. "It depends."

"Depends on…?" Naya felt unsure of the ground beneath her feet. What did he want her to say, to tell him? There was so much that she was uncertain of herself.

Aytal waited a beat, then seemed to resign himself to supplying an answer on his own. "It turns out my uncle Aminon – my mother's brother – is a master archer. He's offered to train me."

"Oh, but that's wonderful," Naya exclaimed, genuinely pleased. "You'll be able to reclaim your gift." Instead of the anger and resentment she'd once felt that he'd renounced his skill with the bow, apparently on her behalf, she now felt happy for him. "How long will the training last?"

"That's just it," Aytal answered. "The training is meant to last for several years."

"Years?" Naya echoed, incredulous. He meant to be away for *years*?

"If I'm serious," Aytal replied, sounding a bit defensive. "Aminon says it takes many seasons to become a true bowman."

"Oh," Naya replied, not knowing what else to say. She looked down, studying the leaf-strewn ground at her feet. An uncomfortable silence ensued.

"You'll be busy," Aytal finally offered. Naya's immediate thought was that, somehow, he'd learned she was pregnant. Her eyes flew to his face in alarm. "What with marrying Perqos," he clarified.

"Oh," she repeated. "Yes, well…" she went on absently, looking away and thus missing the hope in his expression that turned to disappointment when she failed to contradict him. *He doesn't know,* she thought. He didn't know about the child, nor about the consequent uncertainty regarding her marriage prospects, nor about her ambivalence as to wedding Perqos in the first place. How could he, when she'd barely had time to consider the matter herself?

And he doesn't need to know, she decided. After all this time, he was finally free to follow his own path. She mustn't say or do anything to dissuade him. She returned her gaze to his. "Of course you should go," she said, forcing a smile. "And you're right – I'll be busy." She lifted her chin. "I intend to go in search of the red filly – that's the most important thing."

"That's wonderful," Aytal exclaimed, looking as pleased as she'd felt for him a moment earlier. "When will you get started?"

"As soon as… as soon as…" Naya stalled. Just then, she noticed a figure hurrying up the hill towards them. "Look," she pointed. "It's Perqos. He must have news about something."

Side by side, they waited as the figure approached. Amu, tail wagging, trotted down the slope to meet him. "What is it?" Aytal called out once Perqos was within easy earshot. "Has something happened?"

"Good news!" he answered, grinning as he closed the distance and came to a halt in front of them. "The scouts Father sent out a month ago have returned." Turning to Naya, he couldn't hide his excitement. "The red filly," he exclaimed, "we've found her!"

END

A Comment On Language

Proto-Indo-European (PIE) is the language thought by many scholars to have been spoken by the tribes inhabiting the Pontic-Caspian steppe (modern-day Ukraine and southern Russia) during the 4th millennium BCE. Linguists' reconstruction of PIE therefore serves as the inspiration for many personal names, place names, and various terms and expressions appearing throughout the novel. Words derived from PIE are noted in the following glossary. The language spoken by Oyuun and his son Aytal would have been related to Tuvan, a Turkic language spoken by the Dukha, semi-nomadic reindeer herders from the Altai mountains of Mongolia. These words are indicated by (T). The linguistic history of the Caucasus region being rather convoluted, no attempt was made to approximate the language that Naya's mother might have spoken. Ancient myths and legends of the Caucasus, told by the Circassians, Abkhazians and Ossetians and known as the Nart Sagas, offered a source for names. These are denoted by (C) in the glossary. For a fascinating recent discussion of Proto-Indo-European, see **Proto: How One Ancient Language Went Global**, by Laura Spinney (Bloomsbury Publishing, 2025).

Glossary

Character Names
Aknā: 'prickle (PIE)
Amu: 'friend' (PIE)
Árdejā: 'heron' (PIE)
Awija: 'grandmother' (PIE)
Awontlos: 'uncle' (PIE)
Awos: 'grandfather; (PIE)
Aytal: 'one who chooses' (T)
BeHregs: 'brave warrior' (PIE)
Bhermi: 'bear' (PIE)
Bhlaghmn: 'priest' (PIE)
Ceru: 'pike' (PIE) type of fish known for its wiliness
Dayan: 'light/brisk' (T)
Elēn: 'red deer (PIE)
Elōr: 'swan' (PIE)
Glōs: 'sister-in-law' (PIE)
Kawona: 'owl' (PIE)
Kérberos: 'weasel' (PIE) one of Regos's guards
Krnos: 'rotten' (PIE)
Maqā: 'girl' (PIE)
MeHnd: 'wise one' (PIE)
Melit: 'honey' (PIE)
Merkō: 'flimmer' (PIE)
Mikāmi: 'flimmer' (PIE)
Oyuun: 'shaman' (T)
Peikā: 'woodpecker' (PIE) Melit's second brother, a youth of fifteen
summers

Perom: 'feather' (PIE)
Perqos: 'oak' (PIE)
Petsna: 'feather' (PIE)
Potis: 'head of village' (PIE)
Rebhjo: 'rage' (PIE)
Regos: 'king' (from 'regs') (PIE)
Réhda: 'little red head' (from 'reudhos') (PIE)
Reiwos: 'brook' (PIE)
Satanaya: legendary heroine, a beautiful and wise woman (C) Sata and
    Naya share this name
Saurosa: 'sour' (PIE)
Skelos: 'evil' (PIE)
Sunus: 'son' (PIE)
Šuurgan: 'storm' (T)
Swesor: 'sister' (PIE)
Tausos: 'silent' (PIE)
Uksor: 'wife' (PIE)
Unksra: 'shadow' (PIE)
Vedukha: 'foster mother' 'beautiful' (C)
Wailos: 'wolf' (PIE)
Weri: 'water' (PIE)
Zerashsha: beautiful daughter of a water-god (C) Aytal's mother

Deities and religious celebrations
Aiqos: 'even' (PIE) term for either the vernal or autumnal equinox
Cita-Amsus: 'life' and 'creator' (PIE) Awija's term for the Great
    Goddess
Deiwos: 'the shining ones' (PIE) gods in general
Dyēus-Ptēr: 'Sky-Father' (PIE) head deity of the PIE pantheon
Manu /Yemos: 'man' and 'twin' (PIE) Sky-Father's twin sons (PIE
    creation myth)
Mehnot: moon deity (PIE)
Sāwel: sun deity (PIE)
Sāwel-Dom: 'sun' and 'still' (PIE) summer solstice celebration
Trito: 'third man' (PIE) son of Sky-Father, first warrior/cattle raider
Wesr-Admn: 'spring' and 'rite' (PIE) festival similar to Beltane

Tribes / Geographic Features

Antrom-Chelo: 'cave' and 'desire' (PIE) located in the foothills of the
     northern Caucasus
Dān: Don River (from dānus/river) (PIE)
Dānus: 'river' (PIE) steppe tribe of which Ceru is chief of chiefs
Lik: ancient name of the Manych River, tributary of the Don
Plānos: 'flat' 'plain' (PIE) steppe tribe to which Naya's clan belongs
Rā: Volga River (ancient Scythian)

Terms

Ala: 'hello' (PIE)
A't Munar Urug: 'She-Who-Rides-Horses' (T) Aytal's honorary name
     for Naya
Dhugter: 'daughter' (PIE)
Dlkus: 'sweet' (PIE)
Dōsos: 'slave' (PIE)
Dukos: 'leader' (from deuks) (PIE)
Empis: 'insect' (PIE) dragonfly
Etmn itājō: 'soul' and 'journey' (PIE)
Gentis: 'family' / people of the clan (PIE)
Ghosti: 'foreigner' (PIE)
Jai: 'yes' (PIE)
Kóryos: 'war-band' (PIE) a group of young male warriors, often
     identified with wolves
Lāpos: 'heifer' (PIE) unbred female cattle
Lubhjā: 'fragrant herb' (PIE)
Makēn: 'pouch' (PIE)
Miljom: 'red ochre' (PIE)
Moighos: 'pee' (PIE) latrine
Ojt : 'damn' (T)
Ónerjos: 'dream' (PIE) ordinary dream
Piskis: 'fish' (PIE) sturgeon eggs, i.e. caviar
Plowós: 'boat' (PIE)
Skerdā: 'shit' (PIE) expression of dismay
Skortum: 'whore' (PIE)
Sterkos: 'shit' (PIE) term of derision applied to a person
Swopnjājō: 'dream' (PIE) big dream

Tekstlom: 'web' (PIE) dream web, found in shamanic traditions
    world-wide
Tloqai-koljō: 'speak' and 'stick' (PIE) talking-stick, signaling who has
    the right to speak
Uurga: 'lasso-pole' (Mongolian)

Acknowledgements

Many of the same individuals who contributed to the first book in the *She Who Rides Horses* trilogy have also been instrumental in supporting the creation of the second book, *A Clan Chief's Daughter*. Page Lambert continues to be a phenomenal editor, improving my writing and reminding me to listen to my characters, while also believing whole-heartedly in the story. Diana Lancaster, with her talent and vision, once again brought words to life through the cover art. Jane Dixon is a master designer, completing all the finishing touches with skill and efficiency. Kim Esteran and Gail Boone both read various drafts, providing insightful commentary and essential encouragement along the way. Sarah Gibson, M.A., LPC, LAC made sure the emotional tenor of the story rang true, especially in the scenes dealing with sexual assault. As ever, Linda Kohanov served as an inspiration, guide and friend. I'm deeply grateful to all of you.

Three years separate the publication of *She Who Rides Horses (Book One)* from *A Clan Chief's Daughter (Book Two)*. Somewhere along the way, I went from being a part-time writer to working full-time as a novelist and no one questioned the evolution, including me. While winning awards and accolades from critics certainly helped, receiving such a warm and enthusiastic reception from readers of Book One made all the difference in finishing Book Two. Thank you for your eagerness, and your patience, while waiting to learn what happens next in the saga of Naya and the red filly. Book Three is already coming through – I'm as curious as anyone to see how the story ends.

And finally, thank you to my family and friends for believing in this project, and to my horses, for calling me to love them, heart and soul.

www.ingramcontent.com/pod-product-compliance
Lightning Source LLC
Chambersburg PA
CBHW061938130726
47909CB00013B/2043